The Way Home

The Way Home

Henry Handel Richardson

MINT EDITIONS

The Way Home was first published in 1925.

This edition published by Mint Editions 2021.

ISBN 9781513291109 | E-ISBN 9781513293950

Published by Mint Editions®

 MINT
EDITIONS

minteditionbooks.com

Publishing Director: Jennifer Newens
Design & Production: Rachel Lopez Metzger
Project Manager: Micaela Clark
Typesetting: Westchester Publishing Services

Contents

Proem

When, having braved the bergs and cyclones of the desolate South Pacific, and rounded the Horn; having lain becalmed in the Doldrums, bartered Cross for Plough, and snatched a glimpse of the Western Isles: when the homeward-bound vessel is come level with Finisterre and begins to skirt the Bay, those aboard her get the impression of passing at one stroke into home waters. Gone alike are polar blasts and perfumed or desert-dry breezes; gone opalescent dawns, orange-green sunsets, and nights when the very moon shines warm, the black mass of ocean sluggish as pitch. The region the homing wanderer now enters is quick with associations. These tumbling crested marbled seas, now slate-grey, now of a cold ultramarine, seem but the offings of those that wash his native shores; and they are peopled for him by the saltwater ghosts of his ancestors, the great navigators, who traced this road through the high seas on their voyages of adventure and discovery. The fair winds that belly the sails, or the head winds that thwart the vessel's progress, are the romping south-west gales adrip with moisture, or the bleak north-easters which scour his island home and make it one of the windy corners of the world. Not a breath of balmy softness remains. There is a rawness in the air, a keener, saltier tang; the sad-coloured sky broods low, or is swept by scud that flies before the wind; trailing mists blot out the horizon. And these and other indelible memories beginning to pull at his heartstrings, it is over with his long patience. After tranquilly enduring the passage of some fifteen thousand watery miles, he now falls to chafing, and to telling off the days that still divide him from port and home.

On an autumn morning in the late 'sixties that smart clipper the *Red Jacket*, of some seven hundred tons burden, entered the English Channel, and having rolled about for a while, for want of a breeze to steady her, picked up a fine free following wind and forged ahead at a speed of eight and a half knots an hour.

At the eagerly awaited cry of "Land ho!" from the foretop, an excited bunch of cuddy-passengers and their ladies, all markedly colonial in dress and bearing, swarmed to the side of the vessel, and set to raking and probing the distance. Telescopes and spy-glasses travelled from hand to hand, arms were silhouetted, exclamations flew, the female gaze, adrift in space, was gallantly piloted to the sober level of the horizon.

And even the most sceptical convinced that the dusky shadow on the water's rim was, in truth, the goal of their journeying, three cheers were called for and given, the gentlemen swung their hats with an "England forever!" the ladies blew kisses and fluttered their kerchiefs. But, their feelings eased, they soon had their fill of staring at what might equally well have been a cloud or a trail of smoke; and having settled the wagers laid on this moment, and betted anew on the day and hour of casting anchor, they accepted the invitation of a colonial Croesus, and went below to drink a glass to the Old Country.

Richard Mahony alone remained, though warmly bidden.

"The pleasure of your company, Mr. Mahony, sir!"

"Mayn't we hope, doctor, for a few words befitting the occasion?"

He had on the whole been a fairly popular member of the ship's party. This was thanks to the do-nothing life. Here, on board ship, he had actually known what it was to feel time hang heavy on his hands. In consequence, he had come out of his shell, turned sociable and hearty, taking an interest in his fellow-travellers, a lead in the diversions of the voyage. And the golden weeks of sunshine and sea air having made a new man of him—in looks he resembled a younger brother of the lean and haggard individual who had climbed the ship's ladder—he was able for once harmlessly to enjoy the passing hour. Again, a genuine sea-lover, he had found not one of the ninety odd days spent afloat unbearable; and in refusing to be daunted—either by the poor, rough food, or the close quarters; or during a hurricane, when the very cabins were awash; or again in the tropics, when the ship lay motionless on a glassy sea, the cruel sun straight overhead—by making light of inconvenience and discomfort, he had helped others, too, to put a brave face on them. Nobody guessed how easy it came to him. His cheerfulness was counted to him for a virtue, and set him high in general favour; people fell into the way of running to him not only with their ailments but their troubles; looked to him to smooth out the frictions that were the crop of this overlong voyage. So unusual a state of things could not last. And, indeed, with the vessel's first knot in northern waters, he had become sensitively aware of a cooling-off. Let but a foot meet the shore, and the whole ill-mixed company would scatter to the winds, never to reassemble. Well, he, for one, would not feel that his ties with the colony were broken beyond repair until this had happened, and he had seen the last of all these boisterous, kindly, vulgar people.

The liking was chiefly on their part. For though, since setting sail, he had been rid of the big-mouthed colonial boaster, and among runaways like himself, men who were almost as glad as he to turn their backs on Australia—but a single one of the thirty cabin-passengers contemplated returning—this was far from saying that he had found in them congenial spirits. They chafed him in ways they did not dream of. The Midases of the party—it was ruled sharply off into those who had amassed a fortune and those who patently had not; none went "home" but for one or other reason; he himself was the only half tint on the palette—these lucky specimens were forever trumpeting the opinion that the colonies were a good enough place in which to fill your money-bags; but to empty them, you repaired to more civilised climes. And to hear his case—or at least what had once been his intention—put thus crudely made Mahony wince. The speakers reminded him of underbred guests, who start belittling their entertainment before they are fairly over their host's door-sill. At the same time he had to laugh in his sleeve. For where, pray, could Monsieur le Boucher and Monsieur l'Epicier undo their purse-strings to better effect, find a society more exactly cut to their shape, than in the Antipodes, where no display was too showy, no banquet too sumptuous, no finery too loud; and where the man who could slap a well-filled pocket was anyone's equal?—Even less to his taste was the group of lean kine. With nothing to show for themselves but broken health and shattered illusions, these men saw the land of their exile through the smoked glasses of hate, and had not a single good word to say for it. Which of course was nonsense.

And so it came about that Mary was sometimes agreeably surprised to hear Richard, if not exactly standing up for the colony, at least not helping to swell the choir of its detractors. This was unending, went round and round like a catch. People outdid one another in discovering fresh grounds for their aversion. Besides the common grievances—the droughts and floods, the dust winds and hot winds, the bare, ugly landscape, the seven plagues of winged and creeping things—many a small private grudge was owned to, and by the most unlikely lips. Here was a burly tanner who had missed the glimmer of twilight, been vexed at the sudden onrush of the dark. Another grumbler bemoaned the fact that, just when you looked for snow and holly-berries: "Hanged if there ain't the pitches and appricoats ripe and ready to tumble into your mouth!"

"An onnatcheral country, and that's the truth."

"The wrong side of the world, say I—the under side."

Quaint home-sicknesses cropped up, too. On board was a skinny little colonist from the Moreton Bay district, with, as the Irish wit of the company had it, "the face of his own granddad upon his shoulders"— who was, that is to say, more deeply wrinkled than the bewrinkled rest. Where this man came from, dirt was not: the little weatherboard houses were as clean when they dropped to pieces as when first run up. He it was who now confessed to an odd itch to see again the grime and squalor of London town: the shiny black mud that served as mortar to the paving-stones; the beds of slush into which, on a rainy day, the crossing-sweepers voluptuously plunged their brooms; the smoke-stained buildings; monuments tarred with the dirt of ages. He wanted to feel his cheek stung by the mixture of flying fodder and dry ordure that whirls the streets, does the east wind go; to sniff the heavy smell of soot and frost that greets the Londoner's nose on a winter morning— even to choke and smother in a London fog.

No one smiled.

"Aye, it's what one's born to that tells; what one comes back to in the end," nodded a pursy builder, whose gold watch-chain, hung with seals and coins, was draped across his waistcoat like a line of gala bunting. "I knew a man, gents—it's a fact I'm tellin' you!—who could 'a bought out the up-country township he lived in twice and three times over; and yet I'm blessed if this old Johnny-bono didn't as good as turn on the waterworks when he spoke o' the pokey old cottage down Devon way, where he'd been young. Seemed as if all the good smells o' the rest o' the world couldn't make up to him for a bit o' peat burnin' on a still winter's evenin'; or new thatch smellin' in the rains or the softish stink o' the milch-cows' dung in long wet meadow grass."

That white raven, "the man who was going back," held aloof from the sentimentalists. Was he however present at such a sitting, he kept silence, an ambiguous expression on his face. Once only, in a conversation engineered by Mahony out of curiosity, did he speak up. And then it was with a disagreeable overbearing. "I left England, sir, six years since, because man isn't a sprite to live on air alone. My father went half-starved all his days—he was a farmhand, and reared a family o' nine on eleven bob a week. He didn't taste meat from one year's end to another. Out yon "—and he pointed with his cutty-pipe over his shoulder—" I've ate meat three times a day. I've a snug little crib of me own and a few acres o' land, and I've come home to fetch out me old mother and the young fry. They shall know what it is to eat their fill

　　　　　　　　　HENRY HANDEL RICHARDSON

everyday of the seven, and she'll drive to chapel of a Sabbath in her own trap and a black silk gown.—Nay, be sure I haven't loafed around, nor sat with me hands before me. There's not much anyone can learn me in the way of work. But the old country wouldn't either gimme anything to do, nor yet keep me free, gratis and for nothing."—And so on, in a strain dear to the tongues of the lower orders.

These things flitted through Mahony's mind as he stood, chin in hand, elbow on gunwale, gazing over the last stretch of dividing sea. Before him lay an aquarelle of softest colouring, all pale light and misty shadow; and these lyric tints, these shades and half shades, gripped his heart as the vivid hues of the south never had. Their very fleetingness charmed. But a little ago and the day had been blue and sunny, with just a spice of crispness in the air to remind one that it was autumn. A couple of white bales of cloud, motionless overhead, had flung gigantic purple shadows, which lay like painted maps of continents on the glittering sea. But, the breeze freshening, the clouds had been set in motion; and simultaneously the shadow-continents, losing their form, had begun to travel the surface of the water. A rain-shower was coming up from the west: it drew a curtain over the sky, and robbed the sea of its colour. Only in the east did a band of light persist, above which the fringes of the storm cloud hung, sending down straight black rays. And now the squall was upon them; wind and rain hunted each other over the waves; the deck slanted, masts and spars whistled, sails smacked and shrilled.

In the course of that day the vessel was taken in tow, and when, towards evening, the downpour ceased and Mahony again climbed the companion-way, a very different scene met his eye. They now drove through a leaden sea, which the rain had beaten flat, reduced to a kind of surly quiescence. Above them was an iron-grey sky, evenly spread and of a fair height, the lower clouds having withdrawn to the horizon where, in a long, cylinder-like roll, they hung poised on the water's rim. But this cold and stony aspect of things was more than made up for. Flush with the ship, looking as though it had just risen from the waves, was land—was the English shore.

At sight of it Mahony had a shock of surprise—that thrilled surprise that England holds for those of her sons who journey back, no matter whence, across the bleak and windy desert of the seas. Quite so lovely as this, one had not dared to remember the homeland. There it lay, stretched like an emerald belt against its drab background, and was as grateful to sun-tired eyes as a draught of mountain water to a climber's parched throat. Not a rood of this earth looked barren or unkempt: veritable lawns ran down to the brink of the cliffs; hedges ruled bosky lines about the meadows; the villages were bowers of trees—English trees. Even the rain had favoured him: his first glimpse of all this beauty was caught at its freshest, grass and foliage having emerged from the clouds as if new painted in greenness.

Another aspect of it struck Mary who mounted in his wake, gloved, shawled and hatted against the evening chills. With an exclamation of pleasure she cried: "Oh, Richard—how pretty! How. . . how tidy! It looks like. . . like"—she hesitated, searching her memory for the trimmest spot she knew; and ended—"doesn't it? . . . just like the Melbourne Botanic Gardens."

"It looks too good to be true, my dear."

But he understood what she was trying to say. If the landscape before them was lovely as a garden, it had also something of a garden's limitations. There was an air of arrangedness about it; it might have been laid out according to plan, and on pleasing, but rather finikin lines; it was all exquisite, but just a trifle overdressed. And as he followed up the train of thought started by Mary's words, he was swept through by a sudden consciousness of England's littleness, her tiny, tight compactness, the narrow compass that allowed of so intensive a cultivation. These fair fields in miniature!—after the wide acreage of the colonial paddock. These massy hedgerows cutting up the good pasture-land into chequerboard squares!—after the thready rail-and-post fences that offered no hindrance to the eye. These diminutive clusters of houses huddled wall to wall—compared with the sprawling townships set, regardless of ground-space, at the four corners of immense cross-roads. These narrow, winding lanes and highways that crawled their mile or so from one village to the near next—after the broad, red, rectilinear Australian roads, that dashed ahead, it might be for the length of a day's journey, without encountering human habitation. These duly preserved morsels of woodland, as often as not guarded, they too, by a leafy wall where songsters trilled-compared with the immense and terrible bush, bare alike of bird and man: all these forcible contrasts worked in him as he stood gazing on the fair natural garden of southern England; and a sensation that was half wonder, half a kind of protective tenderness, called at the same time a smile to his lips and tears to his eyes. In face of this adorable littleness, this miniature perfection, his feelings were those of the nomad son who, weary of beating up and down the world, turns home at last to rest on the untravelled heart of his mother. Here the familiar atmosphere of his childhood laps him round; and he breathes it greedily—even while he marvels how time has stood still for the home-keepers, and asks himself if he can ever again be one of them. All the tempestuous years of his youth lie between. He has fought fire-spueing dragons, suffered shipwreck in Sargasso, bent the knee at strange shrines. And the sense of an older, tireder wisdom, which makes of him the ancient, of them the young and untried, completes the breach. How, knowing what he knows, can he placidly live through the home day, with its small, safe monotony? How give up forever the excitement of great risks taken and met, on grander shores, under loftier skies?

But a truce to such vapourings! Did the man exist that had it in him to fret and go unhappy, feel pinioned, and a prisoner while, round the cliffs of England, now grey, now white, now red, danced and beckoned the English sea? For who, native to these coasts, would renounce, once having drawn on it, that heritage of vagrancy which has come down to him through the ages? Amphibian among the peoples, has he not learnt to adjust his balance to the sea's tumblings, his sight to its vast spaces?—so that into the English eye has, with time, come a look of remoteness: the sailor-look, which, from much scouring of horizons, seems to focus on near objects only with an effort.—And musing thus, Mahony believed he knew why, for all its smallness, on this little speck of an island rising green and crumbly from the waves, there should have bred a mighty race. It was not in spite of its size, but because of it. Just because the span of the land was so narrow, those whose blood ran high could shove off on the unruly element from their very doorsteps, and whether these looked north or south, faced sunrise or sunset: the deep-sea fishers, the great traffickers, the navigators and explorers, the fighting men of the deep. And with them, so it pleased him to think, no matter for what point they headed, they bore tidings of the mother-country, and of her struggles towards a finer liberty, a nicer justice, that should make of her sons true freemen; for her a difficult task because she lay isolate, shut off by barriers of foam, a prey to hoary traditions, and with no land-frontier across which seditious influences might slip; and yet for her most needful, seeing that the hearts of her people were restless, indomitable—had in them something of the unruliness of her seas. And just as these rovers carried out news of England, so, homing again, either for a breathing-space in the great tourney, or, old and feeble, to lay their bones in English earth, they brought back their quota of things seen, heard, felt on their Odyssey; a fruity crop of experience; so that even the chimney-dwellers in England came by a certain bigness of vision: through the eyes of son or brother they explored outlandish parts, were present at exotic happenings. And now, his thoughts turning inward, he asked himself whether even he, Richard Mahony, in his small way, was not carrying on the great tradition. Having fared forth in his youth, endured in exile, then heard and obeyed the home-call, did not he, too, return the richer for a goodly store of spiritual experience—*his* treasure-trove of life-wisdom—which might serve to guide others on their road, or go before them as a warning? And the idea grew, under his pondering. He saw his race as the guardian of a vast reserve fund of spiritual force, to which all alike contributed—; as each was free at will or at need to draw on it—a hoard, not of the things themselves, but of their ghostly sublimates: the quintessence of all achievement, all endeavour; of failure, suffering, joy and pain. And, if this image held, it would throw light on the obscure purpose of such a seemingly aimless life as his had been; a life ragged with broken ends. Only in this way, he must believe, had it been possible to distil the precious drop of oil that was *his* ultimate essence. Not ours to judge of the means, or in what our puny service should consist: why to one should fall the bugles and the glory—the dying in splendour for a great cause, or the living illustriously to noble issues—to another, a life that was one long blind stumble, with, for finish, an inglorious end. Faith bid us believe that, in the sight of the great Foreordainer, all service was equal. But this we could not know. The veil—a web of steel despite its tenuity—was lowered, and would not rise on the mystery until that day dawned towards which all our days had headed, for which no man had ever waited in vain. And then, pinched of nostril and marble-cold, earth's last little posy in our gripless hands, we should lie supine and—such was the irony of things—no longer greatly care to know.

PART I

I

The ancient little town of Buddlecombe, originally pressed down the mouth of a narrow valley to the sea, from which it is protected by rampart and breakwater, has, in the course of the centuries, scaled the nearer of the two hills that confine it. Nowadays its streets go everywhere up and down. A precipitous lane is climbed by the ridge-like steps of an Italian donkey-path; the old town gardens, massively walled, are built in tiers, so that the apple-trees on the higher levels scatter their blossoms on the gardens beneath. Coming from the upland, three driving-roads drop into the town at a bold gradient; and vehicles, whether they mount or descend, creep like snails. Halfway down the sheerest of the three, the quaint little old houses, that set in oddly enough just where the road is steepest, appear to cling shoulder to shoulder, each a storey or a half-storey lower than the last, their lines all out of drawing with age and the insecurity of their foothold; while those at the bottom of the hill, seen from this point but as a dimpling cluster of gables, dormers, chimneys, look, till you are virtually upon them, as if they were standing in the sea. The roofs of one and all are silvered with the mortar of innumerable repairs, some of their ancient tiles flying off afresh in every rowdy equinox.

The sea-front is crescent-shaped; and a high, wooded cliff, which leaves room for no more than a footpath between it and the surf-rolled shingle, cuts the town in two. The smaller half, grouped about the harbour, includes the old custom-house, a couple of ramshackle magazines and their yards, an ancient inn or two, all bustling places once on a time, when elephants' teeth and gold dust were unshipped here, and the stuffs and linens of England arrived on pack-horses for transit to France; when, too, much lucrative wine and spirit-running went on with the French coast. Now, there is little doing, either here or in the tiny antiquated storehouses and weighing-sheds out on the famous old stone quay that crooks round the harbour. In these sheds children play or visitors shelter while peeping forth at the great waves which, in stormy weather, toss up over the breakwater; and the storehouses are closed and deserted. A claim to notice, though, they still have. More than one of them is tinted a delicate pink; and the rays of the setting summer sun, catching this, reflect it like a rose in the harbour; which sometimes, half full, lies a pool of melted turquoise; sometimes, during the spring-tides, when the moored boats ride level with the quay, has no more colour in it than an empty glass, or a pure sky before dawn.

To get the best view of the town you must row out beyond harbour and mole, or, better still, swim out, on one of those dead-calm days that every summer brings—days when the yellow cliffs across the bay send down perfect golden shadows in the blue mirror of the sea. Then, lying pillowed on this saltest, most buoyant water, glance back to where, grouped in that perfect symmetry that seems the lost secret of old town-builders, the little place on its gun-cliffs lies curved to the bay. Viewed thus, it looks like a handful of grey shells clustered on a silver shingle—pearl, not stone grey—for there is no dourness about Buddlecombe: light and graceful of aspect, it might have suffered bodily transport at the hands of some giant Ifrit, from the French coast over the way. Its silveriness is dashed only by the creeper on the square church-tower—perched, this, too, on the very cliff edge—a creeper which betimes in summer the salt air dyes a blood-red; and by an old jet-black house, tarred and pitched against the breakers which, in a south-west gale, beat to its topmost windows, and hurl roots and branches of seaweed up the slope of the main street.

Above the town the green hillsides are dotted with goodly residences, in which officers on half-pay, and Anglo-Indians in search of clemency, lie snug for the rest of their dormouse days. The houses are as secluded as a foliage of almost tropical luxuriance or walls well over man's height, with great hedges atop of these, can make them; and the loveliness of their jealously hidden gardens is only to be guessed at from peeps through a door left ajar by a careless errand-boy; from the bold application of an eye to a keyhole; or, in midsummer, from the purple masses of buddleia and the wealth of climbing-roses—pink and crimson, yellow and white—that toss over the walls in a confusion of beauty.

In this pleasant spot Richard Mahony had made his home. Here, too, he had found the house of his dreams. It was built of stone—under a tangle of creeper—was very old, very solid: floors did not shake to your tread, and, shut within the four walls of a room, voices lost their carrying power. But its privacy was what he valued most. To the steep road on which it abutted the house turned a blank face—or blank but for entrance-door and one small window—while, in a line with it, up-hill and down, to conceal respectively flower and kitchen-gardens, ran two arms of massy wall. In addition to this, the front door was screened by a kind of sentry-box porch, open only on one side. In this porch was set a tiny glass oval; and here one could stand, secure from rough weather or the curiosity of an occasional passer-by, and watch for mounting postman or expected guest; just as no doubt fifty odd years before, through this very peep-hole, anxious eyes had strained for news-carrier or outrider bringing tidings of sailor son or soldier husband, absent on foreign service in the Great War.

On stepping over the threshold you found yourself at once on the upper floor; for so abruptly did the ground on the farther side fall away that the house was one storey to the road, two to the garden. The living-rooms were on the higher level, with a fine view over town and bay—all but one, a snug little oak-panelled parlour on the ground floor; and here it was that, one autumn morning between eight and nine o'clock, the Mahonys sat at breakfast. Although the air of the young day was mild in the extreme, a generous fire burned in the grate and roared up the chimney, entirely putting to shame, with its scarlet vigour, the wraith-like patch of sunshine that lay across the table.

Mary, seated behind the urn, looked very thoughtful; and this was the more marked because, in obedience to the prevailing fashion, she had swept the heavy bands of her hair off cheeks and forehead, and now wore it braided high in a crown. The change threw up the fine, frank lines of her head and brow; and atoned for the youthful softness it robbed her of, by adding to the dignity and character of her face.

More than once during the meal she had made as if to speak. But as certainly as she opened her lips, Richard, who was deep in The *Times* of the day before, would either absently hold out his cup to her; or attack the muffin-dish anew; or, in turning a richly crackling sheet of the paper, exclaim: "Ha! Here we have it! Mr. Disraeli threatens to resign. The poor Queen will be forced to send for that turncoat Gladstone." And Mary did not wish to spoil his appetite or interrupt his reading.

But when he had pushed cup and saucer from him, wiped his moustache, and driven back his chair, fleetly to skim the less important columns, she felt justified in claiming his attention.

"Richard, dear—I want to tell you something. What we suspected is true. The Burroughs *have* called in Mr. Robinson. Selina says his gig stood outside their house yesterday for quite a time."

She paused, waiting for a rejoinder that did not come.

"And that's not the most annoying thing, either. He has been sent for to 'Toplands' as well."

After this she was no longer in doubt whether he heard her. For though he went on reading, his face changed in a way she well knew. To herself she called it "going wrong"—"his face went wrong" was how she put it—and in the year they had been in England, she had watched what was formerly a casual occurrence turn to almost a habit. Now Richard had always been a very transparent person, showing anger, pride, amusement, all too plainly. But this was something different. It was not so much an expression as a loss of expression; and it happened when anyone laid a chance finger on some sensitive spot he had believed securely hidden. Put thus out of countenance he wore an oddly defenceless, even a hapless air; and it distressed her to see him give himself away in front of strangers. Hence, she had a fresh reason for trying to be beforehand with news of a disagreeable nature. In the old days, she had wished to hinder him feeling hurt; now it was to hinder him showing that he was hurt—which, of the two, she believed he minded more.

In the present case his sole response was a curt: "Well! . . . fools will be fools," as he turned a page of the paper. A moment later, however, he did what she expected: laid the *Times* down and stalked out of the room.

She threw a motherly glance after him, and sighed. Poor old Richard! She had been bound to tell him, of course; but by doing so she had furnished him with a worry for the whole day. It was clear he had set his heart on keeping "Toplands"; and now, after consulting him on and off for a couple of months, the silly people seemed to be going back to that red-nosed, ungentlemanly Mr. Robinson. She couldn't understand it. Still, in Richard's place, she would have taken it calmly. Ten to one turncoats like these would soon come running to him again. Time was needed for people here to find out how clever he was.

Having cleared the breakfast-table, she rang the bell for the servant to take away the tray. But neither her first ring nor a second was answered. For at this moment the girl, her skirts bunched high above a pair of neat prunellas, stood ruefully eyeing the condition of the lower lawn, wondering how she could make her master hear without soiling her boots or indecently raising her voice.

From the dining-room Mahony had stepped out into the garden. This was saturated with moisture. During the night a sea fog had crept up and enmuffled the land; and though by now a watery sun was dissipating the mists—they lingered only about remote objects, like torn handfuls of cotton wool—they had left everything drenched and sodden. As he crossed the grass of the upper lawn, the water came in over the tops of his carpet-slippers; bushes and shrubs against which he brushed delivered showers of drops; and gossamer-webs, spun by the thousand in lovely geometrics that hung whitey-grey and thick as twine, either shattered themselves on his shoulders, or laid themselves fillet-wise round his brow. At the foot of the garden he traversed a second lawn, in which his feet sank and stuck, and climbed three wooden steps set against a side wall. He had hammered these steps together himself, that he might have a view to seaward. A small cutting, in the end wall, as well as all the windows of the house, looked to the town and the row of yellow cliffs beyond. They dated from a time when a land view of any kind was preferred to that of the bare and open sea.

Here he now stood and stared at the palely glittering water. But he did not see it. His mind was busy with the uncomfortable impression left on it by Mary's last statement. At a stroke this had laid waste the good spirits in which he had got up that morning; even if, for the moment, it had done no more than pull him up short, as one is pulled up by a knot in a needleful of pack-thread, or a dumb note on a keyboard. For the feeling roused in him was no such simple one as mere mortification at the rumoured loss of the big house known as "Toplands"; though the dear soul indoors put it down to this, and he should continue to let her think so. No; there was more behind. But only now, when alone with himself, did he mutter under his breath: "Good Lord! What if this place should prove to be Leicester over again!"

He got no further; for here was it that Selina's prim voice broke on his ear. The girl had followed in his steps to say that Jopson, the liveryman, was at the back door and wished to speak to him. A patient also waited in the passage.

Jopson, who was a short man of enormous bulk, had been accommodated with a chair, after his drag uphill. He rose at Mahony's approach, but continued to ease his weight against the doorpost.

"Sarry, surr, but I ca'an't let 'ee 'ave the mare today. 'Er's arff 'er feed. Sarry, surr. T'others is everyone bespoke. No, surr, mine's t' only livery in the town. One o' the inns *might* let 'ee 'ave a turn-out, of a sart; but I dunno as I'd advise 'ee to go to they. They's almighty partiklar, surr, 'ow their 'arses is drove. 'Twouldn't do to bring one o' they whoam along, winded and h'all of a sweat."

"You surely don't mean to insinuate I've been overdriving the mare?"

"Well, surr, and since you mention it yourself, Allfred did say yesterday as 'ow you took 'er h'up ovurr Brandlebury 'Ill faster than 'er 'dd anny mind to go. The 'ills is steep 'ereabouts, surr, and cruel 'aard on the 'arses. An' 'tis naat the furst time neether. If you'll excuse me sayin' so, surr, them 'oove seen it do tell as 'ow you be rather a flash 'and with the reins."

"Well, upon my word, Jopson, this is something new! I drive for show? . . . I overwork a horse? Why, my man, where I come from, it used to be dinned into me on all sides that I was far too easy with them."

"Ca'an't say, surr, I'm sure." Jopson was perfectly civil, but equally non-committal.

"But I can!" gave back Mahony, with warmth. "I had two of my own there, let me tell you, and no beasts were ever better treated or cared for. They certainly hadn't to be walked up every slope for fear they'd lose their wind. They took their honest share of the day's work. For where I come from. . ." At the repetition of the phrase he bit his lip.

"Aye, surr, ahl very well, I dessay, for such a place—Australy, as I unnerstand," answered Jopson unmoved. "But 'twouldn't do 'ere, surr—in England. Thic's a civilised country." And so on to a somewhat acid wrangle, in which Mahony, galled by the doubt cast on his compassion for dumb brutes, was only restrained by the knowledge that, in this matter of conveyance, he was wholly in Jopson's power.

"Really, my dear, if it weren't that the fellow kept his hat in his hand and scattered his 'sirs' broadcast, it might just have been old Billy de la Poer himself I was talking to. *Do* you remember Billy? And how, in his palmy days, one had to wheedle a mount out of him, if he wasn't in the vein to hire? The very same uppish independence! I don't know, I'm sure, what this country's coming to. Though I will say, with all his shortcomings Billy never had the impudence to tell me I couldn't drive."

The woman who was waiting for him brought a summons to one of the lonely little farms that dotted the inland hills.

"Three miles out and only shanks' ponies to get me there just my luck! Imagine, Mary, a place with but a single horse for hire! Tonight I must go thoroughly into the money question again. I shan't be satisfied now, my dear, till I am independent of Jopson and his great fat pampered quadruped. Stable with him? Not I! Not if I have to build on here myself!"

His first visit led him down the main street of Buddlecombe.

It was between nine and ten o'clock, the hour of day at which the little town was liveliest. Shopkeepers had opened their shutters, saw-dusted and sprinkled their floors, picked over their goods, unlocked their tills and tied on clean white aprons. They might now be seen sunning themselves in their doorways, exchanging the time of day with their neighbours, or shooing off the dogs which, loosed from chain and kennel, frolicked, yapped and sprawled over the pavement. Mounted butcher-boys trotted smartly to and fro. A fisherman, urging a sluggish horse and laden cart uphill, cried mackerel at two a penny. And, from big houses and little, women were emerging, on foot or in donkey and pony-chaises, to do their marketing, chat with one another, glean the news that had accumulated overnight. For everyone knew everybody else in Buddlecombe, and was almost more interested in his neighbour's business than in his own. You could not, vowed Mahony, enter a shop for a penn'orth of tin-tacks—the selling of which was conducted as if you had all eternity to spare for it; what with the hunting up of a small enough bit of paper, the economical unravelling of a tangled length of twine—without learning that Mr. Jones's brindled cow had calved at last, or that the carrier had delivered to Mr. Du Cane still another hogshead of brandy-wine. This, together with many a sly inquiry as to where you yourself might be bound for, or the trend of your own affairs. Alongside the rampart stood half a dozen ancient men of the sea, discussing, with vigour, God knew what. A bottle-nosed constable, stationed in the middle of the road to superintend a traffic that did not exist, gossiped with the best.

Down this street Mahony walked, in the surtout, light trousers and bell-topper which he still preferred to the careless attire of a country doctor. He was greeted with bows and bobs and touched forelocks. But the fact of his appearing on foot brought him many a quizzing glance; and there were also shoppers who came at a trot to the door to see and stare after him. Or perhaps, he thought with a grimace, the more than common interest he roused this morning was due to his ill-treatment of Jopson's mare, the tale of which had no doubt already been buzzed abroad. He was really only now, after several months' residence in Buddlecombe, beginning to understand the seven days' wonder with which he must have provided the inhabitants by settling in their midst—he, who bore with him the exotic aroma of the Antipodes! At the time, being without experience of little English country places, he had failed to appreciate it.

His visits in the town paid, he chose to leave it by the sea-front and climb the steeper hill at the farther end, rather than retrace his steps and present himself anew to all these curious and faintly hostile eyes.

Thus began for him a day of fatigue and discomfort. The promise of the early morning was not fulfilled: the sun failed; down came the mist again; and the tops of the hills and the high roads that ran along them were lost in a bank of cloud. He was forever opening and shutting his umbrella, as he passed from rain to fog and fog to rain. Not a breath of air stirred. His greatcoat hung a ton-weight on his shoulders.

He walked moodily. As a rule on his country rounds, he had the distraction of the reins: his eye, too, could range delightedly over the shifting views of lovely pastoral country, fringed by the belt of blue sea. Today, even had the weather allowed of it, he could have seen nothing, on foot between giant hedgerows that walled in the narrow lanes leading from one cottage and one village to the next. Plodding along he first tried, without success, to visualise the pages of his passbook; then fell back on the deeper, subtler worry that was in him. This, sitting perched hobgoblinlike on his neck, pricked and nudged his memory, and would not let him rest. So that, on coming out of a house and starting his tramp anew, he would murmur to himself: "Where was I? . . . what was it? Oh, yes, I know: just suppose this should turn out to be Leicester over again!"

For the present was not his first bid for a practice in England. That had been made under very different circumstances.

II

It was at another breakfast-table, something over a year previously, that Mary, having opened and read it, handed him a letter bearing the Leicester postmark.—"From my mother."

This ran:

> Now my darlings I don't want to hurry you away from all
> the grandeurs and gaieties of the metropolis, and have you
> grumbling oh botheration take that old mother of ours; but
> I do long to see you both, my children, and to get my arms
> round you. Your room is ready, the bed made and aired—
> Lisby has only to run the bed-warmer over the sheets for the
> last time. My home is small as you know, Polly, but you shall
> have a royal welcome, my dears, and I hope will make it yours
> till you have one of your own again.

"A royal welcome indeed, Mary! . . . one may say our first genuine welcome to England," declared Mahony; and threw, in thought, a caustic side-glance at the letters he had received from his own people since landing: Irish letters, charming in phrase and sentiment, but—to his own Irish eyes—only partially cloaking the writers' anxiety lest, as a result of his long absence from the country, he should take Irish words at their face value, take what was but the warm idea of an invitation for the thing itself, and descend to quarter himself upon them. "Now what do you say, love? Shall we pack our traps and be off? Yes, yes, I suppose I shall have to gulp down another cup of these dregs. . . that masquerade as coffee."

"Ssh, Richard! . . . not so loud." Mary spoke huskily, being in the grip of a heavy cold and muffled to the chin. "I should like it, of course. But remember, in engaging these rooms you mentioned a month—if not six weeks."

"I did, I know. But. . . Well, my dear, to speak frankly the sooner I walk out of them for the last time the better I'll be pleased. How the deuce that hotel we stopped at had the effrontery to recommend them staggers me!" And with aversion Mahony let his eye skim the inseparable accompaniments of a second class London lodging: the stained and frayed table linen, cracked, odd china, dingy hangings;

the cheap, dusty coal, blind panes, smut-strewn sills. "Fitzroy Square indeed! By hanging out of the window till I all but over-reach myself, to catch a glimpse of a single sooty tree branch. And the price we're asked to pay for the privilege! I assure you, Mary, though we had fork out rent for the full six weeks, we should save in the end by going. The three we've been here have made a sad hole in my pocket."

"Yes. But of course we've done some rather extravagant things, dear. Cabs everywhere—because of your silly prejudice against me using the omnibus. Then that concert. . . the Nightingale, I forget her name. . . and the Italian Opera, and Adelina Patti. I said at the time you should have left me at home; you could have told me all about it afterwards. What with gloves and bouquet and head-dress, it must have cost close on five pounds."

"And pray are we to be here at last, in the very heart of things, with twenty years' rust—oh, well! very nearly twenty—to rub off, and yet go nowhere and hear nothing? No, wife, that's not the money I begrudge. All the same, just let me tell you what our stay in London has run to—I totted it up at three A.M. when those accursed milk-wagons began to rattle by"—and here he did aloud for Mary's benefit a rapid sum in mental arithmetic. "What do you say to that?—No, I know I haven't," he answered another objection on her part. "But on second thoughts, I've decided to postpone seeing over hospitals and medical schools till I'm settled in practice again, and have a fixed address on my pasteboards. I shall then get a good deal more deference shown me than I should at present, a mere nobody, sprung from the dickens knows where."

He had lighted the after-breakfast pipe he could now allow himself, and pacing the room with his hands in his dressing-gown pockets went on: "This sense of insignificance regularly haunts me. I'm paying, I expect, for having lived so long in a place like Ballarat, where it was easy to imagine oneself a personage of importance. Here, all such vanity is soon crushed out of one. The truth of the matter is, London's too big for me; I don't feel equal to it—I believe one can lose the habit of great cities, just like any other. And sometimes, especially since you've been laid up, Mary—for which I hold myself mainly responsible, my dear, running you off your legs as I did at first. . ."

"Still we can say, Richard, can't we, we've seen all there is to be seen?" threw in Mary with a kind of cheerful inattention. Risen meanwhile from the breakfast-table, she had opened the door of the chiffonier; and her thoughts were now divided between Richard's

HENRY HANDEL RICHARDSON

words and the fresh depredations in her store of provisions that had taken place overnight.

Mahony snorted. "A fiftieth part of it would be nearer the mark!—Well, as I was saying. . . if you'll do me the kindness to listen. . . this last week or so, since I've been mooning about by myself—Gad! to think how I once looked forward to treading these dingy old streets again—half silly with the noise of the traffic. . . upon my word, wife, that begins to get on my nerves, too: it goes on like a wave that never breaks; I find myself eternally waiting for a crash that doesn't come. Well, as I say, when I push my way through all these hard, pale, dirty London faces—yes, my dear, even the best of 'em look as though they needed a thorough scrub with soap and water. . . as for me, if I wash my hands once, I wash 'em twenty times a day; I defy anyone to keep clean in such an atmosphere. All strange faces, too; never one you recognise in the whole bunch; while out there, of course, the problem was, to meet a person you did *not* know. Well, there come times, if you'll believe me, when I've caught myself feeling I'd hail with pleasure even a sight of old What-was-his-name?—you know, Mary, that vulgar old jackanapes on board who was forever buttonholing me. . . my particular *bete noire*—yes, or even sundry other specimens of the *omnium gatherum* we were blessed with."

"Well, I never! And me who thought you were only too glad to ged rid of them."

"Faith and wasn't I? . . . at the time. Indeed, yes." And Mahony smiled; for at Mary's words a picture rose before him of his fellow-passengers as he had last seen them, standing huddled together like frightened sheep on the platform of the great railway terminus: an outlandish, countrified, colonial-looking set if ever there was one, with their over-bushy hair and whiskers, their overloud shepherds'-plaids and massy watch-chains, the ladies' bonnets (yes, Mary's too!) seeming somehow all wrong. Even the most cocksure of the party had been stunned into a momentary silence by the murk of fog and steam that filled the space under the lofty roofing; by the racket of whistling, snorting, blowing engines; the hoarse shouts of cabbies and porters. But the first shock over, spirits had risen in such crescendo that with a hasty: "Come, love, let *us* get out of this!" he had torn Mary from voluminous embraces, bundled her into a four-wheeler and bidden the driver whip up. A parting glance through the peep-hole showed the group still gesticulating, still vociferating, while crowns and half-crowns rained on grinning porters, who bandied jokes about the givers with expectant Jehus and a growing ring of onlookers. Their very luggage, rough, makeshift, colonial, formed a butt for ridicule.

Lost in such recollections—they included the whole dirty, cold, cheerless reality of arrival; included the first breath drawn of an air that smells and tastes like no other in the world; the drive in a musty old growler reeking of damp straw, and pulled by something "God might once have meant for a horse!" to an hotel, the address of which he had kept to himself: "Or we should have the whole lot of 'em trapesing after us!"—sunk in these memories, Mahony let a further remark of Mary's pass unheeded. But when, with a raucous cry, a butcher's boy stumped down the area steps, bearing in his wooden tray the very meat, red and raw, that was to be dished up on their table later on, he swung abruptly round, turning his back on a sight he could not learn to tolerate. "Was there *ever* such a place for keeping the material needs of the body before one? . . . meat, milk, bread! . . . they're at it all day long. My dear, I think I've heard you say your mother's house is not cursed with a basement? Come, love, let us accept her invitation and go down into the country. The English country, Mary! Change of air will soon put you right again, and I could do, I assure you, with a few nights' uninterrupted sleep. Besides, once I'm out of London, it will be easier to see how the land lies with regard to that country practice I've set my heart on."

This last reason would, he knew, appeal to Mary, whose chief wish was to see him back at work. And sure enough she nodded and said, very well then, they would just arrange to go.

For her part Mary saw that Richard's mind was as good as made up: to oppose him would only be to vex him. Of course, it went against the grain in her to be so fickle: to take lodgings for six weeks and abandon them at the end of three! (Vainly had she tried, at the time, to persuade Richard to a weekly arrangement. Richard had *bought* the smile on their landlady's grim face; and she felt certain did not regret it.) But though she hadn't shown it, she had been shocked to hear the sum total of their expenses since landing. Nor was there anything to keep them in London. They had fitted themselves out from top to toe, in order to lose what Richard persisted in calling "the diggers' brand"; and, say what he might to the contrary, they had seen and heard enough of London to last them for the rest of their lives. Museums, picture galleries, famous buildings: all had been scampered through and they themselves worn out, before the first week was over: her ship-softened feet still burned at the remembrance. Yes, for herself, she would be well pleased to get away. Privately she thought London not a patch on Ballarat; thought it cold, comfortless, dreary; a bewildering labyrinth of dirty streets. And the longer she stayed there the more she regretted the bright, clean, sunny land of her adoption.

Thus it came about that before the third week was over, they were in the train bound for Leicester.

It was a wet day. Rain set in at dawn, and continued to fall hour after hour, in one of those steady, sullen, soulless downpours that mark the English autumn. Little could be seen by the two travellers who sat huddled chillily in wraps and rugs, the soles of their feet burning or freezing on tin foot-warmers—seen either of the cast-iron sky, over which drifted lower, looser bulges of cloud, or of the bare, flattish country through which the train ran. On the one side the glass of the narrow window was criss-crossed with rain stripes; on the other, the flying puffs of steam, unwinding from the engine like fleecy cardings, wearisomely interposed between their eyes and the landscape. Now and then Mahony, peering disconsolately, caught a glimpse of a low-lying meadow which, did a brook meander through it, was already half under water. Here and there on a rise he distinguished a melancholy spinney or copse: in its rainy darkness, trailed round by wreaths of mist, it looked as fantastic as a drawing by Doré. On every station at which they halted stood rows of squat, ruddy-faced figures, dripping water from garments and umbrellas, the rich mud of the countryside plastered over boots and leggings. They made Mahony think of cattle, did these sturdy, phlegmatic country-people—the soaked and stolid cattle that might be seen in white-painted pens beside the railway, or herded in trucks along the line. And both men and beasts alike seemed insensitive to the surrounding gloom.

On the platform at Leicester, reached towards five o'clock, so many muddied feet had passed and repassed that, even under cover, not a clean or a dry spot was left. And still the rain fell, hissing and spitting off the edges of the roof, lying as chocolate-coloured puddles between the rails. In the station-yard the wet cabs and omnibuses glistened in the dusk; and every hollow of their leather aprons held its pool of water. The drivers, climbing down from their boxes, shook themselves like dogs; the patient horses drooped their heads and stood weak-kneed, their coats dark and shiny with moisture.

"Good Lord! . . . what weather!" grumbled Mahony, and having got Mary into the little private omnibus that was to bear them to their destination, he watched a dripping, beery-faced coachman drag and bump their trunks on to the roof of the vehicle, and stack the inside full with carpet-bags and hand-portmanteaux. "Yet I suppose this is what we have got to expect for the rest of our days.—Keep your mouth well covered, my dear."

Behind her mufflings Mary vented the opinion that they would have done better to time their landing in England for earlier in the year.

"Yes; one forgets out there what an unspeakable climate this is. The dickens! Look at the mould on the floor! I declare to you the very cushions are damp." Having squeezed into the narrow space left vacant for him, Mahony vehemently shut the door against the intruding rain. And the top-heavy vehicle set to trundling over the slippery cobbles.

But the discomfort of the journey was forgotten on arrival.

The omnibus drew up in a side street before a little red-brick house— one of a terrace of six—standing the length of a broom-handle back from the road. A diminutive leaden portico overhung the door. Descending a step and going through a narrow passage, they entered what Mahony thought would be but a dingy sitting-room. But although small, and as yet unlit by candles, this room seemed all alive with brightness. A clear fire burned in a well-grate; a copper kettle on the hob shone like a great orange; the mahogany of the furniture, polished to looking-glass splendour, caught and gave back the flames, as did also, on the table spread for tea, a copper urn and the old dented, fish-back silver. On the walls twinkled the glass of the family portraits; even the horsehair had high lights on it. A couple of armchairs faced the blaze. And to this atmosphere of cosy comfort came in, chill and numb, two sun-spoiled colonials, who were as much out of place in the desolate, rain-swept night as would have been two lizards, but lately basking on a sun-baked wall.

"Come, this is really *very* jolly, Mary!"

Thus Mahony, toasting his coat-tails before the fire, while their hosts were absent on the last ceremonies connected with tea. And went on, warmed through now, both in mind and body: "I fear you've had a shocking old grizzler at your side of late, love. But I've felt like a fish out of water. Idleness doesn't agree with me, Mary. I must get back to work, my dear. I want a house of my own again too. When I see a snug little place like this, after those unspeakable lodgings, why, upon my word it makes me feel inclined to jump at the first vacancy that offers."

"Oh, that would never do," said Mary with a smile. And their hands, which had met, fell apart at the sound of footsteps.

HENRY HANDEL RICHARDSON

It was also a cheerful evening; one that opened with jest and laughter. For barely were they seated at the tea-table when sister Lisby, who towered head and shoulders above her stout little dot of a mother—Lisby shamelessly betrayed a secret, telling how, while the travellers were upstairs removing their wraps, mother had seized her and danced her round, exclaiming as she did: "Oh, my dear, aren't we grand? . . . aren't we grand? Which I may mention was not intended for you, Polly—I would say Mary. For I feel sure, if you could see inside my mother's heart, you would find yourself there no more than fourteen—the age you were when last she saw you."

They all laughed; and Mother covered her old confusion by picking up the sugar-tongs and dropping an extra lump into Mahony's cup.

"Now give over, miss, will you?" she said affectionately. "Anyone but such a pert young thing as you would make allowance for an old woman's pleasure at getting a son again. Ready-made, too—without any bother. Eight of 'em, Richard my dear, have I brought into this world in my day—a baker's dozen all told, boys and girls together—and not one is left to their poor old mother but this forward young party here. And she'd be off if she could."

"My mother," said Lisby—having filled and handed round the cups, she was now engaged in apportioning a pork pie, performing the task with a nicety that made Mahony think of Shylock and his bond: not a crumb was spilt or wasted—"My mother would have me sit all day at the parlour window, on the watch for some Prince Charming. To him she would gladly resign me. But because I wish to go out into the world and stand on my own feet. . ."

"Lisby! Not woman's rights, I hope?" interposed Mary. And reassured: "Then, mother, I should let her try it. Especially now you've got me to look after you. Lisby, my dear, if you had been in the colony with us in the early days—" and here Mary dilated on some of the hard and incongruous jobs she had seen women put their hands to.

"Now, did you ever?" exclaimed Lisby—with force, but a divided mind. At present she was carving a cold chicken with the same precision as the pie. (Mahony laughed afterwards when, sunk deep in the feathers, he lay watching the gigantic shadows flung by a single candle on the white ceiling, and Mary braided her hair; laughed and said, Lisby's carving made him think of a first-year medical performing on a frog.) "*Never* did I hear tell of such things! I declare, my dear, I am reminded of Miss Delauncey of Dupew. You will remember her, Polly—I would say

Mary." ("I think I do just remember the name," from Mary.) "Well, my dear, what must she do but leave home—against her father's will—to go and be a governess in Birmingham." And now Lisby in her turn held forth on the surprising adventures of Miss Delauncey, who, finding herself in a post that did not suit her, was obliged to take another.

This kind of thing happened more than once during the meal: the ball of talk, glancing aside from the guests' remoter experiences, was continually coming back to Lisby and the world she knew. Her old mother, it seemed to Mahony, was shyer, more retiring. But though she did not say much, it was she who peeped into cups to see if the bottoms were showing; who put titbits on Mary's plate when Mary was not looking; pressed Mahony to a dish of cheesecakes with a smile that would have won any heart. He returned the smile, accepted the cakes, but otherwise, finding no point of contact, sat silent. Mary, with an eye to him through all Lisby's chat, feared her relatives would think him stiff and dull.

But tea over, chairs drawn to the fire, feet planted on the fender, Mother turned her pretty old pink-and-white face framed in lisse cap and bands to Mahony, and seeing him still sit meditative, laid her plump little hand over his long thin one, which rested on the arm of his chair. And as he did not resist, she made it a prisoner, and carried it to her shiny old black silk lap. Sitting in this way, hand in hand with him, she began to put gentle questions about the lives and fates of those dearest to her: John, John's two families of children, and his wives, neither of whom, not the lovely Emma, nor yet soft, brown-eyed Jinny—to whom, through her letters, she had grown deeply attached—could she now ever hope to know on earth. Next Zara, whom she called Sarah: "For the name I chose for her at her baptism I still think good enough for her," with a stingless laugh at her eldest daughter's elegancies. Steady Jerry, who would never set the Thames on fire. Ned, poor dear unfortunate Ned, who had been a source of anxiety to her since his birth—"Ah, but I was troubled when I carried him, Richard!"—from whom she had not heard directly for many a long day. Inquiring thus after her brood, and commenting on what she heard with a rare good sense, she gradually lured Mahony into a talking-fit that subdued even Lisby, and kept them all out of their beds till two o'clock in the morning. Once started, Richard proved regularly in the vein; and Mary no longer needed to fear lest he be thought dull or stand-off. Indeed, she found herself listening with interest. For he told things—gave reasons for throwing up his Ballarat practice, described sensations on the homeward voyage and in London—which were new even to her. At some of them she rather opened her eyes. She didn't want to insinuate that Richard was inventing them on the spur of the moment; but she did think—and on similar occasions had thought before now—that certain ideas occurred to him only when he got fairly wound up: he was like a fisher who didn't always know what he was going to catch.—Besides, there was this odd contradiction in Richard: he who was usually so reserved could, she had noticed, sometimes speak out more frankly, unbosom himself more easily, to people he was meeting for the first time, than to those he lived his life with. It was as if he said to himself, once didn't count.

III

The next-door house, the first in the row, stood at right angles to the rest, and faced two diverging streets of shops and stores. Further, the little leaden rain-shield over the front door was supported by a pair of pillars coloured to resemble marble, between which hung a red lamp. This lamp had burned there, night for night, for over half a Century: the stone of the doorstep was worn to a hollow by the countless feet that had rubbed and scraped and shuffled, under its ruby glow. For the house belonged to old Mr. Brocklebank the surgeon, who was one of the original landmarks of the neighbourhood. He had, in fact, lived there so long that none was old enough to remember his coming—with the possible exception, said Mother, of old Joe Dorgan, for sixty years past, ostler at the "Saddlers' Arms." Joe was now in his dotage, and his word did not count for much; but in earlier life he had been heard to tell of the slim and elegant figure young Brocklebank had once cut, in redingote, choker and flowered gilet; and of how people had thought twice before summoning him, owing to his extreme youth. This defect time had remedied; and so effectually that it soon passed belief to connect youth and slimness with the heavy and corpulent old man. When, for instance, mother came there as a bride, he had seemed to her already elderly; the kind of doctor a young wife could with propriety consult.

The practice had flourished till it was second to none; and he was reported, being a bachelor and very thrifty, not to say close-fisted, to have laid by the thousands which in this town were commonly associated only with leather or hose. But now he had all but reached the eighties; and despite one of those marvellous country-bred English constitutions—founded on ruddy steaks, and ale, and golden cheddars—the infirmities of age began to vex him. For sometime past his patients had hesitated to call him out by night, or in bad weather, or for what he might consider too trifling a cause; though they remained his faithful adherents, preferring any day a bottle of Mr. B. 's good physic to treatment by a more modish doctor. Recently, however, he had let two comparatively simple cases slip through his fingers; while the habit was growing on him of suddenly nodding off at a bedside; what time the patient had to lie still until the old gentleman came to himself again. A blend, too, of increasing deafness and obstinacy led him to shout people down. So that altogether something like a sigh of relief went up when one fine day a great-nephew appeared, and the rumour ran that Mr. B. was retiring: was being carried off to end his honourable and useful career under another's tutelage; to be wheeled to the grave-brink in the humiliating bath-chair to which he had condemned many a sufferer. And house and practice were for sale.

Lisby came primed with the news—brought by the milkman on his early round—to the breakfast-table. And Mother, her first shock over and her eyes dried, fell into a reminiscent mood.

"Dear oh deary me! Old Mr. B. laid on the shelf! Why, it seems only like the other day I saw him for the first time. . . when Johnny was born. Yet it must be nigh on five-and-forty years; Johnny will be forty-five come March. In walks Mr. B.—I'd never needed a doctor till then—and says to me—me, poor young ignorant thing thankful to have escaped with my life—in he comes: 'Here's a fine fish we've landed today, madam! Here's a new recruit for the Grenadier Guards! Twelve pounds if an ounce, and a leg like a three-year-old!' I up on my elbow to see, and he quite gruffly: 'Lie down you villainous young mother, you! Do you want to make an orphan of the brat?' He had always to have his joke had Mr. B. and we were good friends from that day. One after another he brought the whole batch of you into the world.—Deary me, I shall miss him. Many and many's the time he's stepped over the railing with his weekly news-sheet: 'Here's a murder case to make you ladies' blood run cold,' he would say. Or: 'Another great nugget found on the goldfields!'—for he knew the ties I had with the colony. And the last sound I used to hear at night was him knocking out his pipe on the chimney-piece. It was such a comfort to me—after your father went and the boys scattered—to know we'd a man so close. Especially in '59, when those dreadful burglaries took place."

"Now, mother, give over trying to make yourself engaging," was Lisby's comment. "You know the truth is, no one troubled less about the burglars than you. Before my mother went to bed she would lay out all the silver and plate and her rings and brooches, in neat piles on the table, so as to save the robbers trouble should they come."

"So as to save my own skin, you saucy girl!—Well, well! . . . what's past is past. To be sure it wouldn't have done for him to go on doctoring till he lost his memory, and perhaps mixed his drugs and poisoned us all."

"It would not indeed. And for the rest, my dear mother, I tell you what: Mary and I will take up our abode next door and look after you," said Mahony.

At the moment, the words passed as the jest they were meant for. But they sowed their seed. Mahony ate his toast and drained his cup with an absent air; and as soon as breakfast was over made Mary a private sign to follow him upstairs. There, while she sat on the edge of the bed, he fidgeted about the room, fingering objects and laying them down again in a manner that told of a strong inner excitement.

"I spoke without reflection but, upon my soul, it does look rather like the finger of Providence. An opening to crop up in this way at my very elbow! . . . one that's not to be despised either, if report speaks true. Really, wife, I don't know what to think. It has quite unsettled me. Here have I been expecting to have to travel the country, visiting this place and that, answering advertisements that lead to nothing, or myself advertising and receiving no replies—all so much nerve and shoe wear—and a dreary business at best. You see, my dear, what I need first of all is English experience. I mean"—he made an airy gesture—"I must be able to say, when I find the perfectly suitable position I'm looking for: 'I've been practising in such and such a place for so and so many years, and have had a first-class connection there.'—You notice, I hope, I have no intention—should I take the chance offered me, that is, and pop in here—of the making it a permanency. It remains my ambition to live in the country. But if only half what they say of old Brocklebank's affairs is to be believed, a few years here wouldn't hurt me. There are *pots* of money to be made in these manufacturing towns, once a practice is set going—and this has existed for over half a century. Besides, it might even improve under my hands. . . why not, indeed? Such a Methuselah must have been entirely out of date in medicine. I confess it isn't exactly the spot I would have chosen, even to start in, were money and time no object. But considering, Mary, what our expenses have been. . . the lateness of the season, too! Why, it's virtually winter already, and the worst possible time of year to travel about in." And so on, with much more in the same strain, and a final bait of: "Another point we mustn't lose sight of is that here, you, love, would have the company of your mother and sister. And I think I know what a pleasure that would be to you."

"Why, yes, of course, as far as that's concerned," said Mary, who had not interrupted by a word.

"Well, and the rest?" he asked a trifle querulously. "Don't I convince you?"

"Why, yes," she said again, but slowly. "In one way. I agree it might

HENRY HANDEL RICHARDSON

be worth considering. But I wouldn't be in *too* great a hurry, Richard. Look about you. See someother places first."

"Yes, and while I hum and haw and think myself too good for it, someone else snaps it up. The profession is in very different case here, my dear, from what it was in the colonies. It's overcrowded. . . worked to death. I can't afford to be too particular. Must just find a modest corner, slip into it and be thankful.—And let me give you a piece of advice, Mary," he went on more warmly, with the waxing impatience of a man who longs to see his own hesitation overthrown. "It's no earthly use your comparing everything that turns up on this side of the globe, with Ballarat. A practice like that won't come my way again; or at least not in the meantime. *Try*, love, not to let yourself be influenced by the size of a house and the width of a street. I assure you once more, you have no conception what these provincial concerns are worth. If I step into old Brocklebank's shoes, you may drive in your carriage yet, my dear!"

Mary had run through so many considerations in listening, that she had really listened more to herself than to him. Of course, much of what he said was sound. Did he settle here, it would save time and money—and one of her standing fears about the new venture had been that Richard would prove too hard to please. But for him now to rush to the other extreme! Nor was she one to stand out for showiness and style; or rather, she would not be, were Richard a different man. But he, with his pernickitiness! And it was all very well for him to say, don't draw comparisons; how could one help it? To have flung up a brilliant practice, a big house and garden, a host of congenial friends. . . for this a pokey house in a small dull street, in a dull, ugly, dirty town. As for what *she* stood to gain by it, the living door by door with mother and sister, fond as she was of them she could see, even here, drawbacks that were invisible to his man's eye.

However, since the one way to deal with Richard was to give him his head, and only by degrees deftly trickle in doubts and scruples, Mary smothered her own feelings for the time being. Perhaps he was right, said she: the place might do for a start; and she was certainly against him going travelling in winter with the objection he had to flannel. Mr. Brocklebank's advisers might, of course, ask a stiff price for the goodwill of the practice; still, if he got on well for two or three years, that would soon be covered. Thus Mary, trusting to a certain blind common sense that *did* exist in Richard for all his flightiness, if he was neither badgered nor opposed. ("Just the Irish way of getting at a thing backwards!" was how he himself described it.) One point though she insisted on; and that was, he should take an outside opinion on the practice before entering into negotiations.

Entirely pacified, Mahony kissed her and together they went downstairs. According to Mother, who had now to be drawn into confidence, the person to consult would be Bealby the chemist; he had dispensed for Mr. B. ever since the old man grew too comfortable to do it for himself. So Mahony on with his hat and off to Bealby's shop, well content to leave Mary to damp the exasperating flutter into which the news had thrown her relatives. Well, no, he wouldn't say that: in Mother even this was bearable. It was true, declaring you might knock her down with a feather, she had seated herself heavily in her chair by the fire, to think and talk over the plan in detail. But her cheery old mind saw only the bright side of it; while her kindly, humorous smile took the sting from fuss and curiosity. Lisby was harder to repress. She threw up her hands. "No! *Never* did I hear tell of such a thing, Polly—I would say Mary! Going off to buy a practice, my dear, for all the world as if it were a tooth-brush or a cravat!" Richard safely out of the house, Mary felt constrained to come to his defence.

"You must remember, Lisby, it doesn't seem *quite* such an important affair to Richard as it does to you. With all his experience. Living in the colony, too, one learnt to make up one's mind quickly. You had to. Think of shares, for instance. They might be all right when you went to bed, and by the morning have sunk below par; so that you had to decide there and then whether to sell out or risk holding on." The mild amusement with which Richard's behaviour provided Lisby was apt to jar on Mary.

From the chemist Mahony got all the information he wanted—and more. The object of his visit grasped, he was led into a dingy little parlour behind the shop, where, amid an overflow of jars and bottles and drawer-cases, Bealby carried on his ex-business life. And both doors noiselessly closed to ensure their privacy, the chemist—a rubicund, paunchy old man, with snow-white hair and whiskers—himself grew so private that he spoke only in a whisper, and accompanied his words with a forefinger laid flat along his nose. This mysterious air gave the impression that he was divulging dark secrets; though he had no secret to tell, nor would his hearer have thanked him for any. Plainly he was a rare old gossip, and as such made the most both of his subject and the occasion. Mahony could neither dam nor escape from his flow of talk.

However, his account of the practice was so favourable that the rest had just to be swallowed—even disagreeable tittle-tattle about the old surgeon's mode of life. At the plum kept to the last—Brocklebank, it appeared, had actually been called in professionally to the great house of the district, Castle Bellevue—Mahony could not repress a smile; Bealby alluding to it with a reverence that would have befitted a religious rite. Of more practical importance was the information that there were already two candidates for the practice in the field; but that to these, he, Mahony, would no doubt be preferred; for both were young men, just about to start. And: "We want no fledglings, no young sawbones in a position such as this, sir! Now with an elderly man like yourself. . ." Wincing, Mahony contrived soon after to let slip the fact that he was but a couple of years over forty.

"His eyes almost jumped out of his head when I said it, Mary. The fellow had evidently put me down for sixty or thereabouts," he came back on the incident that night. "It made me feel I must be beginning to look a very old man."

"Not old, Richard. Only rather delicate. And the people here are all so rosy and sturdy that they don't understand anyone being pale and thin."

"Well, I'm positive he thought me a contemporary, if not just of old B. 's, at least of his own."

What he did not mention to Mary was the impression he saw he left Bealby under, that lack of success had been the reason of his quitting Australia. Were he only more skilled at blowing his own trumpet! Actually the old fool seemed to think he, Mahony, would be bettering himself by settling in Leicester!

"Well, sir, I can promise you, you will find an old-established, first-class practice, such as this, a very different thing from those you have been used to. England, doctor, old England! There's no place like it." At which Mahony, who had himself, aloud and in secret, rung changes on this theme, regarded the speaker—his paunch, due to insufficient exercise; his sheeplike, inexperienced old face; his dark little living-room, and darker still, mysterious, provincial manner—looked, and knew that he did not, in the very least, mean the same thing anymore.

"COME, GIVE OVER, MARY!" SAID Mother affectionately.

Mother sat by the fire in the twilight, her hands folded placidly in her lap. She was neither a sewer nor a knitter. If not nimbly trotting about the house, in aid of the rheumaticky old servant, she liked best to sit still and do nothing; which Richard said made her a most soothing companion. Her words were addressed to Mary, who was rattling a sewing-machine as if her life depended on it. They also referred to a remark passed in a pause of her handle-twirling. This had constituted a criticism of Richard—or as much of a criticism as Mary could rise to. Which, here, she felt quite safe in making, so surely did she know Richard nested in Mother's heart.

That afternoon—it was December, and night now soon after three o'clock—he had—and not for the first time—stepped over the low railing that separated the garden-plots to say: "Come, Lisby, let us go a-gallivanting!" Nothing loath, Lisby, also not for the first time, laid aside her needle, tied on bonnet and tippet, and off they went arm-in-arm, to prowl round the lighted shops of the town.

Mary's objection was: "But if he's wanted, mother! I shouldn't know where to send for him."

"My dear, Eliza would find him for you in less than half an hour.—Besides, Mary, it's very unlikely anyone would want him in such a hurry as all that."

"Yes, I suppose so. It's me that's silly. But you see, in Ballarat he never dreamt of going out without leaving word just where he was to be found. Indeed, he seldom went out for pleasure at all. He was much too busy."

Mother did not put the question that would have leapt, under similar conditions, to Lisby's lips: "Then, why, in the name of fortune, did he leave it?" She only said: "You must have patience, my dear."

"Oh, it's not me—it's him I'm afraid of. Patience is one of the things Richard hasn't got."

There was a brief silence. Then: "You have a very good husband, Mary. Value him, my dear, at his true worth.—Nay, child, let the lamp be. Can't you sit idle for half an hour?"

She stirred the fire to a blaze which lit up their faces, and the many-folded drapery of their gowns.

"I know that, mother. But he doesn't get easier to manage as he grows older. In some ways Richard is most difficult—very, very queer."

"And pray, doesn't the old tree get knobby and gnarled? . . . Take a hint from your mother, my dear—for though, Mary, you've been so long away from me, I know my own flesh and blood as no one else can. Be glad, child, not sorry, if Richard has his little faults and failings—

even if you can't understand 'em. They help to bind him. For his roots in this world don't go deep, Mary. He doesn't set proper store on the prizes other men hanker after—money and position and influence, and such like." She paused again, to add: "It's a real misfortune, my dear, you have no children."

"Yes, and me so fond of them, too. But I'm not sure about Richard. He's got used, now, to being without them, to having only himself to consider. I'm afraid he'd find them in the way."

"And yet it was of Richard I was thinking," said the old lady gently.

"You say he's hard to manage, Mary," she went on. "But la! child, what does that matter? He's kind, generous, straight as a die—I'm sure I'm right in believing he's never done a mean action in his life?"

"Never! It isn't in him."

"Well, then!" said Mother: and her cheerful old tone was like a verbal poke in the ribs. "He might be easier to manage, Mary—and thoughtless... or stingy... or attentive to other women. You little know what you're spared, child, in not having that to endure. There are some poor wives would think you like the princess in the fairytale, who couldn't sleep for the pea." She fell into a reverie over this, sat looking into the heart of the fire. "Men?—ah, my dear! to me even the best of 'em seem only like so many children. We have to be mothers to 'em as well as wives, Mary; watch over them the same as over those we've borne; and feel thankful if their nature is sound, behind all the little surface tricks and naughtinesses. Men may err and stray, my dear, but they must always find us here to come back to, and find us forgiving and unchanged.—But tut, tut, what a sermon your old mother's preaching you! As if you weren't the happiest of wives," and she laid her soft old hand on Mary's. "I got led into it, I suppose, because of the strong tie between us: you're more like me, Mary, than any of the rest. Another thing, too: I'm a very old woman, my dear, and shan't live to see the end of the day's business. So always remember, love, Mother's advice to you was this: not to worry over small things—the big ones will need all your strength. And you can't do Richard's experiencing for him, Mary, however much you'd like to spare him the knocks and jars of it.—But I do declare, here they come. Now what will they say to finding us gossiping in the dark?"

The shoppers' steps echoed down the quiet street—really sounding like one rather heavy footfall—and turned in at the gate. And then there were voices and laughter and the sound of rustling paper and snipped string in the little room, where Mary lit the lamp, and Lisby displayed her presents—sweetmeats, a piece of music she had coveted, a pair of puce-covered gloves, a new net for her chignon—while Mother tried to prevent the great round pork pie Mahony deposited on her lap, from sliding into the grate.

"You dear naughty spendthrift of a man! Why, the girl's head will be turned."

"Come, mother, let me give her a little pleasure."

"You give yourself more, or I'm much mistaken."

"Pooh! Such trifles! I shouldn't otherwise know what to do with my small change," retorted Mahony. And Mary laughed and said: "Wait, mother, till the practice really begins to move, and then you'll see!"

This nudged Mahony's memory. "Has anyone been?"

"They hadn't when I came over. And Mary Ann has not knocked at the wall.—Oh yes, the boy called with an account from Mr. Bealby."

The news of the empty afternoon, together with Mary's colonialism, grated on Mahony. "*Do* knight him, my dear, while you're about it," he said snappishly.

"Oh well, Bealby then. Though, I really can't see what it matters. And out there, if I *hadn't* said Mr. Chambers, Mr. Tangye, you would have been the one to suffer."

"And I can assure you, my dears, Bealby won't think any the worse of you for turning him into a gentleman," soothed Mother.

"Oh! but Richard is very correct—aren't you, dear?"

Here Lisby had also to put in her spoke.

"And Bellvy Castle, pray?—what of Bellvy Castle? Has still no groom come riding post-haste to summon you?"

Heartily tired of this jest, which he himself had innocently started, Mahony picked up a book and stuck his nose in it. "No, nor ever will."

"Come, Lisby," said Mother, "the kettle's boiling its head off.—Richard, my dear, draw up your chair; you must be cold and famished.—Nay, Mary, I'll not let you go home. We're going to drink a cosy cup together. And afterwards Richard shall tell us more adventures of the early days. I've looked forward to it all the afternoon. It's as good as any book."

Mahony had more than once said to his wife: "Before I knew your mother, Mary, I used to think *you* the warmest-hearted creature under the sun. But now that I know her, love, and can draw comparisons, I declare you sometimes seem to me quite a hard and reasonable young woman."

And then he would fall to musing on the subject of wisdom inborn and acquired. Here was this little old lady, who knew nothing of the world, had never, indeed, travelled fifty miles from her native place, and yet was richer in wisdom—intuitive wisdom, the wisdom of the heart—than any second mortal he had met. He could not picture to himself the situation, however tangled, that Mary's mother would fail to see through, and, seeing, to judge soundly and with loving kindness. Yes, his acquaintance with and affection for her was the one thing that helped him over the blank disappointment of these early weeks.

IV

The surgery was a small, darkish room on the ground floor, a step or two below street level; and the window behind which Mahony spent the greater part of his first English winter was screened from the curiosity of passers-by, by an attorney's brown gauze shade. Across this blind he saw people move like shadows; or like bodies immersed in water, only the tops of whose crowns shewed above the surface. There went the hooded tray and crooked arm of the tinkling muffin-man; and the wares of the buy-a-brooms. There, also, to the deep notes of his bigger bell and his insistent: "To all whom it may concern!" passed the shiny black hat of the town crier. Regularly, too, at dusk, through fog or silvery rain, the lamp-lighter's ladder and torch rose into Mahony's field of vision, flicking alive the little gas flame that set his own brass plates a-glitter.

About this surgery hung a disagreeable, penetrating smell—a kind of blend of the countless drugs that had been housed and mixed there for over half a century—and, air as you might, it was not to be got rid of. It gave even Mary, who was not sensitive to smells, the headache. Otherwise, during Richard's absences she might have used this room, which held a comfortable armchair. As it was, she found herself fairly crowded out. The passage was so narrow that two people were a tight fit in it; and, were more than two in waiting, they had to be furnished with seats in the little parlour to the back, pokier, this, than even the surgery, and very dark—Richard called it the "Black Hole"—giving as it did on a walled-in yard no bigger than a roofless prison cell. Altogether, the accommodation was so cramped that it was like living in a mouse-trap. Still, it would have been folly in the beginning to separate house from practice, when the two had hung together for so long. Time enough later on to make changes. Mary's own idea was to turn the first-floor bedroom into a drawing-room. Richard talked of moving; of knocking two houses into one; even of building for himself. In the meantime he had taken the house on a short lease, preferring to pay a higher rent for a few years than to bind himself for the mystic seven. And so it was mainly in the bedroom that Mary spent her first winter; sewing, sheerly to kill time, garments she did not need, or which she might just as well have "given out." Sitting bent over her needle in the half daylight, she could sometimes almost have smiled did she think of the sacrifices they had made—all for this. But for the most part she felt troubled and anxious. Richard had tied himself down for three years; but not a month had passed before her constant, nagging worry was: how long will he hold out?

Mahony, too, was offended by the atmosphere of his room: though not so much by the drugs, to which his nose was seasoned, as by the all-pervading reek of stale tobacco. This hung about and persisted—though a carpenter speedily prised open the hermetically sealed window—and only became bearable when a good fire burned and the room was thoroughly warm. Cooled off, it had a cold, flat, stagnant smell that turned you sick. His old forerunner must have kept his pipe going like a furnace; have wadded it, too, with the rankest of weeds. Even had the practice been shaping satisfactorily this smell might have ended by driving him from the room; which would also have meant from the house. As things stood, however, it was not worth his while to think of moving. Before a month was up he suspected what two months showed, and three made plain as the nose on his face: the whole affair had been of the nature of a gross take-in.

There he sat, with the last numbers of the medical journals, new books on medicine before him, and was too unsettled to read, or, if he did, to make sense of what he read. The mischief was not only that the practice didn't move properly: what came was of entirely the wrong sort. He had not had half a dozen calls to good houses since starting. The patients who had thus far consulted him were the servant-girls and petty tradesmen of the neighbourhood.

In fits of exasperation, he knew what it was to feel convinced that the entries in the books laid before him at purchase, the rosy tales of Brocklebank's receipts, had been invented for his decoying. If not, what in the name of fortune had become of the practice? In calmer moments, he absolved those about him from the charge of wilful fraud: they had acted according to their lights—that was all. That their way of looking at things was not his, was constantly being brought home to him anew. And how, indeed, could he expect them, who had passed their whole lives fixed as vegetables on the selfsame spot, to know his touchstone for a practice? For example, the visit, famous in local history, paid by old Brocklebank to Bellevue Castle. On closer scrutiny this dwindled into the bandaging of a turned ankle, an ankle belonging to one of the under-servants who had slipped on a greasy cobble while at market. Never had old B. set foot in the Castle: or, at most—little more than a servant himself—had entered it but by the back door. Chagrin was not the only feeling this incident roused in Mahony: he found insufferable the obsequious attitude of mind it spoke to in those concerned. Long residence in a land where every honest man was the equal of his neighbour had unfitted him for the genuflexions of the English middle-classes before the footstools of the great. But he had given up trying to make himself or his views intelligible. For all that those about him understood, he might as well have been speaking Chinese; while any reference to the position and income he had turned his back on, called to their eyes a look of doubt, and even disbelief. They considered him a supremely lucky man to have stepped into old Brocklebank's shoes; and at his door alone would the blame be laid, if he failed to succeed.

And failing he was! So far, he had booked the magnificent sum of slightly over a couple of pounds weekly. Two pounds! It reminded him of his first struggle-and-starve campaign on taking up practice after his marriage. Only under one condition could he have faced the present situation with equanimity; and that, paradoxically enough, was, if he had not seen the colour of the money, and it had stood on account to some of the big houses round about. As it was, it dribbled in, a few shillings here, a few there; which meant that his spending had also to be done in driblets—a habit it was easier to lose than to recapture. Yes! if the handful of shares he had left invested in the colony were not bringing in what they did, he and Mary would at this moment have been reduced to living on their capital.

Talking of Mary: her position here was another bite he could not swallow. It had really not been fair of him to foist this kind of thing on Mary. To begin with, the house—possibly the neighbourhood, too, dark, crowded, airless did not suit her. She looked pale and thin, and had never quite lost the cough she had arrived with. How could she, indeed, when she sat for hours at a stretch stooped over her needle? She had no society worth the name—never a drive, a party, a bazaar. Her sole diversion was tending her mother; undertaking the countless odd jobs the old lady and her rheumaticky maidservant had need of. In one way, of course, this was right and proper; and he did not begrudge her to the mother from whom she had so long been parted. His grudge was aimed at another quarter. Soon after Christmas Lisby had made good her escape, and was now established as resident mistress at a Young Ladies' Seminary, near Leeds. Which wormed, in spite of himself.

No complaint crossed Mary's lips; she sacrificed herself as cheerfully as usual. None the less, he owed one of his chief worries during these weeks to Mary. For he could *feel* that she did not expect him to hold fast, and lived in suspense lest he should throw up the sponge. The consciousness of this galled him—got on his nerves. Yet never had he felt so averse from breaking silence. It was not only self-annoyance at the foolishness he had been guilty of; or anticipation of a resigned, I-told-you-so attitude on Mary's part—she *had* told him so, of course; but it wouldn't be Mary if, when the crisis came, she twitted him with it. No, what tied his tongue was his own disinclination to face the future.

The result was that Mary, too, grew fidgety: it was so unlike Richard to bottle himself up in this fashion. She began to be afraid he was afraid of her and of what she might say. So, one evening, as they sat together over book and needle, she herself broke the ice by asking him point-blank whether he regretted having settled in Leicester. "For I can see the practice is not doing much in the meantime. Still. . . if you otherwise like the place. . ."

At her first word the torrent burst.

"*Like* it? I wish to God I'd never set foot in its hideous red-brick streets! As for the practice not doing much—my dear, it has melted into thin air, and that's all there is to say about it. The great majority of that old horse-doctor's patients have given me the go-by—what on earth has become of the wealthy shoemakers, etc., whose names stood on his books, Heaven alone knows! It can't be that they disapprove of my treatment, for they've never even tried it. Upon my word, Mary, I sometimes think the whole thing was a fake and a swindle. But I can tell you this: if I stop here, I'm on the high road to becoming a sixpenny doctor for the masses. And I will confess to feeling myself a little too good for that."

"I should think so! It's really most unfortunate, Richard. But what's to be done?"

"The only course I can see, is to get out of it. I've made a big mistake, my dear, and the shortest and cheapest way in the end will be to admit it and tot up the balance. I could curse myself now, for not having taken your advice. Over hasty as always! The only excuse for me is, I honestly believed there was money to be made here. And was in a panic at the rate our funds were running away."

"Well, it's no use crying over spilt milk. But since you own you did rush rather blindly into this, be warned and don't, for goodness sake, do the same thing in getting out of it. Give it a year's trial."

But the bare idea turned him cold. Now, too, that he had had his say, he felt doubly resolute. Aloud, he declared that another three months spent in these dark quarters, among this stickiest provinciality, in the mud, wind and rain of this dirty, wet, dismal town, would drive him crazy. "The very smell of the place does for me. Leather and corn and horses—horses and leather and corn! A population of ostlers and grooms and commercial gentlemen, and cattle-dealers and bull-necked farmers. No, thank you, my dear, no more of it for me! Naturally I shall sell at a loss; but the sooner the better, Mary, before the practice falls to pieces altogether." And from this decision he was not to be moved.

The question of what next brought them to another deadlock. Mary had got it into her head that, if he went from here, it should only be to London—and was dumbfounded by the moody silence into which he fell at London's very name.—"It's society you've missed, Richard. Even had you got on well, you couldn't have put up with the lack of that. But if you persist in sticking to your original plan and going to live in some miserable little village, it will be worse than ever. You used to say you felt cut off in Ballarat. But since we've. . ."

"And you? . . . what about you, pray?"

"Oh, for me it's been different"—dear Mary!—"living next door to my mother and all that."

"Well, I can tell you this, wife. I've grown more attached to your mother, her kind heart and sound sense, than I was to anyone in all Australia. And certainly more than I am to my own."

"Surely it's time you proved that? What must they be thinking of you?" ("They? Oh? they'll understand. You forget they're Irish, too, love.") "Well, Richard, my advice is. . . if you're quite determined to move from here. . . go and pay some visits and travel about a bit, as you ought to have done at first."

Than this, no suggestion could have jumped better with Mahony's mood: his cramped soul longed to stretch its wings. Spring was at the door, too: that English spring the marvels of which he had seen so often in imagination—and in imagination continued to catch his only glimpse of them, shut up between brick walls as he was. At Mary's words he had a sudden vision of all the loveliness—green downs rolling to the sea, orchards in blossom, dewy old bird-haunted gardens—that he had missed, in flinging himself hugger-mugger on the business of money-making in this sordid town. And so, overthrowing in his haste his original plan of waiting till he was in more prosperous circumstances

HENRY HANDEL RICHARDSON

to present himself, he packed his carpet-bag and went off to visit his relatives and renew his acquaintance with his *alma mater*, putting the practice up for sale, and leaving a *locum* to hold together what remained of it. According to the innate perversity of things, he had no sooner done this than it showed signs of betterment. His substitute was called in to one of the hosier kings, bespoken by the wife of a wealthy tanner. Mere chance, of course, but it did look as though fate had a special down on him.

THE NOMINAL GOAL OF HIS journey was Dublin; and after that Edinburgh. But when he looked back on the weeks that followed, he saw them solely in the light of a journey into the past. And now, too, he grasped why he had so long postponed embarking on it. He was, he discovered, one of those who have a nervous aversion from returning on their traces.

Alighting from his car at a corner of the square, he stood, bag in hand, and gazed at his old home. It was very early on a gusty, grey, spring morning; and he himself was cold and unslept. Already, too, the spiritual depression that is Ireland's first gift to her homing sons was invading him: looking about him he saw only stagnation and decay. Here now he stood, a worn and elderly wayfarer, over whose head thirty odd years had passed since, as a boy, he light-heartedly trod this pavement. Thirty years! Yet it might have been yesterday. For nothing was changed—or nothing but himself. And, as he moved towards the house, he had—in self-defence as it were—a moment of vision, in which the long trail of his life swept past the eye of his mind: his rich, motley life, with all its blanks and prizes, its joys, pains and compensations, let alone the multitude of other lives with which it had made contact. And to think there had been moments when he counted it a failure!

In the bulging glass flower-case outside the ground-floor window, a familiar collection of ferns and green things pursued their morbid growth. Down in the area stood the empty saucer, placed there full, of a night, for any thirsty beast that passed. Here was the well-known dent in the brass knocker; the ugly crack in the stone coping. As of old, the balcony showed green and mildewed with the water that leaked from a pair of flower-tubs; just as he remembered it, the white carriage step was split asunder—a trap for delicate feet. With this difference, that the mould was thicker, the split wider, the cracks more pronounced.

It was the same with his relatives; they, too, had made giant strides along the road of decay: throats had sagged, eyes grown smaller, knuckles bonier. Of the three, the older generation had worn best. His mother carried herself erectly, was slender—slender to emaciation—and, an inveterate enemy of crinoline, wore clinging, trailing black garments of a style all her own, she and his sisters moving like lank, heavily draped maypoles, where other women bulged and billowed and swam. ("Good Lord, what frights!" was his verdict on this deviation from the norm.) With their ivory faces, long, finely pointed noses, straight Irish eyebrows and pretty, insincere Irish mouths, the three of them looked like replicas of the one cameo (as did also he, could he but have seen himself); and since, in age, there was less than a score of years between the trio, the relationship might have been that of sisters rather than mother and daughters.

Thus dispassionately, and Irishly, he viewed them. As they him. "My beloved son, colony life is disastrous. It ruins the soul. . . as it ruins the body."—From the way they looked at him, as this was said, he saw that they found him unnaturally withered—old for his age. Still, his greying temples and wrinkled brows touched them little compared with the burning question whether he had come home in time to save this soul of his alive. For they were even more deeply rapt than of old in the mysteries and ecstasies of religion. On its conduct they lavished their remaining vitality; while the mother faith, which flourished so abundantly around them, supplied them with an outlet for the bitter hatred which life's hardships had engendered in them. Popery was an invention of the Arch-Fiend; its priests were the "men of sin."— To Mahony, who had learnt to regard all sects and denominations as branches of the one great tree, such an attitude was intolerable.

He stayed with them but for three days; longer he could not have borne the lifeless atmosphere of his old home. But. . . seventeen years, and for three days! There was, however, another reason. Their poverty was such that it wrung his heart to have to watch their shifts and makeshifts. In this big house not a single servant moved; his sisters' thin, elderly hands were hard and seamy with work. The two women rose at daybreak to clean the steps and polish the knocker. Themselves they washed and ironed the finely darned damask; kept bright the massive bits of silver, than which there was little else on the oval surface of a dinner-table built to seat a score of people. They did their scanty shopping in distant neighbourhoods where they were not known, creeping out with their baskets early in the morning, while others of their class were still between the sheets. No! the food they set before him stuck in his throat; it was so much taken from them, who looked so bloodless. Yet, though he grudged himself each mouthful, he did not dare either to refuse what was offered him, or to add to it by a gift of money or eatables—anything that might have shown them he saw how matters stood. Banknotes slipped, unmentioned, into a letter from far Australia had been a different thing. These could be politely ignored— as indeed they had always remained unacknowledged. He imagined the fine gesture with which his mother let them flutter through her fingers, in saying airily to Sophy and Lucinda: "Some nonsense of poor Richard's!" He ventured no more than to buy her a bouquet of cut flowers and a vellum-bound book of devotions. Even hothouse grapes might have exuded a utilitarian flavour. But all he felt went into his gift; and he knew just the nerve in the proud old heart that would be satisfied by it. For though he did not warm to them, yet like spoke to like, blood to blood, directly they met again. He could read their private thoughts, their secret feelings. At a glance he saw through the inventions and excuses, the tricks and stratagems with which they bolstered up their lives; while yet retaining their dignity as great ladies. Again, the flashes of mordant humour, which not your godliest Irishman can ever wholly subdue; or the sudden, caustic, thumb-nail sketch of friend or foe: these were so familiar to him as to seem his own: while the practical Irish habit of stripping things of false sentiment was homely and refreshing. Thus, with regard to Mary's childlessness, his mother queried briskly: "Has fretted for lack of a family? Nonsense! In such a climate she was much better without." Again: "Her relatives will miss you. No doubt they placed great faith in your skill. Besides, your visits cost them nothing." Or her description of a neighbour's state as: "A demi-fortune—cab and one horse!"

Many were the inquiries made after Mary, the regrets expressed at her absence; but he in his heart (as probably they in theirs) felt relieved that she had not accompanied him. For Mary would certainly have put her foot in it. There would have been no keeping out of her face the pity she burned with; she would have made presents where presents were an injury; have torn down veils that were sacred, even between the women themselves; would, in short, have come hopelessly to grief amid the shoals and quicksands through which it was necessary to steer a course. Whereas to him the task was second nature. He took leave of them without regret. Once away, however, he was conscious of a feeling of something like guilt towards them. For he understood now, only too plainly, what the withdrawal of the ninety to a hundred pounds yearly, which in his later, palmy days he had been able to allow them-what the abrupt stoppage of this sum must have meant to them. It had no doubt made all the difference between comparative ease and their present dire poverty. Yet never by so much as a word had they hinted at this. There was surely something great about them, too—for all their oddity.

DID THIS EXPERIENCE GIVE HIM the sensation of a dream in which he, who was alive, went down among those who had ceased to live, his return to Edinburgh and its well-known scenes had exactly the opposite effect: made *him* feel like a shade permitted to revisit the haunts of men. For here was life in all its pristine vigour, life bubbling hot from the source—and aeons divided him from it. Here he found again his own youth—eager, restless, passionate-though encased now in other forms. Other keen young spirits swept from hospital to theatre, and from theatre to lecture-room, as he once had done; and were filled to the brim, they, too, with high purpose and ambition. Never before had it been made so clear to him of what small worth was the individual: of what little account the human moulds in which this life-energy was cast. Momentous alone was the presence of the great Breath: the eternal motor impulse. Each young soul had its hour, followed a starry trail, dreamed a kingship; then passed—vanishing in the ranks of the mediocre, the disillusioned, the conquered—to make room for the new company of aspirants thronging on behind. Many of these lads would, no doubt, in looking back, find as little in their lives to feel proud of as he found in his: nothing accomplished of all they now so surely anticipated. And one or other of them might also, when his time came, hover as an elderly ghost, eyed with a flagrant curiosity by this insolently young throng—how contemptuously would not he himself in old days have stared at the apparition!—hover round the precincts, the real old middle-aged hack, returned for a glimpse at the scenes of his youth.—Such were his feelings, the experience being one that drove his years home to him with a cruel stab.

The result was, he fell into an elegiac mood; and not having Mary at his elbow to nudge his attention to realities, he let day after day slip by without calling on, or otherwise making himself known to distinguished members of the profession. He shirked the necessary explanations. The one attempt he did make turned out poorly. Spelt, too, a good dose of patronage for this untrumpeted doctor from the backwoods.

To Mary he wrote: "I do not see much advancement in physick." But this was in self-excuse. Of a truth new ideas were in the air. The shining lights of his own day, now but a pair of crabbed old invalids, waited each for his mortal release. The man of the hour—or so rumour had it—was a young surgeon in Glasgow; which "Godforsaken" city British and foreign physicians were actually travelling to and settling in, to see demonstrated a new means for hindering germ-putrefaction. At first he himself inclined to side with his old chief, who turned a cold shoulder on young Lister and his experimenting. But after reading up the subject in the Medical Library he changed his mind. Pasteur's theory of the existence of certain spores in the atmosphere might not yet be proved to everyone's satisfaction; but the examples published by this Dr. Lister, illustrating the successful employment of the new method, could not but make a deep impression. In the end, he would for two pins have taken rail himself to Glasgow, where in even the most insanitary hospital wards pyaemia, erysipelas and hospital gangrene had been well nigh stamped out.

It was while he still lingered, ruminating these things, that he saw advertised for sale a practice on the south coast of England, in a locality which was described as lovely, sheltered, salubrious. Something in the wording of the paragraph took his fancy and he wrote for particulars. The reply was so favourable that, instead of either travelling to Glasgow or going back to Leicester, he set out by way of Bristol for the south. To see the place was straightway to lose his heart to it; here, for once was a dream come true. The advertiser turned out to be as young as Brocklebank had been old—a practitioner of but a year's standing. But to the hardy old surgeon as a reed to an oak. For even the soft air of this sheltered nook had not been mild enough for a congenital throat-weakness; and the young man was hieing him to the Cape, where he proposed to settle. Such was his eagerness to be gone that he came a considerable way to meet Mahony in the matter of price.—And now letters passed and telegrams flew between husband and wife; till, even the electric wire proving too circumstantial for Richard's impatience, Mary was bidden to pack her bag and join him there. She came, and was herself charmed with the spot—as, indeed, how could she help being, cried Richard, who was as elated as a child. You might search England through, and not find its equal.

The chief difficulty was to get a house. Young Philips, as a bachelor, had lived in furnished apartments; which of course was impossible for them. But it was literally a case of Hobson's choice. For most people owned their houses—had been born and would die in them like their fathers before them—and in all the place only two were vacant. One was of a type that disfigures many a seaside town: a high, gloomy house—in a terrace of three—standing right on the pavement of a side street. With no garden of its own, it was darkened by the foliage of the big trees in the gardens opposite. Still worse, it turned its back on the sea. A lawyer had lived there; the ground-floor windows bore the hated shades. His widow, planning to move from the neighbourhood, was willing to let the house on lease. But Mahony took a furious dislike to it; and even Mary thought it dull, and rather large for the two of them. The second, much smaller and older—some hundred and fifty years, said report—was, on the other hand, bright and cheerful, and had a charming old-world garden and a magnificent view across the Bay. But it was for sale. Nor was the position it occupied so suitable as that of the lawyer's: it stood above the town, half-way up a steep hill. Still, distances were surely negligible, argued Mahony, in so small a place; and whoever really needed a doctor would summon him, whether it meant fifty yards further or no.

None the less the decision cost him his sleep of a night. Mary was all in favour of the one to be rented: his inclinations leaned to the other. He walked past this a dozen times a day, and went over it so often that the agent suggested him keeping the keys until he had made up his mind. It was ridiculous, he told himself, to think of buying a house before he had sampled the practice; yet seldom had he been so torn. And once again Mary, pitying his distraction, came to the rescue and said, well, after all, perhaps he should just buy and be done with it. For she saw what would happen if he didn't: he would never cease to bemoan his loss, and to find fault with the house he was in. Better for his peace of mind that he should take the monetary risk— and though this meant using up the last remainder of their available ready money. But there was also another unspoken thought at the back of Mary's mind. The knowledge that he had thus involved himself might help him to sit firm, if—and with a person like Richard the contingency *had* to be allowed for—if he afterwards tired of the place.

HENRY HANDEL RICHARDSON

So he bought; and not for a second had he regretted it—anymore than he regretted having pitched his tent in this loveliest of spots. On the contrary he counted himself a remarkably lucky man.

AND THUS TO BUDDLECOMBE.

V

The practice bore out its reputation. The huckster, the publican and the ostler were in the minority here; Mahony's visiting-list was studded with good names. This change for the better, together with the pride he took in his pretty house and garden, sent his spirits up sky-high. And, as was natural, he read his own satisfaction into others. "If I'm not much mistaken, Mary, people here are well pleased to have a medical man of a reasonable age in their midst again." It fell to Mary to keep him gently damped; to prevent him skipping off the earth altogether, in his new-found lightness of heart.

At first, though, even she had to admit there was nothing to complain of.

For if Mahony here felt himself restored to his own level professionally, on the social side—which was important, too—things also promised to run smoothly. Of course, English people were notoriously slow to take you to their hearts; and, even after they had found out all about you, would still go walking round you looking you up and down. Once, however, these sticklers were sure with whom they had to deal, they made rich amends. And so Mary had numerous callers of the right kind; and invitations followed the calls. The vicar's wife took her up—a due appearance at church having been made, and a pew hired—and she joined a circle that sat twice a week to sew for the heathen. Further, she was asked to help in visiting and distributing tracts among the lower orders; in getting up a Penny Reading to raise funds for the promulgation of the Gospel; to take a table at the annual Sunday School Feast: was, in short, made free of all the artless diversions of the parish.

In addition to this, the month was April; and the thousand and one beauties of an exceptionally fine spring unrolled before their eyes. Declared Mahony: to be present at this budding and bursting, this sprouting and flowering, more than made up for the disappointments he had suffered since landing in England. What a feast of tender green, of changing colours, was here spread for eyes sore with the harshness and aridity of the Australian landscape, the eternal grey-green of its skimpy foliage! When he first arrived, every sheltered slope and sunny bank was yellow with primroses; the lesser celandine bedecked the meadow-grass, violets were mauve and purple in the hedgerows; and no sooner did these show signs of fading than the ground became blue with myriads of bells, which, taken in the mass, looked like patches of sky dropped to earth. And the blue in its turn yielded to the ruby-pink of the red campion. Against a background of starry blackthorn blazed the golden gorse. The cliffs were covered with the comical little striped brown pokers of the horsetails, which soon branched out into bristly brooms; and piercing the rust-red carpet of last year's growth, up sprang the straight nimble spears of the bracken. In the high hedges the ruddy cane of the willows was smothered by the succulent green tips of hawthorn and bramble; and on the rolling countryside that belle of trees, the larch, stood out among the copperish buds of the beeches and the first tightly folded leaves of the chestnuts, with a pale green feathery loveliness all its own.

But with the onset of summer, when gardeners were busy netting strawberry-beds and currant-bushes against the greedy thrush; and the blackbird, his wooing done, was omitting the topnotes at the end of his call: by this time, in spite of Mahony's liking for the moderate but sympathetic practice, sly doubts had begun to invade him whether things were really at bottom as satisfactory as they seemed, or whether both in his professional and their twofold social life, there was not a fly in the ointment. In his own case, the suspicion soon deepened to a certainty.—Robinson was that fly.

Of the person who bore his name he had naturally heard nothing at the time of buying. Only by degrees did Robinson come within his ken. A surgeon some years his junior, the fellow had originally, it now turned out, held the whole practice of the place for miles round in his hands. Then, three years previously, he had married a rich widow—report credited her with eight to ten thousand a year—bought a fine property and retired. Since then—again according to rumour—he had spent more time than was fitting in the company of the bottle. However that might be, his former wide professional connection, his wife's money and social standing, combined to make him *persona grata* in all the best houses; while among the townspeople and villagers, slow of wit and opposed to change as only English country-people could be, the memory, or rather the habit of him, had persisted, to the tribulation no doubt of his successors. For there came moments when Mahony mistrusted the throat-weakness alleged by young Philips; or at least wondered whether this was his sole reason for quitting so promising a place after a bare year's trial. And who had preceded Philips? At first what he, Mahony, had to meet was no more than a casual mention of Robinson's name.

"Mr. Robinson said this, or would have done that"; and, at the outset, he had been simple enough to believe it a slip of the tongue for Philips. He soon learned better. A question put, a scrap of gossip retailed by Mary, taught him that Robinson was still a power in the place. For yet a while, however, he ascribed what was going on to hard-dying custom, which might be overcome. The first time he scented actual danger was when one of two spinsters he was attending complained of her sister's slow progress, and said she would ask Mr. Robinson to look in, he understanding their constitutions better than anyone else.

"If you do that, my good woman, you see no more of me!" was Mahony's quick retort. And so he lost a patient.

Thereafter on his rounds he himself began to catch glimpses of the bottle-nosed surgeon—sitting perched in a high gig beside a groom in livery; altogether a very smart turn-out—and this went on until it positively looked as if the fellow intended taking up practice again. . . filching it back from under his very nose. A pretty thing that would be to happen, now he had staked his all on it! A shabby trick and no mistake!—one, too, that ran counter to every known rule of medical etiquette.

The mischief was—with a brain like his—let the door open to one such suspicion, and straightway a dozen others seized the chance of inserting themselves. He next fell to questioning the apparent ease with which Mary and he had entered the polite society of the town. For, the longer he lived there, the more plainly he saw just what a wasps' nest of caste and prejudice they had fallen into. Social life in Buddlecombe was the most complicated affair under the sun: was divided into innumerable grades; made up of a series of cliques, rising one above the other and fitting as exactly as a set of Japanese boxes. No such simple matter, and that was a fact, for a pair of newcomers to find themselves to rights in it. But they in their ignorance had pranced boldly in, where those who knew better, walked warily and with discretion. The vicar's wife had taken Mary up: yes; but by now Mahony had come to see that she would be equally attentive to anyone who might prove useful in helping to run the parish, or in slaving for foreign missions. And he began to doubt whether, often as Mary went to the vicarage, she was invited to the really select parties there given. She had never, for instance, met the Blakeneys of "The Towers," people he knew to be hand-in-glove with the vicaress. Mary either did not notice or, noticing, heed such trivial details she just laughed and said: "Rubbish!" or "You *are* fanciful,

Richard!"—but he most emphatically did, and thanked you for being put off with the second best. And besides her insensitiveness to slights, she was hopelessly obtuse when it came to observing the invisible but cast-iron barriers with which the various cliques hedged themselves round, to keep those a step lower in the scale from coming too near.

"Not shake hands with that nice old Mr. Dandy just because he was once in trade? I never heard such a thing!" In Ballarat Mary had been used to feel flattered did her grocer—rich, influential, a trustee of the church, a member of the Horticultural Society—emerge from behind the counter specially to chat with her. "I think we should just make a beginning."

"Indeed and you'll put your foot in it with a vengeance, my dear, if you try anything of that kind here. . . when I'm still struggling to get a stand."

"Oh well, of course, if you look at it that way. . . But all the same. . . when I think. . ." Her sentence tailed off into a speaking silence.

He understood. "*Tempi passati*, love! Nowadays, we must do as Rome does.—Recollect, too, my dear, these things may seem trifling enough to you. . . and me. . . who have knocked about the world; but to people here they're the very A B C of good breeding—have been sucked in with their mother's milk. We mustn't let ourselves appear ignoramuses of the first water."

"But I've *got* to be friendly with your patients, Richard, whoever they are."

"True. But even you must draw the line somewhere, you know."

"I'm afraid I don't; I'm not clever enough. It doesn't seem human either. For we're all the same flesh and blood."

Yes, for the countless niceties and distinctions of social etiquette, Mary had, as she confessed, little aptitude. It sometimes seemed that, if a mistake was possible, she made it.

The two chief houses in Buddlecombe, the "Hall" and the "Court," were closed when the Mahonys settled there, the families being respectively abroad and in residence in London. During their absence the temporary leader, who gave the sign and set the key, and to whom the vicar deferred with his treacliest smile, was the owner of "Toplands." This was a Mrs. Challoner, a widow with two sons, and a person of great wealth and importance—"Toplands" was really the biggest and most up-to-date place in the neighbourhood, both Hall and Court being cramped by comparison and mouldy with age. But let the Trehernes or the Saxeby-Corbetts show so much as the tips of their noses, and this lady subsided with extraordinary swiftness, collapsed like a jack-in-the-box; for, though her husband's antecedents were irreproachable, there was, on her own side, some shadowy connection with "malt" which could never be forgotten or forgiven her; or at least "only by the grace of God. . . or of the Saxeby-Corbetts."

Mrs. Challoner was a member of the vicarage sewing-circle; and here she met Mary, to whom she seemed to take a liking; for she called, asked her to "Toplands," and, as a special mark of favour, drove her out in her carriage; Mahony being simultaneously summoned to attend the younger of the two sons, a delicate lad of seventeen. Thus, when, in Mary's opinion, the time had come to return the various invitations they had received, by herself sending out cards for a party, she felt justified in including Mrs. Challoner. And, sure enough, had in reply a graceful note of acceptance. So far good. But now it was that Mary let her hospitable impulses outride her discretion. At the vicarage she had made a further acquaintance, in the shape of a Mrs. Johnston-Perkes, a very charming lady who had been settled in Buddlecombe not much longer than they themselves. And having it from this person's own lips that she came of a good Oxfordshire family, besides meeting her where she did—Mrs. Dandy, for example, was not made free of the sewing-club—how was Mary to guess that the Johnston-Perkes were not "in the swim"? Nor could Richard have helped her. For the dark fact, unknown to either, was that in his day the husband's father had had some Connection with a publishing firm; and though Mr. Perkes himself had never soiled his hands thus, yet the business stigma—pray, did not the issuing of books imply the abhorred counter?—clung to him and his lady-wife and tracked them from place to place. What followed proved—according to Mahony—that, though good enough for God and His works—witness the lady's presence at the vicarage!—the Johnston-Perkes were not by any means good enough for the upper crust of Buddlecombe; and the consequence was, Mary's party was a failure. There was no open contretemps; Mrs. Challoner and her satellites behaved with perfect civility. But it was impossible, to Mahony's mind, to misread the crippling surprise writ big on these people's faces; and the atmosphere of the drawing-room remained icy—would not thaw.

Another thing that sent people's eyebrows up was the supper to which Mary sat them down as the clock struck ten. At this date she had not been long enough in Buddlecombe to know it for an unalterable rule that, unless the invitation was to dinner, a heavy, stodgy dinner of one solid course after another, from which, if you happened to be a peckish eater, you rose feeling as though you could never look on food again; except in this case, the refreshment offered was of the lightest and most genteel: a biscuit; a jug of barley-water for the gouty, or lemon-water for the young—at most, a glass of inferior sherry, cellars not being tapped to any extent on such occasions. But Mary had gone at her supper in good old style, giving of her best. And Mahony was so used to leaving such matters entirely to her that it had never entered his head to inferfere. Not until the party was squeezed into the little dining-room, round a lengthened dinner-table on which jellies twinkled, cold fowls lay trussed, sandwiches were piled loaf-high—not till then and till he saw the amazed glances flying between the ladies, did he grasp how wrong Mary had gone. A laden supper-table was an innovation: and who were these newcomers, hailing from God knew where, to attempt to improve on the customs of Buddlecombe? It was also a trap for the gouty—and all were gouty more or less. Thirdly, such profusion constituted a cutting criticism on the meagre refreshments that were here the rule. He grew stiff with embarrassment; felt, if possible, even more uncomfortable than did poor Mary, at the refusals and head-shakings that went down one side of the table and up the other. For none broke more than the customary Abernethy, or crumpled a sandwich. Liver-wings and slices of breast, ham patties and sausage-rolls made the round, in vain. Mrs. Challoner gave the cue; and even the vicar, a hearty eater, followed her lead, the only person to indulge being the worthy gentleman who had caused half the trouble—and *him* Mahony caught being kicked by his wife under the table.

He felt so sore on Mary's behalf that, by the time he had escorted the last guest through the sentry-box porch, he was fairly boiling over. Flinging downstairs to the dining-room, where he found his wife disconsolately regarding her table—it looked almost as neat as when she first arranged it—he flashed out: "Well, you've done it now! What in heaven's name possessed you to sit people down to a spread like this?"

Mary had begun to collect her tartlets—dozens of them—on one large dish, and was too preoccupied to lend him more than half an ear. To herself she said: "What *shall* I do with them?"

"Do? Bury 'em, my dear, in a corner of the garden—hide 'em away out of sight! I wish you could get the memory out of people's minds as easily. *our* supper-party will be the talk of Buddlecombe for many a day to come!"

"Just because I tried to make it as nice as I knew how? I think you judge everyone by yourself, Richard. Because you didn't enjoy it. . ."

"Then why was nothing touched?"

"Perhaps they didn't feel hungry. I oughtn't to have had it till an hour later."

"Nothing of the sort! Though you had given it to 'em at five in the morning, they would still have walked home on empty stomachs. This kind of thing isn't done here, and the sooner you get that into your head the better!"

"Never will I descend to their starvation-diet!" cried Mary warmly.

"Another thing: what in heaven's name induced you to mix those Perkeses up with Mrs. Challoner and her set? That was *faux pas* of the first water."

"I do declare I never seem to do anything right! But you said nothing: you didn't know. For if it comes to that, Richard, you make mistakes, too."

"Indeed and I should like to know how?"—Mahony was huffed in a second.

"I didn't mean to say anything about it. But it appears the vicar took it very badly, the other Sunday, that you went to hear that London preacher at the Methodist Chapel. I overheard something that was said at the last sewing-party—about your perhaps being really a dissenter."

"Well, of all the. . . objects to my going to hear a well-known preacher, just because he belongs to another sect? Preposterous!"

"Yes, if it's anything to do with yourself, it's preposterous. But when it's me, it's mistakes, and *faux pas*, and all the rest of it. Sometimes I really feel quite confused. To remember I mustn't shake hands here or even bow there. That in some quarters I must only say 'Good afternoon,' and not 'How do you do?'—and then the other way round as well. That nice Mrs. Perkes is not the thing and ought to be cold-shouldered; and when I have company I'm not to give them anything to eat. Oh, Richard, it all seems to me such *fudge!* How grown-up people can spend their lives being so silly, I don't know. Out *there*, you had to forget what a person's outside was like—I mean his table-manners and whether he could say his aitches—as long as he got on and was capable. . . or rich. But here it's always: '*Who* is he? How far back can he trace his pedigree?'—and nothing else seems to matter a bit. I do believe you might be friends with a swindler or a thief, as long as his family-tree was all right. And the disgrace trade seems to be! Why, looked at this way there wasn't anyone in Ballarat who was fit to know. Just think of Tilly and old Mr. Ocock. Here they would be put down as the vulgarest of the vulgar. One certainly wouldn't be able even to *bow* to them! And then remember all they were to us, and how fond I was of Tilly, and what a splendid character she had. No, this kind of thing goes against the grain in me. I'm afraid the truth is, I like them vulgar best. And I'm too old, now, to change."

"You too old!" cried Mahony, amazed to hear this, his own dirge, on his wife's lips. "Why, Mary love,"—and from where he sat he held out his hand to her across the table, over the creams and jellies standing like flowers in their cups. "You but a couple of months over thirty, and far and away the best-looking woman in the place! Candidly, my dear, never did I set eyes on such a pack of scarecrows—from the vicaress with her wolf's teeth, up the scale and down."

"You don't feel very happy or at home here, love—I see that," he went on. "And I sometimes doubt, my dear, whether I did right to uproot you from your adopted country."

"I certainly liked being there better than here. Still I'm quite ready, as you know, to put up with things. Only you mustn't scold me, Richard, when I make mistakes I do my best, dear, but. . ."

"We'll lay our heads together, love, and so avoid them. And as a beginning, Mary, we'll stifle the natural feelings of friendliness and goodwill we have always had for our fellow-mortals—no matter what their rank in life. We'll forget that we're all, as you say, the sons of Adam, and are placed on this earth-ball but for a very brief period, in which it would certainly be to our advantage to love our neighbours as ourselves. And we'll learn to be narrow, and bigoted, and snobbish, and mean with our grub. . . eh, Mary? Joking apart, my dear, you see how it is. We've either got to adapt ourselves to the petty outlook of those about us, or be regarded as a pair of boors who've brought home with them the manners and habits of the backwoods. And that means turning out again, love. For I won't stay here to be looked down on. . . when I feel every whit as good as anybody else."

"Now when you talk like that, Richard. . . You know I'm willing to put up with any mortal thing, as long as I can feel sure you're happy and contented. But when I think, dear, of the down *you* used to have on narrowness and snobbishness. . . And this is even worse."

"All the same, I felt I could stand no more of the rough diamonds we had to hobnob with out there."

"Still, some were diamonds, weren't they?"

"What we need, you and I, Mary, is a society that would take the best from both sides. The warm-heartedness of our colonial friends, their generosity and hospitality; while we could do without the promiscuity, the worship of money, the general loudness and want of refinement.— You wonder if I shall be happy here? I like the place, love; it's an ideal spot. I like this solid old house, too: and so far the climate has suited me. I seem to be getting on fairly well with the people; and though the practice is still nothing extraordinary, it has possibilities."

"Yes; but. . ."

"But? Well, I undoubtedly miss the income I used to have; there's little money to be made—compared with Ballarat, it's the merest niggling. And besides that, there was a certain breadth of view—that we'd got used to, you and I. Here, things sometimes seem atrociously cramped and small. But we must remember good exists everywhere and in everyone, wife, if we only take the trouble to look for it. And since the fates have pitched us here, here we must stay and work our vein until we've laid the gold bare. We've got each other, love, and that's the chief thing."

"Of course it is."

And now they were up and doing, he helping her to stow away her feast that it should not meet Selina's eye in the morning. And over this there was a good deal of merriment: they had to eat up some of the more perishable things themselves, which they did to a confession from Mary that she really had not meant to make *quite* so much, but had been lured on from one thing to another, by the thought of how nice it would look on the table. They packed away a decent amount in the larder, for appearance sake; the rest in a cupboard in the surgery.

But afterwards, Mary as she took down her hair, Mahony as he went round the house locking up, each dedicated the matter a further and private refection. She said to herself, astonished: "I do believe Richard is turning radical," and then went on to muse, a little wryly, that the "fates" to which he so jauntily referred were, after all, but another name for his own caprices. He, on the other hand, after justifying an omission to himself with: "No use worrying the poor little soul about that dam fool Robinson!" sent her a thought so warm that it resembled a caress. For at heart his whole sympathy was with Mary and Mary's ineradicable generosity. Alone, and his irritation cooled, he ranged himself staunchly on her side, against the stiff, uncharitable little world into which they were fallen.

VI

Entering the house late one summer afternoon, his pockets bulged with scraps of weed and wild-flower—the country people still gaped at sight of their doctor descended from his trap, a round glass in one eye, poking and prying in the hedgerows—Mahony was turning these specimens out on the hall table when Mary called to him from the dining-room. "Richard! A great surprise!"

He went downstairs to her, pulling off his gloves. "What? . . . the mail in already? I calculated it wasn't due for another week at least."

"And such a big one!"

Mary sat in an armchair, her lap full of envelopes, a closely written sheet of foreign note in her hand. Mahony picked up the several letters bearing his name, and ran his eye over the superscriptions. Their English post-bag was a lean one; but the arrival of the Australian mail more than atoned for it; and the deciphering of the crossed and recrossed pages, the discussing of news from the old home occupied the pair of them for days. Among his pile Mahony found a letter from Chinnery of the London Chartered, another from Archdeacon Long, a third from an old fellow-practitioner; while a bulky envelope promised a full business statement from the agent whom he had left in charge of his affairs. Taking off his greatcoat he sat down to read at his ease.

First, though, he had to hear from Mary the gist of those she had fleetly skimmed, prior to going back and reading them over again, word by word, with a brooding seriousness.

"Just fancy, John writes he's been forced to shut up his house and go and live at the Melbourne Club. *What* a state of things! That lovely house left to go to rack and ruin. It seems the last housekeeper turned out worst of all. She didn't set her cap at him, like Mrs. Perry, but he discovered that she was carrying on improperly with men. To think of a woman like that looking after poor Jinny's children! Now John has put all three to boarding-school. And Josey still the merest baby. How he expects them to thrive, I don't know—with never a proper home, or a mother's care. Then, here's Trotty. . . or Emma as he will persist in calling her. . . accused of being idle and flighty. Trotty flighty! If ever there was a dear, good-hearted little soul. . . easy to manage and open as the day. But John still seems to have his old down on Emma's children.

HENRY HANDEL RICHARDSON

And that brings me to some bad news. Johnny has run away. Listen to this.

"And now I pass to the doings of my son and heir. After keeping the boy to his desk under my own eye for the past twelve months, and endeavouring by precept and severity to make an honest man of him—in vain, Mary, for never a moment's gratification or satisfaction have I had from him; never a thank-you has he given me for all the money spent on him—he was lazy, deceptive, and frequented loose company. . . Richard! At seventeen! . . . Neglected his duties, took more wine than was good for him, played cards for money, and in the end went so far as to abstract his losses from my private drawer.— Isn't it dreadful?—When I taxed him with it, and threatened him with exposure, he as good as whistled in my face; then actually had the audacity to assert he owed me no gratitude, since I had never done anything for him; and the next morning he was missing—his bed had not been slept in. When after the lapse of several weeks I contrived to track him, I learned, to my shame and disgrace, that he had shipped before the mast to that Eldorado of thieves and scoundrels, America. Now he may shift for himself; I wash my hands of him. I have cut him out of my will and shall do the same by Emma, unless she mends her ways. You will scarcely credit it, my dear Mary, but her schoolmistress writes me that the girl—not yet fifteen years of age, Mark you!—has had to be 'publicly rebuked' for coquetting with members of the other sex in a place of worship.—

"Oh, stuff and nonsense, John! Never will I believe such a thing of Trotty. I know the child a great deal better than you. If I were only there, to find out what it all means He winds up with the usual: Thank God, Jane's children are of another disposition. I am confident I shall never be disgraced by them. No, my dear John, they haven't the spirit. But. . . well, I never did!" and Mary let her hand fall flop on the table. "Just listen to this! A postscript—I didn't see it before. He says: Your sister Zara seems about to make a fool of the first water of herself. She is, I hear— for I have seen nothing of her, I am thankful to say—contemplating matrimony.—Richard! And he doesn't even say who to. Isn't that like a man? Can it. . . could it be. . . But there! I believe I saw a letter from Zara herself."

Dropping John's, Mary picked on one of the envelopes in her lap, slit it open and began to fly the lines. "Mm. . . a tirade against John, of course. . . how those two do bicker! They seem to get worse as they grow older. Now where can it be? Mm. . . No one can put up with him any longer. . . Has had to close his house, thus proving—"

"Hullo, my dear, here's news!" cried Mahony and slapped his thigh. He had waited patiently for John's Jeremiad to end. In Zara's pursuit of matrimony he took no interest whatever. "Well, upon my word! . . . who would have dreamt of this? Those *Australia Felixes* . . . you remember, Mary, I bought them rather as a pig in a poke; and they've done nothing but make calls ever since. Now here they are declaring a three-pound dividend. My highest expectations did not exceed thirty shillings and even that would have been handsome. Think what it will be when they get in ten more stamps. Fifty pounds a month, for certain! My dear! we shall end by being moneyed people after all."

"Indeed I hope so," said Mary; and resumed her search for Zara's plum. "It looks as if she's not going to mention it. This is all about her pupils. They dote on her as usual, and she drives out everyday in the carriage. Zara is certainly lucky in her employers.—Oh, here it is— tucked away in a postscript. Other and fairer prospects Beckon, my dear Mary, than those of eternally improving the minds of other people's children. At present I can say no more. but your cleverness will no doubt enable you to divine what I leave unsaid. And that's all. Now I suppose I must wait another three months to hear who it is and how it happened. Oh dear, how *out* of everything we do seem here!"

"They've got the money for the chancel at last," threw in Mahony. "I must write and congratulate Long. Splendid work! They've had the laying ceremony, too, and hope twelve months hence that the Bishop will be up consecrating. The last Fancy Bazaar did the job. Here's a message to you. Mrs. Long's warm love, and she missed your help sadly at the refreshment-stall.—What? Well, I'm hanged! Old Higgins in my place as Trustee. Ha, ha! Listen to this. And now an item, doctor, after your own heart. We recently had with us a disciple and follower of spurgeon—one of the faithful who seceded with the great man from the evangelical alliance. He preached a first time in the Baptist Chapel, but this proved too small to hold a quarter of those who wished to hear him. And so the second time, on a sunday evening, he appeared on the platform of the New Alfred Hall. This was packed to the doors. The consequence was I preached to empty benches. Well! believing that the word of God remains the word of God, no matter under what guise it is presented, I cut my discourse short, doffed my cassock and went home to bed. The worthy fellow called on me next day; wished to exchange bibles—his, I am told, deeply under-scored—but I did not feel justified in going so far as that."

"Oh, Polly's lost her baby, poor thing!" cried Mary, whom the doings of Spurgeon's follower interested but mildly. "I do feel sorry for her. Not but what she takes it very sensibly. And if you think. . . six children and that teeny-weeny house. Still, it's rather sad. She says: Of course nobody misses it or cared anything about it but me. But it was rather a nice little kid Mary, and well formed. I had it at the breast for a day, and felt its little fingers, and it had blue eyes. Now fancy that!—and the rest of them so dark. Polly would think it belonged all the more to her, because of it. She says Ned's keeping a little steadier— that will be good news for Mother. He's clerk in a coal merchant's office now, and brings home his wages pretty regularly. Poor old Ned!" and Mary sighed.

But a message in Mr. Chinnery's made her smile. Tell Mrs. Mahony how much she is missed in society here. Those pleasant evenings we used to spend at your house, doctor, and her famous suppers are still talked of, and will long be remembered. "There, my dear! that's a feather in your cap, and should console you for recent happenings."

With this Mahony's budget was exhausted, and he rose to go to the surgery, where he proposed to make a few calculations in connection with his little windfall. But Mary held him back for yet a moment.

"I declare marrying's in the air. Now here's Jerry gone and got engaged. Who to? He writes: The prettiest girl in all the world and the best as well. Let us only hope that's true. Dear old Jerry! He deserves a good wife, if ever anyone did. But, oh dear me! she's only sixteen— barely a year older than Trotty. That's too young."

"Is it indeed? I know somebody who was once of a different opinion."

"But I was old for my age. Dear Jerry! He's so sensible in other things. If only he has not let his feelings run away with him here!"

"Poor old Mary wife! If only you were there to look after them all, eh? Better as it is, love. You'd have the burden of Atlas on your shoulders again."

"What atlas?" asked Mary absently, having passed to her next correspondent.

But the letter she spent longest over was the one she kept till the last—till Richard had retired to his room. For only to Tilly did she write nowadays with anything approaching frankness; and in this reply, oddly written, indifferently spelt, there might be private references to things she had said, besides the plain truth about all and any it touched on. Afterwards Richard would get, in her own words, all he needed to hear.

BEAMISH HOUSE,
LAKE WENDOUREE,
BALLARAT

My darling Mary,

Yours of 19th was a rare old treat. Job brought it when I wasn't at home—I'd driven out to have a look at the Mare Zoe, who's in foal and at grass in a Paddock of Willy Urquhart's. Didn't I pounce on it when I found it. I read it through twice without stopping, my dear. And didn't know whether to be glad or sorry when I'd done. You write cheery enough, Mary, but it doesn't seem to me you can be really happy in a place like you say leicester is—all damp and dreary, and no garden or space, and so little company. I'm glad it isn't me—that's all. Australy forever, for this chicken. Your description of the rainy season makes me get cold shivers down my spine. Give me the sun, thank you, and horses and a garden, and everything just as Jolly as can be. Fine feathers and blue blood aren't in my line anyhow.

Now for my budget. I'm still the gay old Widder I was when you heard last, and haven't felt tempted to change my state. To tell the truth, Mary, though I gad about as usual and don't sit at home and pull a long face, I still miss dear old Pa. It was so homey to hear him say: "Now then, what's my girl been up to today?" Whenever I came in, and the joy of my life to help him set his will against monseer H.'s. Well, he can't say he's forgotten. I've put him up the grandest monument in all the new cemetery. Pa in a sort of nightshirt, Mary, with wings attached, flying off, and a female figure all bowed up and weeping on the ground. This is all right for me, but sometimes I think Pa would rather have been took just sitting on a log and smoking his pipe. But Henry and the man as done it wouldn't hear of such a thing, said it wouldn't be ideel.

The chief news of this establishment is that Tom and Johnny has moved out. I was for keeping them on—we're none of us chickens anymore—but Henry pecked and nagged at me about propriety, till I gave in for sheer peace sake. They're boarded out, poor boys, and Tom comes over every morning to see after the fowls. One of these days I shall have to put my foot down and squash Henry—I see that. For it was the same with the weeds. Pa used to say: "Wear no weepers for me, Tilda!"—meaning veils and hangers and all that—"you've nothing to grieve for, old girl." And I to comfort him: "Right you are, old Jo! If my memory lasts so long, that is, for you'll beat Methuselah yet!" But when Henry heard of it, he all but stood on his head—my dear, he has agnes going round with a flounce of crepe a yard wide on her skirts. And indeed, Mary, I don't think I could have faced walking up the aisle of a sunday without a black bonnet and all complete; Though between ourselves it makes me feel a proper crow. Don't tell, but when I drive out into the bush I stuff a shady old hat in a basket under the seat, and as soon as I get far enough, I off with the bonnet and on with the hat. The weepers do draw the flies so. Aye, and flies of another colour too, Mary, if you'll believe me. But they come to the wrong shop here; none of your long-nosed fortune-snufflers for me. And that reminds me—what do you think Henry's latest is? says I ought to have someone to live with me—That it isn't commy faut for an attractive young Widder-woman to live all alone! ha ha! Do you see any green in this child's eye? I think I can be trusted, don't you, Mary, to look after myself. But I enjoy keeping Mossieu Henry on the quake. What he's afraid of is that all I got from poor old Pa won't fall to his and agnes's kids when I hop the Twig. Talking of agnes, I don't see Miladi once in a Blue Moon nowadays. I hear she's "Not at all well." It's my private belief something's wrong there, Mary. They've changed doctors three times, tell your husband, since he left. Louise Urquhart's presented her husband with the eleventh. How she keeps it up so regular beats me. But there's ructions in that family at present. Willy's been unusual gay. This time it was a governess, a real young spark they had up to Yarangobilly to teach the kids.

She got bundled out double-quick at the end, and Willy's looked meek as a sucking-lamb ever since. I drop in to see Ned's Polly now and again—you've heard I suppose she lost her last. And a good thing too. She's got more than she can manage as it is. I heard from her, young Jerry's the newest candidate for the Holy Estate. They do say the bride elect still plays with dolls. Lor, Mary! What will these infants be up to next? Another piece of news is that that obstinate old brute in Melbourne has gone and put all poor Finn's blessed little nippers to boarding-school. That does hit me hard, Mary. But I get even with him in another way, my dear. I've won over the old vinaigrette here—She needed new Globes, etc. for her schoolhouse—And we have a kind of agreement, all unbeknownst to the honourable, that the kid Trotty can come home with me of a saturday afternoon instead of spending the day on the backboard. She's a nice little kid, full of life, though young enough for her age, and I try to give her a good time. But what she likes best is to make butter, so I pin an apron on her and turn her into the dairy with Martha, among the milk-pans and churns. But let me tell you this, my dear. The honourable John needn't indulge any fool ideas about economising in housekeepers when her schooling's over—As old prunes and prisms tells me. Someone a great deal younger and handsomer than him will whip her off. She's much too pretty for the single life.

I think that's all my news. We had great church festifications lately and look forward to more when the chancel's built. I say, the doctor had some "Australia Felixes," hadn't he? I hear they've struck the reef. But this is a fearful long scrawl, and yet not half so comfortable as even a quarter of an hour's good yarn would be. When shall we have that again, Mary darling? I don't lose hopes for someday. And as you know I've sworn never to cross the water, it must mean the other way about. Yes, I still believe I shall see you back again: And when you do come, you'll find you are not forgotten by your devoted Old Crony—Tilly.

VII

The end of September brought day after day of soft, steamy mists, which saturated everything with moisture, and by night fell as a fine rain that turned low-lying parts of the garden to a bog. Did you mount to the roads on the high level you were in the clouds themselves; they trailed past you like smoke. There was no horizon seaward. At a little distance from the shore the grey water became one with a bank of vapour; the yellow cliffs vanished; suns neither rose nor set.

It was exasperating weather. These eternal sea fogs, which never a puff of wind came to chase away, seemed literally to bury you alive. They brought out the sweat on the flagged floors and passages of the old, old house; a crop of mould sprang up in the corners of the dining-room; the bread mildewed in the bin. Did the back door stand open, frogs took advantage of it to hop in and secrete themselves; slugs squeezed through cracks and left their silvery trail over the carpets. Mary began to fear the house would prove but sorry winter quarters; and she had ample leisure to indulge such reflections, the bad weather confining her almost wholly within doors. Here was no kind friend with buggy or shandrydan to rout her out and take her driving; and ladies did not walk in Buddlecombe: the hilly roads were too steep, the flat roads too muddy. So, once more, she sat and sewed, faced by the prospect of a long, dull, lonely winter. Calls and invitations had rather dropped off, of late. . . as was not unnatural. . . and she would have been for seeing nothing peculiar in it, had she not connected it in some obscure way with Richard and the practice. This had also declined; was failing, it was plain, to live up to its early promise.

She was unaware that no sooner had the "Court" reopened for the winter than the tale—in a garbled version—of the innovations attempted by the "new doctor's wife" had been carried to the ears of its mistress. And Mrs. Archibald Treherne pinched a pair of very thin lips and further arched already supercilious eyebrows. That was all; but it was enough. And, in consequence, from the choicest entertainments of the autumn the Mahonys found themselves conspicuously omitted.

Their only personal connection with the big house was due to an unhappy contretemps of the kind that was given to rankling forever after in Mahony's mind.

On learning of the family's arrival, both he and Mary privately thought an exchange of courtesies would follow. Hence when one day a footman was found to have handed in cards during Mary's absence—his mistress keeping her seat in her carriage at the foot of the hill—the visit did not take them by surprise. Within the week Mary drove out in a hired vehicle to return it.

A bare half-hour later she was home again, looking flushed and disturbed.

"Richard! . . . a most *awkward* thing has happened. Those cards were not meant for us at all. It was the footman's mistake. He ought to have left them at the next house down the road—that little thatched cottage at the corner. They were for a Mrs. Pigott, who's staying there."

"What? Well, upon my word!"

Leaning back in his chair Mahony stared at his wife, while he took in the significance of her words. "And does that mean to say the woman doesn't intend to call on you. . . as well?"

"Evidently not." Mary was crestfallen.

"*What?* But will call on this Mrs. Pigott?—living in a farmer's thatched cottage?" And Mary not replying, he burst out: "You will never, with my consent, set foot in that house again!"

"Indeed, I don't want to," said Mary, and sitting down untied her bonnet-strings and threw them over her shoulders. "I don't know *when* I've felt so uncomfortable. I was ushered into the drawing-room—it seemed crowded with people—and there she sat, holding our cards and looking from them to me and back again. I heard something about 'the new doctor's wife' as I went in. Then she asked to what she owed my visit, said she hadn't the pleasure and so on—all in front of these other people—the Brookes of 'Shirley' I think they were—that retired old General. . . you met him once, you know, and thought him very stuck-up. I had to explain how it had happened; I felt my face getting as red as fire. I didn't know whether to walk out again or what, and she didn't help me—didn't get up, or shake hands, or anything. Fortunately a very nice person—a sort of companion, I think—asked me to rest a little after my drive, and I thought it would make things less awkward for everybody if I did so; so I just sat down for a minute and said a word or two, and then bowed and left. She came with me to the door—the companion, I mean."

White with anger Mahony shuffled and re-shuffled the papers that lay before him on the writing-table. "We've never been treated like this in our lives before, Mary, and I for one won't put up with it! Damn the woman and her insolence! Talk about breeding and blue blood—give

HENRY HANDEL RICHARDSON

me ordinary decent feelings and a little kindness, and you can keep the blood, thank you! I snap my fingers at it." In imagination he saw his Mary, faced by a like predicament, doing her utmost to smooth over the embarrassment of the moment and set the unfortunate intruder at ease.

And time did not lessen his resentment. Rudeness to Mary—such a thing had never before come within the range of his experience—stung him, he found, almost more than rudeness to himself. But was the thrust not actually aimed at him. . . through her? What had the object of it been but to drive home to him the galling fact that, on this side of the world, the medical profession carried with it no standing whatever? In the colonies, along with the Parson and the Police Magistrate, he had helped to constitute the upper ten of a town. Here the doctor—and quite especially the country doctor—stood little higher in the social scale than did the vet and the barber. Oh, those striped poles! Tradition died so hard in this slow-thinking, slow-moving country. Ingrained in people, not to be eradicated, was a memory of the day when the surgeon had been but the servant, the attendant lackey of the great house.

Grimly cogitating, he prepared in advance for further snubs and slights by going about with his chin in the air, looking to the last degree stiff and unapproachable. For, that Mary's misadventure would remain a secret, he did not for a moment believe. There were all too many mouths in Buddlecombe agape for gossip—it would be threshed out over every tabby's tea-table—and those already inclined to look down their noses at him and Mary would have a fresh excuse for so grimacing. Anything was possible in such a petty-minded, tittle-tattling place. Hence, it did not surprise him to hear that Robinson had been called to the "Court." The trouble was, of course, that the townspeople and lesser folk were faithful in imitation of their betters; and soon it began to seem to him that he was not occasionally, but everlastingly getting out of Robinson's way. And as he sat at home over the fire—Mary kept fires going to drive the damp out; though, in order to breathe, you had to leave the windows wide open to mist and fog—his thoughts were anything but cheerful. There was not work enough for two—or money either. As it was, he was having to depend more than he cared for on his Australian dividends.

It was at this juncture that the report reached his ears of illness at "Toplands," where the younger son lay prostrate with gastric fever. But his services were not requisitioned.

Then came that morning when Mary, grave and worried, broke the news to him that Robinson's gig had been seen at the gates of "Toplands"; the morning when, unable to hire a horse for his rounds, he was tormented, as he trudged the country lanes, by the idea that, like the last, this practice also was threatening to peter out.

Late that evening as he sat reading, there came a loud rat-tatting at the front door. The doctor in him pricked up his ears at the now unfamiliar sound: it was like an old-time call to action—in the land of cruel accident and sudden death. The visitor admitted, an excited voice was heard in the passage, and Mary's in reply; after which Mary herself entered the surgery, shutting the door behind her and looking irresolute and uncomfortable. The elder of the two Challoner boys had, it seemed, come driving down post-haste from "Toplands." His brother lay dying. Would Dr. Mahony come back with him—the dogcart was at the door—and meet Mr. Robinson?

"Meet *Robinson?* Not if I know it!"

"I told him I couldn't be sure. But, Richard, there's nobody else—unless he rides all the way to Brixeter. And there and back would take him at least four hours. His brother might be dead by then. Their mother is almost out of her mind, poor thing."

"Poor thing, indeed! After the way she's treated us. But you haven't a scrap of pride in you."

"Not when it's a case of life or death I haven't. Dear, don't you think you could manage to overlook what's happened? . . . not stand on etiquette? If the boy should die, you'd reproach yourself bitterly for not having gone."

"You never will understand these things, Mary!—and though you live to be a hundred. Little did I dream," he said with violence, as he slapped his book to and ungraciously rose to his feet, "when I settled here, that I should ever come down to playing second fiddle in this fashion."

"It may be your chance to play first again—if you cure him."

Mahony pshawed.

Off he drove though, as she had known all along he would; and did not get back till four in the morning. Then, half a glance was enough to show her that he was in a state of extreme nervous exasperation. So she asked only a single question: did the lad still live? But Richard could not contain himself; and as he moved about the bedroom, winding up his watch and letting his collar fly, he burst out: "Nothing on earth will induce me to stop in this place, Mary, to be insulted as I have been tonight! This is worse—a hundred times worse!—than the colony."

From under her lashes Mary shot him a swift look he did not see: a look full of motherly tenderness—and yet triumphant. Aloud she merely said: "But think what a feather in your cap it will be, if the boy recovers, . . . the prestige you will gain."

"Prestige? Pah! Robinson will say he did the curing, and I stepped in and took the credit. A fat lot of prestige to be got from that! Mary, there's been a dead set made against me here—I've felt it now for sometime, though why, I knew no more than Adam. Tonight I believe I got a clue. It's Australia if you please!—the fact of my having practised in Australia is against me." And at Mary's vigorously expressed disbelief: "Well! just listen to this, my dear, and judge for yourself. First of all, they prefer Robinson *fuddled*, to me sober. Yes, it's the truth. When I get to 'Toplands' I find him tight—stupidly tight—standing by the bed staring like an owl. Quite devoid of shame he evidently is not though, for no sooner did he see me than off he bolted—leaving me as much in the dark as ever. I tried to get some information from the womenfolk about the earlier stages of the complaint; but not one was capable of giving a connected answer. . . I'd sent the other young fellow off for leeches and the barber. Young Leonard lay convulsed and insensible. And yet, if you'll believe me, Robinson had been telling them it was gastric, and plying him with brandy. Inflammation of the membranes of the brain, Mary!—and the fool killing him with stimulants. While I was making mustard poultices for his feet and legs, back comes Robinson and attempts to feel his pulse. I said: 'Now look here, my good man, if you don't give me some particulars of this case, I shall proceed to treat it without you.' He answered not a word. Then I turned to her. 'Now, madam,' said I, 'I'm not going to stand this. Either he or I must leave the room—or indeed the house—and, until you decide which, I go downstairs.' She followed, all but clawing at my coat. He lurches after us, shouting abuse. . . for the whole house to hear. And what, pray, do you think he said? . . . amongst other scurrilous trash. 'Very well, if you prefer the opinion of this old quack to mine, take it and abide by the consequences. Australia! We all knows what *that* means. Ask him what other trades he's plied there. Make him turn out his credentials.' It was as much as I could do to keep from knocking him down. Only the thought of the lad upstairs restrained me. *She* was very humble and apologetic, of course; besought me to take no notice; almost grovelled to me to save her son, etc. etc. I made short work of her, though."

"Besides, you can surely afford to smile at such nonsense, Richard?" Mary strove to soothe him. "It would be beneath your dignity to notice it. Especially as he wasn't himself." Distressed though she felt at this return for Richard's kindness, Mary was also unpleasantly worked on by his interlarded "My good man!" and the general hoity-toity air of his narration. What a peppery fellow he was! How could he ever expect to succeed and be popular? That kind of tone would not go down here.

"I make allowance for his condition. . . of course I do. . . but all the same it does not incline me, my dear. . . If such are the tales that are going the round about me, Mary—charlatan and quack, a colonial ne'er-do-well trading on a faked diploma and so on; if it's a blot on my reputation to have lived and practised in the colonies, instead of mouldering my life away in this miserable village—then much is explained that has been dark to me. Anyhow, it came over me with a rush tonight: I go from here. They don't want me; I'm not good enough for them—a man who has held a first-class practice in the second city of Victoria not good enough for the torpid livers of Buddlecombe! Very well, let them get someone else. . . I'm done with 'em. Really, Mary, I sometimes feel so sick and tired of the struggle that I fancy throwing up medicine altogether. What would you say, love, to taking a small cottage somewhere and living modestly on the little we have?"

Now what *would* he say next? wondered Mary with an inward sigh. But the present was not the moment to combat such vagaries. Richard was sore and smarting; and in this mood he just tossed off suggestions without thinking; letting his anger out in them as the hole in the lid of a kettle lets out steam. So she only said: "Let us first see what happens here. Is there any chance of Lenny Challoner recovering?"

"Frankly, I don't think there is. I give him till the coming midnight. He'll probably die between then and dawn."

But this prediction was not fulfilled. The boy weathered the night; and after sixty hours' unconsciousness spoke to those about him, though with wandering wits.

Buddlecombe was all a-twitter and agog: the affair was discussed over counters by tradesmen and goodwives; at mahogany dinner-tables; in the oaken settles of inns. Everyone knew to a T everything that had happened. . . and a good deal more: were for and against the two doctors in their feud. "'Tis a'anyway little better'n boo'tchers a hoald t'lot of un," thus Raby, the town crier, summed up the matter to his cronies of the "Buddlecombe Arms." "Bu'ut if us was ca'alves, 'tis the ha'and us knows as us 'ud ra'ather die by."

Yes, chiefly against him, felt Mahony: and it screwed him stiff as a rod. The majority sided with the townsman who had lived among them for years; who was rich enough to spend freely in their shops, subscribe heavily to their charities; besides being an expert in the right admixture of joviality and reserve necessary to make his failings go down.

Mary fought this idea with all her might. Richard was just reading his own feelings into other people, as usual. She herself clung to the belief that the sick boy would pull through, now he had held out so long. Which would be a veritable triumph for Richard. If only he did not spoil things by his uncompromising behaviour! For he was in a most relentless frame of mind. More than one of Robinson's patients subsequently sent for him. But he, riding the high horse, declined to touch a single other of the enemy's cases. They should apply for relief, said he, to Mr. Jakes of Brixeter.

Meanwhile, of course, he did not spare himself over the patient he had taken in hand. But eventually, in spite of his care, the boy died, killing Mary's hopes, and enabling Robinson to go about cockahoop, boasting that wrong treatment had finished him off. It *had* been "gastric," after all!

And now, as he stalked his way or drove his gig about the hilly roads and narrow streets, Mahony felt himself indeed a marked man.

"Till Christmas. . . not a day longer! I was never built for this." And as he said it, his thoughts flew back to a time when the merest hint that his skill was doubted had shaken his roots to their depths. Here, where he had as yet hardly put out a sucker, the wrench was easier, and at the same time a hundredfold more destructive.

VIII

B ut before Christmas came, Mary's hope that things would somehow right themselves burned up anew—if hope that could be called which ran so counter to her own inclinations, and to the possible issue she now thought she descried.

With the onset of November it was the turn of "Buddlecombe Hall" to reopen. And now a wave of new life seemed to run through the sluggish little town. The Saxeby-Corbetts, returning, as it were took possession of the place; and they had this advantage over the Trehernes—a childless couple—that they counted a baker's dozen in family all told. Their arrival was after the fashion of crowned heads. First came dragloads of servants, male and female, and of varying ages—from the silver-headed butler down to young scullery and laundry-maids— after which the windows of the great house were flung up, the chimneys belched smoke, hammerings and beatings resounded; while various elderly women in the town tied on rusty black and went off to give obsequious aid. Footmen in livery lounged about the inns; grooms rode swathed horses out to exercise. The tradespeople wellnigh lost their wits with excitement. One heard of nothing, now, on entering a shop, but "the family," its needs and preferences.

"I've never seen anything to equal it!" cried Mahony exasperated. "The way these poor creatures burn to prostrate themselves."

The list of young people would not be full till the holidays began; but donkey and pony-carts were met with containing the smaller children, their attendant governesses and nursemaids. The squire himself, a ruddy-faced man in early middle age, mounted on a fine chestnut, might be observed confabbing with the farmers; and lastly came his lady, driving herself in a low chaise: a bony-jawed, high-nosed woman, whose skin told of careless exposure to all weathers. Dressed anyhow, too, said Mary, who had once seen her in the town with an old garden-hat perched on her head, a red flannel spencer thrown over her bodice.

And now, at the sound of wheels, grocer and butcher would prick up their ears and pop from their respective doors, merely on the off chance of pulling their forelocks, and (as likely as not) receiving in return a snub from the lady of the "Hall." For in spite of what Mahony called their "piteous desire" to please, she was never satisfied, and hurled at their heads, in vigorous language, her frank opinion of their wares.

"Now, Johnson, this will not do! That last meat you supplied to the servants hall was tough as my boot. If the next is no better, I shall come and superintend the slaughtering myself. It's my belief, my man, you don't know a heifer from a leather-gutted milch-cow!"

And Johnson, doubled in two with relish of her "ladyship's" joke, could be heard right down the street vowing there should be no further ground for complaint; though a visit from her "ladyship" to his humble establishment would at anytime be reckoned as an honour—and so on.

To mark his disapproval of this fawning, and for fear any hint of patronage or condescension might come his way, Mahony had all his armour on, all his spines out, when he was unexpectedly summoned to the "Hall" to attend one of the children, sick of a feverish cold. Mary saw him go, with many misgivings; but it actually seemed as if, for once, his lordly manner went down. By his own account he successfully faced the imperious dame: "Who, if you please, was for herself pronouncing on the ailment—it turns out to be chicken-pox—and had nurses and maids dancing like puppets to a string. I soon let her see that kind of thing wouldn't do with me, Mary. And she took the hint fast enough, changed her tone, and behaved like any other decently bred woman.—I had certainly rather though," he added, "have her for a friend than an enemy."

Oh, if this could only be, thought Mary. It might alter everything. And it was here, with him daily at the "Hall," where the nursery in a body succumbed to the pox, that her confidence bloomed anew. For in a way Richard even became a kind of protege of its mistress: she would keep him, after his professional visit was paid, to chat about the colonies and hear his impressions of England. Even Mary herself received a call, and though it was one of a somewhat quizzing inspection and Madam was "not at home" when she returned it, yet Richard was pleased, which was the main thing. He himself was twice bidden to dinner—a little informal dinner, at which only another man or two was present; a state of things that seemed to mark as true the report that the dame had small liking for the company of her own sex.

Yes, Richard's fortunes seemed at last to have taken a definite turn for the better, when of a sudden the blow fell which put an end to hopes and fears alike. What was behind it Mary did not know, and never learned. But one morning at breakfast he blurted out in summary fashion that he had resolved, overnight, to shake the dust of Buddlecombe off his feet. And before she had recovered from the shock of this announcement, the house was up for sale, and she hard at work sorting and packing. Coming as it did on top of her renewed confidence, the decision hit Mary hard. It also gave a further push to her tottering faith in Richard's judgment. Of course, it was clear something unpleasant had happened at the last dinner-party. But she could get nothing out of Richard—absolutely nothing—except that he was done "for all eternity" with place and people. In vain she reasoned, argued, pleaded. . . and even lost her temper. He remained obstinately silent, leaving her to her own conjectures—which led nowhere. Leicester? . . . well, compared with this, his bolting from Leicester had been as easy to understand as A B C—an ugly town with no practice worth speaking of, and the little there was, of the wrong kind. But here where she had thought his first irate "Till Christmas!" was gradually being overlaid; here she could only put his abrupt determination down to one of his most freakish and wayward impulses.

Mahony saw her trouble; saw, too, how rudely her trust in him was shaken. But he did not enlighten her—he would rather have cut his tongue out. For what had happened concerned Mary first of all; and though there was a chance she might have taken it less tragically than he—in real "Mary-ish" fashion—yet he felt as averse to bringing the words over his lips as to letting her see how deeply it had mortified him.

Another informal invitation to dine at the "Hall" had reached him—at least, he took it to be such, since Mary was not included. At the entrance to the great house, however—six o'clock of a frosty December evening—he ran into old Barker, a retired Anglo-Indian, just dismounting from his hired fly; and to his amazement saw that, this time, Barker had his ladies with him. Becoming involved in their entrance, he was waiting with the Colonel for wife and daughters to rejoin them, when the old valetudinarian found that he had left his jujubes in the pocket of his greatcoat. Standing thus alone, close to the half-open drawing-room door, Mahony suddenly heard his own name spoken and in the harsh, grating voice of their hostess.—"Yes, from the colonies. I can tell you I *was* put out, when I came back and found what had happened. I wrote off at once to that sheep, young Philips, and gave him a sound rating for letting himself be frightened away, after the trouble I had been to, to get him here." At this a gentler voice murmured a query; to which the answer rang shrill and dear: "Oh, well, *he* is quite presentable!"

This it was that stuck in Mahony's throat. And on getting home shortly after midnight he did not go down the passage to the bedroom, but turned into the surgery, which faced the hall-door. No sound came from Mary; she was evidently asleep.

He did not strike a match: feeling his way to the window, he raised the blind and leaned his forehead on the glass. The sea lay still and black as ink, under a starlit sky—as starlight went here. Presently the moon, now entered on her last quarter, would come up from behind the cliffs and throw a lurid light—lurid, because the light of decay—over the cold sea and sleeping town, picking out the line of silvery shingle that edged the beach, and making the odd old curved breakwater look as though it were built of marble.

He had been at white heat all the evening. Again and again amid the desultory talk, both at the dinner-table and afterwards in the drawing-room, the rasping voice had rung in his ears: "*He* is quite presentable!"—while he could imagine, though he had not seen, the impudent shrug that accompanied the stressing of the pronoun. Thus wantonly did mortals glance at, sum up and dismiss one another. The jar to his pride was a rude one. For, ingrained in him, and not to be eradicated was the conviction that he was gentleman first, doctor second: slights might be aimed at his profession, but not at him in person.—And yet, in comparison, the patronising "presentable" affixed to himself left him cold. It was the sneer at Mary that stung him to the quick. That was something he would never be able either to forget or forgive. Did he contemplate this great heart, full to the brim of charity, of human kindness; this mine of generous impulse; this swift begetter of excuse and explanation for everything in others that was not as fair and honest as in himself; did he consider that, to assist in their need any of these purblind souls who sat so lightly in judgment on her, she would have stripped the clothing from her back: then he burned with a wrath too deep for words. He did not know one of them worthy to tie up her shoe-lace. And yet, such a worm for truth existed in him, so plaguy an instinct to get to the root of a matter, that even as he burned, he found himself looking Mary up and down, viewing her from every angle, and with a purely objective eye. He saw her at home, in church, in the company of others; saw her gestures, her movements, her smile; heard her laughter, the tones of her voice and her way of speaking: all these, for the first time, as things for themselves, detached from the true, sound core of her. And as he did so, he was forced to own that, in a way, these people were justified of their criticism: she *was* different. But not as they meant it. Her manner had a naturalness, her gestures a spontaneity, which formed only too happy a contrast to their ruled and measured restraint. Indeed as he studied her, it began to seem to him that into all Mary did or said there had crept something large and free—a dash of the spaciousness belonging to the country that had become her true home. She needed elbow-room. Her voice was deeper, fuller, more resonant than theirs; she fixed a straight, simple gaze on people and things; walked with a freer step, was franker in her speech, readier with her tongue; she stood up to members of the other sex as women emphatically did *not* do here, and they did not belong to the class of "Madam of the Hall." No connection between Mary and the pursed-up mouth, the downcast, unroving, unintelligent eye, the hands primly folded at the waist, the short, sedate steps, of the professing English lady. For that, the net of her experience had been too widely cast. She had rubbed shoulders with all sorts; had been unable to afford the "lady's" privilege of shutting an eye to evil or wrong-doing and pretending it did not exist. And if, in the process, she had come to be a shade too downright in her opinions, too blunt for the make-believe of antique conventions. . . well, he thought he might safely leave it to Him who had broken bread with publicans and sinners, to adjudge which was the worthier attitude of the two.

Thus he reasoned; but ever and again his mind veered back to the personal thrust. Mary vulgar! . . . Mary, of whom he had felt so fondly proud, having grown to middle age hearing on all sides that she had not her equal in those attributes that make a woman blessed. "Out there" he had seen her courted, made much of; none had approached her in popularity. And from this happy state he had torn her away. . . for what? For the privilege of being looked down on as not quite a lady. . . had uprooted her from the country she loved best and fitted best into, to make her a stranger on the face of the earth. So much for Mary. But did he himself feel anymore at home here than she? Not a bit of it! Nor had he been a jot apter at adjusting himself. They stood out, the pair of them, like over-large figures on a miniature background. The truth was they had lost the knack of running in a groove: life, in its passage, had hammered them out into citizens of the world. So that, by now, an indelible stamp was on them. And, with this as their dower, cured forever of an excessive insularity, they had come back to find an England that had not budged by an inch; where people's outlook, habits, opinions were just what they had always been—inelastic, uninspired. Worse, these islanders seemed to preen themselves on their very rigidity, their narrow-mindedness, their ignorance of any life or country but their own; waving aside with an elegant flutter of the hand, everything of which they themselves had no cognisance. And into this closed circle he and Mary—especially Mary—had come blundering, trampling on prejudice, surrounded by an aura of adventure. . . and unsuccessful adventure at that! Was it indeed any wonder they found themselves outside the pale?

Well, this ended it. He could not picture himself going on living there with a nervous eye eternally cocked at Mary to see how she was comporting herself, or how what she did struck the wretched group of snobs he had been fool enough to dump her down amongst; the while he winced at idiosyncrasies he yet grudged to admit. No, the wider the distance he could put between himself and Buddlecombe the better he would be pleased. But where to go? . . . what next? Back to some sordid manufacturing town, with its black mud and slippery cobblestones, to act as medical adviser to a handful of grooms and servant girls? Or to another village to see exclusive country-folk turn up their noses at your wife, and watch the practice in which you had invested your hard-earned hundreds melting away, filched by one whose chief merit was never having been out of England? Not if he knew it!—There now remained only London to consider—Mary would no doubt harp anew on the openings to be found there. But at the mere thought of London he shrank into himself, as he had shrunk under his first physical impression of it. What he had then suspected he now felt sure of. Great cities were not for him: he was too old to stand the strain of their wear and tear. And therewith the list of possibilities on this side of the globe was exhausted. Would he had stayed on the other! Civis Britannicus Sum—that knowledge should have been enough for him. Instead of which, burning to prove his citizenship, he had chased back, with, in his heart, the pent-up feelings of his long, long absence. He laughed did he now recall the exultation with which he had descried the outlines of the English coast. "Out there," he had seen this old country through the rose-red spectacles of youthful memory. Now he knew that the thrill he had experienced on again beholding it—his pleasure in its radiant greenness—was the sum total of the satisfaction he would ever get from it. No sooner ashore—and not even Mary had fathomed his passionate desire to stand well here—than he had felt himself outsider and alien. England had no welcome for her homing sons, or any need of them: their places were long since filled.

But stay! let him be frank with himself. Had he liked the motherland any better than it liked him? He had not. Indeed his feelings were a great deal more active than any want of liking. He hated it—yes! hate was not too strong a word—and had done, from the first moment of landing. His attempt at transplanting himself had been a sad and sorry failure. Returning full of honours and repute, he found that the mere fact of his having lived and practised in Australia cast a slur on his good name. Again, he had come back on what he believed to be but the threshold of middle age—and without being greatly troubled by it; for, "out there," men of his own years had kept pace, gone along with him—and everywhere had been made to feel himself well over his prime, if not indeed—thanks to Australian pallor and wrinkles—an old man: one of those broken-down adventurers who limp home, at long last, to eke out the remainder of a wasted life.

But what next?—what in all the world next? To this question he could find no answer. Nor was he helped by staring at the sea, or the golden, lemon-shaped moon that now came up on its back from behind the dark mass of the cliffs. The purchase of a third practice was beyond him: if he went from here he went empty-handed. Possibly he might get for the house what he had given for it—though he had discovered that it was both damp and in need of repair—but this sum would not suffice to set him up anew. No, the outlook was darker than, a moment before, the night had been; no moon rose for him. And he lay long wakeful, grappling in a cold sweat with the many small practical details of the break—details which it is so easy to overlook in the taking of sweeping decisions, yet which afterwards rise up like mountains—and following the square of silver that flooded in through the uncurtained window, and slowly moved across the bed on its passage from wall to wall. With the glimmer of the material dawn, however—red behind those cliffs that had delivered up the moon, great Jupiter hanging like a globe of silver above them—there came to him, too, the dawning of a possible solution. But at the first hint of it he flung restlessly over on his side, unable to bear its weight. A bolder hand than his was needed, to sweep away the cobwebs of prejudice and nervous aversion in which he had spun himself. It took Mary to do it; and she did; though not till she had talked herself hoarse in an attempt to make him see reason, begging him to hold the field and show fight; till her head swam with listening to his monotonous: "What now? Where can I go?" Then, abruptly determined, she cut the knot by facing him and answering squarely: "Why, home again!"—words which first made Mahony wince, then snort with contempt. But he had no other suggestion to offer—or none but the fatuous one Mary had already smiled at, that, he having given up practice, they should retire to some tiny cottage, do without domestic help, see no company, and live on the slender sum that came to them from Australia. "I think we could be very happy and content, love, living so—just you and I." If a soul can be said to laugh, then, in spite of her trouble, Mary's soul rocked with laughter at this fresh sample of Richard's fantasy. Oh, was there ever such an unpractical old dreamer? . . . such an inability to see things as they were. No doubt he pictured a show cottage, wreathed in roses and honeysuckle, where they would pass idyllic days. The slow death-in-life of such an existence, the reaction of his haughty pride against the social position—or want of position—that would be forced upon them, was hidden from him. Perhaps mercifully hidden. . . and Mary sighed.

But she did not falter. . . either at his first disdainful sniff, or, later on, when his eyes came stealing back to hers; came tamed, all the scorn gone out of them. "Only do not call it home," was his unspoken request. Short of a miracle that name would never, he believed, cross his lips again. No place could now be "home" to him as long as he lived. He was once more an outcast and a wanderer; must go back in humiliation to the land that had eaten up his prime, and there make the best of the years that were left him.

As time wore on, however, and their preparations for departure advanced; as, too, the prospect of a change of scene hoisted its pirate flag again, this sense of bitterness subsided; the acute ache turned to a dull pain that was almost a relief. And worked on by this, as by the joy which, for all her anxieties, Mary could not quite conceal, the relief also imperceptibly changed its character, and grew to be a warm spot in his heart.

And one evening, when the supper dishes had been pushed aside to make room for Mary's desk—she was methodically noting the contents of a tin trunk—Mahony in watching her and thinking how the frequent coughs and colds she had suffered from, since landing in England, had thinned her down, spoke his thought aloud. "Well, love, whatever happens, you at least will grow fat and well again, and be the healthy woman you always were."

"Now don't start to worry about me. I'm all right," said Mary. "It takes time to get used to a strange climate." She entered a few more items in her clean, pointed writing, then laid her pen down and put her chin on her hand. "The thing I like to think of, Richard, is how soon I shall be seeing them all again—Ned and Jerry and Tilly, and the dear children. I can hardly believe it. I *have* missed them so."

"Poor little wife! And shall I tell you what I dwell most on? 'Pon my soul, Mary, it's of getting my teeth into a really sweet apple again—instead of a specimen that's red on one side only. I believe England will stick in my mind, for the rest of my days, as the land where the fruit doesn't ripen."

"And yet costs so much to buy."

"And if I know you, my dear, it's the Abernethy biscuit and thin lemon-water you won't forget. Well, well, madam! you'll soon be able to pamper your guests once more to your heart's content."

"Perhaps. But I shall at least see who it is Jerry thinks of marrying."

"See? . . . yes. But don't hug the belief you'll be able to influence him in his choice."

"I may not want to. And then there's Johnny to try and find out about, poor boy, and to keep Zara from making a goose of herself. Oh! now that we're going home, I feel how dreadfully cut off from them all I have been here."

"And they'll everyone hail you joyfully, my dear, rest assured of that! . . . be literally foaming with impatience to make use of you again. I should only like to know how they've got on without you." Mahony had risen from his chair and was standing on the hearthrug with his back to the fire. Having meditatively warmed his coat-tails for a moment he added: "There's another thing, Polly, I don't mind telling you I look forward to, and that is seeing a real sunrise and sunset again. On this side of the world. . . well, as often as not the sun seems just to slip in or out of a bank of clouds. There's none of that sense of a coming miracle. . . that uplifting effect of space. . . or splendour of colouring. Why, I've still in my memory evenings when half the field of the sky was one pink flush—with a silver star twinkling through—or a stretch of unreal green deepening into yellow—or mauve. . . And the idea has come to me that it must have been from glories of this kind that the old Greek scribe drew his picture of the New Jerusalem. . . Yes, I must say, things here—colouring, landscape, horizon—have all seemed very dull and cramped. . . like the souls of the people themselves."

Again he fell into thought. Then warmed by these confidences, went further. "Mary, love, let me confess it: I realise what a sad fool I've made of myself over this whole business. My ever leaving Ballarat was a fatal mistake. If I'd only had the sense to take your advice! I was run down—at the end of my tether—from years of overwork. A twelve-month out of harness would have set me right again: a voyage to this side; fresh surroundings and associations—and no need to stint with the money either, for we should now have been going back to our old ample income. Instead of having to face another start on as good as nothing. . . eat humble pie before them all, too. For they will certainly grasp what has happened.—No, I can see it now; I was too old for such a drastic break. One's habits stiffen with one's joints. You've noticed I've been hurt by people here implying I'm out-of-date, old-fashioned—good enough for the colonies but not for the home-country—but, upon my word, Mary, I don't know if there isn't some truth in it. I stopped too long in the one place, my dear; with the result that I ought to have stopped there altogether.—Well, well! . . . there's only this about it: fiasco though it has proved, it has not hit me as hard as it might have done, considering the exaggerated expectations I came home with. Which in itself is enough to show me age is rendering me indifferent. Actually, my dear, I believe much of the sting is taken from what has happened by the sight of your satisfaction at returning. Never should I have brought you here—never! I thought to find myself among a different set of people altogether. In memory, I confused good breeding with tact and kindliness. Whereas, now, if it comes to a choice between blue blood and inborn goodness of heart, then what I say is: give me nature's gentlefolk all the time. There's as little likeness between them as between this eternal clammy drizzle and some of those cloudless winter days we knew on the Flat."

"Richard! Don't forget how you hated the climate there. And how poorly the sun made you feel."

"Nor do I. And in spite of the mizzle, and damp, and want of sun, I've thriven in this country. But one can't live on climate alone. And when I let my mind dwell on the way I—we—have been treated here; the stodgy lack of goodwill. . . animosity even. . . the backbiting and gossip, I tell you this, love: there's but one person I shall regret when I leave; one only of whom I shall carry away a warm remembrance;

and that's, as you know, your dear old mother. But can you guess why? Upon my word, I believe it's because there's something in her warm-heartedness and generosity, her overflowing hospitality, that reminds me of the people we lived among so long."

"Well! it's late. . . we must to bed," he went on, after a silence which Mary did not break, there seeming really nothing left for her to say. "I've no plans, my dear, nor have I at present the spirit to make any. It seems best at this moment to leave the future in the laps of the gods. I know this much though: I'm cured of castle-building forever."

Mary nodded and acquiesced; or at least again said nothing; and she kept to this attitude in the weeks that followed, when, as was only natural, Richard's mind, far too active and uneasy to rest, began to play round the plans he *might* have made, had he not forsworn the habit. These included settling somewhere by the sea; either near Melbourne or at one of the watering-places on the Bay—Dromana or Schnapper Point. Mary let him talk. She herself was persuaded that the only rational thing for him to do was to return to Ballarat. It was of no use his riding the high horse: feelings of pique and pride must yield to practical considerations. He was known from one end of Ballarat to the other; and the broken threads could there be picked up more swiftly and with greater ease than anywhere else. It would, of course, no longer be a case of Webster Street—unless the doctor to whom he had sold the practice had failed, or proved otherwise unsatisfactory. But Richard would find room somewhere; even if it had to be on the Redan, or at Sebastopol, or out at Buninyong. And though he could now never hope to occupy the position he had wilfully abandoned—oh, the unspeakable folly of man!—never hope to give up general practice for that of consultant or specialist, yet with care something might still be saved from the wreck of the past. And nursing these schemes, Mary set her lips and frowned with determination. Never again in the years to come, should he be able to say he repented not having taken her advice. This time she would set her will through, cost what it might.

HENRY HANDEL RICHARDSON

PART II

I

The good ship *Florabella*, eighty-four days out from Liverpool, made the Australian coast early one spring morning; and therewith the faint, new, spicy smell of land wafted across the water.

Coming up from below to catch a whiff of it, her passengers blinked dazzled eyes at the gaudy brilliancy of light and colouring. Here were no frail tints and misty trimmings; everything stood out hard, clear, emphatic. The water was a crude sapphire; the surf that frothed on the reefs white as milk. As for the sky, Mahony declared it made him think of a Reckitt's bluebag; while a single strip of pearly cloud to the east looked fixed, immovable—solid as those clouds on which, in old paintings, cherubs perch or lean.

Outside the "Rip" the vessel hove to, to take up the pilot; and every neck was craned to watch his arrival; for with him would come letters and news—the first to reach the travellers since their departure from England. Hungrily was the unsealing of the mail-bag awaited.

Mary's lap would hardly hold the envelopes that bore her name. They were carried to her by the grizzled old Captain himself, who dealt them out, one by one, cracking a joke to each. Mary laughed; but at the same time felt a touch of embarrassment. For her to receive so large a share of the good things—under the very noses, too, of those unfortunates who got none—seemed not in the best of taste. So, the tale told, she retired with her budget to the cabin; and Mahony, having seen her below, went back to read his own correspondence on deck.

But she had done no more than finish John's note of welcome and break the seal of Tilly's, when a foot came bounding through the saloon, off which the cabin opened, and there was Richard again—Richard with rumpled hair, eyes alight, red of face, looking for all the world like a rowdy schoolboy. Seizing her by the hands he pulled her to her feet, and would have twirled her round. But Mary, her letters strewing the floor, protested—stood firm.

"What *is* the matter?"

"Mary! Wife! Here's news for us! . . . here's news. A letter from—" and he flourished a sheet of paper at her. "I give you three guesses, love. But nonsense!—you couldn't. . . not if you guessed till Doomsday. No more pinching and scraping for us, Mary! No more underpaid drudgery for me! My fortune's made. I am a rich man. . . at last!"

"Richard dear! What is it now?"

Mary spoke in the lightly damping tone which Mahony was wont to grumble she reserved for him alone. But today it passed unnoticed.

"Here you are, madam—read for yourself!" and he pushed a crumpled letter into her hand. "It's those *Australia Felixes* we have to thank for it. What a glorious piece of luck, Mary, that I should have stuck to them and gone on paying their wretched calls, when everyone else let them lapse in despair. John will be green with envy. And this is only the beginning, my dear. There's no telling what they'll do when they get the new plant in—old Simmonds says so himself, and he's not given to superlatives as you know.—Yes, it's goodbye to poverty!"—and forgetting in his excitement where he was, Mahony flung round to pace the floor. Baulked by the narrow wall of the cabin, he had just to turn to the right-about. "It means I can now pick and choose, Mary—put up my plate in Collins Street East—hold my head as high as the best."

"Oh, dear, how glad I am! . . . for your sake." The tears sprang to Mary's eyes; she had openly to wipe them away. "But it's so sudden. I can hardly believe it. Are you sure it's *really* true?" And now she stroked the page smooth, to read for herself.

"You for my sake. . . I for yours! What haven't you had to put up with, my poor love, through being tied to a rolling old stone like me? But now, I promise you, everything will be different. There's nothing you shall not have, my Mary—nothing will be too good for you. You shall ride in your own carriage—keep half a dozen servants. And when once you are free of worries and troubles you'll grow fat and rosy again, and all these little lines on your forehead will disappear."

"And perhaps you won't dislike the colony so much. . . and the people. . . if you can feel independent of them," said Mary hopefully. Could he have promised her from this day forth a tranquil and contented mind, it would have been the best gift of any.

When he had danced out—danced was the word that occurred to her to describe the new spring in his step, which seemed intolerant of the floor—had gone to consult the steward about the purchase of a special brand of champagne, which that worthy was understood to hold in store for an occasion such as this: when Mary sat down to collect her wits, she indulged in a private reflection which neither then nor later did she share with Richard. It ran: "Oh, how thankful I am we didn't get the letter till we were safely away from that. . . from England. Or he might have taken it into his head to stop there."

Mahony felt the need of being alone, and sought out a quiet spot to windward where he was likely to be undisturbed. But news of the turn of his fortunes had run like wildfire through the ship, started by the steward, to whom in the first flush he had garrulously communicated it. And now came one after another of his fellow-passengers to wring his hand and wish him joy. It was well meant; he could not but answer in kind. But then they, too, had changed. From mere nondescripts and undesirables they were metamorphosed into kindly, hearty folk, generous enough, it seemed, to feel almost as elated at a fellow-mortal's good luck as if it were their own. His hedge of spines went down: he turned frank, affable, easy of approach; though any remaining standoffishness was like to have been forgiven him, who at a stroke had become one of the wealthiest men on board.

He could see these simple souls thought he took his windfall very coolly. Well! . . . in a way he did. Just for the moment he had been carried off his feet—as indeed who could fail to be, when by a single lucky chance, one spin of fate's wheel, all that had become his which half a lifetime's toil had failed to give him? Yet ingrained in him was so lively a relish, so poignant a need for money and the ease of mind money would bring, that the stilling of the want had something almost natural about it—resembled the payment of an overdue debt. Yes, affluence would fit him like a second skin. The beggardom of early days, the push and scramble for an income of later life—these had been the travesty.

Next came a sense of relief—relief unspeakable. Alone by now in his windy corner, he could afford to let his eyes grow moist; and the finger he passed round inside his collar trembled. From what a nightmare of black care, a horde of petty anxieties, did the miracle of this day not set him free! To take but a single instance: the prospect of having to explain away his undignified return to the colony had cost him many a night's sleep. Now he was the master of circumstance, not its playball. And into the delights of this sensation he plunged as into a magic water; laved in it, swam, went under; and emerged a new man. The crust of indifference, the insidious tiredness, the ennui that comes of knowing the end of a thing before you have well begun it, and knowing it not worth while: all such marks of advancing age fell away. Youthfully he squared his shoulders; he was ready to live again, and with zest. And under the influence of this revival there stirred in him, for the first time, a more gracious feeling for the land towards which he was heading. What he had undergone there in his day, none but himself knew; but, if his sufferings had been great, great, too, was the atonement now made him. Indeed the bigness of the reward had in it something of the country's own immensity—its far-flung horizons.

"And perhaps, after all... who knows, who knows! .... I myself... the worm that was in me... that ceaseless hankering for—why, happiness, of course... the goal of man's every venture... the belief in one's *right* to it... the fixed idea that it must be waiting for one somewhere... remains but to go in search of it. So, it is not conceivable... thus made wiser... all fear for the future stilled, too—*how* fear lames and deadens!—independent, now... beholden to nobody"—such were some of the loose tags of thought that drifted through his brain.

Till one or other touched a secret spring, and straightway he was launched again on those dreams and schemes with which he believed his last unhappy experience had forever put him out of conceit. Oh, the house he would build! .... the grounds he would lay out... the books he would buy... and buy... till he had a substantial library of his own. All the rare and pretty things that should be Mary's. The gifts they would make her dear old mother. The competency that should rescue his own people from their obscure indigence. The deserving strugglers to whom he would lend a hand. Even individuals he disliked or was fretted by— Zara, Ned, Ned's encumbrances—sipped from his overflow. Indeed he actually caught himself thinking of people—poor devils, mostly—who had done him a bad turn, and of how he could now requite them.

Over these imaginings the hours flew by—hours not divided off each from the next, but fusing to form one single golden day: of a kind that does not come twice in a lifetime. Meanwhile the vessel was well advanced up the great Bay, and familiar landmarks began to rise into view. He had sometimes wondered, on the voyage out, what his feelings would be, when he saw these familiar places again and knew that the pincer of the "Heads" had snapped behind him. Now, he contemplated them with a vacant eye; did not take up the thread of a personal relationship. Or once only: at sight of a bare old clump of hills behind Geelong. Then he impulsively went below to fetch Mary—Mary was packing the cabin furniture, sewing up mattresses in the floor-carpeting, the mirror in the blankets—and she, good-naturedly rising from her knees, for today she had not the heart to refuse him anything, tied on her bonnet and accompanied him on deck. There, standing arm-in-arm, they thought and spoke of a certain unforgettable evening, now years deep in the past.

HENRY HANDEL RICHARDSON

"What greenhorns we were then, love, to be sure! So mercifully ignorant of all the ups and downs in store for us."—But his tone was light, even merry; for today the ups had it.

"Yet you seemed to me very old and wise, Richard. I suppose it came of you wearing that horrid beard."

"And what a little sprite you were!—so shy and elusive. There was no catching you. . . or getting a word in edgeways—thanks to that poor old chattering Mother B and her two bumpkins."

"Whom you couldn't tell apart. . . how that did make me laugh!" said Mary To add with a sigh: "Poor Jinny! Little did we think she would have to go so much sooner than the rest."

"My dear, a good half of that party is dust by now."

But no melancholy tinged the reflection. In his present mood, Mahony accepted life, and the doom life implied, with cheerfullest composure.

HARDLY A LETTER RECEIVED BY Mary that morning but had besought them to regard the writer's house as their own: they had only to make their choice. "Yes, and give umbrage to all the rest. Nonsense, Mary! We'll just slip off quietly to a hotel. We don't need to consider the expense now, and shall be much freer and more comfortable than if we tied ourselves down to stay with people."

But Mahony's plan miscarried.

What a home-coming that was! No sooner had the ship cast anchor than rowing-boats began to push off from the pier; while one that had been lying on its oars made for them with all speed. Mary, standing hatted and shawled for landing, looked, looked again, rubbed her eyes and exclaimed: "Why, I do declare if it isn't Tilly! Oh, *Richard*, what a difference the weeds make!" And sure enough a few minutes later Tilly's head came bobbing up over the side, and the two women lay in each other's arms half laughing, half crying, drawing back, first one, then the other, the better to fix her friend. Certainly Tilly had never shown to more advantage. In old days her hats had been flagrant, her silks over-sumptuous, her jewellery too loud. Now, the neat widow's bonnet with its white frill and black hangings formed a becoming frame for her yellow-brown hair, tanned skin and strong white teeth; the chains, lockets and brooches of twenty-two-carat Ballarat gold had given way to decorous jet; the soft black stuff of the dress moulded and threw up every good point in the rich, full-bosomed figure. Silently

Mary noted and rejoiced. But Tilly, one glance snatched, blurted out: "Well, I must say England 'asn't done much for you, my dear! In all my days, Mary, never did I see you look so peaked and pasty. Seasickness? Not it! It's that *horrible* climate you've 'ad to put up with. I declare your very letters—with their rain, rain, and fog, fog—used to gimme the blue devils. Well! you've come back 'ere to the finest climate in the world. We'll 'ave you up to the mark again in a brace o' shakes."

Further she did not get, for here now was John arriving—a somewhat greyer and leaner John than they had left, but advancing upon one, thought Mahony, with the same old air of: I am here; all is well. Having cordially embraced his sister, John wrung his brother-in—law's hand: "It would be false to pretend surprise, my dear Mahony, at your decision to return to us." On his heels came none other than Jerry and his wife: a fair, fragile slip of a girl this—Australian-born and showing it, in a skin pale as a white flower. Mary put her arms round the child—she was scarcely more—and kissed her warmly; while in one breath the little wife, who was all a-flutter and a-tremble, confided to her how very, very much afraid she had felt of this meeting, knowing Mary to be dear "Harry's" favourite sister; and how she hoped dear Mary, please, wouldn't mind her calling him Harry, but she had once had a dog named Jerry, a white dog with a black patch over one eye; and it seemed so droll, didn't it? to call your husband by the same name as a dog, especially such a funny-looking dog; although if dear Mary wished it very, very much. . . all this gabbled off like a lesson got by heart. Mary promptly reassured her: it was her good right to call her husband by whatever name she chose, so long as he did not mind; and that—with a loving glance at Jerry—she would guarantee he didn't. Then she turned to her brother. The same steady old sober-sides; but now grown quite the man: broad of shoulder, richly whiskered, and, as could be seen at a glance, the most devoted of husbands. Did his young wife speak to someone, he tried to overhear what she was saying; watched the effect of her words on the other; smiled in advance at her little jokes, to incite the listener to smile, too—for all the world after the fashion of a fond mother playing off her child. And when, sprite-like, the girl ran to the other side of the ship, he took the opportunity before following her to squeeze his sister's hand and murmur: "*what* do you say to my little Fanny, Mary? Isn't she perfect?"

"Dear, dear Jerry! If she's only half as good as she's pretty. . . and I can see she is," said Mary returning the squeeze.

Meanwhile quite a crowd had collected on the wharf, to which the party was rowed in a boat so laden that, at moments, the ladies instinctively held their breaths to lighten the load, and the little bride shrank into the crook of her husband's arm. Here stood Zara fluttering a morsel of cambric: she had feared an attack of *mal de mer*, she whispered, did she embark on so choppy a sea. ("We could hardly, I think, love, expect Zara to consider us worth the half-guinea the boatmen were charging!" was Mahony's postprandial comment.) Here were Agnes Ocock and Amelia Grindle with sundry of their children, and the old Devines, and Trotty, advanced to a hair-net, and John's three youngest in charge of their schoolmistress; besides many a lesser friend and acquaintance who had made light of the journey to the port. Hand after hand was thrust forth with: "I trust I see you in prime health, ma'am?" "Dear, dearest Mary! *How* we have missed you!" or: "Thought you'd never hold it out over there, sir." "Delighted, doctor, I'm sure, to welcome you back to our little potato-patch!" And those who could not get near enough for more, along with a sprinkling of curious strangers, enjoyed just forming the fringe of the crowd. It was a pleasant break in the monotony of colonial life to catch a glimpse of arrivals from overseas; to note the latest fashion in hair and dress; to hear news and pick up gossip.

Mary had just stooped to the youngest of the children, marvelling at its growth, when her ear caught an oddly familiar sound, an uneven, thumping footfall, and turning quickly, whom in all the world should she see but Purdy, out of breath and red in the face, but otherwise looking just the same as of old, or at least "not very different"—a phrase with which Mary had already covered a marked change in more than one present: John's singular spareness of rib, Zara's greying front, Agnes's florid cheeks, the wizened-apple aspect of Amelia Grindle. In Purdy's case it cloaked a shining-through of the cranium, did he bare his head; more than a hint of coming stoutness; a cheap and flashy style of dress. First, though, she shot a lightning glance at Richard: how would he take this sudden apparition? The look reassured her: he was today uplifted above all ordinary prejudice. There was just an instant's hesitation, and then he himself stepped forward, both hands outheld, one to grasp Purdy's right, the other to clap on his shoulder; while his: "Dickybird, my boy! How are you? . . . how are you?" came simultaneously with Purdy's: "Dick, old man, I heard your tub was in. I thought I'd just trot along and give you a pawshake."—And thus the old bond was cemented anew.

Thought Mary: was there any end to the good things with which this day was full?

Drawn to the group, Purdy came in for his share of the welcome. For he had not been back to Ballarat since his abrupt departure some years previously; and his former friends and acquaintances hailed him with the lively interest and curiosity peculiar to people who see but few fresh faces, and never forget an old one.

He shook hands all round. When it came to Tilly: "I need hardly introduce you two, I think!" said Mary slyly.

Tilly burst into a roar. "I should say not, indeed! Why, my dear, I can remember 'im when 'e was only *so* 'igh,"—and she measured a foot from the ground.

Purdy capped her fiction. "Is that all? Why, you lisped your first prayer at my knee."

But the children grew peevish; it was time to make a move. At the first breathing of the word hotel, however, such a chorus of dissent broke out that Mahony's plan had there and then to be let drop. Not a guest-chamber, it seemed, but had been swept and dressed for them—John's excepted, John still leading a bachelor life at the Melbourne Club. Even Jerry and his bride had made ready their tiny weatherboard; and here Jerry put his lips to Mary's ear to say how inconsolable little Fanny would be if they went elsewhere: she had sat stitching till past midnight at wonderful bows for bed and window-hangings—a performance which, in the young husband's eyes, far outweighed the fact of their living miles out, at Heidelberg, to which place a coach ran but at ten of a morning; so that the present night would have to be spent in Melbourne, under the bride's father's roof. Had Mary been free to please herself, she would have waived all other considerations rather than disappoint the youthful pair. But Richard! She could hear his amused and sarcastic ha-ha, at the idea of "camping out" with utter strangers for the pleasure of next morning being "carted off" to Heidelberg. Meanwhile, on her other side Fanny was whispering: just fancy, Harry hadn't been able to tell her what dear Mary's complexion was, whether blonde or brunette. She had chosen pink for her bows, because pink suited most people, and she had clapped her hands on finding she was right; but she thought she would have sunk through the floor, had she hit on blue. And when Mary laughingly declared that blue was one of her favourite colours, and that even in yellow or green the trimmings would have been equally appreciated, little Fanny

HENRY HANDEL RICHARDSON

bit her lip and looked as if she were going to cry.—All this in a rapid aside.

The Devines won the day—after a heated discussion in which everybody spoke at once. These good people had actually a carriage-and-pair in waiting, that the travellers might be spared the brief railway journey from port to town; as well as a spring-cart for the baggage. There was no standing out against Mrs. Devine's persuasions, seconded as they were by the M.L.C. himself, who from a modest place in the background threw in, whenever he got the chance: "My 'ouse is entirely at your disposal, sir. We beg you and your good lady will do us the honour."

"Indeed and I'll *not take no*!" declared his wife; and, under a pair of nodding, hearse-like plumes, her fat, rosy face beamed on those about her, after the manner of a big red sun. "'Tis a great hempty barn, that's what it is, and I've looked to this day to fill it. Why, dearie, so's not to 'ear quite so much of me own footsteps, I've been and taken in one o' Jake's sister's 'usband's sister's children."

Thus the Mahonys found themselves rolling townwards in the Devines' well-hung landau, on their knees a picnic-basket containing port wine and sandwiches with which to refresh and sustain the inner man.

Mahony fell silent as the wheels revolved; a smile played round his lips. He was laughing at himself for having imagined that it would be necessary to explain away his reappearance in these people's midst. One and all had followed John's lead in finding his return to Australia—Australia *facile princeps*!—the most natural thing in the world.

At South Yarra they became the occupants of the largest guest-chamber in a brand-new mansion, which counted every comfort and luxury the upholsterers had known how to cram into it, and now only needed really to be lived in. Its stiff formality reminded Mary, the homemaker, of the specimen rooms set out in a great furniture warehouse; rooms in which no living creature has yet left a trace. Her fingers itched to break up the prim rows of chairs ranged against the walls; lightly to disarrange albums; to leave on antimacassars the impress of a head.

Mrs. Devine having finally satisfied herself that they had everything they had everything they required—; down to a plump and well-studded pincushion on which the pins wrote "Welcome!"—for: "I've no faith in them giddy girls, dearie,"—husband and wife were at last alone together.

"Whew!" breathed Mahony, and sinking into an armchair he fanned himself with his handkerchief. "Well! I sincerely hope you're satisfied, Mary. Royalty itself could not ask for a warmer welcome than you have had, my dear." But he smiled again as he spoke; and the usual edge to his words was wanting.

"You, too," said Mary, who was fighting the lock of a carpetbag. Then she laughed. "As if royalty ever got hugged, and kissed, and slapped on the back! But indeed, Richard, I shall never, never forget the kindness that's been shown us. And what a lovely house this is! I mean, could be made."

"My dear, you shall have as good—and better. Rather much oilcloth here for my taste. The grounds, too, struck me as stiffish, what I saw of them." Rising to take another look through a raised slat of the venetian, he turned and beckoned his wife. "What do you say to this, Mary?" Peeping over his shoulder she saw their host, in comfortable corduroys, without his coat, his shirt-sleeves rolled up above his elbows, trundling a loaded wheelbarrow. Said Mahony: "Seems to have turned into a very decent sort of fellow indeed, does our good Cincinnatus."

"Who? . . . Mr. Devine? Yes, hasn't he? I thought it most tactful of him to be quiet in the carriage, when he saw you didn't want to talk."

Below, on a dinner-table built to accommodate a score, a veritable banquet had been spread. They sat down to it at six o'clock, a large family party. For on the wharf Mrs. Devine, as winner, had scattered her invitations broadcast, even insisting on Tilly exchanging her hotel for the second-best spare room. Zara was there, together with Jerry and his wife, and John, and Trotty, who hung on one of Aunt Mary's arms as did pretty Fanny on the other; and the health of the home-comers and the happy change in Mahony's fortunes were drunk to in bumpers of champagne. By everyone but the master of the house; before whose plate stood a jug of barley-water. In the intervals of signalling to the servants where to put the dishes, and whose glass or plate stood empty, Mrs. Devine, purply moist with gratification and excitement, drew Mahony's attention to this jug with a nudge and a wink.

"Your doin', doctor. . . all thanks to you. Jake took the pledge that time you know of, and never 'as 'e broke it since, no matter where 'e is or in 'oos company." She actually laid her pudgy hand on Mahony's and gave it a warm squeeze.

"Very creditable. . . very creditable indeed," murmured Mahony, stiff with embarrassment lest his host should overhear what was being said.

But Mrs. Devine had already telegraphed to her husband down the length of the table; and the good man smiled and nodded, and sipped his barley-water in Mahony's direction.

The ladies withdrawing and Jerry sidling out soon after, the three men pulled their chairs closer; and now colonial affairs took the place of family gossip and perfunctory inquiries about "home." As fellow-members of the Legislative Council, John and Devine had become fast friends. It was also in the wind, it seemed, that Devine might be called on to form a ministry. Puzzled by the many changes, the new men and new names that had come up during his absence, Mahony acted chiefly the listener; but the interested listener, for it was gratifying to find himself once more at the fountain-head. His companions' talk, ranging over a great variety of topics, harked back yet and again to the great natural catastrophe in the face of which legislation was powerless—the unprecedented drought which, already in its fourth year, was ruining the squatters, compelling them to part with thousands on thousands of dying sheep, for the price of the skins alone.

In listening Mahony eyed the two men up and down. His bearded host looked sound as a bell. But it was otherwise with John—"He's a shocking bad colour,"—and knowing his brother-in-law to be of temperate habits, he resolved to have a word with him in private.

It grew late: for over an hour John's horses had pawed the gravel of the drive. Finally Mahony excused himself on grounds of fatigue and ran upstairs. But he might have saved his haste. For Mary had taken her hairbrush and gone to Tilly's room. There, a fresh log having been thrown on the whitewashed hearth, the two women sat and talked far into the night.

Mahony's first lightning plan of putting up his plate at the top of Collins Street, among the bigwigs of the profession, was not carried out. For when, the day after landing, he went to interview Simmonds, his man of business, he found his affairs in even more brilliant condition than Simmonds' letter—written a fortnight back to await the ship's arrival—had led him to believe. That had put the sum lying to his credit at between ten and eleven thousand pounds. By now, however—a second company in which he was interested choosing the self-same moment to look up—combined dividends were flowing in at the rate of twelve to fifteen hundred pounds a month. And this, despite the enormous outlay incurred by the Australia Felix Company in sinking a fourth shaft, lighting the mine throughout with gas, erecting the heaviest plant yet seen on the goldfields.

In the conveyance that left Collins Street at midday for South Yarra, Mahony sat feeling mildly stunned by the extent of his good fortune, as by Simmonds' confident prediction of still grander things to come; sat with far-away eyes, absently noting the velvety black shadows that accompanied vehicles and pedestrians up and down the glaring whiteness of the great street. He had already drawn attention to himself by smiling broadly at thought of the news he was taking home to Mary. Now, as a fresh idea struck him, he uttered a smothered exclamation and tried to slap his knee a gesture that entangled him with a stout party whose crinoline overflowed him, and gave a pimply faced youth sitting opposite a chance to exercise his wit.

"Fy, matey, fy! What 'ud our missis say?"

The vehicle—a kind of roofless omnibus—started with a lunge that sent the two rows of passengers toppling like ninepins one against another. Mahony alone raised his voice in apology: he had lain on the shoulder of the fat woman. The man on her farther side angrily bade her take her danged feathers out of his eye. The greater number recovered their balance by thrusting forth an elbow and lodging it firmly in a neighbour's rib.

Even in his present holiday mood this promiscuity was too much for Mahony. He regretted not having accepted Devine's offer of a buggy; and half-way to his destination dismounted, and covered the rest of the distance on foot.

This was better. In the outlying district where he found himself, no traffic moved. Roads and paths were sandy and grass-edged. The scattered houses lay far back in their gardens, screened by rows of Scotch firs. He met no one, could think in peace; and over a knotty point he stopped short and dug with his stick in the sand.

The brilliant idea that had flashed through his mind in the omnibus was: why go back into harness at all? Retire! . . . retire and live on his dividends. . . here was the solution. From now on be free to devote himself to the things that really mattered, in which he had hitherto had no share.

He threshed the scheme out as he went, and was plain-spoken with himself. I am now a middle-aged man: forty-three and a quarter to be exact in point of time, but a good ten years older with regard to bodily health. . . and disillusionment: considerably more than halfway, that is, on my journey to the green sod. And what have I so far had of life? It has been but one long grind: firstly to keep my head above water, and then, to live up to my neighbours; while every attempt to free myself has failed, the last great wild-goose chase most completely of any. Yes, the real trouble has always been want of money—of money and time—or of money enough to have time. Now that the one has fallen to me, should I not be a fool beyond compare if I failed to master the other? Think of all the wonders of this world I shall die without knowing—the books I shall not have read, the scientific discoveries, the intellectual achievements I shall never have heard of. Oh! the joy of devoting one's remaining years to a congenial occupation. One cannot love one's work, the handle one grinds by—the notion that such a thing is possible belongs to a man's green and salad days. Though perhaps if one climbed to the top of the tree. . . But for the majority of us, the fact that we labour to earn our bread by a certain handiwork wears all liking for it threadbare. It becomes a habit—like the meals one eats. . . the clothes one puts on of a morning.—Ambitions to be sacrificed? But are there? I had them once; in plenty. Where are they now? Blown into thin air—spent like smoke. The fag of living was too much for them. And so, in following my bent, I should sacrifice nothing—or nothing but the possibility of fresh humiliations. . . and much unnecessary pother. . . an infinitude of business. . . Thus he reasoned, thus justified himself to himself, arriving at the house with his arguments marshalled ready to be laid before Mary. The walk, however, had taken longer than he expected; the afternoon was now far advanced and he footsore and hungry. But though he could hear the servants chattering in the kitchen, none came to offer him so much as a cup of tea. They would of course suppose him to have lunched; or else Madam D. had the keys of the larder in her petticoat pocket. The big house yawned inhospitably still and empty—but for a common-looking child in copper-toed boots and oilcloth apron, which he unexpectedly ran across: it fled from him like a startled cat. Mary was out driving with her hostess and did not get back till close on dinner-time. There was another party that night; they sat down fifteen to table and went to bed only in the small hours. He could do no more than skim the cream off his interview for her benefit, before retiring.

His chance came next morning.

Ten o'clock had struck, but Mary was still in bedgown and slippers, her hair tied in its nightly bunch of half a dozen little plaits on the crown of her head. This state of undress did not, however, imply that she had newly risen—as a matter of fact she had been up and doing for a couple of hours. But it was one of the rules of this extraordinary house that visitors did not breakfast till after ten; the longer after, the better, but at any moment *past* the hour, provided that the servants did not know beforehand what it would be: they must be kept up to the mark, hover perpetually alert for the ringing of the dining-room bell: and many and scathing were Richard's comments on the practice of using your guests as the stick with which to belabour your slaves. Mrs. Devine herself, clad in a voluminous paisley gown, her nightcap bound under her chin, was early astir: she gave her husband, who rose at dawn to work among his flowers—as he had once worked among his market produce—breakfast at eight, before he left for town. But if you belonged to the elite, were truly *bon ton*, you did not descend till the morning was half over, and even then must appear "stifling elegant yawns, which show the effort it has been to tear your high-born limbs from the feathers!"—so ran another of Richard's glosses. The first morning he and Mary had blundered in this respect; on the second they were wiser; and now loitered chilly and hungry above-stairs. Chafing at the absurdity and fretting for his breakfast, Mahony grumbled: "Was there ever such a fudge? As if the woman didn't know I used to have to be up at daybreak, if necessary. . . was in my consulting-room hours before this."

Mary, who had been writing letters and sewing, began to dress her hair. "Do try not to fuss so, dear. After all, it's only a little thing. It pleases her to imagine she's up in the ways of good society. Besides, every house has its peculiarities."

"Then give me my own, thank you. But what absurd nonsense you do talk, Mary! I'm sure, when you had 'em, you never tyrannised over guests in this stark fashion. You were their drudge, my dear; danced to their tune. But I believe you'd sacrifice the last scrap of your personal comfort to pander to the foibles of other people."

"Nonsense!" said Mary stoutly. "But we can't possibly let her see we don't like it."

She had unbound her hair: freed from its plaits, it hung all crinks and angles. Now she set, with long, smooth sweeps, to brushing it to its customary high gloss.

Mahony pulled a chair to the window, threw up the sash and leant his elbow on the sill. The morning was warm and balmy, after a bitterly cold night. By midday the sun would have gained almost summer strength, gradually to fade through the autumn of the afternoon till, with darkness, you were back in a wintry spring. The orange-blossom scent of the pittosperums, now everywhere in flower, filled the air. Sunning himself thus, he fell to informing Mary yet once again what he had made up his mind to; spoke shortly and impatiently and with decision. For this time at least he knew that his planning involved his wife in no hardships: he was not asking her to shoulder fresh burdens.

Practised hand though she was at concealing surprise, and rightly attributing Richard's snappishness to the want of a good hot cup of coffee, Mary could not help echoing his words, her hairbrush suspended in the air. "Give up practice altogether?" And, at his emphatic affirmation: "But, Richard, you'd soon get tired of having nothing to do."

"Nothing to do indeed! I, who all my life have longed for a little leisure to follow my own pursuits! Haven't I told you, Mary, again and again, that if I were to read from sunrise to sundown, for the rest of my days, I shouldn't get through a quarter of the books that are waiting for me?"

"Oh, dear, don't talk such rubbish. As if you could spend all the rest of your life reading! Why, I've often heard you say, after sitting with your head in a book for even a few hours running, that it felt like a boiled turnip."

"But, good God! . . . I shall have a garden, I suppose? . . . and a decent horse to ride?"

"Now, Richard, it's no use mincing words: you do tire easily of things—much more easily than other people. And I'm sure you'd tire of idleness as well. After working as you have."

"Oh, go on acting the brake on the coach. I suppose that, too, is a mission in life."

"How you do snap one up! There's this about it, of course, you *could* go back into practice at anytime if you wanted to." ("Thank you, never again for me!") "You only say that now, Richard. In a couple of years you may have completely changed your mind. No, it's not a bit of good getting angry. I think it's a step that requires most careful consideration. Besides you promised, remember, not so *very* long ago, to be guided next time by what I thought."

"So I did. But here the case is different—entirely different. Not twopenceworth of risk is entailed. I have no intention of speculating further, as you ought to know—if you know anything at all about me— and, well invested, this money that has fallen to us is enough to keep us in comfort to our lives' end."

But Mary refused to be rushed into a decision.

The long, elaborate breakfast over: they had to eat their way through chops and steaks, eggs and rissoles, barracouta and garfish, fruit, hot rolls, preserves, tea and coffee: breakfast coped with, Mary waited, dressed for driving, for the carriage to come round, and for her hostess to cease goading on her several maidservants and tracking down their misdeeds. Propping her chin in her hand and poking with the tip of her parasol at one of the fruit-and-flower baskets enworked in the maroon ground of the Brussels carpet, Mary wrestled with the problem of their future. Richard's present project called for a readjustment of all her private plans for his benefit. These had never wavered; remained those she had hatched on the morrow of the Buddlecombe fiasco; and throughout the voyage she had listened in silence to his fluid plannings and imaginings what he was going to do next—had just listened and let him talk. Ballarat had seen his beginnings; seen his rise to one of its most popular medical men: it should also, she was resolved, learn to know him as the moneyed consultant who could afford to see as few patients as he wished. It was ridiculous for him to think of starting all over again in a strange place, when there, in Ballarat, was his old reputation waiting for him. What was the point of success either, if it did not come to you among the friends of your less palmy days?

But his intention to retire into private life cut clean through these

　　　　　　　　HENRY HANDEL RICHARDSON

aspirations. And yet, for the first time, Mary hesitated. The difference was, what he now proposed made a subtle appeal to her. For, to be nothing, to have neither trade nor profession, to fold one's hands and live on one's income—that was the *ne plus ultra* of colonial society, the ideal tirelessly to be striven after. Work brought neither honour nor glory where all too many had been manual labourers, the work itself of a low or disreputable kind. And the contingency of Richard ending as the private gentleman, the leisured man of means, had never been wholly absent from Mary's mind—or wouldn't have been, had he not so quixotically cut his career in half.

There was another point, too: was anybody better fitted than he to live as the gentleman? Where so many floundered like fish out of water, he would be entirely in his element. If *only* she could have felt surer of him! But thanks to Buddlecombe she knew that, no matter how fixed he seemed, at the first trifling unpleasantness—a hint, for example, that medically he was on the shelf—he would be up and off to prove the contrary; perhaps again, as on the last occasion, not even condescending to tell her where the trouble lay. Oh dear! it *would* be nice to have a husband who saw things sensibly and practically—as one did oneself. How the two of them could then have put their heads together. Instead of her always having to make allowance for unreckonable impulses.

One comfort: there was no more talk on his part of going "home" with his fortune. The old foolish idea that he would be happier in England had been knocked on the head. At considerable expense, and much worry and trouble, poor old Richard! Still, if he *would* buy his experience in this costly fashion. . . Here, however, her musings were cut short by the entrance of Mrs. Devine in shawl and bonnet, and struggling to button a magenta kid glove across a palm not built for such a covering: it bulged through the opening, creased and rolled with fat. The good lady was keyed up to a high pitch with domestic disasters—a chipped wineglass, a scrap of flue found under a bed— "Liars and deceivers everyone, dearie!" But the great red face beamed with goodwill. No malice was in it; only the delights of the chase; so that the onlooker was reluctantly driven to conclude that Mrs. Devine heartily enjoyed her slave-driving.

And her private doubts and scruples notwithstanding, Mary could not but feel pleased and proud, for Richard's sake, at the stir caused by the announcement that he had no further need to practise medicine. Congratulations showered on him. Himself, he laughed, in his new, happy fashion. "I declare, so much fuss they make, I might have discovered the North Pole." And having got him safely away from the tyrannic rules Mrs. Devine considered essential to his comfort—or the comfort of his blue blood—and settled in a furnished house near the Carlton Gardens, Mary prepared to guide him gently and imperceptibly along the road she thought it for his good he should go. In doing this, however, she found herself up against a stone wall, in the shape of a hitherto unsuspected trait in Richard: a violent aversion from returning on his traces. When it dawned on him that she was still hankering after Ballarat, he lost his temper, and vowed with the utmost vehemence that *when* he was done with a place he *was* done, and wild horses shouldn't drag him back to it.

"Good God, Mary! one's dead self would confront one at every turn. Here one did this, there that. You don't stock-take, my dear, when you're going on living in a place; but a break—and even a brief one—forces you to it. . . in murderous fashion. I should thank you for the constant reminder how life is flying, and how little one has made of it, and what a fool one was in the past, and yet how full of hopes and aspirations."—With cobwebby stuff such as this, there was no coming to grips.

No, it was to be Melbourne this time. What was more, he had resolved to build his own house. He was sick to death of suiting his needs to those of other people.

Build? . . . well yes, there was something to be said for it: Mary hastily swallowed her dismay, seeing his feathers rise in earnest. Build? . . . before he knew anything about a locality? Why, a neighbour's fowls only needed to cackle or crow too early of a morning, railway-whistles or church-bells sound too plainly, and all his peace and pleasure would be gone. She was not going to risk any such contingency as that, thank you! And having wormed the information out of him that he leaned to the district lying between St. Kilda and Brighton, she took John into confidence, and John and she laid their heads together to circumvent his harebrained scheme. A string or two was pulled; and one day, while Richard and she were driving round looking for a site, they happened, as if by chance, on the very house to suit them. One, too, that was not yet in the public market. As John had foreseen, Richard lost his heart to it on the spot, and before the week was out had become its owner.—Well! buying offhand was bad enough; but a good deal less risky than building.

Houses in Melbourne were of two types: either spacious, white, two-storeyed buildings almost as broad as they were long, with balcony and verandah to the front, and needing but to stand in a sandy compound to advertise their origin; or low, sprawly villas a single storey high, Covering much ground space, and wearing their circlet of verandah like a shady hat. Mahony's purchase was of this latter kind.

Built some ten years previously, by a wealthy squatter who was now about to become a permanent absentee, it stood within half an hour's walk of the Brighton beach, on a quiet, sandy road the edges of which were fringed with grass and capeweed. The grounds, running to between four and five acres, were well stocked and fully grown; and included kitchen and flower-gardens, a couple of croquet lawns and a fair-sized orchard. From the gates, no glimpse of the house could be caught, so thick were the protecting shrubberies, so closely set the Scotch firs. These grounds turned the scales for Mahony. To get a garden—and such a garden!—ready-made, instead of having to wait for it to grow. In the house itself the only alteration he planned was a large study to be thrown out on the orchard side. Otherwise it suited them to a nicety.

III

While Richard haunted his new property and egged on the workmen, or sat drawing up a list of books for dispatch to an Edinburgh bookseller, Mary devoted herself to unravelling the knots and tangles into which the several members of her family had tied themselves. And after for two years having had to deal exclusively with a difficult, faddy person like Richard, she found this a comparatively simple job. Those to whose aid she now came saw things from the same angle as herself, and they spoke a common language.

Zara had first innings. Seated in the drawing-room of the Carlton house, Zara poured out her woes, with much drying of eyes and the old, old recriminations against John. Never, she wept, had she met anyone so hard, so self-centred. He was also too stingy to lift a finger to help you; and, in her opinion, richly deserved the misfortunes that had befallen him—Emma's untimely death, and the loss of Jinny; the disgrace of Johnny's flight and Trotty's misdemeanours. Who could wonder at it, if he treated wives and children as he was now treating her?

"But, Zara. . ."

Oh, John had the influence, could do it *easily* if he chose. But for that, he was too down on the match. As if his own second marriage had been anything to boast of! Pray, who was Jinny? A publican's daughter. . . and, if the truth were told, common as dirt. But— "I'm still utterly in the dark, Zara. Who is it John objects to. . . that you want to marry?"

"Not I want to marry, if you please, Mary!" Zara's tone was acid as a lemon. "It's *quite* the other way about. If it only rested with me. . ."

"Yes, but *who?*"

"Haven't you wits enough to guess, my dear? Who is it that has followed me and pestered—yes, *pestered!*—me with his attentions, ever since my first visit to Ballarat?"

Ballarat? Her first visit? "Zara! You surely don't mean. . ."

"My dear, I have not a heart of *stone*—like *some* people I could mention! I can stand out no longer against his prayers and persuasions. Year after year, year after year—not *many* women, Mary, can boast of having inspired such devotion. He worships the very ground I tread—and has done ever since those early days. . . though I was then little more than a child. Of course, I am aware he is not my equal. . ."

"Oh, good gracious, what does that matter if you really care for him? I've no patience with nonsense of that kind."

Mary spoke with a robust heartiness; but her thoughts were elsewhere, and travelled swiftly. In the two years that had elapsed since last she saw her, Zara had crossed a subtle boundary, and, from being a youngish person who looked a trifle worn and tired, had turned into an elderly person who looked young for her age: which made all the difference in the world. For, alas! Zara's features were not of that well-boned type, whose cameo outlines show up even better in the middle years than under the plump padding of youth. Short, irregular, piquant, they had depended on freshness and round contours for their charm. Now that the dimples had run to lines, the cheeks hollowed, the skin sagged, Zara wore the pathetic aspect of a faded child. When she drooped her fine eyes, it was really sad, to one who loved her, to see how haggard and old she looked. Poor Zara! All her choice offers and good chances come to nothing. She had dangled them too long; been over fastidious; and now it was too late. Mary could read this out of what she said: this and more. Even the posts open to her as finishing-governess were not, it appeared, what they had once been. Younger women, competent to teach the new—fangled "callisthenics," and dull, dry pieces by "Mosar" instead of the tuneful *Morceaux* in which Zara excelled, were now getting the plums. It did seem a shame, considering Zara's talents, and her long experience but so it was. Perhaps she had grown a trifle "scratchy" with the years. Her elegant sprightliness was certainly deserting her, giving place to a kind of fixed pettishness. And so, having turned the matter over, Mary soothed her by promising to do all she could to further the marriage. She would beard John in his den, and urge him to use his influence—according to Zara he was on friendly terms with a prominent member of the Baptist Union—to procure for her intended, who was still but an unsalaried "helper," the pastorate that would enable them to wed.

"Meanwhile, you must bring Hemp. . . Mr. Hempel to see us."

As visiting John at the Melbourne Club was out of the question, Mary took the only slightly less bold step of calling at the great warehouse in Flinders Lane. And having climbed a dark, steep stair to the first storey, and passed through various rooms where clerks, perched on high stools, stole curious glances at the apparition of a silk-and-velvet-clad lady whispered to be the senior partner's sister: this ordeal behind her, she arrived, a trifle pink and confused, at the door of John's sanctum.

John himself emerged to meet her.

"Yes, John, quite alone. . . I hope you won't mind. But I wanted very much to see you." And having regained breath and composure, Mary lost no time in going straight to the core of Zara's business.

John listened, with a patience he would have shown no one else, his dark eyes, so like Mary's own, yet so much older in worldly wisdom, turned intently on her.—"Objections to her marrying? My dear girl, as far as I personally am concerned, my sister Zara may wed a navvy if she chooses—always provided he has the means to support her, once the knot is tied. But this Methody-fellow now. . . have you seen him? No? Then pray do so, without delay. After which, let me hear if you are still of the same mind."

"Your sister Zara," he went on, "admits to having laid by, in the course of her governessing, some five hundred pounds: knowing her as we do, seven or eight hundred would, I make no doubt, be nearer the mark. This sum, well invested, will ensure her yearly some eighty or ninety pounds—not a princely income, I dare say, but sufficient for the requirements of an unmarried female. Should she, however, fritter away her savings on this what's-his-name, it would, in the event of his decease, fall to her relatives to support her. Which I for one am not disposed to do."

Mary had refrained from interrupting. Now, nothing daunted, she insisted on John viewing the case from Zara's standpoint: the very natural desire of an ageing woman for a home and a husband; the dreaded stigma of old-maidism; the weariness and monotony of going on teaching other people's children year after year; the mortification of seeing younger women chosen over your head, and your salary steadily decreasing as you grew older. And finally, by dint of what she afterwards described to Richard as "this, that, and the other thing," she got John so far as to promise that if, after seeing the bridegroom-elect, she still thought the marriage should go forward, he would do what lay in his power to procure for Hempel the pastorate in the little up-country township of Wangawatha, on which Zara had set her heart.

This accomplished, Mary drew on her gloves, which she had removed for the sherry and biscuits brought forth by John from a cupboard, with a "Both dry unfortunately, my dear girl, since I am not often honoured by visits from the sweet-toothed sex."

"And does business flourish, John?"

"It does, Mary. Yes, on that score I have nothing to complain of—

nothing whatever. As you will have observed, we have recently made considerable additions to the premises, and young MacDermott has been definitely taken into partnership. Still, as far as I myself am concerned, I confess there come moments when in spite of everything I look round me and ask: *cui bono*? For whom do I build? . . . since there is no one to step into my shoes when I am gone."

John and *cui bono*! . . . John to talk of being "gone"! Mary's eyes widened and darkened. But she did not let the opportunity slip. "Look here, John, what I have always been meaning to say: I firmly intend to try and find out what has become of Johnny—and if possible get him home again. It seems dreadful to me that a boy of that age, and one I was so fond of, too, should just disappear and perhaps never be heard of again. I feel convinced there was nothing radically wrong; and can't help thinking he'd be ready to come back after this taste of hardship, and settle down, and make you proud of him."

Was it fancy, or did a new expression flit over John's face at her words?—a kind of hope look out of his eyes? If so, it was gone again at once, drowned in the harsh expression he seemed to reserve for poor Emma's children. "Nay, I have washed my hands of him, Mary. He has publicly disgraced me. And from all I hear, I fear his sister is about to follow the example he has set her."

At this Mary laughed outright. "Really, John! I'm surprised at you: letting yourself be imposed on by the tales of some prim old schoolmarm. You wait; I mean to have Trotty down to stay with me; and then I'll very soon find out the truth about her. Besides, you know you *can't* wash your hands of your children like this; it's unnatural. I wish to goodness I could see you comfortably settled in your own house once more, with them all about you. This is very well, but it *isn't* home."— And Mary's glance swept the leaded windows, the cobwebbed corners, the white dust on books and papers, the dimness of the office furniture; to end with John himself. To her eye he had a rather uncared-for appearance nowadays; looked unbrushed, much less spruce than of old.

"Well, well!" John, his elbows on the arms of his chair, lightly met his ten fingers and tipped them, to a shrug of the shoulders. "Ah! had it pleased the Almighty to make women other than they are—yourself excepted, my dear Mary, always excepted. But that reminds me. I have been intending for sometime past to ask you to drive out and go over the house, and report to me on its condition. The last person I placed in charge proved as untrustworthy as the rest."

Stowing away the key in her petticoat pocket, Mary gladly undertook the commission. And as she jogged homewards in a wagonette, she felt well satisfied with what she had achieved; and not on Zara's score alone. "Poor old John! He doesn't *know* how lonely and uncomfortable he is. Or how, in his heart of hearts, he's fretting for that boy."

Meanwhile, after considerable shilly-shallying, Zara had introduced Hempel afresh, in what proved an exceedingly painful visit.

"I declare," said Mary afterwards, "everytime I spoke, I seemed to put my foot in it."

To begin with, it was plain at once what John had meant by his: wait till you have seen him! Hempel was now but the shadow of his former self, shrunken, emaciated, with over-bright eyes, and a dry cough that took him in paroxysms, at the end of which he withdrew a spotted handkerchief from his lips.

Zara looked so annoyed when this happened that Mary tried to seem unobservant. But after one particularly violent explosion, the words: "Oh, what do you do for it?" escaped her in spite of herself.

"It's *nothing* in the world but dust," cut in Zara smartly. "I vow Carlton to be the dustiest suburb in all Melbourne. How you came to select it amazes me—positively it does!"

"I look upon it as a righteous affliction, ma'am," said Hempel loudly and slowly, and as though Zara had not spoken. "Such things are sent to try us. 'Oom the Lord loveth 'e chasteneth."

"Besides he is perfectly well able to control it if he chooses."—Zara was so caustic that Mary hurriedly made a diversion by inviting her upstairs. And curiosity to hear a detailed account of the interview with John got the better of Zara's patent reluctance to leave the two men alone together.

"He looks dreadfully delicate, Zara," said Mary dubiously, when the bedroom door had shut behind them.

"My dear Mary, a change of climate is *all* that is necessary. We have taken the very *best* medical advice. I truly hope Richard will not go putting any far-fetched notions into his head." And overriding Mary's delicate inquiries with a dramatic: "The happiness of my life is at stake!" Zara declined a chair, swept her crinoline about the room, and having greedily extracted the gist of John's promises, knew no peace till they returned to the parlour.

Hempel—he now wore a short, woolly beard round face and

throat—had certainly improved in his way of speaking. Still he did have lapses; and these Zara accentuated and underlined in distressing fashion. Throughout the visit she sat bolt upright on the extreme edge of her chair, almost prompting the words into Hempel's mouth; while, at every misplaced or unaccomplished "h," she half-closed her eyes and drew in her breath with a semi-audible groan, as if the aspirate were a missile that had struck her. Hempel alone remained undisturbed by her behaviour. Richard, Mary knew, would be fuming inwardly at such tactlessness; and her own discomfiture was so acute that she trebled the warmth of her manner towards the unfortunate man.

"And what are we to call you?" she asked, as Zara rose to go. "Mister sounds too stiff altogether for a relation."

Instantly she saw that, with this well-meant question, she had made another mistake. Zara turned a dark red, and flashing a warning glance at Hempel began a hurried babble of adieux. But Hempel was either too dense or too obstinate to see.

"My name, ma'am, is Ebenezer." ("Edgar, Mary, Edgar is what I call him!") "Yes, Miss Turn'am 'ere"—and so saying, Hempel signified Zara, without looking at her, by an odd little outward jerk of the elbow and a smile that struck even Mary as malicious—"Miss Turn'am don't cotton to it, and wants to persuade me to fancy names. But I say the one as my parents chose for me in the name of the Lord is good enough for me. So I'll be obleeged by Ebenezer, if you please."

"It's in the Bible, too, isn't it?" threw in Mary, feeling, if she did not see, the silent laughter with which Richard was shaking. And to herself she thought: "Oh dear, won't he catch it when he gets outside!"

"Ha ha! Serves her right. . . serves her very well right. Mrs. Ebenezer! Why, of course, it comes back to me now." ("I felt sure it was Edward— or I shouldn't have asked," said Mary ruefully. "And now I shan't know what to call him.") "But I can tell you this, my dear: Zara is about to commit a monstrous folly. The fellow is far gone in phthisis. If she wants a job as sick-nurse, she'll get it—and upon my word, Mary, I don't know that she won't be better employed in seeing the poor chap decently and comfortably into his coffin, than in grafting her insincerities and affectations on the young. A more lukewarm bridegroom, though, it has seldom been my lot to meet."

"How hard on her you are! Yes, both you and John. Every woman *naturally* wants a husband. . . and a good thing, too, or where would the world be? Besides if she doesn't marry, you men are the first to twit her with being an old maid. But if she shows any inclination for it, it's considered matter for a joke. . . or not quite nice."

"Hear, hear! Why, love, at this rate we shall soon have you clad in bloomers and spouting on a platform for women's rights."

"Richard! Don't speak to me of such horrors. But we're talking about Zara. I must say, after seeing Hempel I agree with John, it's a ridiculous match. He really doesn't seem to care *that* much for her. . ."

"Which is but natural. At his stage of the disease a man is entirely occupied with his own health. . . and his God."

"And I thought Zara most cutting with him. No, I'm afraid she's taking him just to be married."

But, even as she said it, Mary had a glimpse into depths that were closed to her menkind. Just to be married! It meant that solace of the woman who was getting on in years—the plain gold band on the ring finger. It meant no longer being shut out from the great Society of Matrons; no longer needing to look the other way were certain subjects alluded to; or pretending not to notice the nods and winks, the silently mouthed words that went on behind your back. It was all very well when you were young; when your very youth and innocence made up for it: as you grew older, it turned to a downright mortification—like that of going in to dinner after the bride of eighteen.

"Besides we *can't* dictate to Zara as if she were still a child. She has a right to buy her own experience. . . even if it's only with a poor creature like Hempel."

Another unspoken thought that lurked comfortably at the back of Mary's mind was of the more than liberal pin-money Richard was now giving her. He had said expressly, too, she need render no account of how she spent it. Thus, should the worst happen, she would be able to see to it that neither he nor John had to put hand to pocket.

A last attempt to bring Zara to reason, however, she made. And having only succeeded in fanning the flames—sister-wise, Zara took interference less well from her than from anyone—Mary tilted her chin, and sighing: "Well, we must just make the best of it!" forthwith requested John to do his share.

One thing, though, she did not yield in: she went off by herself to town and bought the stuff for Zara's wedding-dress. For Zara, she could see, was meditating satin and orange-blossoms; and against this all Mary's common sense rose in arms. "For a place like Wangawatha! And with not even a Bishop to entertain. . . I mean, Hempel being a

Baptist." So she chose Madras muslin—finest Madras, which cost a good deal more than satin—and a neat bonnet trimmed with lilac.

"For these you can wear to chur—to chapel, Zara, you know, when the hot weather comes." But Zara was so angry that she forgot to thank Mary for the gift, and tried the texture of the muslin between thumb and finger as if it were a bit of print.

And so a quiet wedding was celebrated at the Carlton house, a ceremony in which the only hitch was a somewhat lengthy pause for the bridegroom to recover his breath after a fit of coughing; a glass of champagne was drunk to the health of the newly wedded; and off they went in a shower of rice which Mary took care was thick enough to satisfy even Zara. Nor was a satin slipper forgotten for the back of the carriage-and-pair, all flowers and favours, which Mahony had provided to drive the happy couple to the steamboat on which they would sail to Sorrento.

The very last thing, upstairs in the bedroom, Mary pressed a small wad of notes into Zara's hand. "A bit of my wedding present to you, dear Zara. Now don't stint on your honeymoon. Put up at the best hotel and enjoy yourselves. Remember, one is only married once."

"*Merci, ma bonne Marie, merci!*" said Zara: in the course of the past hour she had gradually taken on the allures of an elder married woman towards her junior. "But I should have done so in any case."

THE RICE SWEPT UP, THE hundred and one boxes of wedding cake dispatched which should intimate to even the least of Zara's acquaintances that she had quitted the single state, Mary turned to her next job, and drove one morning to St. Kilda to inspect John's house. She went by herself, for she thought John would thank you to have other eyes than hers quizzing his neglected home. And she was glad indeed no one else was present when, the coachman having unlocked the front door and drawn up the blinds for her, she was free to wander through the deserted rooms. The house had stood empty almost as long as she had been absent from the colony; and, in such a climate as this, two years spelt ruin. No window or door had fitted tightly enough, when hot winds and their accompanying dust-storms swept the town. The dust crunched gritty underfoot; lay in a white layer over all tables and polished surfaces; made it impossible to look out of the windows. The cobwebs that hung from the corners of the ceilings, and festooned the lustred chandeliers, were thick as string with it. You could hardly see yourself in the mirrors for fly-specks, or see the wax flowers under their shades. Everywhere, in hundreds, flies and blowflies lay dead. Moths had ravaged each single woollen article she laid hands on. The beautiful Brussels carpets were eaten into holes, as were also curtains and bed-hangings, table-covers and the backs of wool-worked chairs. It was truly a scene of desolation.

In John's bedroom she chanced to open a leaf of the great triple-fronted mahogany wardrobe, to look if any clothes had been left hanging to share in the general dilapidation; and there, the first thing she lighted on was a shawl of "poor Jinny's"—or what had once been a shawl, for it was now riddled like a colander, and all but fell to pieces as she touched it. For a moment Mary stood lost to her surroundings. What memories that shawl called up! Of softest white cashmere, with a handsome floral border, it had been John's present to Jinny on the birth of their first child: "And if the next's a boy, Jane, I promise you one of richest India silk, my love!" But, even so, this gift had filled Jinny's cup to the brim. Mary could only remember it tied up with ribbons in tissue paper, and smelling of camphor to knock you down—Jinny had hardly dared to wear it for fear the dust should discolour it, or the sun fade the bordering. There had been quite a quarrel one day, when John and she were staying with them in Ballarat, because Jinny had visited the Ococks in her second-best. "Far from me be it, Mary, to inculcate an extravagant spirit in Jane, or encourage her to run up bills at the milliner's. But she is now my wife, and it is her duty to dress accordingly," had been John's way of putting it. Well, poor Jinny, she might just as well have worn her finery and worn it out. . . as only have had it on her back some dozen times in all. She was gone where no shawls were needed.

"It's really a lesson not to hoard one's clothes, but to use and enjoy them while you can. Not to get anything too grand, either, which makes it seem a pity to wear."

"John ought to have given all such things away," she aid to herself a few minutes later. For a nudge of memory had drawn her to a lumber-room, where four zinc-and-wood saratogas were lined up in a row. These held all that remained to mortal eyes of "poor Emma." For Jinny had once soon after marriage confessed to a wild fit of jealousy, in which she had packed away every scrap of her predecessor's belongings.—Fifteen years dead! The things were now, no doubt, mere rags and tatters, for the box-lid was not made that could keep out the moth. Some day

HENRY HANDEL RICHARDSON

she, Mary, must make it her business to run through them, to see if no little enduring thing was left that could be handed on to Trotty, as a memento of her long-dead mother.

"Regular Bluebeard's chambers," was Richard's comment, when she told him of her discoveries.

But Mary had on her thinking-cap, and sat wondering how she could best reduce John's affairs to order. The house must be opened up without loss of time, scrubbers and cleaners turned in, painters and paperhangers and then. . . A few days later she came home radiant.

"I've got the very *person* for John!" and undoing her bonnet-strings, she threw them back with an air of triumph. It was a hot November afternoon.

"What! . . . yet again?" and having kissed her, Mahony laid his book face downwards and prepared to listen. "Tell me all about it."

"Quite one of the most sensible women I've ever met."

"Then, my dear, you do *not* mean pretty Fanny!"

For Mary had been out spending a couple of days with the young pair at Heidelberg, to pay her overdue respects to the cottage of which she had heard so much.

"It really is a dear little place. And kept in apple-pie order."

She had soon discovered, though, that the prevailing neatness and nicety were not the result of any brilliant housewifely qualities in the little bride. The good genius proved to be an aunt—"Auntie Julia"— who had had charge of the motherless girl since birth.

"One of those neat, brisk little women, Richard, who do everything well they put their hands to. Her hair's grey, but she is not really old. What struck me first was when she said: 'Now please don't imagine I'm a fixture here, Mrs. Mahony. I just came to help my little Fan over her first troubles in setting up house. I don't hold with old aunts—or mothers either—quartering themselves upon the newly wed. Young people should be left to their own devices. No, poor old Auntie Julia's job is done; she's permanently out of work.'"

It was here Mary thought she saw a light in John's darkness. Taking the bull by the horns, she there and then told Miss Julia the story of her brother's two marriages, and of his vain attempts to live in peace and harmony with Zara.

"Poor fellow, poor fellow! Dear Mrs. Mahony, I agree with you: relatives are not the easiest people in the world to get on with. They are either so much alike that each knows all the time just what the other is thinking—and that is fatal; for, if you won't mind my saying so, the private thoughts we indulge in, even of our nearest, are not of a fit kind to be made public." ("But with such a merry twinkle in her eye, Richard, that it took away anything that might have sounded sharp or biting.") "Or else brothers and sisters are so different that they might have been born on different planets."

Mary next enumerated the long line of housekeepers who had wandered in their day through John's establishment. "In at one door, and out at the next!"

"Aha! You needn't tell me where the shoe pinched there. I see, I see. Each of 'em in turn thought she was *the* one chosen by fate to fill your poor sister-in-law's place. May I speak frankly? If I take the post, you may make your mind perfectly easy on that score. I'm not of the marrying sort. Some men are born to be bachelors; some women, bless 'em, what's known as old maids. I can assure you, my dear Mrs. Mahony, I am happiest in the single life. Nor have I missed a family of my own, for my little Fan here has been as much mine as though I had borne her." Here, however, seeing Mary's rather dubious air, she laid a hand on her arm and added reassuringly: "But don't be afraid, my dear. I do not noise these views abroad. They're just between you, me and the tea-caddy."

"It was really said very nicely, Richard—not at all indelicately."

"All the same, I should give her a hint that such radical ideas would be fatal to her prospects with his lordship," said Mahony, who had recently smarted anew under his brother-in-law's heavy-handed patronage.

"She won't talk like that to a *man*. And I feel sure I'm right; she's the very person."

And so she was. No sooner had John, on Mary's recommendation, made definite arrangements with Miss Julia than tangles seemed to straighten of themselves. Hers was a master mind. In less than no time the house was cleaned, renovated, repaired; efficient servants were engaged; John was transferred from his uncomfortable Club quarters to a comfortable domesticity. And Miss Julia proved herself of an exquisite tact in running the establishment, in meeting John's wishes, in agreeing with him without yielding a jot of her own convictions. And thereafter John—"He couldn't, of course, let the credit for the changed state of affairs go out of the family!"—John went about singing Mary's praises, and congratulating himself on being the possessor of so capable a sister.

Next, Jinny's three mites were brought home from boarding school;

and together Mary and Miss Julia stripped them of their "uniforms," undid their meagre little rats'-tails, and freed their little bodies from the stiff corsets in which even the infant Josephine was encased. Three pleasant-faced, merry-eyed little girls emerged, who soon learned to laugh and play again, and filled the dead house with the life it needed. They adored Auntie Julia: and were adored by their father as of old.

There remained only Trotty—or Emmy, as she was now called. Mary had confabbed with Miss Julia, and they had shaken their heads in unison over John's extraordinary attitude towards his first family. But, on meeting the girl, Miss Julia struck her palms together and cried: "What! stand out against *that?* . . . my dear, have *no* fear! Just let your brother grow used to seeing such a daughter opposite him at breakfast, and he'll soon miss her if she chances to be absent. *Exactly* what he needs to preside over his dinner-table. It shall be my task to train her for the post."

In the meantime, however, Mary kept Emmy at her own side, in order to renew acquaintance with one she had known so well as a child.

IV

Emmy also served to fill a gap.

As always when forced to live at haphazard, without a fixed routine, Mahony was restless and ill at ease. He had not even a comfortable room to retire to: his present den was the dull little back parlour of a town house. Books, too, he came very short in; it did not seem worth while unpacking those he had brought out with him; and the newly ordered volumes could not be expected to arrive for months to come. Nor did he see much of Mary: what time she had to spare from her relatives was spent in endless discussions with decorators and upholsterers.

The company of his young niece was thus a real boon to him. Emmy had no obligations, was free to go with him when and where he chose. What was more, with neither the cares of a family nor of house-furnishing on her mind, her thoughts never strayed. And a sound friendship sprang up between the oddly matched pair. No longer afraid of her uncle, Emmy displayed a gentle, saucy, laughing humour. Mahony hired a little horse for her and they rode out together, she pinned up in Mary's old habit; rode out early of a morning while other people were still fast asleep. Their destination was invariably the new house, to see what progress had been made since the day before: holding her habit high, Emmy would run from room to room, exclaiming. Thence they followed quiet, sandy tracks that led through stretches of heath and gorse to the sea. Or they strolled on foot, Emmy hanging on her uncle's arm and chattering merrily: a simple-hearted, unaffected girl, as natural as she was pretty, which was saying a good deal, for she promised to be a regular beauty. "Strawberries and cream" was Mahony's name for her. She had inherited her mother's ripe-corn fairness and limpid, lash-swept eyes; but the wildrose complexion of the English-born woman had here been damped to palest cream, in which, as a striking contrast, stood out two lovely lips of a vivid carnation-red—a daring touch on the part of nature that already drew men's eyes as she passed. In person, she was soft and round and womanly. But the broad little hands with their slyly bitten nails were still half a child's. She was childishly unconscious too, of her attractions, innocent in the use to which she put them; and blushed helplessly did anyone remark on her appearance—as the outspoken people who surrounded her were only too apt to do.

HENRY HANDEL RICHARDSON

Without being in the least clever, she had a bright open mind, and drank in with interest all Mahony could give her: tales of his travels or of the early days; descriptions of books and plays; little homilies on the wonders of nature. If he had a fault to find with her, it was that she seemed just as sweetly grateful for, say, "Auntie Julia's" enjoinders how to hold her crotchet-needle, or hints on dress and deportment, as to him for his deeper lore. Yes, the child had an artless and inborn desire to please, and dissipated her favours in a manner that belonged very surely to her age. . . and her sex. For he might say "child," but let him remember that his own little Polly-Mary had been but a couple of months older, when he ran her off from among her playmates and friends.

Altogether there was much about John's daughter—no! not thus would he put it—about Mary's niece, that reminded him of Mary herself, as a little mouse of a bride long years ago. And not the least striking point of resemblance was this whole-hearted surrender of attention. It would, of course, be unreasonable to expect the faculty to persist: life in its course brought, to even the fondest of wives, distractions, cares and interests of her own. But there was no denying it, this lack of preoccupation it was, this freedom—even emptiness if you would—of mind, into which oneself poured the contents, that rendered a very young woman so delightful a companion.

And when, at length, the move to the new house was made, and Mahony set about unpacking, arranging and cataloguing the books he had, and planning where those to come should be shelved, Emmy was still his right hand. Mary, busy with strange servants, with the stocking of kitchen and larder, could do no more than occasionally look in to see how the two of them were getting on, and keep them supplied with refreshment. Good-naturedly she yielded Emmy entirely to Richard, who now passed to overhauling his minerals, plants and butterflies, all of which had made the journey to England with him and back. And glass cases, stacks of blotting-paper and sheets of cork were set up afresh in this big, pleasant room, the windows of which looked down a vista cut through spreading oleanders to where, in the orchard, peach and almond-blossom vied in pinkness against a pale blue sky.

But it was not very long before Emmy was spirited away to grace her father's table. Then, his own affairs in order, domestic appointments running smoothly, Mahony drove out with Mary in the neat brougham he had given her, to return some of the visits that had been paid them.

Later on, too, he accompanied her to dinners, balls and soirees; or played the host at his own table, which Mary soon filled with guests.

The society in which they here found themselves had a variety and a breadth about it that put it on a very different footing from either the narrow Ballarat circle of earlier years, or the medieval provincialism into which they had stumbled overseas. And moments came when, squarely facing the facts, Mahony admitted to himself he might go farther and fare worse: in other words, that he could now never hope to know anything better. The most diverse tastes were catered for. There was the ultra-fashionable set that revolved round Government House and the vice-regal entertainments; that covered the lawns at Flemington and Caulfield; drove out in splendid four and six-in-hands to champagne picnics at Yan Yean; overflowed the dress circle at the Theatre Royal, where Bandmann was appearing in his famous roles; the ladies decked for all occasions—lawn, theatre, picnics, dusty streets alike—in the flimsiest and costliest of robes. At the head of this aristocracy of wealth stood those primitive settlers the great squatter-kings, owners of sheep-runs that counted up to a hundred thousand acres: men whose incomes were so vast that they hardly knew how to dispense them, there existing here no art treasures to empty the purse, nor any taste to buy them had they existed. Neither did travel tempt these old colonists, often of humble origin, whose prime had been spent buried in the bush; while it had not yet become the fashion to educate sons and daughters "at home."

Since, however, fortunes were still notoriously precarious—flood or fire could ruin a man overnight—and since, too, the sense of uncertainty that characterised the early days had bitten too deep ever to be got out of the blood, "spend while you may" remained the motto men lived by. And this led to a reckless extravagance that had not its equal. Women lavished money on dress, which grew to be a passion in this fair climate; on jewellery with which to behang their persons; on fantastic entertainments; men drank, betted, gambled; while horse-racing had already become, with both sexes, the obsession it was to remain. This stylish set—it also included fabulously lucky speculators, as well as the great wool-buyers—Mahony did not do much more than brush in passing. His sympathies inclined rather to that which revolved round the trusty prelate who, having guided the destinies of the Church through the ups and downs of its infancy, now formed a pivot for the intellectual interests of the day—albeit of a somewhat non-progressive, anti-modern kind. Still, the atmosphere that prevailed in the pleasant rooms at Bishopscourt was the nearest thing to be found to the urbane, unworldly air of English university or cathedral life. Next in order came the legal luminaries, Irishmen for the most part, with keen, ugly faces and scathingly witty tongues; men whose enormous experience made them the best of good company. And to this clique belonged also the distinguished surgeons and physicians of the eastern hill; the bankers, astutest of financiers; with, for spice, the swiftly changing politicians of the moment, here one day, gone the next, with nothing but their ideas or their energy to recommend them, and dragging with them wives married in their working days. . . well, the less said of the wives the better.

Such was the society in which Mahony was now called on to take his place. And the result was by so much the most vivid expression of his personality he had yet succeeded in giving, that it became *the* one that imprinted itself on men's minds, to the confusion of what had gone before and was to come after: became the reality from which his mortal shadow was thrown.—"Mahony?" would be the query in later years. "Mahony? Ah yes, of course, you mean Townshend-Mahony of 'Ultima Thule,'" this being the name he had bestowed on his new house.—Mary regarded him fondly and with pride. Certain it was, no matter in what circle she moved, whose dinner-table he sat at, whose hearthrug he stood on, he was by far the most distinguished-looking man in the room. And not only this: a kind of mellowness now descended on him, a new tolerance with his fellowmen. The lines of work and worry disappeared; he filled out both in face and figure, and loved to tease Mary by declaring he was on the high road to growing fat. He brushed up his musical accomplishments, too; and his pleasant tenor, his skill as a flute-player, brought him into fresh demand. Miss Timms-Kelly, Judge Kelly's daughter, who had quite the finest amateur voice in Melbourne, was heard to say she preferred Richard's second in a duet to any other; and many an elaborate aria, full of shakes and trills, did she warble to his *obbligato* on the flute.

How happy all this made Mary, she could not have told. To know Richard even moderately contented would have satisfied her; to see him actually taking pleasure in life caused her Cup to run over. She had now not a care left, hardly a wish unfulfilled. And she showed it. The eclipse in health and good looks she had suffered by reason of her transplantation was past: never had she felt better than at present; while in appearance she bloomed anew—enjoyed a kind of Indian summer. At thirty-two, an age when, in the trying climate of the colony, a woman was, as often as not, hopelessly faded, Mary did not need to fear comparison with ladies ten years her junior. Her skin was still flawless, eye as brilliant, her hair as glossy as of old. In figure she inclined to the statuesque, without being either too tall or too full: arms and shoulders were unsurpassed in their rounded whiteness. A certain breadth of brow alone prevented her, at this stage of her life, from being classed among the acknowledged beauties of her sex: it lent her a thoughtful air, where she should have been merely pleasing.—But, after all, what did this matter? Her real beauty, as Richard often reflected, consisted in the warmth and loving-kindness that beamed from her eyes, illuminating a face which never a malicious thought had twisted or deformed. Her expression was, of course, no more one of utter unsuspicion— experience had seen to that—just as her mind was no longer afflicted with the adorable blindness that had been its leading trait in girlhood. Mary now knew very well that evil existed, and that mortals were prone to it. But she would not allow that it could be inborn; held fast to her unconquerable belief in the innate goodness of every living soul; and was never at a loss to exonerate the sinner. "No wonder he's what he is, after the life he has been forced to lead. We mightn't have turned out any better ourselves, with his temptations." Or: "She has never had a chance, poor thing! Circumstances have always been against her."

With her anxieties on Richard's behalf, Mary's ambitions for him— that he should climb the tree, make a name—also gradually sank to rest. Her mind was thus at liberty to follow its own bent. Fond though she was of her fellow-creatures, the formal round of social life had never made a very deep appeal to her: she liked to see people merry and enjoying themselves, but she herself needed something more active to engross her. Her house, well staffed, well run, claimed only a fraction of her attention. Hence she had plenty of time to devote herself to what Richard called her true mission in life: the care of others—especially of the poor and suffering, the unhappy and unsure. And many a heart was lightened by having Mary to lean on, her strong common sense for a guide. Her purse, too, was an unending solace. Even in the latter years in Ballarat, she had had to dispense her charities carefully, balancing one against another. Now her income was equal to all the calls made on it. . . and more. . . Richard generously bidding her add to her own pin-money anything left over from the handsome cheque he gave her for housekeeping expenses. And since he, mindful of his promise, never inquired what she did with it, she was at last free to give as royally as she chose. . . in any direction. But if he did not ask to see her pass-book, neither did she see his: he would not have her troubling her head, he said, about their general expenditure. At first she rather demurred at this: she would have liked to know how their outlay per month tallied with the sum at their disposal; and she missed the talks they had been used to have, about how best to portion out their income. But Richard said those days were over and done with: she would lose her way, he teased her, among sums of four figures—for, in a twinkling, his late-found affluence had thrown him back on the traditional idea that money affairs were the man's province, not the woman's. For her comfort, he stressed once more the fact that he did not intend to speculate; also that at long last, he would, despite the enormous premium, be able to insure his life. In the event of anything happening to him, she would be well provided for, and thus might spend what he gave her freely and without scruple. Yielding to these persuasions, Mary acquiesced in the new arrangement, and gradually slipped into the delightful habit of taking money for granted. After all, the confidence was mutual: he trusted her not to run up bills at milliner's or jeweller's; she, too, had to trust in her turn. She valued his faith in her, and was careful not to abuse it. Her own accounts were scrupulously kept: just as in the old days, she wrote down every shilling she spent, and knitted her brows over the halfpennies; with the result that she soon began to accumulate a tidy little nest-egg.

Her charities were her sole extravagance, her personal wants remaining few and simple. Besides, Richard was forever making her presents. It could not be said of him that his tastes did not expand with his purse. He put his men-servants into livery, stocked his cellars, bought silver table-appliances and egg-shell china, had his crest stamped wherever it could find a place. And the things he bought for her were of the same costly nature. In addition to the carriage, which she had to admit was both useful and necessary, his gifts included jewellery (which she wore more to please him than because she had any real liking for it)—rings and chains, brooches and bracelets—all things *his* wife ought to have and never had had: curling ostrich feathers for hat and fan; gold-mounted mother-of-pearl opera-glasses; hand-painted fans; carved ivory card-cases; ivory-backed brushes and silver vinaigrettes: any fal-lal, in short, that struck his eye or caught his fancy.

There came a day on which he fairly outdid himself. Soon after inscribing their names in the visiting-book at Government House, they received invitations to a ball there, in honour of two men-of-war that were anchored in the Bay—a very select affair indeed: none of your promiscuous May Day crushes! As it would be their first appearance in style, Mahony—a trifle uncertain whether Mary would do the thing handsomely enough—insisted on fitting her out. The pale blue silk he chose for her gown was finest Lyons, the cost of which, without making, ran to thirty pounds: Mary had never seen a silk like it. It was got privatim through John, who had it direct from the French factory. John, too, was responsible for the crowning glory of Mary's attire. For after Richard had added a high, pearl-studded Spanish comb for her hair, John one day showed him a wonderful shawl that had just come into the warehouse, suggesting it would look well on Mary. And for once Mahony found himself in agreement with his brother-in-law. Of softest cashmere, supple as silk—and even softer to the touch—the scarlet ground of the shawl was well-nigh hidden by a massive white Indian embroidery; so that the impression gained was one of sumptuous white silk, broken by flecks of red. It was peaked, burnous-like, to form a hood, and this and the corners were hung with heavy white silk tassels. So magnificent an affair was it that Mary had severe qualms about wearing it: in her heart she considered it far too showy and elaborate. But Richard had no doubt paid an enormous price for it, and would be hurt into the bargain if she said what she thought.

He himself was charmed with the effect, when she draped it over the sky-blue of the gown. "Upon my word, my dear, you'll put every other woman in the shade!"

But even he was not prepared for the stir that ran through the ballroom on their arrival. In among the puces and magentas, the rose-budded pinks and forget-me-notted blues came Mary, trailing a bit of oriental splendour, and wearing it, as only she could, with a queenly yet unconscious air. Seated on a dais among the matrons—for nowadays she danced only an occasional "square," leaving round dances to the young—Mary drew the fire of all eyes.

And it was not the opera-cloak alone.

"A skin like old Florentine ivory!" declared an Englishman fresh from "home." The guest of the Governor, he was wandering through this colonial assembly much as a musical connoisseur might wander through a cattle-yard. Till Mary caught his eye... And when she dropped the cloak, for the honour of a quadrille with his Excellency, this same visitor was heard to dilate on the tints cast by the blue on the ivory. . . to murmur of Goya. . . Velasquez.

Subsequently he was introduced, and sat by her side for the better part of an hour.

At two o'clock, when Mahony handed her to the carriage, it was with something of the lover-like elan that even the least fond husband feels on seeing his wife the centre of attraction.

"Now, madam! . . . wasn't I right? Who was the success of the evening I should like to know?"

"Oh, Richard. . . Put up the window, dear, it's cold. If there can be any talk of a success. . . then it's the cloak you mean, not me."

"It took you to carry it off, love. Not another woman in the room could have done it. Made it seem very well worth the price I had to pay for it."

"Which reminds me, you haven't yet told me what that was."

"My business, sweetheart! Yours to play the belle and get compared to the old masters by admiring strangers."

"*Really*, Richard!" Mary made the deprecating movement of the chin with which she was wont to rebuke extravagances. "Why, dear, he was so high-falutin I didn't know half the time what he was talking about." Then fearing she had been too severe, she added: "Of course I'm very glad you were pleased,"—and hoped that was the end of it. Compliments, even from one's husband, were things to be evaded if possible. "Well, I must remember poor Jinny and not hoard it up for the moths to get at." But there was more than a dash of doubt in Mary's tone, and she sighed. Not merely for Jinny. She did not know when another opportunity so splendid as this evening's would arise. For an ordinary one, such finery would certainly be out of place.

"Wear it or not as you please, love. It has served its end. . . stamped itself on a moment of time," said Mahony; and fell therewith into a brown study.

But as he helped her from the carriage he stooped and kissed her. . . which Mary was very much afraid the coachman saw.

V

Than queening it at balls, she felt more in her element seated in a rather dingily furnished drawing-room, holding poor Agnes Ocock's hand. Although it had struck five and the worst heat of the day was over, Agnes was still in her bedgown—she had been lying down with the headache, she said—nor could Mary persuade her to exchange this for bonnet and shawl, and drive out with her in the brougham that stood at the door.

"Another time, dearest, if you do not mind. Today I have no fancy for it."

Mary was shocked by the change the past six months had worked in her friend; and disagreeably impressed by the common-featured house in which she found her: it had no garden, but stood right on the dusty St. Kilda Parade. Agnes was growing very stout; her fine skin looked as creased as her robe, her cheek was netted with veins, her hair thin, under a cap set awry. Mary knew the rumours that were current; and her heart swelled with pity.

"Just as you like, dear. And how are the children? Are they in? May I see them?"

"Oh, yes, the children. Why. . . the truth is, dearest Mary, I haven't. . . they are not with me. Henry thought. . . he thought. . ."

Agnes's voice broke, and after a painful struggle to compose herself she hid her face in her hands.

Leaning forward Mary laid an arm round her shoulders. "Dearest Agnes, won't you tell me your trouble? Is it the little one you. . . you lost, you are fretting over?"

And now there was no sound in the room but that of crying—and such crying! It seemed difficult to connect these heavy nerve-racking sobs with the lovely, happy little Agnes of former days. Holding her close, Mary let her weep unstintedly.

"Oh, Mary, Mary! I am the most miserable creature alive."

Yes, it was the loss of the child that was breaking her heart. . . or rather the way in which she had lost it.

"It was the finest baby you ever saw, Mary—neither of the others could compare with it. They were all very well; but this one. . . His tiny limbs were so round and smooth—it was like kissing velvet. And dimples everywhere. And he was born with a head of golden hair. I never knew Henry so pleased. He said such a child did me credit. . . and this used rather to make me wonder, Mary; for Baby wasn't a bit like Henry. . . or like the other two. He took after my family and had blue eyes. But do you know who he reminded me of most of all? It was of Eddie, Mary. . . and through Eddie of Mr. Glendinning. When Eddie was born he used to lie in my lap, just as soft and fair. . . and sometimes I think I forgot, and imagined this baby *was* Eddie over again. . . and that made me still fonder of him; for one's first is one's first, love, no matter how many come after. And then. . . then. . . He was five months old, and beginning to try to grasp things and take notice—oh, such a happy babe! And then one morning, I wasn't feeling well, Mary—the doctor said the nursing of such a hearty child was a great strain on me; then a giddy fit took me—I had been giving him the breast and got up to lay him down—nurse wasn't there. I must have been dizzy with sitting so long stooped over him—and he was heavy for his age. I got up and came over faint all of a sudden—the doctor says so. . . and I tottered, Mary, and Baby fell—fell out of my arms. . . on his little head—I heard the thud—yes, the thud. . . but not a cry or a sound. . . nothing. . . nothing. . . he never cried again."

"Oh, my poor Agnes! Oh, you poor, poor thing!"

Mary was weeping, too; the tears ran down her cheeks. But she made no attempt to palliate or console; did not speak of an accident for which it was impossible to blame yourself; or of God's will, mysterious, inscrutable: she just grieved, with an intensity of feeling that made her one with the bereft. Things of this kind went too deep for words; were hurts from which there could be no recovery. Time might grow its moss over them. . . hide them from mortal sight. . . that was all.

As she drove home she reflected, pitifully, how strange it was that so soft and harmless a creature as Agnes should thus be singled out for some of life's hardest blows. Agnes had so surely been born for happiness—and to make others happy. Misfortunes such as these ought to be kept for people of stronger, harder natures and with broader backs; who could suffer and still carry their heads high. Agnes was merely crushed to earth by them. . . like a poor little trampled flower.

But before she reached the house, a fearful suspicion crossed her mind.

Tilly nodded confirmingly.

"The plain English of it is, she was squiffy."

And went on: "It was hushed up, my dear, you bet!—kept dark as the grave. . . doctor changed, etc. etc. They actually 'ad the face to put it down to the nurse's carelessness: said nurse being packed off at once, *handsomely remunerated*, mind you, to hold 'er tongue. An' a mercy the child died; the doctor seemed to think it might 'ave been soft, 'ad it lived—after such a knock on the pate—and can you see Henry dragging the village idiot at 'is heels? *never* was a man in such a fury, Mary. Ugh! that white face with those little pitch-black eyes rolling round in it—it gave me the fair shakes to look at 'im. 'Pon my word I believe, if 'e'd dared, 'e'd 'ave slaughtered Agnes there and then. His child, *his* son!—you know the tune of it. 'E'll never forgive 'er, mark my words he won't! . . . the disgrace and all that—for of course everybody knew all about it and a good deal more. She was odd enough beforehand, never going anywhere. Now she's taking the sea-air at St. Kilda, and, if you ask me, she'll go on taking it. . . till Doomsday."

"The very way to drive her to despair!" cried Mary; and burned.

Tilly shrugged. "It's six of one and 'alf a dozen of the other to my mind. I'd almost rather be put away to rot like a poisoned rat in a hole, than live under the whip of Mossieu Henry's tongue—not to mention 'is eye!"

"Agnes shall not die like a rat in a hole if I can help it."

"Ah, but you can't, my dear! . . . don't make any mistake about that. You might as well try to bend a bar of iron as 'Enry.—And I must say, Mary, it does sometimes seem a good deal of fuss to make over one small kid. She can 'ave more for the asking."

"*Tilly!*" Mary looked up from her sewing—the two women sat on the verandah of Tilly's house in Ballarat, where Mary was visiting—in reproof and surprise at a speech so unlike her friend. It was not the first either; Tilly often wore a mopy, world-weary air nowadays, which did not sit naturally on her. "Each child that lives is just itself," added Mary. "That's why one loves it so."

"Oh, well, I s'pose so. And as you know, love, I'd 'ave 'ad a dozen if I could. It wouldn't 'ave been one too many to fill this 'ouse."

Mary believed she read the answer to the riddle. "Look here, Tilly, you're lonely. . . that's what's the matter with you."

And Tilly nodded, dumpily—again unlike herself.

"Fact is, Mary, I want something to *do*. As long as dear old Pa lived, and I 'ad the boys to look after, it was all right—I never knew what it was to be dull. But now. . . P'r'aps if they'd let me keep Tom and

Johnny. . . or if I could groom my own 'orses or ride 'em at the stakes. . . No, no, of course, I know it wouldn't do—or be *commy faut*. It's only my gab."

"I wonder, Tilly," said Mary, "I wonder if. . . have you never thought, dear, at times like these that. . . that perhaps you might some day marry again?" She put the question very tentatively, knowing Tilly's robust contempt for the other sex.

But Tilly answered pat: "Why, that's just what I 'ave, Mary."

"Oh!" said Mary. And to cover up her amazement, added: "I think it would be the very best thing that could happen."

There followed a pause of some length. Mary did not know what to make of it. Tilly was humming and hawing: she fidgeted, coloured, shifted her eyes.

"Yes, my dear," she said at length, in answer to Mary's invitation to speak out: "I *Have* something on my chest. . . something I want to say to you, Mary, and yet don't quite know, 'ow. Fact is, I want you to do me a good turn, my dear. No, now just you wait a jiff, till you 'ear what it is. Tell you what, Mary, I've found meself regularly down in the mouth of late—off me grub—and that sort of thing. No, Pa's death has nothing whatever to do with it. I was getting on famously—right as a trivet— till. . . well, till I went to town—yes, that time, you know, to meet you and the doctor." And as Mary still sat blank and uncomprehending, she blurted out: "Oh, well. . . till I saw. . . oh, *you* know!—till I met a *Certain Person* again."

"A certain person? Do you. . . Tilly! Oh, Tilly, do you *really?* Purdy?"

Tilly nodded, heavily, gloomily, without the ghost of a smile. "Yes, it's a fact—and not one I'm proud of either, as you can guess. And yet again I ask meself why not? I need someone to look after, Mary. . . and that's the truth. 'E's down on *his* luck, as always; can't get the money to stick; and I've more than I know what to do with. And to see 'im there, lookin' so poor and shabby, and yet keeping 'is pecker up as 'e did—why, I dunno, but it seemed some'ow to 'urt me *'ere!*"—and Tilly, her aitches scattering more wildly than usual under the stress of her emotion, laid her hands, one over the other, on her left breast.

"But Tilly—"

"Oh! now don't go and but me, Polly, like the dear good soul you are and always 'ave been. If you mean, am I going to let 'im make ducks and drakes of poor old Pa's money, I can truly say no—no fear! Not this child. But. . . well. . . look 'ere, Mary, I 'aven't spit out the whole truth yet. You'll laugh at what I'm going to tell you, and well you may do; it sounds rum enough. But you know they do say old folks fall to playing again with toys, cuddling dolls and whittling chips. Well, a *Certain Person* 'ad a bit of hair, Poll, that used to curl behind 'is ear—many and many's the time in the old spoony days I've sat and twiddled it round me finger. Now, 'is hair's wearing thin on top, but the curl's still there—and I. . . would you believe it? . . . yes, I'm blessed if my finger didn't itch to be at it again. And what's worse, *has* itched ever since. 'Ere I go, properly in the dumps and the doldrums, and feeling as if nothing 'ull ever matter much anymore if I can't. Oh, there's no fool like an old fool, Mary love! . . . and nobody knows that better than the old fool 'im—herself."

"Oh come, Tilly, you're not quite so ancient as you try to make out! As to what you say. . . it's been the living alone and all that, it's come of."

But though she spoke in a reassuring tone, Mary was none the less genuinely perturbed: her robust, sensible Tilly reduced to such a foolish state! Why, it was like seeing one's dearest friend collapse under a sudden illness.

"P'r'aps. And p'r'aps not. But what I want you to do for me, old girl, is this. Ask me down to stop for a bit, and ask him to the house while I'm there. The rest I'll manage for myself. Only you won't let on to the doctor, will you, love, what I've told you? I don't want the doctor to know. 'E'd look down 'is nose at me with that queer look of his—no, I couldn't stand it, Poll! Henry, too—I shall keep 'Enry in the dark till it's too late. 'E'd raise Cain. For, of course 'e thinks what Pa left's safe to come to his brats. While, if I fix things up as I want 'em"—she lowered her voice—"I may 'ave kids of my own yet."

"Indeed and I hope so. . . from the bottom of my heart."

Tell Richard? No, indeed! As that same afternoon Mary drove in Tilly's double buggy down the dusty slope of Sturt Street, and out over the Flat, she imagined to herself what Richard would say—and think—did she make him partner in Tilly's confidences. What? . . . try to trap a man, and an old friend to boot, into a loveless marriage, merely because you want to twist a bit of hair round your finger? He would snort with disgust at such folly. . . besides thinking it indelicate into the bargain. As she was afraid she, Mary, did a little, too. The difference was: she saw, as he never would, that loneliness was at the bottom of it; loneliness, and they want of someone to care for, or, as Tilly put it, of something to do. It might also be that the old girlish inclination had never quite died out, but only slumbered through all these years. Not that that would count with Richard; indeed, it might count in just the opposite way. For he was more than straitlaced where things of this kind were in question; had a constitutional horror of them; and he would not consider it at all nice for the seeds of an old attachment to have stayed alive in you, while you were happily married to someone else. Another point: if Purdy yielded to the temptation and took Tilly and her money, Richard might always think less well of him for doing so; which would be a thousand pities, now a first move towards a reconciliation had been made. Whereas if the engagement seemed to come about of itself. . . And in this respect there was really something to be said for it. Purdy once married and settled, the foolish barrier that had grown up between the two men would fall away, and they again become the friends they had been of old.

Reasoning thus, Mary arrived at a row of mean little weatherboard houses, in one of which Ned lived. She did not knock, but stepped across the verandah, turned the door-knob and went down the passage. It was a Monday, and washing day. The brick floor of the kitchen overflowed with water, in which the young fry played. Polly, turning from the tubs, ran her hands down her arms to sluice off the lather, before extending them, all moist and crinkled, in an embrace. By the copper sat Ned—poor Ned—convalescent from the attack of acute bronchitis which had brought Mary in hot haste to Ballarat a few weeks previously. Ned's chest and shoulders were wrapped up in an old red flannel petticoat, pinned under the chin; his feet, well out of the damp's way on an upturned sugar-box, were clad in down-at-heel felt slippers. His thick ringletty hair and curly beard hung long and unkempt above the scarlet drapery, forming a jet-black aureole from which his face, chastened to a new delicacy, looked out beautiful as a cameo.

Pouncing on Mary he talked volubly, in the hoarse whisper that was all the voice his illness had left him. It was the same old Ned, holding forth in the same old way: on the luck that had always been against him, the fair chance he had never yet had; man and theme lit up by the same unquenchable optimism. He had today a yarn to tell of the fortune he might have made, not three months back, had he only at the critical moment been able to lay hands on the needful: men had gone in and won who had not a quarter of his flair. How much of this was truth and how much imagination, Mary did not know or greatly care—unlike Polly who, rasped beyond measure, clicked an angry tongue and lashed out at Ned's "atrocious lies."

Striving to keep the peace by dropping in soothing words, Mary sat and pondered how best these poor souls could be helped. On the voyage out, she had seriously considered adopting one—perhaps even two—of the black-haired brood. But again Polly made short work of the suggestion. Not even to Mary whom she dearly loved, would she give up her children.

"They're me own and I'll stick to 'em, come what may! For they're all I've got, dearie. . . all I'll ever get from the whole galumphing galoot." With which Mary was forced to agree; and though seven lived and a ninth was on the way.

Nor could Polly be induced to part from them even for the benefit of their education.

"Ta, love, you mean it kindly, but I'll not have 'em brought up above their station. They're a working-man's kids, and such they'll remain. Besides, you may be sure there'll be *some* of Ned's blowfly notions in some of their heads. And the State School's the best place to knock such nonsense out of 'em." Which, duly reported by Mary, Richard said was a gross example of parental selfishness. What right had a mother to stand in the way of her offspring? No child with any true affection would grow up to despise his parents. On the contrary, as he understood the sacrifice they had made for him, his love for them would deepen and increase. But this was just Richard's high-flown way of looking at things.

No, what Ned and Polly wanted was money, and money alone. This piece of knowledge was accompanied, however, by so disagreeable a sensation that Mary was thankful Richard was not there to share it. Not only were they ready to take every shilling offered. . . poor things, no one could blame them for that, pinched and straitened as they were. . . it was their manner of accepting that wounded Mary. They pocketed what Richard sent them almost as a matter of course, frankly inspecting the amount, and sometimes even going so far as to wrinkle their noses over it. Which was really hardly fair; for Richard was very generous to them; considering they were no blood relations of his, and he felt they didn't like him. Nor did they: there was no getting away from that; they showed it even to the extent of begrudging him his good luck. . . without which he would have been unable to do anything for them! Poor Ned's eye was hot with envy whenever Richard's rise in the world was mentioned. While Polly alluded to it with an open sneer.

"I say, *infra dig*, isn't it and no mistake, for a heavy swell like he is, to have such low-down connections. . . people who take in other people's washing!"

Mary could not bring herself to sit in judgment on them: for all his tall talk, Ned had never harmed a fly; and Polly's was just a generous nature warped and twisted by poverty and an imprudent marriage. All the same she took great pains not to let Richard know how the wind blew. Her letters to him, on Ned and Polly's behalf, were full of the warm gratitude she herself would have felt had she stood in their shoes.

VI

For the first time in his life Mahony found himself in possession of all the books he wanted: rare books hard to get; expensive books he had till now never felt justified in buying. And Mary, his social conscience, being absent, he fell into depths of abstraction from which there was nothing to rouse him.

His two old arch-enemies time and money—or rather the lack of them—had definitely ceased to plague him. His leisure was unbounded, the morrow well provided for, and the material comfort of his present surroundings such as he had hitherto known only in dreams. No domestic sounds rasped his ear, scattered his attention; his spacious study, book-lined from ceiling to floor, stood apart from the rest of the house, and was solidly built. Was cool and airy, too; even in the heat of midday he caught a whiff of the sea. The garden with its shrubberies and lawns of buffalo-grass, its spreading figtrees and dark firs, rested and refreshed the eye. His meals appeared on the table as by clockwork, served as he liked them, cooked to a turn. And so greatly did the hermit's life he now led jump with his mood, that invitations to social functions grew fly-spotted on the chimney-shelf, or were swept up by the housemaid from the floor.

He first undertook to examine the great moderns: those world-famous scientists and their philosophic spokesmen who dominated the intellectual life of the day. So far he had read their works only in snatches, and at random. He now re-read them systematically; followed step by step the presentment of their monumental theories—the idea of evolution, the origin of species, the antiquity of man—as well as the constructive or subversive conclusions deduced therefrom.

Thus weeks passed. At the end of this time—Mary being still from home—he emerged heavy-eyed and a trifle dazed, from sittings protracted late into the night, and paused to take his bearings. And it was now, on looking back over what he had read, that he became aware of a feeling of dissatisfaction. Chiefly with regard to the mental attitude of the writers themselves. So sound were their arguments that they might well, he thought, have refrained from the pontifical airs they saw fit to adopt; having been a shade less intolerant of views and beliefs that did not dovetail with their own. Riding on the crest of the highest wave of materialism that had ever broken over the world, they

HENRY HANDEL RICHARDSON

themselves were satisfied that life and its properties could be explained, to the last iota, in terms of matter; and, dogmatically pronouncing their interpretation of the universe to be the only valid one, they laid a crushing veto on any suggestion of a possible spiritual agency. Here it was, he parted company with them. For the same thing had surely happened before, in the world's history, bodies of learned men arising at various epochs in divers lands, and claiming to have solved the great riddle once and for all? Over and above this, did Huxley's inflamed outbursts against the "cosmogony of the semi-barbarous Hebrew"; his sighs that the "myths of Paganism, dead as Osiris or Zeus," had not been followed to their graves by the "coeval imaginations current among the rude inhabitants of Palestine"; his bald definition of science as "trained and organised common sense"—*did* Huxley's type of mind, or yet that of another well-known savant, who declared that one should decide beforehand what was possible and what not, incline you to trust these men's verdict on the spiritual issues of human existence? In his own case, certainly not. He believed and would continue to believe it impossible wholly to account for life and its phenomena, in terms of physiology, chemistry and physics.

Another thing that baffled him was: why, having advanced to a certain point, should they suddenly stop short, with a kingly gesture of: "Thus far and no farther"? Devoting decades of laborious research to the *origin* of life on this globe, its age, its evolution, why should they leave untouched two questions of still more vital import: life's ultimate goal, and the moral mysteries of the soul of man? Yes, the chief bone he had to pick with them was that they had no will to fathom such deeps; plumed themselves instead on cold-shouldering them; flaunted as their device: *ignoramus et ignorabimus*. Arrogantly sure of themselves, carried away by a passion for facts, they covered with ridicule those—the seers, the poets, the childlike in heart—who, over and above the rational and knowable, caught glimpses of what was assumed to be unknowable; declaring, with a fierce and intolerant unimaginativeness, that the assertion which outstripped the evidence was not only a blunder, but a crime. Strange, indeed, was it to watch these masters toiling to interpret human life, yet denying it all hope of a further development, any issue but that of eternal nothingness. For his part, he could not see why the evolution-formula should be held utterly to rule out the transcendental-formula. But so it was; every line of their works confirmed it. . . confirmed, too, the reader's opinion that, in their bigoted attitude of mind, they differed not so very markedly from those hard-and-fast champions of orthodoxy who, in the rising flood of enlightenment, remained perilously clinging to the vanishing rock of dogma and tradition. On the one hand, for all answer to the burning needs and questions of the hour, the tale of Creation as told in Genesis, the Thirty-nine Articles, the intolerable Athanasian Creed; on the other, as bitterly stubborn an agnosticism—each surely, in the same degree, stones for bread. One would have liked to call to them: Fear not to turn the light of research on the conception of that immortality which you affirm. . . which you deny.

Thus it came about that, little by little, Mahony found himself drifting away from the barren conclusions of science: just as in earlier years he had cast loose from a too rigid orthodoxy. Occult subjects had always had a strong fascination for him, and he now turned back to them; read ancient screeds on alchemy and astrology; the writings of Paracelsus and Apollonius of Tyana. Thence he dived into mysticism; studied the biographies of Saint Theresa, Joseph Glanvill, Giordano Bruno; and pondered anew the trance history of Swedenborg. Men and women like these, living their lives as a kind of experiment, and an arduous and painful experiment at that, were yet supported and uplifted by the consciousness of a mighty power outside, and at the same time within themselves: a bottomless well of spiritual strength. Out of this inspiration they taught confidently that all life emanated from God (no matter what form it assumed in its progress), to God would return, and in Him continue to exist. Yes, spirituality outstripped intellect; there were mysteries at once too deep and too simple for learned brains to fathom. Actually, the unlettered man who said: "God is, and I am of God!" came nearest to reading the riddle of the universe. How cold and comfortless, too, the tenet that this one brief span of being ended all. Without faith in a life to come, how endure, stoically, the ills that here confronted us? . . . the injustices of human existence, the evil men did, the cruelty of man to his brothers, of God to man? Postulate a Hereafter, and the hope arose that, some day, the ultimate meaning of all these apparent contradictions would be made plain: the endless groping, struggling, suffering prove but rungs in the ladder of humanity's upward climb. Not for him the Byzantine Heaven of the churches, with its mental stagnation, its frozen immobility, wherein a jealous God, poorer in charity than the feeble creatures built in His image, spent Eternity damning those who had failed to propitiate Him.

HENRY HANDEL RICHARDSON

Nor yet the doctrine of the Fall of a perfect man from grace. Himself he held this present life to be but a portal, an antechamber, where dwelt an imperfect but wholly vital creation, which, growing more and more passionately aware with the passing of the ages of its self-contained divinity, would end by achieving, by being reabsorbed in, the absolute consciousness of the Eternal.

Yes, old faiths lay supine, stunned by the hammer blows of science; and science had nothing soul-satisfying to offer in their place. Surely now, if ever, the age was ripe for a new revelation: racked by doubts, or cut to the heart by atheistic denial, it cried aloud for a fresh proof of God's existence, and of God's concern with man.—Restlessly feeling his way, Mahony set himself to take the measure, where he had so far only dabbled in it, of the new movement spiritualism, which, from its rise in a tiny American hamlet, had run like a wildfire over Europe. If what its followers claimed for it was true—and among them were men of standing whose words could not be dismissed with a shrug—if the spirits of those who had crossed the bourne were really able. . . as in the days of Moses and the prophets. . . to return and speak with their loved ones—then it meant that a new crisis had arisen in man's relation to the Unseen, with which both science and religion would eventually have to reckon. Unlike the majority, he was not put off by the commonplace means of communication employed—the rappings and the tappings, the laborious telling over of the alphabet—nor yet by the choice, as agents, or the illiterate and immature. He recalled the early history of Christianity: the Chaldean shepherds; the Judean carpenter's shop; the unlettered fishermen; the sneers and gibes of Roman society. God's ways had never been, never would be man's ways. Why, even as it was, some found the practice of conventional Christianity none too easy, thanks to the frailty of the human channels through which the great message had to pass: the supercilious drawl of a ritualistic parson; one's inability to admit that a bad priest might read a true Mass; the fact that the celebrant from whom you received the Eucharist was known to be, in his spare hours, drinker and gambler, or one of those who systematically hunted small animals to death. Measured by such stumbling-blocks as these, the spiritualists' sincere faith and homely conduct of their seances did not need to shirk comparison. Indeed, there would sometimes seem to be more genuine piety at their meetings than at many an ordinary church service. But, however one looked at it, the question to be answered remained: was it possible to draw from this new movement proofs of the knowledge one's soul craved—the continuity of existence; the nearness, the interwovenness, of the spiritual world to the material; the eternal and omnipotent presence of the Creator?

Mary wrote: What in all the world are you doing with yourself Richard? The carters quite expected you last wednesday, and the rentouls had a place laid at dinner for you on friday evening. Both write me hoping you were not kept away by illness. I think it's time I came home to look after you.

To which Mahony replied: Nonsense, my dear, I am getting on capitally—servants most attentive, and cook dishing me up all manner of good things. Do not hurry back on my account.

Mary's next letter bore the heading "Yarangobilly," and ran:

You see where I am now. The Urquharts insisted on my coming out—and Tilly with me. There's a large party here as usual, and picnics, dancing, music and singing go on all the time. I was sorry to leave ballarat, which is as lovely as ever, and everyone just as kind. Willy is just the same; so full of life and fun you really can't help liking him, however much you may disapprove. Both he and Louisa seem pleased to have me and are full of regrets that you are not with me. I think it is a great pity you didn't take my advice and come too. Ever so many people have inquired after you.

Not I! was Richard's response. They never wanted me when I was among them; why on earth should they miss me now? . . . When they've had ample time to forget all about me. It's only your own imagination.

And Mary: What rubbish you do talk, dear! I believe you're growing odd and fanciful through being so much alone. Do go out more, and not coop yourself up so.—Well, we're still here. Louisa won't hear of our leaving; It's quite a change for her to have friends of her own in the house—the others are mostly Willy's. Poor Louisa through never getting away—I mean with all the babies, etc. makes hardly any. She looks far older than her age, and "very" dowdy. She needs someone to take her in hand and freshen her up. I've made her promise to spend at least a month with me after I get back—the last baby's well over a year now, and there are no fresh expectations in the meantime, thank goodness. . . twelve are surely enough. I intend to stitch a rose in her bonnet, and teach her how to do her hair. Also get her into one of the new bustles—her dresses are in the style of the year one. She would still be quite pretty if nicely dressed, and I think that would be much more effective than sitting moping and fretting, and not caring how she looks. Fretting about Willy, I mean. I'm afraid he's incurable. he's very much epris again at present. This time it's a fascinating widow who's stopping here—a very charming person, and interested unfortunately in everything Willy's interested in—horses, dogs, riding, driving, cattle and sheep—to cut it short, all Louisa isn't.

A week later. I had a long talk with Mrs. Marriner—that's the widow-lady I mentioned in my last. She's really much attached to Louisa, and would be her friend if only Louisa would let her. (Now I'm not imagining this!) But L. is so jealous that she can hardly be civil. There was quite a scene last night. It ended by poor Louisa going to bed in floods of tears. Of course I can see it from her side, too. It must be very hard to know that another woman pleases your husband better than you do. Still, Willy has had so many fancies in his day, I think Louisa needn't take this one too seriously. Gracey—Mrs. Marriner, that is—was quite upset about it herself. She is really very charming and it isn't exactly her fault: She can't help pleasing. And so sensible, too. We had a talk, she and I, about poor agnes and her failing—she knows all about it—and she quite agrees with me, it's really someone's duty to tackle Mr. Henry.

And again: Oh no, Richard, you've got quite a false idea of her. She's anything but designing—not one of those widows who go about setting their caps at men. But you'll be able to see for yourself; for she talks of taking a House at Brighton. And I'm sure you'll like her, and get on well with her—she's so clever. You should have heard her yesterday evening discussing the reform of gaols and penitentiaries with a gentleman who's staying here. We other ladies felt our noses quite put of joint.

Back in ballarat, Mary wrote: Well! I've done the deed, dear. I thought it best not to mention it beforehand, for I knew you would write about minding one's own business, not interfering between husband and wife, etc. Tilly and I came back to "Beamish House" at the end of the week, and on wednesday off I went and paid a visit to Mr. Henry. He couldn't have received me more Civilly. He told his clerk he would see nobody else while I was there, and had wine and biscuits fetched—I can tell you, paid me every attention. He also asked most kindly after you.—As you may guess, I approached the subject of agnes very gingerly. Just hinted I had seen her and how sorry I was to find her in such a poor state of health. He was rather reserved at first. But when I gave him to understand she had confided in me, and how broken-hearted she was and what reproaches she was making herself, and when I sympathised with him over the loss of such a beautiful child. . . Why, then he quite thawed and came out of his shell. Indeed all but broke down. Think of that with Mr. Henry, who has always been so cold and stern! you'll perhaps say it is chiefly his pride he has been hurt in: But don't you think that's hard enough, for a man like him? Well, one thing led to another, and before long we were talking quite freely about poor little agnes and her terrible weakness. He admitted he was at his wits' end to know what to do with her. Had had some thoughts of putting her in a home, under a doctor's care: but shrinks from the publicity and disgrace. then he fears her bad example on the children—The boy Georgy is seven now, and sharp as a needle. One thing I made him promise and that was, to let agnes leave that dreadful house and come to us for a bit, where she can have the children with her again. (I'll take good care they don't disturb you, dear.) When I came away he took both my hands and shook them and said: "God bless you, my dear Mrs. Mahony! I shall never forget your great kindness in this matter. Nor do I know another soul—certainly not one of your sex—to whom I could have spoken as I have to you." Think of that from Mr. Henry! Tilly hasn't got over it yet. She says it comes of me having worn my best bonnet (the gay one with the flower in, that you like). But of course that's only her nonsense. And I do feel so glad I went and didn't let myself be persuaded not to.

I hope the silk vests are a great success, and that you remember the days for changing them.

VII

"My papeh dotes on music. Positively, I have known my papeh to say he would rather go without his port at dinner than his music after dinner. My papeh has heard all the most famous singers. In his opinion, no one could compare with Malibran." Thus Miss Timms-Kelly; and at his cue the chubby, white-haired old Judge, surreptitiously snatching forty winks in a dark corner of the drawing-room, would start, open his eyes, and, like a well-trained parrot, echo his daughter's words.

"Malibran? . . . ah, now there was a voice for you!—Pasta could not hold a candle to her. As a young man I never missed an opera when she sang. Great nights, great nights! The King's Theatre packed to suffocation. All of us young music-lovers burning with enthusiasm. . . our palms tingling from applause." Here however, at some private sign, the speaker abruptly switched off his reminiscences, which threatened to carry him away, and got to the matter in hand.—"My dear, give us, if you please, *casta diva*. Though I say so myself, there is something in my daughter's rendering of that divine air that recalls Malibran in her prime."

A musical party at the Timms-Kellys' tempted even Mahony forth. On such evenings, in company with other devotees, he would wander up Richmond Hill and through the wooden gates of Vaucluse, where a knot of houses stood sequestered in a grove. The French windows of the Timms-Kellys' drawing-room were invariably set wide open; and guests climbing the hill could hear, while still some way off, the great voice peal out—like a siren-song that urged and cajoled.

Miss Timms-Kelly herself bore the brunt of the entertainment; occasionally mingling in a duo with some manly second, or with the strains of Mahony's flute; but chiefly in solo. For the thin little tones of the other ladies, their tinkly performances of "Maiden's Prayers" and "Warblings at Eve," or the rollicking strains of a sea ballad (which was mostly what the gentlemen were good for) stood none of them an earthly chance against a voice like hers. It was a contralto, with, in its middle and lower registers, tones of a strange, dark intensity which made of it a real *voix sombre*; yet of such exceptional compass that it was also equal to *or sai chi l'onore* and *non mi dir, bell' idol mio*. Mahony used to say there was something in its lower notes that got at you, "like fingers feeling round your heart." Ladies, while admitting its volume and beauty, were apt to be rendered rather uncomfortable by it; and under its influence would fall to fidgeting in their seats.

In person Miss Timms-Kelly matched her voice: though not over tall she was generously proportioned, with a superb bust and exquisitely sloping shoulders. Along with this handsome figure went piquantly small hands and feet—she boasted a number three shoe—white teeth, full lips, a fresh complexion. But her chief charm lay in her animation of manner: she was alive with verve and gesture; her every second word seemed spoken in italics. Amazing, thought and said all, that one so fascinating should have reached the brink of the thirties without marrying; society had known her now for twelve years, and during this time the marvellous voice had rung out night for night, her old father faithfully drawing attention to its merits, the while he grew ever whiter and sleepier in his corner of the drawing-room.

But the little court that surrounded Miss Timms-Kelly consisted chiefly of married men and bachelors well past marrying age: greybeards who, in listening to the strains of *Norma* or *Semiramide*, re-lived their youth. Eligible men fought a little shy of the lady and after a couple of visits to the house were apt to return no more. Happily, Miss Timms-Kelly did not take this greatly to heart. Indeed she even confessed to a relief at their truancy. "All my life, love, I have preferred the company of *elderly* gentlemen. They make one feel so *safe.*"

In process of dressing for such an evening, Mary remarked: "Of course, it's very nice of Lizzie to say that. . . and most sensible. But all the same it *is* odd—I mean the fact of her never having married. Not only because of her voice—one doesn't just marry a voice. But she really is a dear, warm-hearted creature. And so generous." At which Mahony stopped shaving his chin to throw in: "That's precisely it. Your marriageable man instinctively fears not being able to live up to the fair singer's generosity."

"*Really*, Richard! . . . it takes you to say queer things. Now I believe it comes of Lizzie never having had a mother to go about with. She's been obliged to put herself too much forward."

But for all his two-edged comments, let Miss Timms-Kelly but open her mouth to sing, and Mahony was hopelessly her slave. His natural instinct for music had outlived even the long years of starvation in this country, where neither taste nor performance was worth a straw. Under the present stimulus, his dormant feelings awoke to new life: when the great voice rang forth he would sit rapt. . . absorbed. And where others, but faintly responsive to the influence, listened with only half an ear, the while they followed their own trains of thought, musing, gently titillated: "How fine the moon tonight!" or "I shall certainly succeed, if I carry through that deal," or "Perhaps after all Julia will hear my suit," he surrendered thought for emotion, and climbed the ladder of sound to a world built wholly of sound, where he moved light-footedly and at ease.

"Upon my soul, I would walk ten miles to hear her rendering of an aria by Mozart or Verdi!"

This was all very well in its way—its musical way. But now something happened which brought him with a bump to earth. And, ever after, he twitted and blamed himself with having been the innocent cause of a most unnecessary complication.

Towards the close of her stay in Ballarat, Mary had a second meeting—a chance one, this time—with Mr. Henry Ocock. And Ocock, in his new role of friend and adviser, let fall a hint with regard to a certain mining company in which he believed Mahony held shares. This was not the case; but Mary rather thought John did, begged Richard to find out, and if so, to let him know what was being said. As Mr. Henry's information had been *sub rosa*, Mahony thought it wise to pass it on by word of mouth, and wrote John saying he would drop in for a moment the following evening, on his way to Richmond: he was bound with his flute for Vaucluse. In the morning, however, John's groom brought a note asking him to take pot-luck with the family at six o'clock. Such things were possible in John's house nowadays, under the fairy rule of Miss Julia. And so he found himself that night at John's dinner-table.

As usual at this stage, when he had not seen his brother-in-law for a time, Mahony's chief sensation on meeting John was one of discomfort. Without doubt, some great change was at work in John. Lean as a herring, yellow as a Chinaman, he had been for months past. But the change in his manner was even more striking. Gone was much of the high-handedness, the pompous arrogance it had once been so hard to stomach; gone the opulent wordiness of his pronunciamentos. He was now in point of becoming a morose and taciturn sort of fellow; prone, too, to fits of blankness in which, staring straight before him, he seemed to forget your very presence. So much at least was plain: John was not taking the universe by any means so much for granted, as of old.

Money troubles? . . . such was the first thought that leapt to Mahony's mind. Then he laughed at himself. John's business flourished like the green baytree: you never heard of it but it was putting forth a fresh shoot in a fresh direction. No lack of money there!—the notion was just a telling example of how one instinctively tried to read into another, what had been one's own chief bogey. Besides, the warning passed on by Mary left John cold: he waved it aside with a gesture that said: a few thousands more or less signified nothing to him. Could the wife's idea that he was fretting over the loss of his boy be the right one? Again, no: that was just a woman's interpretation: *he* jumped to money, she to the emotional, the personal. Then after all it must be John's health that was causing him anxiety. But a tactful question on this score called forth so curt a negative that he could not press it.

Not till the nuts and port were on the table did John shake off his abstraction. Then his trio of little girls ran into the room—with the playful antics of so many tame white mice—ran in and rubbed their sleek little comb-ringed heads against their father's, and climbed over him with their thin little white-stockinged legs. And John became solely the fond parent, gathering his children to him, taking the youngest on his knee and holding her to his watered-silk waistcoat, letting them play with the long gold chain from which depended his *pince-nez*, count his studs with their little fingers, disarrange the ends of his tie. At the lower end of the table Emmy, who had presided over the meal a radiant vision in white muslin and blue ribbons, flushed, drooped her head, and looked as though she were going to cry. For though the lovely girl had throughout dinner hung distractingly on her father's lips, he had never so much as glanced in her direction.

In watching her, Mahony fell into a reverie, so vividly did she remind him of her dead mother, and the one—the only—time he had seen John's first wife. It was here, in this very room, that the gracious Emma, the picture of all that was comely, had dandled her babes. One of the two, like herself, had vanished from mortal eyes. The other, a full-grown woman in her turn, was now ripe for her fate.

When Emmy shepherded the little girls to their nursery, he turned to John. "Upon my soul, it makes a man realise his age, to see the young ones come on as they do."

Something in this reflection seemed to flick John. His response was more in his old style. "You say so? For my part I cannot admit to feeling a day older than I did ten years back. I am not aware of any decrease of vigour. I still rise at six, take a cold shower-bath, and attend to business for a couple of hours before breakfast. I have needed neither to diet myself for a gouty constitution, nor to coddle myself in flannel. Age? Bah! At forty-six a man is in the prime of his life!"

After this one outburst, however, he relapsed into his former moody silence; and they sat smoking, with scant speech, till Mahony rose to leave. Then it turned out that John had forgotten the existence of a previous engagement on Mahony's side, and now made a lame attempt to overthrow it. ("Looks as if he didn't want to be left to his own thoughts!") This being impossible, Mahony suggested that John should accompany him, and undertook to guarantee him a hearty welcome: it would be well worth his while to hear Miss Timms-Kelly sing. At first John pooh-poohed the suggestion; musical evenings were not in his line; and though he had knocked up against old Timms-Kelly at the Club, he had never met the daughter. However, in the end he allowed himself to be persuaded; and off they went, in company.

"And that, my dear, was how it came about in the first place. I dragged him with me, like the fool I was. And, once there, the game was up. From the moment John entered the drawing-room, your friend Lizzie made what I can only describe as a dead set at him. She never took her eyes off him. She talked to him, she talked at him; she sang for him, asked his opinion of her selections; and there sat John, who doesn't know doh from re, or a major key from a minor, tapping his foot to the tune and looking as if he had been a judge of music all his life. On two occasions afterwards, I found him there. Mind you, only two. Then came that unfortunate evening at *Ernani*. It's no use asking *me*, Mary, how the muddle occurred. I can't tell you; I had nothing to do with it. All I know is, after the opera Mrs. Vance had to be escorted back to North Melbourne; and this job naturally fell to me, John not being the man to shoulder unpleasant duties if he can, with propriety, put them off on someone else. Well, we hired a wagonette and drove away—in a violent thunder-shower—leaving the other three outside the theatre. But it appears that somehow or other, what with the rain and the crush, the two of them lost sight of the old man. According to John's account they stood waiting for him to turn up till Miss Lizzie's teeth were chattering with cold. There seemed nothing for it but for him to call a cab and drive her home. He did so, and the next morning I'm hanged if he doesn't get a furious letter from the father, accusing them of having slipped off alone on purpose. John heads straight for Vaucluse to apologise; and when he gets there the old man hammers the table, declares his daughter has been compromised, and ends by demanding to know John's intentions. Now I ask you, what could John—what could any man with the feelings of a gentleman—do, but offer the only reparation in his power and at once propose for her hand? Therewith, of course the old boy cools down. . . becomes amiability itself. I don't know, my dear, whether John was really guilty of an indiscretion—that's his affair. But if you want my candid opinion, I think the whole thing was a put-up job. Your friend Lizzie is a veritable Leyden jar."

Mary, whom the news of John's engagement had brought flying home from Ballarat, here uttered a disclaimer. "Tch! There you go, Richard. . . jumping to conclusions. . . as usual. Still, I must say. . . I'm confident, as far as John was concerned, he had no idea of marrying again. I really don't know what to think."

"Ah! but such a dear, kind, generous creature. . ."

"Why, so she is. But. . ."

"But it's another story, eh, when John the Great comes in question?"

"Don't be sarcastic! You know quite well I'm very fond of Lizzie. But poor John was so comfortably settled—I mean with Miss Julia to look after him. It seemed as if he was going to have peace at last. And then, think of the upset again for those poor dear children."

"Indeed and I do. Though, on the other hand. . . stepmother to two families. . . I shouldn't care, love, to take on the job. But there's another thing, Mary. Your brother is decidedly queer just now—I mean in his manner. . . and appearance. He looks a tired man. My own opinion is, he's seen the best of his health. Of course, he's lived a strenuous life—like all the rest of us—and isn't as young as he was. But that's not enough. . . doesn't account for everything. And makes what has happened very disturbing. If only I'd let well alone that evening. . . he'd probably never have set eyes on the woman. It is certainly a lesson to mind one's own business—even when it's a question of doing a kindness. . . or what one thinks a kindness."—"My dehling Mary! So we are to be sisters, love—actually sisters! I cannot say how overjoyed I am. Never have I had such a surprise, dehling, as when my papeh informed me your brother had declared himself. I said: 'Papeh, are you *sure* you are not mistaken?' For never had I imagined, love, that such a clever and accomplished man as your brother would select *me*, from all the ladies of his acquaintance. My heart still flutters when I think of it. I walk on air.—Yes, dehling! Though how I shall ever manage to leave my dear papeh, I do not know."

HENRY HANDEL RICHARDSON

"Dear Lizzie! I, too, am very glad.—But what about the children? Have you thought if it will suit you to be a stepmother? Emmy is a grown girl now—turned seventeen."

"Mary! The dehlings! The poor neglected lambs! Why, I yearn, dearest, simply yearn to show them a mother's love."

But on Emmy being presented, Lizzie's fervour suffered a visible abatement. Even to Mary's eye. And an embrace given and received, her stepmother-to-be looked the girl up and down, with a coolness which not even her extreme warmth of manner could conceal.

"My dehling! Why, Mary, love, I had no idea—positively I had not. . . I declare it will be like having a younger sister.—My dehling girl! And I will show you how to dress your hair, love—two puffs, one on each side of the parting—it will be a *great* improvement to your appearance. That will please papeh, won't it? His dear *pet*, I feel sure. Who will be able to tell me *all* his little ways."

Emmy wept.

"I *hate* the way she does her hair, Aunt Mary. I wouldn't wear mine like that—not for anything! And I'm *not* going to show her how papa likes things done.—Oh, couldn't I come and live with you and Uncle Richard? I shall never be happy here, anymore. Why does papa want to get married? Auntie Julia always promised me I should keep house for him, and he would learn to like me in time. And now. . . now. . ."

It was not for a daughter to sit in judgment on her father, and Mary gently rebuked Emmy, even while she reflected that the girl had really a great deal of John's own spirit in her. Lizzie would not find her new position a bed of roses. For neither did the little ones take to her. They clung to Auntie Julia's hands and skirts—although, to these children who were without personal beauty, their future mother was still more gracious than to Emmy. At first, that was. Afterwards, remarked Mahony who was present at the introduction: afterwards when she saw that they were not to be cozened into friendliness, she made him think of a pretended animal lover, who, on a dog failing to respond to his advances, looks as though he will presently kick it on the sly. But then Richard had flown to the other extreme, and become both prejudiced and unfair, not being able to get over the march that had been stolen on him.

But to such a bagatelle as the likes or dislikes of a parcel of children Miss Timms-Kelly paid small heed. She had other and more important fish to fry. The engagement was to be as brief as propriety admitted; and she was hard put to it to get her trousseau bought, furniture chosen, the affairs of her maidenhood set in order. Through the apartments of her new home she swept like a whirlwind. . . like a whirlwind, too, overthrowing and destroying. Painters and paperhangers were already hard at work. For much company would be seen there after the wedding, great receptions held: as the Honourable Mrs. Turnham she would move not only in musical circles, but in the wider world of politics. John's prospects were of the best: it was an open secret that, for his services in the Devine ministry, he would probably receive a knighthood. And small wonder, thought Mary, that Lizzie found the house shabby and antiquated. Nothing had been done to it since the day on which John, in his first ardour, had dressed it for his first bride.

Now, drastic changes were in progress. The old mahogany four-poster with its red rep curtains—"Jinny's bed," as it persisted in Mary's mind—was to be replaced by one of the new French testers, with canopy and curtains at the head only. (A rather risky innovation at John's age!) Oval plate-glass mirrors in gilt frames, with bunches of candelabra attached, were hung round the drawing-room walls: a splendid Collard and Collard ousted the old piano; bouquets of wax flowers and fruit under glass shades topped the whatnots; horsehair gave way to leather. And the nursery, which stood next John's own bedroom, was requisitioned by Lizzie as a boudoir, the children being relegated to the back of the house.

And John?—To the four eyes that watched him, with curiosity and a motherly anxiety, John's attitude came as a surprise and a relief. He was regularly caught up in the whirl; and, for once leaving both business and politics in the lurch, danced attendance on his affianced from morning till night. Though he still had a haggard air, and certainly nowadays looked what he was, an elderly man, yet a wave of new life ran through him. In his attire he grew almost as dapper as of old. It seemed as if he was determined to carry the affair off with a high hand. He spared no expense, baulked at no alteration; and the ring that sparkled on Lizzie's plump finger was, even in this land of showy jewellery, so costly and magnificent as to draw all eyes. Nor would he have been human, had he not at heart felt proud of the fine figure cut by his bride-elect. He *was* proud, and showed it. More: when he returned from his wedding-trip to Sydney and the Blue Mountains, everyone could see that he was very much in love.

VIII

It was a promise of long standing that, once fairly settled in her new house, Mary should invite to stay with her those of her friends to whom she lay under an obligation. She had plenty of room for them, plenty of time; all that remained to do was to fix the order of their coming.

First, though, she charged herself with Emmy and the children: to get them out of the workpeople's way, and after the wedding—it was celebrated at All Saints, Brighton, and proved a very swell affair indeed, John's four daughters following the bride up the aisle—to leave Miss Julia free to give the final touches to the house. Emmy cried bitterly when the day came to return to it: all Mary's reasoning and persuading had not succeeded in plucking from the girl's heart the sting this third marriage of her father's had implanted there. A great hope had been dashed in Emmy; and she went back hot with resentment against the intruder. The young ones were easier to manage. The excitement of the wedding, new frocks, new dolls, helped them over the break. For them, too, this would not be so complete. Miss Julia proposed to open a select school for the daughters of gentlemen, at which the three little girls were to be day-pupils.

Not a word had passed between Mary and Miss Julia in criticism of John's marriage. Their eyes just met for a moment in a look of complete understanding ("Oh, these men. . . these men!"). Then with a nod and a sigh they set resolutely to making the best of things—a task, said Mahony, in which the wife had at last found her peer.

John's affairs having thus once more slipped from her grasp, Mary devoted herself to the long line of visitors who now crossed the threshold of "Ultima Thule."

Louisa Urquhart headed the list. Louisa arrived one afternoon at Spencer Street railway station, and was drawn from the train, her bonnet askew, her cheeks scarlet with excitement at having undertaken without escort the four-hour journey from Ballarat. And after Louisa, who far outstayed her welcome, came Agnes Ocock and her children and her children's nurses; came Zara and her husband, in search of expert medical advice; Jerry and his Fanny, the latter in a delicate state of health; a couple of Ned's progeny; Amelia Grindle and a sickly babe; came Mrs. Tilly: not to speak of other, less intimate acquaintances.

Mahony groaned. It was all very well for Mary to say that, if he wished to be alone, he had only to go into his study and shut the door. He could and did retire there. But, like other doors, this, too, had a handle; and since Mary could never get it into her head that to be busy among your books was to be seriously busy, the petty interruptions he suffered were endless. Take, for example, the case of Louisa Urquhart. This was by no means exhausted with the stitching of a rose in a drab bonnet. Louisa had lived so long in semi-invalid retirement that she was little better than a cretin with regard to the small, practical affairs of life. She did not know how to stamp a letter or tie up a newspaper for the post; could not buy a pair of gloves or cross a crowded street without assistance. They had to accompany her everywhere. She also lived in a perpetual nervous flutter lest some accident should happen at Yarangobilly while she was absent: the house catch fire, or one of the children take a fit. "That Willy will not do a bolt with a less dismal party than she, it would be rash indeed to assume! Of all the woebegone wet-blankets. . ." Mahony was disgruntled: it spoilt his appetite for breakfast to listen to Louisa's whining, did she learn by the morning post that one of her infants had the stomach-ache; or to look on at the heroic efforts made by Mary to disperse the gloom. (The wife's tender patience with the noodles she gathered round her invariably staggered him afresh.) Then parties must needs be given in Louisa's honour—and the honour of those who came after; the hours for meals disarranged, put backwards or forwards to suit the home habits of the particular guest.

Even more disturbing was the visit of Mrs. Henry which followed. Here, he could not but share Mary's apprehensions lest something untoward should happen which might give servants or acquaintances an inkling of how matters stood. As for poor Mary, she grew quite pale and peaked with the strain; hardly dared let Agnes out of her sight. At dinner-parties—and the best people had to be asked to meet the wife of so important a personage as Mr. Henry—her eye followed the decanters their rounds with an anxiety painful to see. (Between-times, she kept the chiffonier strictly locked.) During this visit, too, the servants made difficulties by refusing to wait on the strange nursemaids, who gave themselves airs; while, to cap all, a pair of the rowdiest and worst-behaved children ever born romped in the passage, or trampled the flower-beds in the garden. No walls were thick enough to keep out their noise; anymore than the fact of being in a stranger's house could improve their manners. The walls were also

HENRY HANDEL RICHARDSON

powerless against Zara's high-pitched, querulous voice, or the good Ebenezer's fits of coughing, which shook the unfortunate man till his very bones seemed to rattle. Later on, for variety, they had the shrill screaming of Amelia Grindle's sick babe (with Mary up and down at night, preparing bottles); had Ned's children to be tamed and taught to blow their noses; pretty Fanny tumbling into faints half a dozen times a day. Of course, there was no earthly reason why all these good people should not make his home theirs—oh dear no! If Jerry got a fortnight's holiday, what more natural than that he should choose to spend it in his sister's comfortable, well-appointed house, rather than in his own poky weatherboard? If Mrs. Devine wanted to take sea-air ("And, really, Richard, one *has* to remember how extraordinarily kind she was to us on landing"), the least one could do was to beg her to exchange Toorak for Brighton-on-Beach. Only the fact of John's house being but a paltry half-hour's walk distant, and the ozone both families breathed of the same brand, saved them from having John and Lizzie quartered on them as well.

Yes, Mary's hospitality was rampageous—no other word would describe it. He had given her *carte blanche* and he kept to his bond; but as time went on his groans increased in volume, he was sarcastic at the expense of "Mrs. Mahony's Benevolent Asylum," and openly counted the days till he should have his house to himself again. A quiet evening was a thing of the past; he was naturally expected to escort the ladies to their various entertainments. Besides, he was "only reading." What selfishness to shut yourself up with a book, when a visitor's amusement was in question! For, as usual, Mary's solicitude was all for others. Much less consideration was shown him personally than in the old Ballarat days. Then, he had been the breadwinner, the wage-earner, and any disturbance of his life's routine meant a corresponding disturbance in their income. Here, with money flowing in without effort, and abundantly—as it continued to do-there was no such practical reason to respect his privacy. And so it was: "Richard, will you answer these cards for me?" "See to the decanting of the port?" "Leave an order at the fruiterer's?" "Book seats for *East Lynne*, or *Maritana?*"

In this hugger-mugger fashion week after week, month after month ran away. Then, however, things seemed to be tailing off, and he was just congratulating himself that he had bowed the last guest out, when Tilly arrived, and back they fell into the old atmosphere of fuss and flutter. Tilly had originally stood high on Mary's list. Then, for some reason which was not made clear to him, her visit had been postponed; and he had comfortably forgotten all about it.

Once she was there, though, it was impossible to forget Tilly, even for an hour. Her buxom, bouncing presence filled the house. There was no escape from her strident voice, her empty, noisy laugh. The very silk of her gowns seemed to rustle more loudly than other women's; and she had a foot like a grenadier. The truth was, his old aversion to Tilly, and the type she represented, broke out anew directly she crossed his door-sill. And three times a day he was forced to sit next her at meals, attend to her wants, and listen, as civilly as he might, to her crude comments on people and things.

In vain did Mary harp on Tilly's sterling qualities. Before a week was out, Mahony swore he would prefer fewer virtues and more tact. Goodness of heart could be rated too highly. Why should not quick-wittedness, and sensitiveness to your neighbour's tender places, also be counted to your credit? Why must it always be the blunt-tongued, the hob-nailed of approach, who got all the praise?

It was at the dinner-table where, in the course of talk, the burning question of spirits and spirit-phenomena had come up; and Mary—Mary, not he: it would never have occurred to him to dilate on the theme before such as Tilly!—had told of the raps and movements of furniture that were taking place at the house of a Mrs. Phayre, a prominent member of Melbourne society. Now Tilly knew very well he did *not* belong to those who dismissed such happenings with a smile and a shrug. Yet the mere mention of them was enough to send her off into an unmannerly guffaw.

"Ha, ha! . . . ha, ha, ha! To see your furniture jumping about the room! I'D pretty soon nab the slavey—you take my word for it, Mary, it's the slavey—who played such tricks on me. I'D bundle 'er off with a flea in 'er ear."

A glance at Richard showed him black as thunder. Mary adroitly changed the subject. But afterwards she came back on it.

"It's all very well, Richard, but you can't expect a common-sense person like Tilly *not* to be amused by that sort of thing."

"And pray do you mean to imply that everyone who does not mock and jeer is devoid of sense?"

"Of course not. Besides, I didn't say sense; I said common sense."

"Well, since you yourself bring in the 'common,' I'll quote you the dictum of a famous man. 'Commonplace minds usually condemn everything that is beyond the scope of their understanding.'"

"How sweeping! And so conceited. But Tilly is *not* commonplace. In many ways, she's just as capable as her mother was. But I don't think we ought to be discussing her. While she's our visitor."

"Good God! Is one to go blind and dumb because a fool is under one's roof?"

"Well, really! I do wonder what you'll say next." Mary was hurt and showed it.

But Mahony did not try to conciliate her. He had a further ground for annoyance. Ever since Tilly had come to the house, that side of Mary's nature had prevailed with which he was least in sympathy. Never had she seemed so deadly practical, and lacking in humour; so instinctively antagonistic to the imaginative and speculative sides of life. Her attitude, for example, to the subject under discussion. At bottom, this was no whit different from Tilly's. "*That* sort of thing," said as Mary said it, put her opinion of the new movement in a nutshell.

Out of this irritation he now demanded: "Tell me: are we never in this world to have our house to ourselves again?"

"But, Richard, Tilly *had* to come! . . . after the time I stayed with her. And now she's here—even though you despise her so—we've got to do all we can to make her visit a success. I should hate her to think we didn't consider her good enough to introduce to our friends."

"Among whom she fits about as well as a porpoise in a basin of goldfish."

"As if a porpoise could get inside a basin! How wildly you do talk! Besides you don't mean it. For if ever there was a person particular about paying debts, it's you."

Late one afternoon he came in from the garden, where he had been superintending the laying out of a new shrubbery. Only the day before he had found, to his dismay, that a gap in the screening hedge of lauristinus and pittosporums allowed of errand-boys and nursemaids spying on a privacy he had believed absolute. The thought was unbearable. But the change had cost him a fierce tussle with his pig-headed Scot of a gardener, who held there were already too many shrubs about the place. Now he felt hot and tired.

As he crossed the verandah Mary came rustling out of the dining-room. She looked mysterious, but also, if he knew his Mary, a trifle uncomfortable. "Richard! I've got a surprise for you. I want you in the drawing-room."

"Well, I suppose it will keep till I've washed the dust off." The drawing-room spelt visitors; and he had looked forward to pipe and book.

In course of making a hasty toilet, however, he pricked up his ears. Down the passage came the tones of a voice that seemed strangely familiar. And, sure enough, when he entered the room he found what he expected: the visitor Tilly was entertaining with such noisy gusto was no other than Purdy.

Purdy sat on the circular yellow-silk ottoman, in the easiest of attitudes. With one leg stuck straight out before him, he hugged the other to him by the knee, rocking his body backwards and forwards as he told what was evidently a capital story—to judge by his own roars of laughter and Tilly's purple face and moist eyes, at which she made feeble dabs with her pocket-handkerchief.

The shock of the encounter drove the semblance of a hearty greeting out of Mahony. But with this he had exhausted himself; Purdy and he could find no points of contact; and after a few halting remarks and awkward pauses, Purdy faced round to Tilly again and took up the broken thread of his yarn. And from now on, both there and at the high tea to which Mary presently led them, Mahony sat silent and constrained. For one thing, he disdained competition with Tilly in her open touting for Purdy's notice. Again, as he looked and listened, he understood Mary's discomfort and embarrassment. On the occasion of last seeing Purdy, they had both been giddy with excitement. Now the scales fell from his eyes. This, his former intimate and friend? This common, shoddy little man, already pot-bellied and bald?—whose language was that of the tap-room and the stable; who sat there bragging of the shady knowledge he had harvested in dark corners, blowing to impress the women; one of life's failures and aware of it, and, just for this reason, cocksure, bitter, intolerant—a self-lover to the Nth degree. In the extravagant fables they were asked to swallow, he, Purdy, had seen the best of everything, the worst of everything, had always been in the thick of a fray and in at the finish.

Well! one person present seemed to enjoy the tasteless performance, and that was Tilly, who hung on his lips. She even urged him to repeat some of his tallest stories, for the benefit of Mary who had been out of the room.

"Oh, love, you *must* 'ear that yarn of the splitter and the goanna. I've laughed to burst my sides. Go on, Purd, tell it again. It was a regular corker." And, belonging to the class of those who pre-indulge, Tilly hee-hawed at full lung-strength in anticipation of the coming joke. After which Mahony had to listen for the second time to some witless anecdote, the real point of which was to show Purdy in his role of top dog.

Was it possible that he had ever enjoyed, or even put up with this kind of thing? Had Purdy always been a vainglorious braggart, or had the boasting habit grown on him as he went downhill? Of course he himself had not become more tolerant as the years went by; and he could afford to yield to his antipathies, now that no business reasons made civility incumbent. But there was more in it than this. In earlier days a dash of the old boyish affection had persisted, to blind him to Purdy's failings; just as the memory of their boyhood's standing—he the senior, Purdy the junior—had caused Purdy to look up to him and defer to his opinion. Now, nothing of this remained. On either side. Long-suffering, deference, affection had alike been flung on time's scrap-heap—at least, during the two distasteful hours spent in Purdy's company, not even the ghosts of such feelings stirred. Then what had brought him back? Mere tuft-hunting? Where, too, in the name of Christendom had Mary fished him up, who would have been so much better left in obscurity? Had she really fancied she would give him, Mahony, a pleasure thereby? *Poor Mary!*

But the thin smile of amusement that curled his lips at the thought faded, when he heard her pressing Purdy to come again. And the first time he got her alone—it was not till bedtime—he took her soundly to task.

"Your surprise this afternoon was a surprise indeed—in more ways than one. But what possessed you, Mary, to ask him to repeat the visit? My dear, you must surely see for yourself we cannot have the eyesore he has become, about this house?"

Mary paused in the act of slipping the rings off her fingers and on the branches of her ring-tree, and looked surprised. "*What*, Richard? Your *oldest* friend?" But Mahony, versed in every lightest expression that flitted across the candid face before him, felt the emphasis to be overdone. Like himself it was plain Mary had suffered something of a shock.

So he swallowed a caustic rejoinder, and said dryly: "I know your intentions were of the best. But. . . well, frankly, my dear, I think it's bad enough if you fill the house with *your* old friends."

He was right. Her discomfiture showed in the way she now flared up. "Fill the house? . . . with only one person here at a time, and never more than two? But—since you put it that way, Richard—I think it's rather a good thing I do. If we are ever to see anyone at all!"

"Give me books and I don't want people."

"Oh, I've no patience with such a selfish standpoint. Whatever would be the good of all this—I mean the nice house, and our not needing to worry about expense—if we didn't ask other people to share it with us?"

"Pray, have I hindered you from doing so?"

"Well, not exactly. But why start to grumble now, when it's a question of your best friend?"

At the repetition his patience failed him. "Best friend! Oldest friend! Good heavens, Mary! do think what you are saying. How can one continue to be friends with a person one never sees or hears of? Surely the word implies somebody with whom one has at least *half* an idea in common? People don't stand still in this world. They're always growing and changing—up or down or off at a tangent. *Panta rei* is the eternal truth: *Semper idem* the lie we long to see confirmed. And to hug a sentimental memory of what a mortal once was to you, and go on trying to bolster up an intimacy on the strength of it—why, that's to drag a dead carcase behind you, which impedes your own progress.—No, the real friend is one you pick up at certain points in your life, whose way runs along with yours—for a time. A time only. A milestone on your passage—no more. Few or none march together the whole way."

"Milestones? Why not tombstones while you're about it?" cried Mary hotly, repudiating a theory that seemed to her wholly perverse "Of course, you're able to use words I don't understand; but I say, once a friend, always a friend. I know I'D be sorry to forget anyone I had ever liked—even if I didn't find much to talk to them about. But you must always have your own ideas. I declare you're going on now about people just as you do about places, about not wanting to see them again once you've left."

"Yes, places and people—one as the other. Let me face forward—not back. But to return to the matter in hand: I don't mind telling you I'd gladly *pay* our visitor of this afternoon to stop away. . . and drink his tea elsewhere."

"I never heard such a thing!" Then, however, another thought struck her. "You're not letting that silly old affair in Ballarat still prejudice you against him?"

Mahony laughed out loud. "Good Lord, no! The grass has been green over that for what seems like half a century."

"Then it's because he drank his tea out of his saucer—and things like that."

"Tch!" On the verge of letting his temper get away with him, Mahony pulled up. "Well, my dear. . . well, perhaps you're not altogether wrong. I'll put it even more plainly though. Mary, it's because he spoke and looked like what I veritably believe him to be: an ostler in some stable. Horsey checks, dirty nails, sham brilliants; and a mind and tongue to match. No, I stick to what I've said: I'd offer him a ten-pound note to stop away."

"I never knew anyone so hard on people as you."

"Come, *do* I need to mix with ostlers at my time of life? . . . and in my present position. It's not my fault that I've gone up in the world and he down."

"No, but all the more reason not to turn your back on somebody who hasn't had your luck."

"I deny that I'm a snob. I'd invite my butcher or my baker to the house any day, so long as he had decent manners and took an interest in what interests me."

"My dear Richard, you only say that because you know you'll never have to! And if you did, you wouldn't like them a bit better than you do Purdy. But I'm sure I sometimes don't know what's coming over you. You used to be such a stickler for remembering old friends and old kindnesses, and hadn't bad enough to say about people who didn't. I believe it was the going home that changed you. Yet when you were in England, how you railed at people there for letting themselves be influenced by a person's outside—how he ate peas, or drank his soup, and things like that."

"England had nothing whatever to do with it. But it was a very different thing in Ballarat, Mary, where my practice brought me up against all sorts of people to whom I was forced to be civil. Now, there's no such obligation. And so I decline, once and for all, to exhibit the specimen we saw today to our social circle. If you're absolutely bent on befriending him—and I know doing good is, to you, the temptation strong drink is to others—although in my opinion, my dear, you'll end by *over*doing it: you've not looked yourself for weeks past. If you must have Purdy here, kindly let it be when no one else is present, and if possible when I, too, am out of the way. What you're to say about me?

Anything you like. He won't miss me so long as your friend Tilly is at hand to drink in his words. You certainly hit the bull's-eye this time, my dear, in providing her with entertainment. Purdy's egregious lying was pabulum after her own heart."

With which Richard slung a towel round his neck and retired to the bathroom, leaving Mary to the reflection that, if ever there was a person who knew how to complicate the doing of a simple kindness, it was Richard. Here he went, detesting Tilly with all his old fervour and dead set from the start against Purdy and his coming to the house. (It was true Purdy had got rather loud and bumptious; but a sensible woman like Tilly might be trusted soon to knock the nonsense out of him.) Meanwhile she, Mary, had somehow to propitiate all three; and in particular to hinder Richard from showing what he felt. For if the match came off, Purdy would become a rich and important personage to whom every door would open. And then Richard, too, would come round—would have to. If, that was, she could meanwhile contrive to keep him from making lifelong enemies of the happy pair.

IX

Tilly said:

"My dear! the minute I set eyes on 'er, I knew she was a fraud. And I thinks to myself: 'Just you wait, milady, till the lights go out, and I'll cook your goose for you!' Well, sure enough, there we all sat 'and-in-hand in the dark, like a party of kids playing 'unt-the-slipper. And by-and-by one and another squeals: 'I'm touched!' What do I do, Mary? Why, I gradually work the hand I'm 'olding in me right, closer to me left, till I'd got *them* joined and me right 'and free. (It's as easy as Punch if you know 'ow to do it.) And when the man next me—oh, 'e *was* a solemn old josser!—when 'e said in a voice that seemed to come from 'is boots: 'The spirits 'ave deigned to touch me'—as if 'e'd said: 'God Almighty 'as arrived and is present!'—I made one grab, and got 'old of— now what do you think? I'm danged if it wasn't 'er false chignon I found in my hand. I thought she was going to give me the slip then, after all: she wriggled like an eel. But I held on like grim death and, luckily for me, she'd a few 'airs left still clinging to her cranium. She squeals like a pig. 'Up with the lights,' says I; 'I've got 'er!' 'Turn up the lights if you dare,' cries she: 'it'll kill me.' Over goes a chair in the scrimmage, and then they did turn 'em up, and there was she squirming on the floor, bald like an egg, with I don't know how many false gloves and feathers and things pinned on to 'er body!"

Tilly sat by the fire in Mary's bedroom, her black silk skirts turned back from the blaze. She was in high feather, exhilarated by her own acumen as by the smartness with which she had conducted the exposure. Opposite her Mary, her head tied up in red flannel, crippled by the heavy cold and the face-ache that had confined her to the house, listened with a sinking heart. It was all very well for Tilly to preen herself on what she had done: Richard would see it in a very different light. He had gone straight to his study on entering; and hurrying out in her dressing-gown to learn what had brought the two of them home so early, Mary had caught a glimpse of his face. It was enough. When Richard looked like that, all was over. His hatred of a scene in public amounted to a mania.

It was most discouraging. For a fortnight past she had done everything a friend could do, to advance Tilly's suit; plotting and planning, always with an anxious ear to the study-door, in a twitter lest Richard should suddenly come out and complain about the noise. For the happy couple, to whom she had given up the drawing-room, conversed in tones that were audible throughout the house: a louder courtship Mary had never heard; it seemed to consist chiefly of comic stories, divided one from the next by bursts of laughter. Personally she thought the signs and portents would not be really favourable till the pair grew quieter: every wooing *she* had assisted at had been punctuated by long, long silences, in which the listener puzzled his brains to imagine what the lovers could be doing. However, Tilly seemed satisfied. After an afternoon of this kind she went into the seventh heaven, and leaning on Mary's neck shed tears of joy: it *was* a case of middle-aged lovesickness and no mistake! True, she also knew moments of uncertainty, when things seemed to hang fire, under the influence of which she would vehemently declare: "Upon my soul, Mary love, if *he* doesn't, I shall! I feel it in my bones." A state of mind which alarmed Mary and made her exclaim: "Oh no, don't, Tilly!—don't do that. I'm sure you'd regret it. You know, later on he might cast it up at you."

And now Tilly had probably spoilt everything, by her hasty, ill-considered action.

Fortunately for her she didn't realise how deeply she had sinned; though even she could see that Richard was angry. "Of course, love, the doctor's in a bit of a taking. I couldn't get a word out of 'im all the way 'ome.—Lor', Mary, what geese men are, to be sure! . . . even the best of 'em. Not to speak of the cleverest. To see all those learned old mopokes sitting there tonight, solemn as hens on eggs. . . it was enough to make a cat laugh. But even if 'e *does* bear me a bit of a grudge, it can't be helped. I'm not a one, love, to sit by and see a cheat and keep my mouth shut. A fraud's a fraud, and even if it's the Queen 'erself."

"Of course it is. I feel just the same as you. It makes my blood boil to watch Richard, with all his brains, letting himself be duped by some dishonest creature who only wants to make money out of him. But. . . when he once gets an idea in his head. . . And he's not a bit *grateful* for having his eyes opened."

Grateful, indeed! When, after an hour's solitude which might really have been expected to cool him down, he came into the bedroom, his very first words were: "Either that woman leaves the house, or I go myself!"

For all Mary's firm resolve to act as peacemaker, this was more than she could swallow. "Richard, don't be so absurd! We can't turn a visitor out. Decency forbids."

HENRY HANDEL RICHARDSON

"It's *my* house, and for me to say whom I'll have in it."

"Tilly's *my* friend, and I'm not going to have her insulted." Mary's tone was as dogged as his own.

"No! but she is at liberty to insult mine. . . and make me a laughing-stock into the bargain. Such a scandalous scene as tonight's, it has never been my lot to witness."

"However did it happen that you held a seance? The invitation only said cards and music. I'd have kept her at home if I'd guessed, knowing her opinion of that sort of thing."

"I wish to God you had! You talk of decency? You need hardly worry, I think, in the case of a person who has so few decent feelings of her own. If you could have heard her! 'I got 'er! Up with the gas! I'm 'olding 'er—by 'er false 'air!'"—Mahony gave the imitation with extravagant emphasis. "I leave it to you to imagine the rest. That voice. . . the scattered aitches. . . the gauche and vulgar manner. . . the medium weeping and protesting. . . your friend parleying and exclaiming—at the top of her lungs, too—glorying in what she had done as if it was something to be proud of, and blind as a bat to the thunder-glances that were being thrown at her. . . no! I shall never forget it. She has rendered me impossible—in a house where till now I have been an honoured guest."

The exaggeration of this statement nettled Mary. She clicked her tongue. "Oh, *don't* be so silly! Surely you can write and explain? Mrs. Phayre will understand. . . that you had nothing to do with it."

"Who am I that I should have to explain and apologise?—and for the behaviour of a person she did us the courtesy to invite."

"But considering the woman *was* a fraud? Tilly vows she had all sorts of contrivances pinned to her body."

"There you go! Ready, as usual, to believe anyone rather than me! She was no more a fraud than I am. She came to us well attested by circles of the highest standing. Yet in spite of this, an ignorant outsider, who is present at a sitting for the first time in her life, has the insolence to set herself up as a judge.—Mary! I've put up with the job lot you call your friends for more than a twelvemonth. But this is the last straw. Out she goes, and that's the end of it!"

But this flicked Mary on the raw. "You seem to forget *some* of the job lot were my own relations."

"Oh, now get touchy, do! You know very well what I mean. But enough's enough. I can stand no more."

"You talk as if you were the sole person to be considered. As usual, think of nobody but yourself."

"Ha! I like that," cried Mahony, exasperated. "I think I'm possessed of the patience of Job, if you ask me. For there's never been a soul among them with whom I had two ideas in common."

"No, you prefer these wretched mediums and the silly people who are taken in by them. I wish spiritualism had never been invented!"

"Don't talk about what you don't understand!"

"I *do*. I know nearly everytime we go out now, I have to sit by and watch you letting yourself be humbugged. And then I'm not to open my mouth, or say what I see, or have any opinion of my own."

"No! I should leave that to the superior wits of your friend."

"I think it's abominable the way you sneer at Tilly! But if you do it just to get her out of the house, you're on the wrong tack. She's *not* going just now, and that's all about it. Anyone but you would understand what's happening. But you're so taken up with yourself that you never see a thing—not if it's under your very nose!"

"Pray what do you mean by that? *What* is happening?" Pierced by a sudden suspicion Mahony swung round and faced her. "Good Lord, Mary!" . . . his voice trailed off in a kind of incredulous disgust. "Good Lord! You don't want to tell me you're trying to bolster up a match between this woman and. . . and Purdy?"

Mary tightened her lips and did not reply.

Mahony's irritation burst its bounds. "Well, upon my soul! . . . well, of all the monstrous pieces of folly!" After which he broke off, to throw in caustically: "Of course if it comes to that, I'll allow they're well matched. . . in manners and appearance. But the fellow's an incorrigible waster. He'll make ducks and drakes of old Ocock's hard-earned pile. Besides, has he shown the least desire for matrimony? Are you not lending yourself to a vulgar intrigue on the woman's part? If so, let me tell you that it's beneath your dignity—your dignity as my wife—and I for one decline to permit anything so offensive to go on under my roof. Not to speak of having to see you bear the blame, should things go wrong."

"No, really, Richard! this is too much," cried Mary, and bounced up from her seat. "For *goodness* sake, let me manage my own affairs! To hear you talk, anyone would think I was still a child, to be told what I may and mayn't do—instead of a middle-aged woman. I'm quite able to judge for myself; yes! and take the consequences, too. But you blow me up just as if I wasn't a person for myself at all, but only your wife. Besides, I think you might show a *little* confidence in me. I shan't disgrace you, even if I am fool enough to bring two people together again who were once so fond of each other. Which you seem to have quite forgotten. Though your own common sense might tell you. Tilly's alone in the world, and has more money than she knows what to do with. And he has none. I think you can safely leave it to her to look after her own interests. She's a good deal sharper than any of us, you included. And Purdy, too. You sneer at him for an ostler and a ne'er-do-well. He's nothing of the sort. For six months now he's worked hard as a traveller in jewellery." ("Ha! . . . *that* explains the sham diamonds, the rings, the breastpins.") "There you go! . . . sneering again. And here am I, struggling and striving to keep the peace between you, till I don't know whether I'm standing on my head or my heels. And as far as you're concerned, it's not the least bit of good. I think you grow more selfish and perverse day by day. You ought to have lived on a desert island, all by yourself. Oh, I'm tired. . . sick and tired. . . of it and of everything!"—and having said her say, passionately and at top speed, Mary suddenly broke down and burst out crying.

Mahony's anger was laid on the instant. "Why, my dear! . . . why, Mary. . . what's all this about? Come, come, love!"—as her sobs increased in violence—"this will never do. There's nothing to upset yourself over. The fact is, as you say, you're tired out. We shall be having you ill in earnest if this goes on. And small wonder, I'm sure. I declare, as soon as you're rid of your cold I shall shut this place up and take you away from everybody, on a trip to Sydney and the Blue Mountains."

"I don't want to go to Sydney. I only want to be left alone, and not have my friends insulted and turned out of the house."

"Good God, wife! . . . surely you can give me credit for some small degree of tact? But now, enough. You lie still and go to sleep. Or as I say, we shall have you really ill."

"Oh, leave me out of it, do. I shall be all right in the morning."

But this was not the case. Mary coughed and tossed, and went from hot to cold and cold to hot, for the greater part of the night. In the morning her head felt a ton weight on the pillow. It was no good chafing; in bed she had to stay. Mahony and Tilly faced each other in glum silence across the length of the breakfast-table.

The next few days bringing no improvement, Tilly had the good sense to pack her trunks and return to Ballarat. And it was one crumb of comfort to Mary that, thanks to her indisposition, this departure was accomplished without further unpleasantness.

Leaning over the bed for a farewell embrace, Tilly answered her friend's hoarse whisper with a shake of the head. "But don't you bother, love. My dear, you'll see what you do see! I'm no chicken, Mary, nor any mealy-mouthed schoolgirl to lose me chance for want of opening me mouth. But whatever happens, I'll never forget how you tried to pull it off for me, old girl—never! . . . not so long as I live."

And now, the nervous strain she had been under of lying listening for sounds of strife and warfare—this removed, Mary was left at peace in her dimity-white bed, and gave herself up to the luxury of feeling thoroughly out of sorts. Richard found plenty to say in admonition, as the days went by and she continued low and languid, unable to shake off what seemed but a heavy cold. He also laid down many a stringent rule to safeguard her, in future, from the effects of her inexhaustible hospitality.

Then, however, the words died on his lips.

WHEN THE TRUTH DAWNED ON them that Mary's illness could be ascribed to a purely natural cause, and that, at long last, she was to bear a child, husband and wife faced the fact as diversely as they now faced all vital issues. In Mahony's feelings, bewilderment and dismay had the upper hand. For though, at one time, Mary's childlessness had been a real grief to him, so many years had passed since then that he had long ceased either to hope or to regret. And when you had bowed thus to the inevitable, and arranged your life accordingly, it was disquieting, to say the least of it, to see your careful structure turned upside down. Rudely disquieting.

And this sense of inexpediency persisted long after Mary was up and about again, her old blithe self, and the two of them had more or less familiarised themselves with the idea of the drastic change that lay in store for them. The truth was: he no longer wished for children. One needed to be younger than he, still in the early years of married life, to accept their coming unconcernedly. (Nor was he enough of a self-lover to crave to see himself re-duplicated, and thus assured of an earthly immortality.) He felt old; *was* old: too late, now, to conjure up any of the dreams that belonged by rights to the coming of a child. His chief sensation was one of fear: he shrank from the responsibility that was being thrust upon him. A new soul to guide, and shield, and make fit for life! . . . when he himself was so unsure. How establish the links that should bind it to the world around it?—as to the world unseen. How explain evil? . . . and sin? . . . the doctrine of reward and punishment?—and reconcile these with the idea of a tender, all-powerful Creator. For though one might indulge in theory and speculation for one's own edification, one dare not risk them on a child. Another more selfish point of view was that he looked forward with real apprehension to the upheaval of his little world: the inroads on, the destruction of that peace and solitude with which he had fallen so deeply in love.

A bright side to the affair was that they were now, for the first time in their united lives, really able to afford the outlay involved. They could make comfortable, even extravagant preparation for the new arrival; and only too gladly did he bid Mary spend what she chose. For though his own pleasure in the prospect of fatherhood was severely tempered, it warmed his heart to see her joy. "Radiant" was the only word that described Mary. No irksome thoughts of responsibility bore her down. She would have laughed at the notion in regard to a child of her own. But then, there never was less of a doubter than Mary: no hypercritical brooding over man's relation to God, or God's to the world, had ever robbed her of an hour's sleep. She accepted things as they were with a kind of simple, untroubled faith. Or was it perhaps just the reverse—the absence of any religious spirit? Sometimes he half believed it—believed there existed in Mary more than a dash of the pagan. Well, however that might be, the coming of a babe would set the crown on a life which, in spite of its happiness, had so far lacked the supreme gift. For women's arms, like their bodies, were built to cradle and enfold the young of the race.

Mary wrinkled her brow over none but the most practical considerations. Enough to occupy her was the burning question which rooms to take for nurseries, in a house where all rooms had long ago had their use allotted them.

Mahony laughed at her worried air. "Why, build 'em, my dear, and as many as you choose! I'll not grudge the expense, I promise you."

But this was just one of Richard's harebrained schemes. The house was amply big enough as it stood; and any additions would spoil its shape. Time enough, too, to think of extra accommodation when all was happily over. Thus Mary: deciding eventually that the guestrooms were those that must be sacrificed: they were large, cool, airy; and once the baby was there, she would have scant leisure for entertaining.

At least, in the beginning. And with this resolution, which was at once put into effect, Mary's overdone and tiresome hospitality found its natural end.

Next came the question of furnishing. And here Richard proved to have ultra-queer notions about what would be good for a child—his child—and what wouldn't. The nurse was not even to share a room with it—and this, when most nurses slept with their charges in the same bed! Then he tabooed carpets as dust-traps, so that there was no question of just covering the floor with a good Brussels; and curtains must be of thinnest muslin—not rep. In the end Mary had the floors laid in polished wood, on which were spread loose strips of bamboo matting; and dark green sunblinds were affixed to the outsides of the windows. The walls were distempered a light blue. In place of the usual heavy mahogany the furniture was of a simple style, and painted white. The little crib—it had to be made to order, for Richard would have none of the prevalent rocking-cradles, which, he declared, had rocked many a babe into convulsions—was white as well. When all was finished the effect was quite fairylike, and so novel that tales of the nurseries got abroad, and visitors invariably asked before leaving if they might be allowed a peep at them. Meanwhile, Mahony did his share by hunting up pictures on which the infant eye might rest with pleasure. He also bought toys; and would arrive home with his pocket bulging. Mary bore with him as long as he confined his purchases to woolly balls and rag dolls. But when it came to his ordering in an expensive rocking-horse, she put her foot down.

"*Really*, Richard! Just suppose anything. . . I mean it will be more than time enough for things like these a year or two from now."

"Oh, the doctor expects *his* kid to come into the world able to walk and talk. . . like a foal or a calf. Never will such a miracle have trod this old earth!"

And as Tilly—she had come down on her own initiative, solely to be near Mary over her confinement—as she drove back to the hotel at which she was putting up, she hummed the popular refrain:

> *Oh, la, la!*
> *What fools men are!*

For besides making a donkey of himself over his purchases, Mahony was haunted, now the end drew nigh, by a memory, by the fear of another disappointment. He hardly trusted Mary out of his sight; hardly let her put one foot before another,—"As jumpy as a Persian cat! You'd never think 'e'd 'elped hundreds of brats into the world in 'is day!"

Mary sat in a rocking-chair on the shady side of the verandah, and waved a palm-leaf fan to keep the flies off. More often she was surrounded by yards of muslin, real India muslin, which she fashioned into robes and petticoats, on which she frilled and tucked and embroidered, sewing every stitch by hand.

"A regular trousseau!" said Tilly; and enviously fingered the piles of gossamer garments.

On the ordeal that lay before her, Mary herself was not given to brooding: for one thing, she was much stronger than she had been as a girl. And the first discomforts of her state over, her health was well maintained. But when December, with its livid heat, had slipped into the greater heats of January and her time came, she gave birth as hardly as on that first occasion long years ago; all but paying with her own for the new life she was bringing into the world. Well-known specialists, hastily summoned, performed a critical operation, Mahony's trust in his own skill deserting him as usual where Mary was in question. And though the operation was successful and the child born alive, days of acute anxiety followed before it was certain that Mary would pull through. Tilly and Mahony buried the hatchet in the long hours they spent together in that darkened bedchamber, where Mahony moved a pale, distraught shadow, and Tilly sat weeping silently, her handkerchief to her eyes. In the dining-room John and Jerry strayed aimlessly to and fro among the furniture; and outsiders like Mrs. Devine would drive up early, and remain sitting in their carriages to hear the latest bulletin. In the end Mary's sound constitution triumphed, and she was gradually won back to life; but over a week passed before she even asked to see her child. Then, in sudden impatience, she tried to raise herself on her elbow—a movement that sent Tilly and the nurse flying to lay her flat again. Tilly it was who, going to the crib, carried to her on a pillow one of the tiniest babies ever seen: a waxen doll, with black hair an inch long, and the large black eyes of Mary's own family.

It was a boy. At his baptism, where John, Jerry and Lizzie stood sponsors, he received the name of Cuthbert—in full was to be known as Cuthbert Hamilton Townshend-Mahony.

PART III

I

These unlooked-for children—the following year twin girls were born, thus rounding off a trio—came too late to form the bond between their parents they might once have done. For that, the attitudes adopted towards them by father and mother, themselves now branched so far apart, were too dissimilar. In Mahony's case, once his children were there in the flesh before him, all his puny fears of personal upset and mental pother fell away. He had only to feel tiny soft fingers straying over his face, to become the tenderest of fathers, loving his babies wholeheartedly. Now he feared only for them, in their frailty and helplessness. Did he wake in the night and think he heard a cry, he was out of bed in an instant; and the nurse, entering from the next room to make sure of her charges, would find her master there before her—a tall, dressing-gowned figure, shading a candle with his hand. Often, too, when wakeful, he would rise and steal into the night-nursery to take a peep at his little ones, lying relaxed in sleep. Yes, he was passionately solicitous for them—and not for their bodily health alone. He would have wished to shield their little plastic minds from all impressions that might pain or harm; have had them look only at beautiful and pleasant things, hear soft voices and kind words; on no child of his might hand be laid in anger. The result was that the children, dimly conscious of his perpetual uneasiness, were rendered uneasy by it in their turn, and, for all the deep affection from which it sprang, never really warmed towards their father.

Instead, they sunned themselves in their mother's love, which knew nothing of fears or apprehensions. Mary laughed at Richard's exaggerated anxiety; though she rejoiced to see him so fond. A self-centred person like him might well have found children a nuisance and in the way.

To her they were all in all; and on them she lavished that great hoard of mother-love which, till now, she had spent on the world at large. Had they been born shortly after her marriage, she, who was then little more than a child herself, would have been a child along with them; and the four would have grown up together in a delightful intimacy. Of this there was now no question. Coming when they did, the children stood to her only for possessions—her most precious possessions—but still, something absolutely her own, to do with just as she thought good.

Through them, too, she believed she would some day gratify those ambitions which, where Richard was concerned, had proved so stark a failure. He had had no desire to walk the high paths she had mapped out for him. Her children would—and should. In the meantime, however, ambition lay fallow in love; and it was to their mother the babies ran with their pains and pleasures, their discoveries and attainments. She alone gave them that sense of warmth and security in which very young things thrive.

Their devotion to her was the one feature the three had in common. The twins—they soon earned the nickname of "the Dumplings"—were mere rolypoly bundles of good nature and jollity, who rarely cried, and were as seldom ill as naughty. Mary boasted: the most docile children in the world. Passionately attached to each other said Mahony, it was as though a single soul had been divided between two bodies—they toddled through babyhood hand in hand; faithfully sharing all good things that came their way; sleeping in the same crib, face to face, each with an arm flung protectively about the other's neck. To look at they were as like as two peas, blue-eyed, fair-haired, dimpled, lovely to handle in their baby plumpness, and the most satisfying of armfuls. Their development, too, kept equal pace they walked late, owing to the burden of their little rotundities and long remained content with inarticulate sounds for speech.

The boy was of quite another fibre: as hard to manage as they were easy; as quick as they were slow. Tilly early said of him: "Lor', Mary! the doctor 'imself in frocks and petticoats." But this referred chiefly to little physical tricks and similarities: a certain faddiness about his food, his clothes, his belongings. A naughty child he was not—at first. He, too, began life as a placid infant, who slept well, did not cry, and accepted philosophically the bottle—substitute that was put to his lips. This meant that, in spite of his midget-size at birth, he was sound and healthy—in a fragile, wiry way. He continued small, but was neatly formed. To his mother's colouring he added his father's straight features; and even in babyhood had the latter's trick of carrying his head well back, and a little to one side. He walked before he was a year old, talked soon after; and, to his parents' pride, was able to pick out a given letter from a play-alphabet before he either walked or talked.

His precocity showed itself in other ways as well. For a year and a quarter he was King of the House, the pivot of his little world, sole occupant of his mother's knee. Then came the sudden apparition of his sisters. In the beginning, Cuffy—thus he named himself—did not pay much heed to this pair of animated dolls, who moved their legs and arms when bathed, and rode out in a carriage beside his, but for the most part lay asleep and negligible. Only gradually did it dawn on him that his privileges were being invaded; that not only, indeed, was his reign as sole ruler at an end, but that the greater favours were falling to the newcomers' share. And one day the full knowledge of what had happened burst through, with disastrous results, Cuffy being then something over two years old. Dressed for driving Mary entered the nursery; and Cuffy clamoured to be set upon her knee.

"Not now, darling, I've no time. You must wait till Mamma comes back."

But the nurses appearing at this moment with the babies, all warm and fragrant from their afternoon nap, Mary was not able to resist holding out her arms for them. She even lingered, fondling them, after the carriage was announced.

Cuffy had docilely retreated to a corner, where he played with a stuff elephant. But on seeing this—seeing his mother, who had been too busy for him, petting the twins who had not even *asked* to be nursed—at this he planted himself before her and regarded her with his solemn black eyes. ("I do declare, Master Cuffy seems to look right through you and out behind, when he stares so," was a saying of Nannan's.)

Relinquishing her babies Mary stooped to him. "Say goodbye to Mamma."

To her amazement, instead of putting up his face for a kiss, Cuffy darted at her what she described to Richard as "a dreadfully naughty look," and going over to his rocking-horse, which, though he was not yet allowed to mount it, was his dearest treasure, started to beat it with both hands, and with such force that the patient effigy swung violently to and fro.

Shocked at this fit of temper, Nannan and Mary exclaimed in chorus: "Master Cuffy! Well, I never did! Such tantrums!"

"Cuffy! What *are* you doing? If you are so naughty, Mamma will never take you on her knee again."

The child's back being towards her, she did not see how at these words the little face flushed crimson, the eyes grew round with alarm. Cuffy at once left off hitting the horse; just stood stock-still, as if letting what his mother had said sink in. But he did not turn and come to her. Mary told Richard of the incident as she buttoned her gloves. And

Richard had Cuffy brought to him. Laying aside his book he lifted the child to his knee.

"Papa is sorry to hear Cuffy has been naughty. Will Cuffy tell Papa why?"

Unwinkingly the great eyes regarded him. But there was no response.

"Fy, fy! To hit poor horsey. . . when it had done nothing to deserve it."

"Cuffy's 'orsey—own norsey."

"But, just because it is Cuffy's—Cuffy's very own—he must be kind. . . all the kinder. . . to it. Never wreak your temper or your vengeance, my little son, on a person or thing that is in your power. It's ungenerous. And I want my Cuffy to grow up into a good, kind man. As careful of the feelings of others as he is of his own."

Something in his father's voice—grave, measured, tender—got at the baby, though the words went over his head. And then Mahony saw what he long remembered: a fight for self-control extraordinary in one so young. The black eyes filled; the little mouth twitched and trembled. But the child swallowed hard in an attempt to keep back his tears. And when at last they broke through, he turned and hid his face against his father's coat. Not, Mahony felt sure, seeking there either comfort or sympathy. Merely that his distress might be unobserved. Taking in his own the two little hands, which were locked in each other, Mahony drew them apart. Both palms were red and sore-looking, and no doubt still tingled hotly. The child had hurt himself most of all.

But Cuffy's tears soon dried. After a very few seconds he raised his face, and, this having been patted with his father's handkerchief, slid to the floor and trotted back to the nursery. And then, said Nannan, what a to-do there was! Master Cuffy dragged his little chair up beside the horse, climbed on the chair and put his arms round the animal's neck, talking to it for all the world as if it was a live creature and could talk back.

"Wos 'oo 'urt, dea' 'orsey?—poor 'ickle 'orsey! Cuffy didn't mean to. Wot 'oo say, 'orsey? 'Orsey 'oves Cuffy double-much? Dea' 'orsey! Cuffy 'oves 'orsey, too—much more better zan Effalunt."

And having deposited horsey's rival upside-down in a dark cupboard, he begged a lump of sugar from Eliza the under-nurse, and rammed it in between the steed's blood-red jaws; where it remained, until a trail of white ants was discovered making a straight line for it from the window.

To Mary, Mahony said: "If I were you, my dear, I should be careful to distribute my favours equally. Don't let the little fellow feel that his nose has been put out of joint. He's jealous—that's all."

"Jealous? Of his own sisters? Oh, Richard! . . . I don't think that augurs very well for him.—And surely he can't learn too soon that it's for him to give way to them—as little girls?"

For almost the first time in his knowledge of her, Mahony seemed to sense a streak of hardness in Mary; for the first time she did not excuse a wrongdoer with a loving word. And this her own child!

"He's but a baby himself. Don't ask too much of him," he soothed her. And added: "Of course, I only give you my idea. Do as you think best."—For Mary had proved as capable as a mother as at everything else: she solved problems by sheer intuition, where he would have fretted and fumbled. Even the children's early religious training had, when the time came, fallen to her. Here again she had no bothersome theories: just the simplest practice. The question whether Cuffy and his sisters should be taught to pray or not to pray, to invoke a personal or an impersonal Deity, never entered her head. As soon as they could lisp their first syllables, they knelt night and morning at her knee to repeat their "Gentle Jesus!" and "Jesus, tender Shepherd!" And as long as the great First Cause was set forth in this loving and protective guise, Mahony saw no reason to interfere. He contented himself with forbidding the name of God ever to be used as a threat, or in connection with punishment: the children were taught that the worst that could befall a sinner was a temporary withdrawal of God's love. Nor would he have the Thou God Seest Me! fallacy—this reduction of the Omnipotent and Eternal to the level of spyer and peeper—instilled into their young minds; while such a purely human invention as the Devil—"That scapegoat on which man piles the blame for the lapses in his own nature!"—was never to be so much as mentioned in the nursery.

These few simple rules laid down, he retired into the background. The comfortable knowledge that his children were in the best of hands left his mind free.

Until now it had been plain sailing. Now. . . well, Mary invariably dated the beginning of the real trouble with Cuffy from the day on which he flew into such a naughty passion with his horse. Exactly an easy child to manage he had never been; he was too fanciful for that. There was no need for Richard to fuss and fidget about keeping ugly things from him. Cuffy himself would have none of them. Before he was a twelve-month old, did he, in looking at his "Queen of Hearts" story-book, draw near the picture of the thieving knave, you saw his eyes getting bigger and bigger. And if he could not contrive, with his baby hands, to turn two pages at once—and nobody else might do it for him—he would avert his eyes altogether, or lay his palm flat over the wretch's ugly face. The Doré illustrations to his big fairy-book had a kind of horrid fascination for him. There he would sit staring at these dense and gloomy forests, these ruined, web-hung castles surrounded by their stagnant moats—and then, when bedtime came, he turned frightened. It was of no use trying to shame him with: "A great boy like you! Why, the Dumplings aren't a bit afraid." Or cheerily assuring him: "There are no such things, darling, as witches and giants. They're only made up to amuse little children."

Cuffy knew better—when the lamp was out and Nannan had left the nursery. Then the picture he feared most: Hop-o'-my-Thumb, a creature in petticoats, no bigger than himself, leading a long string of brothers and sisters into a forest black as ink: this picture *would* rise up before him. Not only so, but he himself must join the tail, fall in after Hop-o' and follow into that dreadful wood, where the ogre lived. Since he could not resist its attraction, the book had to be locked away.

The eldest, and a boy, to be such a baby! Mary felt quite abashed for Cuffy, and lost no chance of poking fun at his fears. But it did not help; and eventually she saw that she must leave it to time to drive this nonsense out of him. There were other, more actively disturbing traits in his nature, on which time might have the opposite effect. For example, for such a little child he was far too close and reserved; he kept his thoughts and feelings buttoned up inside himself. He had a passionate temper—"Cuffy's temper" it was called, as though of a special brand that belonged to him alone—but he did not often give it play. Was he hurt or offended or angry, he would retire to a corner, and stay there by himself. If he had to cry, he cried in a corner; he did not want to be petted or comforted; and he would also in nine cases out of ten not say—Richard declared would perhaps not be able to say—why he cried. Mary saw him growing up very unfrank and secretive; which, to her, spelt deceitful.

Again, it wormed in her that he was not a friendly or a trusting child—one of those who indiscriminately hold out their arms, or present a cheek. Cuffy would not go to strangers or always give his kiss when bidden. Nor was he generous; he did not willingly share his toys,

HENRY HANDEL RICHARDSON

or his picture-books, or his lollipops. The things that belonged to him belonged absolutely. Really, he seemed to look upon them as bits of himself, and hence not to be parted with. His favourite animals—horse and elephant—might be touched by no one. Was there a children's party in the nursery special playthings had to be provided, or only those used that were the Dumplings' property. To Mary, bound by but gossamer threads to all things material, her little son's attitude was something of a mystery; and many a time did she strive with him over the head of it. His inability to share with others stood to her for sheer selfishness. She trembled, too, lest the Dumplings should learn to copy him in this, and cease to be the open-hearted, open-handed little mortals they were. For they looked up to Cuffy with adoring eyes—Cuffy who walked while they still drove; was present at dessert in the evening, while they were put to bed; wore knickerbockers instead of skirts. But, try as she might, by teaching and example, she could not influence the boy, let alone master him; while the usual nursery proceeding of making a child's naughty fit end with an expression of contrition shattered on Cuffy's obstinacy. If he did not feel sorry, he would not say he was; and in the battle royal that ensued he generally came off victor. The fact was, in the dark-eyed mite she had now to deal with, Mary ran up against more than a dash of her own resolute spirit; and naturally enough failed to recognise it.

"He's got a shocking will of his own. And what troubles me, Richard, is, if he's as set as all this when he's not much more than a baby, whatever will he be when he grows up?"

"Set? Nonsense, my dear! The child's got character. Give it scope to expand. Try to influence him and work on his good feelings instead of bullying him."

"It's all very well for you. You don't have to deal with him a dozen times a day. I must say, I sometimes think you might help a little more than you do." It was a sore point with Mary that Richard would not rise to his responsibilities as a father, but went on leading the life of a bookworm and a recluse. "Especially as the child takes more notice of you than of anyone else."

But Mahony was not to be bought. "My dear, you've the knack and I haven't. Now don't worry. As long as he's honest and truthful, he'll be all right."

Honest? . . . truthful? That went without saying! It was only that Mary wanted her first-born to be so much more: sunny, lovable, transparent, brave—and a hundred other things besides. He was Nurse's darling though. You had only, said Nannan, to beware of knocking up against any of his funny little fads, such as undressing him before people, or asking him to eat with any but his own silver fork and spoon.

"What Master Cuffy needs is just a bit of managing. I can twist him round my little finger." But it did not tally with Mary's ideas that a child of that age should have to be "managed" at all.

Turning from these traits in her son of which she could not approve, she dwelt with pleasure on his marked quickness and cleverness. Cuffy had sure fingers and a retentive memory. At an early age he could catch a ball and trundle a hoop; could say his prayers without prompting; learn nursery rhymes at a single hearing; could eat nicely, keep himself clean, button up those of his buttons which were within reach: in short do everything in this line that could be expected of so young a mortal.

And in addition he had one genuine talent. For some reason or other—"a throwback to his grandmother," supposed Mahony—Cuffy had been dowered with a natural gift for music. He learnt tunes more easily than he learnt his letters; could hum "Rock of Ages" and "Sun of my Soul" before he uttered a word. His ear was extraordinarily good, his little voice sweet and true. And knowing that Mary's intonation was but faulty, that of the nursery faultier still, Mahony here put in his single spoke in Cuffy's education. He had the boy brought to his dressing-room of a morning; and there, while he dressed, Cuffy with his elephant would sit perched on a corner of the table, singing songs old and new. Together Mahony and his son practised "Oft in the Stilly Night" and "The Land o' the Leal," and with such success that, was there company to dinner, Cuffy in his best velvet tunic would be stood on a chair at dessert, to perform to the guests. And as he gave forth, in baby language, such ditties as:

> *A temple to friendship,*
> *Cried Laura, enchanted,*
> *I'll build in my garden*
> *The thought is divine!*

The ladies uttered rapturous exclamations; while the gentlemen, mostly without a note of music in them, declared: "'pon my word, very remarkable, very remarkable indeed!" and Aunt Lizzie, from whom cuffy had picked up this song by ear, hailed him as an infant prodigy, and painted for him a future that made Mary's heart swell with pride.

Such were Mahony's children.

II

Mrs. Marriner, the youngish widow whose acquaintance Mary had made while visiting on the Urquharts' station, was a person of character. In the matter of dress, for example, she defied the prevailing fashion; wore her light brown hair swept straight back from her brow (which was classic), and, employing neither net nor comb, twisted it in a Grecian knot on the nape of her neck. She also eschewed crinoline, and wandered a tall, willowy form, the eyed of all beholders.

"Out and away too conspicuous!" was Mahony's verdict. "The woman must *want* people to stare at her. Though I will say, Mary, it's something of a treat to behold the natural female figure again, after the unnatural bulgings we've put up with. And a very fine figure, too!"

For this he had to admit: there was nothing unfeminine or forbidding about the lady. She was as handsome as she was striking. A full eye, a Grecian nose, a slim waist: such were her charms; to say nothing of a white, dimpled hand, and a well-turned ankle. And yet everyone who knew her agreed that she captivated less by reason of her comeliness, than by the ease and elegance of her manner.

She was just as popular with her own as with the sterner sex. Which said a good deal; for, wherever she went, she was run after by "the gentlemen." And small wonder, thought Mary. For Gracey was up in any subject, however dry; had brains really equal to "gentlemen's conversation."

Richard said: "It's not the least piquant thing about her that after she has been holding forth, supremely well, on one of those learned themes ladies as a rule fight shy of, she will suddenly lapse into some delightful feminine inconsequence. That, my dear, gives us men back, for a finish, the sense of superiority we need." But here you just had one of the satirical remarks Richard was so apt at making—especially in the early stages of an acquaintance. Afterwards he generally had to eat his words, or at least water them down.

Mrs. Marriner rented a villa within easy driving distance of "Ultima Thule." This was in the early days of the nursery, while the twins were still babies in arms, and Mary went out but little. It fell to the newcomer to pick up the threads; and she did so with a will, calling frequently and entering wholeheartedly into Mary's interests. She was devoted to children; and sometimes, as they sat on the verandah, Nannan would

HENRY HANDEL RICHARDSON

bring Cuffy out to them. And then it was a pretty sight to see the tall, handsome woman on her knees before the little child, rolling his woolly ball to him, or playing at peek-a-bo.

The merry voices lured even Mahony forth from his den. And having tossed his son in the air, he lingered for a word with his wife's guest. This happened more than once; after which, as Mary had foreseen, his sarcasms died away. Mrs. Marriner had travelled widely, and owned a large collection of photographs of famous beauty-spots; and the first time Mahony went to her house was when he and Mary drove over one evening to view these through a stereoscope. Dotted about the rooms they found many another interesting memento of her travels. On the chimney-piece were candelabra of Dresden china. Coloured prints of Venice by night and the blue grotto of Capri adorned the walls. A statuette of Christ by a Danish sculptor stood on the lid of the piano. She had a very fair assortment of books—serious works, too: essays, poetry, history—both old and of the newest; and Mahony carried away with him a couple of volumes by a modern writer of verse named Browning.

In addition she was musical. Not in sister Lizzie's superb, almost professional fashion; but singing in a clear, correct voice, and playing the pianoforte with neatness and skill. Her performance of Mendelssohn's *Songs Without Words* was most enjoyable. And now it was Mahony's turn to suggest inviting her; after which he went back to sing duets, and listen to her execution of a sonata by Haydn. He relished, too, a conversation that for once rose above the affairs of the nursery.

For, the piano closed, the lady and he dropped into talk. And having skimmed the surface of various subjects on which they found themselves in marvellous accord, they came round to the one which still engrossed Mahony's attention. Of spiritualism Mrs. Marriner was ignorant; she begged the doctor to enlighten her. And the rough sketch he gave her interested her so much that she expressed a strong wish to know more. He promised to bring her an armful of literature; and then, if her interest still held, to procure her the entree to a sitting at the house of that arch-spiritualist, Mrs. Phayre, where remarkable phenomena took place. Weird noises might be heard there at dead of night: furniture was moved by unseen hands from its place against the wall.

The next day he carried over the books; and Mrs. Marriner read them with what seemed to him a rare and unfeminine insight: that is to say, she was neither alarmed, nor derisive, nor stupidly obstinate: and, so far, except for members of the inner circle, he had known no woman whose state of mind towards the question was not one of these three. She also jumped at his offer of introducing her at a seance. Later on, learning that he was eager to find an unprofessional medium with whom he might experiment in private, and on whom no shadow of suspicion could be held to rest, she herself proposed sitting at a small table in her drawing-room. And after a few fruitless hours, during which he had every reason to admire her patience, they met with success: the table tilted under their hands and a pencil, delicately sustained by the lady's fingers, wrote words that could be read. It was plain she was possessed of the power.

He went home to Mary in high feather.

"Now, perhaps, you'll believe there's something in it!"

"I never said there wasn't *something*. It's only that. . ."

"You can hardly suspect your friend of being an impostor?"

"Good gracious no! The idea!"

And Mary meant it. Gracey was no more capable of downright fraud than she herself. And yet. . . yet. . . say what you liked, there was a part of you that simply would not accept the conclusions you were asked to draw. To think, because a table stood on two legs, or a pencil wrote: "I am here," that dead people—people who lay mouldering in their graves!—were speaking to you. . . no, that she would never be able to believe, not if she lived to be Methusalah. Why, you might just be leaning a little too heavily on your side of the table without knowing it. Or your hand write things down in a kind of dream, and you imagine somebody or something else was doing it. And still be the most truthful person alive. Like Richard. Who again and again let himself be imposed on.—The truth was: if people wanted to believe such things, believe they would: the wish was father to the thought. Well, at least this new hobby of Richard's had one advantage: it gave him something to do. Which was just what he needed. Instead of always sitting humped up over his books.

Under the stimulus he began to look more like his old self. He spruced up his dress; and the daily ride to Gracey's gave him beneficial exercise. As time went on, their sittings proved so satisfactory that he began to think of publishing a small pamphlet, embodying the results. And though Mary would rather it had been on a less outlandish subject, she hailed the idea and encouraged it. For looking after

Richard became, year by year, more like minding a fidgety child, who had always to be kept on the go. He had been such a worker in his day. And the old fear could still wake in her at times that, being without active employment, he might all of a sudden turn restless and declare himself tired of their lovely home.

But then came that afternoon when Lizzie let drop an item of news which successfully routed Mary's peace of mind.

They did not see much of Lizzie nowadays; she and John were always in society; out night after night at concerts, dinners, balls. Or else entertaining lavishly in their own home. It was an open secret that the longed-for knighthood would very soon set the crown on John's labours for the colony.

Stateliness in person, gauzes and laces floating from arms and shoulders, trinkets and chains a-jingle, Lizzie swept through the hall, a majestic figure indeed. No wonder John was still unable to refuse her anything.

Then, just about to step into her carriage, she paused. "Mary, dehling. . . I vow I all but forgot it! I have something to tell you, love, that I think will interest you. Mary! I met a gentleman on Friday who was once acquainted with our friend—the charmin' Gracey. And *what* do you think? My dear, she is not a widow at all."

Mary was thunderstruck. "Not a widow? Lizzie! Then—"

"My dehling, her husband is still alive. He left her, love—deserted her for another woman. . . the lowest of the low! At this very moment he lives with the creature. . . in his lawful wife's stead."

As always, Mary's first impulse was to protect. . . defend. "Oh, poor Gracey! . . . how terrible for her!"

"Well, love. . . I thought you ought to know. Since dear Richard is so friendly there. And considering the ultra-strict views he holds."

"Yes, of course. But, Lizzie, it's not her fault, is it? *She* can't help the man she married turning out a scoundrel."

But though she spoke up thus, Mary was greatly perturbed and her mind became a sea of doubts where no doubts had been. She found herself looking at Gracey with other eyes. The fact was, a divorced or legally separated woman—even one who was just living apart from her husband—was by no means the same as a widow. . . and never could be. Gracey knew that well enough; else why, to a close friend like herself, had she made a mystery of her state? And though not a shadow of blame should rest on her (and Mary was sure it didn't), it meant, none the less, that she had been through all sorts of unpleasant matrimonial experiences, which a properly married or widowed woman would know nothing about. Something of them might have remained clinging to her. . . the old saw about touching pitch would run in Mary's head. It was dreadful. Such a dear, nice woman as Gracey. And yet. . . deep down in Mary's heart there dwelt the obstinate conviction that once married was always married, and that as long as your husband lived you belonged at his side. Did you sit firm and hold fast to your rights as a wife, it seemed incredible that another woman could ever usurp your place. Had Gracey perhaps gone off in a tantrum, leaving the coast clear? Yes, doubts would up, and the result was, she found herself considering, with a more critical eye, the friendship that had sprung up between Richard and Grace over their table-tilting. Never before had she known Richard so absorbed by anyone outside his home. Now suppose, just suppose Gracey, thanks to her wretched married life, had come to regard things—serious things, sacred things—more lightly than she ought? What if, because of her own unhappy past, she should not hold the marriage-tie to be binding? Why was she so attractive to gentlemen? Did they know or suspect anything? In reply to which there flashed through Mary's mind a memory of her last visit to Yarangobilly: Willy Urquhart's infatuation and the state poor Louisa had worked herself into. Of course there was really no comparison between the two cases—none whatever! Willy was a notorious flirt: Richard a gentleman. And poor Louisa's morbid, distorted outlook would never be hers.

Richard. . . The question that teased Mary was, should she tell him what she had heard, or keep it to herself? In one way she agreed with Lizzie that he ought to know, he being so fastidious in his views. Besides, if he heard it from someother source, he might feel aggrieved that she had held back. On the other hand, his knowing would probably curtail, if not put a stop altogether to his and Gracey's experiments: he wouldn't want to give people food for talk. And that would be a pity. Would it be disloyal to say nothing? Disloyal to Gracey to tell what she so plainly wished to keep dark? But Richard came first.—And here again, unlike poor Louisa, Mary felt she could weigh the matter very calmly; for in her was a feeling nothing could shake: the happily married woman's sense of possession. It was not only the fact of Richard being what he was. Their life together rested on the surest of foundations: the experiences of many, how many years; the trials and tribulations they had been through together; the joys they had shared; the laughs they had had over things and people; a complete knowledge of each other's prejudices and antipathies—who else could unlock, with half a word, the rich storehouse of memories they had in common? Homelier things, too, there were in plenty, which bound no less closely: the airing and changing of your underlinen; how sweet or how strong you drank your coffee; how you liked your bed made; your hatred of the touch of steel on fruit; of a darn in a sock.—Deeper down though, pushed well below the topmost layer of her consciousness, just one unspoken fear *did* lurk. If she told Richard what she had heard, and he did not take it in the spirit he had hitherto invariably shown towards irregularities of this kind, Mary knew she would feel both hurt and humiliated. Not for herself—but for him.

THE SITTING AT AN END, the table was put back in its place against the wall.

"You will smoke, doctor? Nay, please do. . . I like it. Here are matches.—Down, Rover! Not yet, Fitz!" For at her movement a red setter had sprung up from a corner, and now stood, his front paws on her knee, ingratiatingly wagging his tail; while observing his comrade's advance an immense black cat, which had been dozing in an arm-chair, rose and dropped a kind of bob-curtsey with its hind quarters. "Behold my two tyrants! They think it time for a run.—Oh, yes, Mr. Fitz comes too."

"You are very fond of animals?"

"I should be lost without them. They are such dear companions, in their dumb way." As she spoke Mrs. Marriner fondled a silky ear, letting it slip through a pretty, dimpled hand.

"Well do I know it. In my bachelor days, living in a bark-hut the whole of which would have gone into this room, I kept no less than three." And casting the net of his memory Mahony told of his long-forgotten pets, and of their several untimely ends.—"After that I took no more."

"You had not the heart?" Now could any but a genuine animal-lover have put this question?

"Not exactly. But as a hard-worked medico, with a growing practice. . . the burden of them, you see, would have fallen on my wife. And she does not much care for animals."

"Dear Mary. And now, of course, she has her babies."

"Yes, and all a mother's fears for them, with regard to the four-footed race."

"That is but natural. While they are so tiny." In the kindly indulgence of her tone, the speaker seemed to take all mothers and their weaknesses under her wing. "And yet, doctor, if I had been blessed with little ones, I think I should have brought up babies, puppies and kittens *en masse*... as one family party. Correct me though, if I speak foolishly. Perhaps, when children come, they are all in all."

"It *is* amazing how the little beggars twine themselves round one's heart. Before my boy was born, my chief feeling was a sense of the coming responsibility. I can laugh at myself now. For my wife has shouldered everything of that sort... I leave the children entirely to her."

"I think dear Mary quite the most capable person I know."

What a handsome creature she was, to be sure, full-bosomed yet slender, her neat waist held by a silver girdle, her face alight with sympathy and understanding! Mahony answered heartily: "There have, indeed, been few situations in life Mary has not proved equal to."

The words set a string of memories vibrating; and a silence fell. Unlike many of her sex, who would have babbled on, the lady just smiled and waited; and even her waiting was perfect in tact.

Mahony felt drawn to unbosom himself. "Talking of my children... it is sometimes a sorry thought to me that my acquaintance with them can only be a brief one. I mean, the probability is I shall see them but to the threshold of their adult life—no further. And would like so well to know what they make of it."

His meaning was grasped... and with ease. "I understand that... especially in the case of such a gifted child as your sweet little Cuffy."

"Yes, I do think the boy is quick beyond the common run."

"Without doubt he is. Look at his musical ability."

"Ah, there you mention the one bit of his education I take a hand in. For Mary has no ear for music. Nor even any particular liking for it."

"And it is so important, is it not, that the ear should be well trained from the first? The spadework done before the child is even aware of it." (Here spoke your true musician.) "But, doctor, if our findings are correct, you may still have the joy of watching over your little brood from the other side... *n'est-ce-pas?*"

"Ah!... if that might be. If one could be sure of that." And on the instant Mahony mounted his hobby-horse and was carried away. "With this, my dear lady, you put your finger on what seems to me one of the vital points of the whole question. Have you ever reflected what a difference it would make, did we mortals *seriously* believe in a life to come? . . . I don't mean the Jewish-Byzantine state of petrified adoration that the churches offer us. . . I mean a life such as we know it: a continuation of the best of this earthly existence—mental striving, spiritual aspiration, love for our neighbour. If we did so believe, our every perspective would alter. And the result be a marked increase in spirituality. For the orthodox Christian's point of view is too often grossly materialistic—and superstitious. The tenacity with which he clings to a resurrection of the flesh—this poor cankered flesh! . . . after countless years deep in its grave—that grave on which he dwells with so morbid a pleasure. Or his childish fear of death—despite the glories that are promised him on the other side. . . do these not remind you of the sugar-candy with which an infant is bribed to take its pill? Against all this, set the belief that in dying we pass but from one room to another of the house of life—Christ's 'many mansions.' The belief that an invisible world exists around us—the spirit counterpart of this we know. That those we have lost still live and love and await us. . . on the other side of a veil which already a few, of rarer perceptions than the rest, have pierced.—But forgive me! When once I get going on this subject I know no measure. And I confess. . . so few opportunities to talk of it arise. My wife has scant sympathy with the movement; sees, I fear, only its shady side."

"Dearest Mary. She is so practically minded."

"Yes. She is often genuinely uneasy at the hours I spend over my books; would rather have me up and doing—and though but riding for pleasure along the seashore. Books to her are only a means of killing time."

Mrs. Marriner turned the full weight of a grave, sweet smile upon him. "While we book-lovers. . . well! as far as I am concerned, doctor, my life would be a blank indeed, without the company of the printed page."

"And what of me? . . . whose dearest dream it was, while I slaved for a living, to be able to end my days in a library. I declare to you, it is still a disturbing thought that I shall die leaving so many books unread."

"Let me comfort you. My dear father, who lived to a ripe old age, was given to complaining towards the end that he had 'read all the books'— or at least all that were worth reading."

"Of course; as one grows older; and harder to please. . . Myself though, I seem still far from that. The lists I send my bookseller grow longer, not shorter. And it's not the unread books only. While we're on these ghost-thoughts—we all have them, I suppose—let me confess to another, and that is that I shall probably need to go, having seen all too few of the grandeurs and beauties of this world. Pass on to the next without knowing what the Alps or the Andes are like, or the torrents of the Rhine."

"But doctor. . . what hinders you? I don't mean the Andes,"—and Mahony was the recipient of a roguish smile. "But travel is so easy nowadays. One packs one's trunks, books one's berth—*et voila*! What hinders you?"

Ah! what. . . what, indeed? Mahony hesitated for a moment before replying. "The truth is, the years we spent in England were thoroughly uncongenial. . . to us both. We were glad, on getting back to the colony, to settle down. And having once settled. . ."

Yes, that was it: of his own free will he had saddled himself with a big, expensive house, and all that belonged to its upkeep: men-servants and maid-servants, horses and carriages. Mary had taken root immediately; and now the children. . . their tender age. . . But darker than all else loomed Mary's attitude. . . or what might he expect this to be, if—"The truth is, my wife does not. . . I mean she has gone through so many upheavals already, on my account, that I should hardly feel justified. . . again. . . so soon. . . Still there's no denying it: I do sometimes feel like an old hulk which lies stranded. But there! All my days I've been gnawed by the worm of change—change of any sort. As a struggling medico I longed for leisure and books. Pinned to the colony, I would be satisfied with nothing but the old country. Now that I have ample time, and more books than I can read, I could wish to be up and out seeing the world. And my dear wife naturally finds it difficult to keep pace with such a weathercock."

"I think it is with you as the German poet sings: 'There, where thou art not, there alone is bliss!'"

"Indeed and that hits my nail squarely on the head. For I can assure you it's no mere spirit of discontent—as some suppose. It's more a kind of. . . well, it's like reaching out after—say, a dream one has had and half forgotten, and struggles to recapture. That's baldly put. But perhaps you will understand."

A lengthy silence followed. The clock ticked; the dog sighed gustily. Then, feeling the moment come, the lady rose and swept her skirts to the piano. "Let me play to you," said she.

HENRY HANDEL RICHARDSON

Mahony gratefully accepted.

Once the music had begun, however, he fell back on his own reflections; they were quickened rather than hampered by the delicate tinkling of the piano. He felt strangely elated: not a doubt of it, a good talk was one of the best of medicines, particularly for such a dry, bottled-up old fogy as he was on the verge of becoming. Of course, did you open your heart you must have, for listener, one who was in perfect tune with you; who could pick up your ideas as you dropped them; take your meaning at a word. And mortals of this type were all too rare; in respect of them, his life had been a sandy waste. Which had told heavily against him. Looking down the years he saw that, all through, his most crying need had been for spiritual companionship; for the balm of tastes akin to his own. It was a crippling reflection that never yet had he found the person to whom he could have blurted out his thoughts without fear of being misunderstood. . . or disapproved. . . or smiled at for an oddity. Here, having unexpectedly tapped a woman's quick perception, a woman's lively sympathy, he had a swift vision of what might have been—that misty picture that inhabits the background of most minds. To know his idiosyncrasies fondly accepted—his mental gropings accompanied, his roving spirit gauged and condoned. . . not as any fault of his own, but as an innate factor in his blood! Ah! but for that to come to pass, one would need to leave choosing one's fellow-traveller on the long life-journey until one's own mind and character had formed and ripened. How could one tell, in the twenties, what one would be on nearing the fifties?—in which direction one would have branched out, and set, and stiffened? At twenty all was glamour and romance; and it seemed then to matter little whether or no a heart was open to the sufferings of the brute creation; whether the written word outweighed the spoken; in how far the spiritual mysteries made appeal—questions which gradually, with time, came to seem more vital than all else. In youth one's nature cried aloud for companionship. . . one's blood ran hot. . . the mysteries played no part. And then the years passed and passed, and one drifted. . . drifted. . . slowly, but very surely. . . until. . . well, in many a case, he supposed the fact that you *had* drifted never came to your consciousness at all. But should anything happen to pull you up with a jerk, force you to cast the plummet; should you get an inkling of something rarer and finer: then, the early flames being sunk to a level glow, you stood confounded by your aloofness. . . by the distance you had travelled. . . the isolation of your state. But had he, in sooth, ever felt other than lonely, and alone? Mary was—had always been—dearest and best of wives. . . yet. . . yet. . . had they, between them, a single idea in common? . . . Did they share an interest, a liking, a point of view?—with the one exception of an innate sobriety and honesty of purpose. No, for more years than he cared to count, Mary had done little, as far as he was concerned, but sit in judgment: she silently censured, mentally condemned all those things in life which he held most worth while: his needs, his studies, his inclinations—down to his very dreams and hopes of a hereafter.

Lizzie said: "My dear, our lady friend is in hoops now, if you please! Nothing extreme, of course, considering from whom she takes her present cue. *Just* the desired *soupcon!*—Mary, she went about as a Slim Jane only because the *cavalier* of the moment approved the simplicity of the human form divine. Today she is a rapping and tapping medium—as we very well know. Tomorrow, love, the wind will shift to another quarter, and we shall hear of the fair lady running to matins and communicating on an empty stomach. Or visiting in a prison cell got up as a nursing sister, *A la* Elizabeth Fry."

Hoops. . . nothing extreme. . . considering from whom she takes her present cue. At these words, and even while she was standing up for Gracey's sincerity, there leapt to Mary's mind, with a stab of real pain, Richard's nervous hatred of the exaggerated—the bizarre. And whether it was hoops, or hooplessness.

HENRY HANDEL RICHARDSON

III

These rather waspish comments—Lizzie never seemed able to resist having a thrust at Gracey—were made in the drawing-room at "Ultima Thule," where the two wives sat waiting for their husbands to rejoin them. John and Lizzie were dining there at John's express request: the groom had ridden over after lunch with a line from John, asking if he and Lizzie might take pot-luck with them that evening. Richard said: "Wonders will never cease," and a refusal was not to be thought of; but Cook had been very put out by the shortness of the notice; so much so that Mary had driven to town to fetch delicacies; thinking as she went, how in the old days *she* would have run up a dinner for four, and one well worth eating, too, in less than an hour. Her hands did sometimes itch to show such a fair-weather worker as Cook what could be done.

By now the evening was more than half gone, and still the gentlemen lingered; though Lizzie had sung all Richard's favourite songs and pieces, some of them more than once. To pass the time, she had also sung to Cuffy; for—as had happened ere this when she was dining there—Nannan had knocked to say Master Cuffy could not be got to sleep, for thinking his Auntie might sing to him. Cuffy as audience was better than none, so Lizzie begged for the child to be brought in; and thereupon Cuffy appeared on Nannan's arm in his little red flannel nightgown, his feet swathed in a crib—blanket, his eyes alight with expectation. Seated on his mother's knee he drank in: "There was a Friar of Orders Grey," and the sad ditty of "Barbara Allan," himself rendering "Sun of my Soul" before, soundly kissed and cosseted by his aunt, who had a great liking for the little man, he was carried back to bed.

Towards ten o'clock, Lizzie could no longer conceal her yawns. Mary and she had talked themselves out: and where she had first surreptitiously peeped, she now openly drew her watch from her belt. This, John's latest present to her, was a magnificent affair, crusted back and front with diamonds, while tiny brilliants sprinkled the long gold chain on which it hung. Unlike most women, Lizzie could wear any quantity of jewellery without looking overloaded. At the present moment a little heap of rings and bracelets lay on the lid of the piano; for, in despair, she had re-seated herself at the keys and begun anew to sing.

At the best of times Mary found it hard to fix her mind on music for five minutes together; and on this evening she had had more than enough of it, and could now let her thoughts stray in comfort. She wondered what could be keeping the two men. . . it was certainly rather impolite of Richard. . . wondered if Nannan had at last got Cuffy to sleep. The dinner had been very nice; Cook needn't have made so much fuss beforehand. But there! When they undertook anything of this kind, it usually went off well. The house, of course, had something to do with it. This room, for instance, how well it lighted up! Richard declared he much preferred it to John's, and Mary's eyes wandered lovingly round walls and furniture, lingering on the great gilt-edged mirror, which reached to the ceiling; the lovely girandoles, a present from Richard; the lustred chandelier; the glass-shaded ormolu clock. The carpet, too, was of a most uncommon lemon colour; the suite, in a brocade to match, had a pattern of French lilies on it. She loved every inch of the place. *What* a happy ending to all their ups and downs! . . . to be settled at last in such a home. Did she look back on the "Black Hole," or the snails and damp of Buddlecombe, she felt she did not always fully appreciate her present good fortune.

But Lizzie here striking up a tune Mary knew, her thoughts came back with a jerk. She eyed the singer in listening, and: "Handsomer than ever" was her mental comment; although by now Lizzie was embarked on that adventure which, more than any other, steals from a woman's good looks. What with her full, exquisitely sloping shoulders—they stood out of the low-cut bertha as out of a cup—her dimpled arms and hands, the fingers elegantly curled on the notes of the piano; her rich red lips, opening to show the almond-white teeth; her massive throat, swelling and beating as she sang. . . yes, Lizzie had indeed thriven on matrimony. It was otherwise with John. One had grown gradually used, as time passed, to the loss of that air of radiant health, of masterful assertion, which had formerly distinguished him. But since his marriage he had turned almost into an old man. Thin as a lath, he walked with a slight stoop, and hair and beard were grey. His face seemed to have grown longer, too, more cadaverous; his eye had an absent, inturned expression. At dinner he had been very silent. He had just sat there listening to Lizzie, hanging on her lips—really, if he went on like this when the two of them were at a stranger's house, it would not be quite the thing.

Afterwards, in the drawing-room, Lizzie had made open complaint

HENRY HANDEL RICHARDSON

of his inertia; discussing him in that barefaced way of hers which plumed itself on calling a spade a spade.

"Yes, he is growing stodgy, dehling—stodgy and slow! I said to him the other day, I said: 'John, love! this will *never* do. *Where* is the man I married?' Will you believe it, Mary, he actually wished to stop at home from Government House Ball last night? While this evening, if you please, he throws up an important dinner-party at Sir Joshua Dent's, to come here. Not but what it has been a *charmin'* evening, dehling. But a man in John's position has not the right to pick and choose."

"Are you sure he is quite well, Lizzie? He looks very thin to me."

"Oh, dear, yes! Perfectly well. John was never made to be fat."

The laggards at length appearing, Lizzie crashed out a chord and rose from the piano-stool to hail and reproach them. "A pretty pair to be sure," cried she playfully yet not without malice, the while she slid on rings and clicked the catches of bracelets; a pretty pair of husbands to prefer the society of their pipes to that of their wives! She had been so looking forward to a duo with Richard. It was evident she had reckoned without her host! Richard made one lame attempt to fall in with her tone, John none at all. He seemed only in haste to go; asked for the carriage to be brought round at once; himself rang the bell and gave the order.

Lizzie might be too full of her own grievances to notice how the wind blew; but Mary had eyes in her head. She saw that something was seriously amiss the moment the two men entered the room. Richard looked pale and distracted—and as for John! Whatever could be the matter? Had they quarrelled? . . . had a scene?

Then, in coming along the passage from the bedroom, with Lizzie enshawled at her side, she caught a murmured word of Richard's that was evidently meant only for John's ear. And when she had seen her guests off she did not re-enter the house, but stood on the verandah, anxiously awaiting Richard who had gone to open the gate.

At the crunch of his feet on the gravel, she moved forward, exclaiming impetuously before she was level with him: "What's the matter? What was wrong with John tonight?"

"Matter? What on earth do you mean?" He stooped to pick up something; was exaggeratedly casual and indifferent.

"Now, dear, you needn't put on that tone to me. I saw directly you came into the room. . . have you and he fallen out?"

"Good God, no! What have you got in your head now?"

"Well, then what is it? You can't deceive me, Richard. . . you don't look like that for nothing."

"Who wants to deceive you, I'd like to know?" He was very short and gruff.

"Is John ill?"

"My dear Mary, don't try and *pump* me, if you please! You know my aversion to that kind of thing."

"Richard, I heard with my own ears what you said to him in the hall. . . about a possible loophole. What did you mean? Oh, *don't* be so obstinate! Very well, then! I shall go over and see John myself, the first thing in the morning."

"Indeed and you'll do nothing of the sort."

"He's my brother. I've a right to know what's happened."

"A confidence is a confidence; and I'm hanged if I'll be hectored into betraying it."

"Anyone would think I was asking out of mere curiosity," cried Mary; and tears of vexation rose to her eyes. "I know—I have the feeling— there's something wrong. And you go on talking about confidences. . . and your own pride in not betraying them. . . when John looked to me as if he'd got his death sentence."

Richard's start did not escape her. He retorted, though less surely: "But it is at his own urgent request, Mary, that I hold my tongue!"

"Then he *did* come to consult you about his health? Oh, Richard, please! . . . don't keep me in suspense. What is it?"

"My dear, if you had gone through what I did tonight! I suppose I may as well out with it; for as usual with your wild shot you have hit the bull's-eye. The fact of the matter is, what I had to tell John did amount to a sentence of death."

"Then. . . then it is. . ."

"The worst. I examined him. A growth in the liver. No, too late now, for anything of that kind. My private opinion is he hasn't more than six months to live."

"*Richard!* . . . though I think I've been afraid of something like this. . . it's just as if, inside me, I had felt what was coming."

"And I suspected it. But you know, Mary, what John is. . . so unapproachable. I must say this though: I was moved this evening to a profound admiration for him. He took the verdict like a man. . . without flinching."

"Yes, yes. But what does that matter now? The thing is, you've let him go home alone—with this on his mind—and only Lizzie beside him. . . who cares for no one but herself." Mary had not known she thought this of Lizzie; it just popped out.

"A great spider! . . . that's what the woman is, if you want my opinion," cried Mahony angrily. "But what could I do?—Besides, at heart, I'm one with him. There are crises in a man's life that are best fought through alone."

"Not while I'm here. Where I'm going? Why, to him, of course!"

"At this hour of night? Indeed I advise you very strongly, Mary, to do nothing of the kind. Not only will he resent—and rightly too—my having broken my word, but he won't thank you either for intruding.—And he'll have gone to bed. How can you knock him up? What excuse have you?"

Mary reached for a wrap and threw it over her shoulders. "John won't be in bed. And I'll make it all right about you; don't be afraid.—No, no, I'll just walk over. As for intruding. . . I've always understood John better than any of you. Besides, I don't see how people can care whether they do or not at a time like this."

"Well, at least put on a pair of sound walking-boots and take a shawl. Of course I am. If you must go, I go with you."

Stepping out of the gate they plodded through the sand of the road that led past now a large garden, now a wild, open space covered with gorse and heath. Masses of firs stood out black and forbidding. In the distance could be heard the faint lapping of the sea.

They walked in silence. Once only did Mary exclaim aloud, out of the many conflicting thoughts that were going round in her head: "Lizzie, of course, must know nothing. The last thing John will want is for her to be worried or upset."

And Mahony: "It will not be long now before she and everyone else has to know."

"When I think. . . how. . . how proud she has been of it all—I mean John's position. . . and their entertainments. . . and his future—how she has looked forward to the title coming. . . Oh dear, oh dear! If only Jinny were beside him now. . . or poor dear Emma."

On reaching the house they unlatched the gate with care, and crept like a pair of conspirators over the grass, to avoid the noise their steps would have made on the gravel. The venetian blinds were down, but bars of light filtered through them in Lizzie's bedroom on the one side, and in John's sanctum on the other. Mary tiptoed round the verandah, and tapped on her brother's window-pane.

"It is I, John. . . Mary."

There was a moment's pause, then the French window was noiselessly opened, and she disappeared inside the room.

On the front verandah a rocking-chair had been left standing. Mahony sat down in it and waited. . . and waited. Time passed; an hour. . . two hours. . . and still Mary did not return. Lizzie's light had long ago gone out; not a sound came from the house; nor did any living thing move in garden or road. So absolute was the stillness that, more than once as he sat, he heard a petal drop from a camellia in the central bed. John had a fine show of these stiff, scentless flowers. They stood out, white and waxen, against the dark polish of their leaves.

It was spring, and a night warm enough to release the scents of freesia and boronia; though as usual the pittosporums outdid all else. There was no moon; but the stars made up for that; the sky was powdered white with them—was one vast field of glittering silver. Leaning back in his chair Mahony lay looking up at them and thinking the old, well-worn thoughts that besiege a mortal at sight of the Creator's prodigality. Pigmy man's insignificance in face of these millions of worlds; the preposterousness of the claim that his tiny existence can engage the personal notice of Him who has strewn the Milky Way; and yet the bitter reality of his small, mad miseries, the bottomless depths of his mental anguish: pain, as the profoundest of life's truths, the link by which man is bound up with the Eternal. . . pain that bites so much deeper than pleasure, outlasting pleasure's froth and foam as granite outlasts thistledown.

And now John's link was being forged. . . his turn had come to taste pain's bitterness—John who, all his days, had looked haughtily down on weakness and decay, as touching others, not himself. The material things of this world had been his pride and his concern. His soul, that poor soul which Mary, once more the comforter, was standing by in its black hour, had gone needy and untended. Now he was being called on to leave everything he prized: marriage and happiness, wealth, a proud standing, ambition crowned. Never, in his forward march, had John looked deeper; though in his own way he had walked according to his lights: a man of enterprise and energy, upright in business, grappling with the hardships of a new country, a pathfinder for those who would come after.—Yet for all this, a strangely unsympathetic nature! It was not alone the absence of the spiritual in him. It was the cold, proud, narrow fashion in which he had lived enclosed in his earthy shell,

HENRY HANDEL RICHARDSON

keeping the door rigidly shut on intruders. No one had really known John—known what manner of man housed within. Perhaps he had acted thus out of fear; had been afraid of the strange fears that might be found in him. Afraid of his fellows discovering that he was hollow, a sham and a pretence, where they had imagined wonderful strength and lovely virtues.

Well! . . . be that as it might. The time was past for probing and conjecturing. John's hour had struck; and the phantom which had thus far borne his name, striding confident and alert through the world of men, would soon be blotted out. However one looked at it, it was a melancholy business. The swiftness of the blow made one realise, anew, on the edge of what an abyss one walked. Life was like a procession that trooped along this perilous margin, brimful of hope and vigour, gay, superbly unthinking; and then of a sudden there was a gap in the ranks, and one of the train had vanished, had pitched head-foremost into the depths, to be seen no more—by mortal eyes at least. Such a disaster must surely say—to those who had pinned their hearts to this world, with no more than a conventional faith in one to come (which amounted to little or none)—must surely seem to say: take all you can get while there is still time! A little while and it may be too late. Even in himself, who had won through to the belief that life was a kind of semi-sleep, death the great awakening, it called up the old nervous fear of being snatched away before he was ready to go. One lived on. . . *he* lived on. . . inactive as a vegetable. . . and at any moment the blow might fall, and his chance be gone forever—of doing what he had meant to do, of seeing what he had meant to see. And now, sitting there under the multitudinous stars, Mahony let the smothered ache for movement, the acute longing for change of scene that was smouldering in him, come to full consciousness. Yes, there was no denying it: the old restlessness was strong on him again; he was tired of everything he knew—tired of putting on his clothes in the morning and taking them off at night; tired of nursery talk and the well-known noises about the house, and the faces he saw everyday. Tired of his books, too, and of his own familiar company. He wanted fresh scenes and people; wanted to open his eyes on new surroundings; be on the move again—feel a deck under his feet, and the rigours of a good head wind—all this, while health and a semblance of youth were left him. Another few years and he would be past enjoying it. Now was the time to make the break. . . cut his bonds. . . front Mary's grief and displeasure.

Mary. At her name the inner stiffening, the resistance, with which his mind had approached her, yielded; and in its place came a warm uprush of feeling. Her behaviour this very night—how surely and fearlessly she had come to the stricken man's aid, without a single hampering thought of self! There was nobody like Mary in a crisis: happy the mortal who, when his end came, had her great heart to lean on. That was worth all else. For of what use, in one's last hour, would be the mental affinity, the ties of intellect he had lately so pitied himself for having missed? One would see these things then for the earth-trimmings they were. A child faced with the horrors of the dark does not ask for his fears to be shared, or to have their origin explained to him. He cries for warm, enfolding arms with which to keep his terrors at bay; or which, if met these must be, alone can help him through the ordeal. Man on his death-bed was little more than such a child; and it was for the mother-arms he craved, to which he clung in passing, until, again like a child, he had dropped to sleep. Hope, faith and love, these three. . . yes, but needed was a love like Mary's, compounded of utter selflessness, and patience, and infinite forbearance—a love which it was impossible to sin against or overthrow. . . which had more than a touch of the divine in it; was a dim image of that infinite tenderness God Himself might be assumed to bear towards the helpless beings He had created. Measured by it, all other human experience rang hollow.

HENRY HANDEL RICHARDSON

IV

Mamma and Papa were going away; Master Cuffy would need to be a *very* good boy and do everything he was told; so that Mamma would be pleased with him when she came back. Thus Nannan, while Eliza and she gave the three children their morning bath; and four blue and two black eyes were turned on her in curiosity and wonderment. Cuffy, extending his arm to have the raindrops rubbed off it, echoed her words: "Mamma and Papa goin' away!" It sounded exciting.

After breakfast he broke the news to Effalunt, who, though now in his old age, hairless, and a leg short, was still one of the best beloveds; for Cuffy had a faithful heart.

Going away? What would it be like? Hi-spy-hi in the garden? . . . or a pitchnick? . . . or Mamma putting on a pretty dress wif beads round her neck?

He played at it during the morning: he got under an opossum-rug and was a bear to the Dumplings, and go'ed away. Later on, he was allowed to crawl inside a leather trunk that stood in Mamma's bedroom, and have the lid *nearly* shut over him.

The carriage came round after lunch; the trunk was hoisted to the roof; Mamma and Papa had their bonnets on.

There stood Nannan, a Dumpling's hand in each of hers. The babies, though o-eyed, were serene; but Cuffy by now was not so sure. He had watched Mamma's dresses being put into the trunk and Eliza sitting on it, to make it shut; and the thing that worried him was, how Mamma could get up in the morning if her clothes were locked inside the big box. He began to feel uncomfortable. And so, now the moment had come, he was busy being a horse, capering up and down the verandah, stamping, tossing his head.

The Dumplings obediently put up their faces and offered their bud-mouths. Cuffy had to be called to order.

Said Mary: "Why, darling, aren't you coming to kiss Mamma and Papa goodbye? Or be a little sorry they're going?"

Sorry? Why? He hadn't been naughty! Perfunctorily Cuffy did what was required of him, but his heart went on being a horse.

It was not till night that the trouble broke. Then, as often as Nannan entered the nursery, he was sitting bolt upright and wide-eyed in his crib, his little face looking each time wanner and whiter as he piped: "Is Cuffy's Mamma and Papa tum 'ome yet, Nannan?"

"There you have it!" said Nurse to Eliza. "This is what happens when gentlemen get to interfering in things they don't understand. If the doctor 'ud just 'ave let me say they were gone to a party, there'd 'ave been none of this. Master Cuffy knows well enough what a party is, and though it 'ad lasted for weeks it wouldn't 'ave made any difference to him, bless 'is little heart! It's the things they *don't* understand that worries children. This fad now that they must 'ave nothing but the truth told 'em. Lord bless you! If we did that, there soon wouldn't be anymore children left. . . nothing but little old men and women."

And to mark her disapproval of Mahony's methods, Nannan kept the forbidden lamp alight, and sat by the cribside with Cuffy's hand in hers till he fell asleep.

MEANWHILE MARY AND RICHARD HAD taken the afternoon train to Ballarat. For the date set for Tilly's marriage had come right in the middle of the trouble about John.

Seated in a saloon carriage Mary undid her bonnet-strings and put her feet up on the cushions. Off at last! And opposite her sat Richard—a morose and unamiable Richard, it was true, who made it abundantly plain that he was being dragged to Ballarat against his will. Still, there he was, and that was the main thing. Up to the last minute she hadn't felt sure of him.

She had early determined that it was his duty to be present at Tilly's wedding, and had spared no pains to win him over. Hadn't it to a certain extent been his fault that Tilly's plans had failed, the time she stayed with them before Cuffy was born? If he had not been so down on her, the plot she was hatching might then and there have come to a head. As it was, one thing after another had happened to delay the issue. Misunderstanding Tilly's abrupt departure, Purdy had disappeared up-country again, on his commercial rounds. Then, still up-country somewhere, he had been in a frightful buggy-accident, pitching out head-foremost, and all but breaking his neck. For months nothing could be heard of him, he lying at death's door with concussion and broken bones, in a little bush hospital. When Tilly did finally contrive to run him to earth, he was literally at his last farthing, and a sick and broken man. Tilly had behaved like her own splendid self: waiving any false pride, she had journeyed straight to see him; and at

HENRY HANDEL RICHARDSON

their very first meeting they had arrived at an understanding (Mary could make a shrewd guess how) and were now to be man and wife. An even more urgent reason why Richard should appear at the wedding was, it would greatly improve Purdy's social standing, if it became known that Dr. Mahony had travelled all the way from Melbourne to be present. And Purdy, poor fellow, could well do with such a lift. Even she, Mary, who had known him in so many a tight fit, had felt shocked at his condition after his last adventure.

Thus she reflected as she watched the landscape slip past: yellowish-grey flats, or stone-strewn paddocks tufted with clumps of brown grass, all of which she had seen too often before to pay much heed to them. Still she never wanted to read in a train. So unlike Richard, whose idea of a journey was to bury himself in a book from start to finish. At the present moment he was deep in a pamphlet entitled: "The Unity, Duality or Trinity of the Godhead?"—Tch, what questions he did vex his head with! . . . he must always be trying to settle the universe. If only he would sometimes give his poor brains a rest.

He was looking pale and washed out, too, not by any means his best. . . for meeting all the old friends. But what could you expect if he *would* spend his life cooped up indoors?—never leaving the house except to attend long, hot seances; or sittings with Gracey. And these had rather fallen off of late. Mary didn't know why, and he said nothing; but Lizzie as usual was prolific in hints. Poor old Richard! She did hope things would go smoothly for him during the next three days. She would feel relieved when they were over.

But no sooner did they reach Ballarat than the trouble began. On the platform stood Tilly, wreathed in smiles, open-armed in welcome, but gone, alas, was the decent and becoming black to which, as "old Mrs. Ocock," she had been faithful for so long. In its stead. . . well, there was no mincing the fact: she looked fit for *Punch!* Her dress, of a loud, bottle-green satin, was in the very latest mode, worn entirely without crinoline, so that her full form was outlined in unspeakable fashion; her big capable hands were squeezed into lemon-coloured kid gloves, tight to bursting, and on her head perched a monstrous white hat, turned up at the side and richly feathered.

"Oh dear, oh dear!"

For Mary knew very well that neither the genuine sincerity of Tilly's greeting, nor her multitudinous arrangements for their comfort, would suffice to blot from Richard's mind the figure she cut this day.

Climbing to the driver's seat of an open buggy, all her feathers afloat, Tilly trotted a pair of cream ponies in great style up Sturt Street. Of course everybody in Ballarat knew her, so it didn't matter for herself what she looked like. It was Richard who was to be pitied.

The next thing to provoke him was the arbitrary way in which she disposed of his personal liberty. She had it all fixed and settled that, directly supper was over, he should go back to town, to "Moberley's Hotel," and there spend the evening with the bridegroom-elect.

"She wants them to be seen in public together," thought Mary as she helped Richard on with his overcoat and muffled him up in a comforter; for the air on this tableland struck cold, after Melbourne's sea-level. "And for that, of course, there's no better place than Moberley's Coffee Room."—Aloud she said reprovingly: "Ssh! She'll hear you. You know, dear, you needn't stop long." But Richard, chilly and tired from the railway journey, looked as though he could cheerfully have consigned Tilly and her nuptials to Hades.

"And now you and I can 'ave a real cosy evening, love, while the lords of creation smoke and jaw about early days," said dear blind old Tilly. Or perhaps she was not quite so blind as she seemed; and just wanted to be rid of Richard and the atmosphere of glacial politeness that went out from him. Anyhow off he set, with a very bad grace, and the two women retired to Tilly's bedroom. Here a great log fire burned on the whitewashed hearth; and Tilly kept the poker in her hand with which to thump the logs, did the blaze threaten to fail. This dyed the dimity-hangings of the fourposter; made ruddy pools in the great mahogany wardrobe.

Said Tilly: "Well, here we are again, Poll, you and me, like so often before. . . and the day after tomorrow's me wedding-day. 'Pon my word it's hard to believe; and yet. . . I don't know, dearie, but somehow it seems no time since us three bits of girls used to sit over the fire and gas about all the grand things that was going to happen to us. That's ages back, and yet, except that we're grown a bit hulkier you and me, it might be only yesterday. I don't feel a day older and that's the truth; which is odd when you come to think of it. . . with pa and ma and Jinn and poor old Pa all gone, these ever so many years! I say, *do* you remember, Poll, how Purd used to ride down from Melbourne? And how, when 'e'd gone, I'd count the days off on me fingers till 'e'd come again?"

"I think you're a very lucky woman, Tilly, to get your heart's wish like this. I do hope it will bring you every happiness."

HENRY HANDEL RICHARDSON

"I think it will, Poll. I'm not going into it with my eyes shut, or any of the flighty notions one has as a young girl—heaven on earth and bunkum of that sort. But now, listen to me, dearie, there's things I want to say to you. First of all, Mary, I've fixed, once we're spliced, for Tom and Johnny to come back to this house—which they never ought to 'ave left. I won't say it 'asn't taken a bit of managing. But my mind was quite made up. It's gone to my heart, all these years, to see how badly those poor lads were cared for. Enough to make poor old Pa turn in 'is grave."

But Mary had raised her eyebrows. For all its kindness, she thought the plan a most unwise one. Just suppose Purdy should turn nasty! In subtle connection the question sprang to her lips: "What about the money side of it—settlements, and all that?"

Tilly nodded. "Ah! I can see what you're thinking, love—writing me down a lovesick old fool who's going to let Pa's good money be made ducks and drakes of. It's true, most of what I've got *will* pass to Purd, to do as 'e likes with. But somehow I don't believe 'e'll be a waster. A man who's gone short as long as him. . . However, just in case, Poll"—here Tilly sank her voice to a mysterious hiss—"the fact is, love, I've got a reserve fund of my own, a nest-egg so to speak, which I don't mean to let on one word about. . . no, not to anybody. Except you. I've laid something by, my dear, in the last few years, made a bit at the races; sold out of *Blazing Diamonds* in the nick of time; and the long and the short of it is, Mary, I've between seven and eight thousand by me at this very minute. What's more, I intend to keep it; just let it lie, have it to draw on, in case of trouble. One never knows. I've got a small tin box, my dear, and out in the dairy, going down the ladder into the cellar, a flag's come loose, which just leaves room for it. There's no chance there of fire, or thieves either—no one but myself even sets foot in the place. And if anything happens to me, it's there you'll find it. The boys are to have it, if I go first. For as you can see, love, with no blood-tie between them and me, there wouldn't be much call on Purd, would there, to support 'em after my death?"

Indeed that was true; nor could Purdy be blamed, if he failed to recognise the obligation. It said a good deal for him that he was willing to accept, as inmates of his house, these two middle-aged men, one of whom was a confirmed drunkard with lucid intervals, the other little more than an overgrown child. As for Tilly's plan of keeping a large sum of money on the premises, risky though it seemed, Mary faltered in her criticism of it. For she knew too well the advantage of a private purse into which you could dip at will. Instead of having to run to your husband with all the little extra expenses that *would* crop up, spare as you might. These were never kindly greeted. Richard, too, had been the most generous of husbands, and she a fairly good manager. Tilly on the other hand was lavish and lordly with money, Purdy still a dark horse in respect of it.

Another thing, as long as Purdy and Mr. Henry knew nothing, Tilly could neither be wheedled out of her savings nor bullied into reinvesting them.

When at the end of an hour the two women kissed goodnight, Tilly uttered her usual request: "Now mind, not a word to the doctor!"

Oh dear no! (*How* Richard would have jeered!) Besides, when he got home some half-hour later, he was so full of a new grudge against Tilly that every word had to be weighed, for fear of fanning the flames. It seemed that on reaching Moberley's, he had found Purdy the centre of a rowdy party, whose noise and laughter could be heard even before he entered the hotel. More: his appearance was totally unexpected. Purdy looked as if he couldn't believe his eyes; exclaimed: "What, Dick? You here already?" and then turned back to his companions—the motley collection of commercial travellers and bar-haunters he had gathered round him. Ten minutes of this were enough for Mahony; he slipped unobserved from the room. Recognising, however, that the appointment had been a ruse on Tilly's part to get rid of him, he did not come back to the house, but took a long walk round the lake in the dark. There, at least, he could be sure of not meeting anyone he knew.

He seemed to have this idea of dodging familiar faces on the brain. Did ever anyone hear the like? . . . on his return, for the first time, to the place where he had spent a third of his life. . . where he had been so well known and sought after. But really *just* how odd Richard had become, Mary did not grasp till now. And before the following day was out, she was heartily sorry she had not left him at home. One of his worst bad nights did not help to mend matters. He vowed he had not missed the striking of a single hour; but had tossed and turned on a too hard bed, in a too light room, listening to the strange noises of a strange house, and wakened for good and all long before dawn, by the crowing of "a thousand infernal roosters." Before anyone else stirred he was up and out, on a long tramp bushwards.

There was nothing to be done with him. Summoned to the drawing-room to greet Amelia Grindle and Agnes Ocock, who drove over immediately after breakfast "for a glimpse of our darling Mary," he was so stiff and found so little to say that poor Amelia, timid and fluttery as ever, hardly dared to raise her eyes from her boots. Thereafter Mary left him in peace on the back verandah, and sought to waylay Tilly, whose main idea of hospitality—poor old Tilly!—was continually to be bothering him with something to eat.

The person who did not look near was Purdy; and this was an additional source of offence. The least he could have done, said Richard, was to ride out and make up for his offensive behaviour of the night before. Didn't the fellow grasp that he, Mahony, had come to Ballarat solely with the object of doing him a good turn? Privately Mary thought it very unlikely that Purdy, or Tilly either, saw Richard's presence in this light. Aloud she observed that he must know it would not be considered proper for the bridegroom to hang about the house, the day before the wedding. But Richard said: propriety be hanged!

He also flouted her suggestion that he should himself pay some visits—look up the Archdeacon, or Chinnery of the National, or those colleagues on hospital or asylum with whom he had once been intimate.

"Not I! If they want to see me, let *them* make the overture."

"Don't be silly. Of course they'd like to see you again."

"I know better."

"Then why, if you're so sure of it, feel hurt because they don't come? For that's what you are," said Mary bluntly. She wore a large cooking-apron over her silk gown, and looked tired but content. She had helped to set the wedding-breakfast on long trestle-tables running the length of the hall; had helped to pack and strap the bride's trunks for the journey to Sydney; had baked some of her famous cakes, and laid the foundation for the more elaborate cream dishes that were to be whipped up the first thing next morning.

She went on: "Personally, I don't see how you can expect people to run after you, when you've never troubled to keep up with them. . . written a line or sent a message." And just because she herself thought *some* of Richard's old friends might have done him the compliment of calling, Mary spoke very warmly. Adding: "Well, at least you'll take a stroll round the old place now you're here, and see how it's grown."

"Indeed and I'll do nothing of the sort! . . . now don't start badgering me, Mary. Why on earth should I go to the trouble of soldering old links, for the sake of a single day? I'll never be here again."

"Tch, tch!" said Mary. "With you it's always yourself. . . nothing but I, I, I!"

"Well, upon my word! . . . I like that. After me dragging all this way, , , not to speak of being perched up tomorrow before a churchful of people, for them to stare at!"

At this Mary laughed aloud. "Oh, Richard! As if they would ever think of looking at anybody but the bride! . . . or bridegroom."

But Richard, it seemed, suffered from an intense nervous conviction that he would be a target for all eyes.

Something before three o'clock the following afternoon, Mary stood on the front verandah, which was white and scrunchy with flowers and rice, and watched him, carpet-bag in hand, make a dash for gate, trap, and the train that was to carry him back to town. Indoors the guests still lingered: you could hear a buzz of talk, the clink of glasses, the rustle of silk; and she herself was not leaving till next day, having promised Tilly first to see the house restored to order. But nothing would persuade Richard to stop a moment longer than was necessary. He fled.

Tossing hat and bag on the cushions of the railway carriage, Mahony fell into a seat and wiped his forehead. Doors slammed; a bell rang; they were off. Well, *that* was over, thank God! . . . and never, no, never! would he let himself be trapped into this kind of thing again. To begin with, he had been inveigled here on false pretences. It no doubt buttered Tilly's vanity to see his name topping the list of her wedding-guests. But as far as all else was concerned, he might have stayed comfortably at home. Purdy had not cared a threepenny-bit one way or the other. As for it ever dawning on the fellow that he was being given a leg-up—a social safe-conduct, so to speak—all such rubbish originated in Mary's confounded habit of reading her own ideas into other people. At his expense.

But while he could dismiss Tilly and her folly with a smile, Purdy's bovine indifference roused a cold resentment in him. Consciously he had washed his hands of the connection long since. And yet it seemed as if a part of him still looked for gratitude—or at least a show of gratitude—did he exert himself on Purdy's behalf. Which was absurd.— And anyhow Purdy had never been famous for delicacy of feeling—a graceless, thankless beggar from the start. In his heyday, a certain debonair blitheness had cloaked his shortcomings. Now, time having robbed him of every charm, he stood revealed in all his crudity: obese, loose-mouthed, with an eye grown shifty from overreaching his fellow-men: *how* he plumed himself on his skill as a Jeremy Diddler! Oh, this insufferable exaggeration!—this eternal bragging. . . even while they were waiting in church for the arrival of the bride, he had been unable to refrain. Mary said: "Do have patience. Mark my words, Tilly will knock him into shape." But Mahony doubted it. Once a boaster, always a boaster!—besides, the fair fat Tilly was too far gone in love to wish to chip and change her chosen. Her face had been oily with bliss as she stood with her groom before the altar, he in a check the squares of which could have been counted from across the road, draped in a watch-chain on which he might have hanged himself; she, puce-clad, in a magenta bonnet topped with roses the size of peonies, which sat crooked over one ear. (Mary, cool and pale in silver grey, looked as though sprung from a different branch of the human race.)

What a farce the whole thing had been! . . . from beginning to end. The congratulations he had had to smirk a response to on "his friend's" marriage, "his friend's" good fortune. Then old Long's flowery periods, which would have well befitted a dewy damsel of eighteen, but bordered on the ludicrous when applied to Tilly, who would never see forty again, and had been through all this before. Henry Ocock "giving away" his mature stepmother and her money-bags, his father's money-bags, those bags that should by rights have descended to *his* son: in spite of his sleek suavity, it was not hard to imagine the wrath that burned behind Henry's chalky face and boot-button eyes. He was ageing, was Henry; white hairs showed in his jetty beard and the creasing of his lids made him look foxier than ever. But so it was with all of them. Those he had left young were now middle-aged the middle-aged had grown old. Like Henry's, their faces had not improved in the process. Time seemed to show up the vacancy that had once been overlaid by rounded cheeks and a smooth forehead. Or else the ugly traits in a nature, ousting the good, had been bitten in as by an etcher's acid. He wondered what secrets his own phiz held, for those who had eyes to see. The failures and defeats his prime had been spent in enduring—had each left its special mark, in the shape of hollow, or droop, or wrinkle? Oh, his return to this hated place called up bitter memories from their graves: raised one obscene ghost after another, for his haunting. Here, he was to have garnered the miraculous fortune that would lift him forever out of the mud of poverty; here had dreamt the marriage that was to be like no other on earth; here turned back, with a big heart, to the profession that should ensure him ease and renown—even the cutting himself loose, when everything else had miscarried, was to have heralded the millennium.—No! one's past simply did not bear thinking about. Looking back was wormwood and a wound. It meant remembering all the chances you had not taken; the gaudy soap-bubble schemes that had puffed out at a breath; meant an inward writhing at the toll of the years flown by, empty of achievement—at the way in which you had let him get the better of you. Time, which led down and down, with a descent ever steeper and more rapid, till it landed you. . . in who knew what Avernus?—Nervously Mahony unclasped his bag and rummaged a book from its depths. To lose himself in another's thoughts was the one anodyne left him.

The train was racing now. They had passed Navigator, white and sweet with lucerne; and the discomforts and absurdities of the past forty-eight hours were well behind him.

CUFFY, PLAYING THAT EVENING ON the front verandah, was surprised by the sudden advent of his father, who caught him up, tossed and soundly kissed him with a: "And how is my little man? How is my darling?" But at three years old even a short absence digs a breach. Cuffy had had time to grow shy. He coloured, hung his head, looked sideways along the floor; and as soon as he was released pattered off to Nannan and the nursery.

HENRY HANDEL RICHARDSON

V

The old mahogany fourposter with the red rep hangings had been brought out from among the lumber, and set up afresh in John's study. And soon after his interview with Mahony John shifted his quarters to this room, on the pretence of sleeping poorly and disturbing his wife. Lizzie raised fierce objections to the change. It took Mary to mollify her, and to insist that she must now place her own health and comfort above everything. Save in this one point, it was true, Lizzie needed small persuasion. The household danced to her whims.

Emmy's room was only a trifle nearer the study than the other bedrooms; but in everything that touched her father the girl's senses were preternaturally acute. And so it happened that she started out of her first sleep, wakened she did not know by what, but conscious, even as she opened her eyes, of sounds coming from her father's room—the strange, heart-rending sounds of a man crying. Sitting up in bed, her hands pressed to her breast, Emmy listened till she could bear it no longer: stealthily unlatching the door, she crept down the passage to the study. And there, on this and many another night, she lay crouched on the mat, her heart bursting with love and pity; while John, believing himself alone with his Maker, railed and rebelled, in blind anguish, against his fate. Yes, Emmy knew before anyone else that some disaster had come upon her father. And in the riot of emotion the knowledge stirred in her, there was one drop of sweetness: she alone shared his secret.

The feeling of intimacy this engendered did much to help her over the days of suspense that followed; when she waited from hour to hour for the unknown blow to fall. She confided in no one—not even Aunt Mary. Her father himself she dared not approach. Papa was so stern with her. Once, after a night when she really thought her heart would break, she ventured a timid: "Papa, if there is anything. . . I mean, Papa. . . if I could. . ." But he stared so angrily at her that she turned and ran from the room, for fear of bursting out crying—as much at the sound of her own words and the feeling of self-pity they roused in her, as at his cold repulse. She did not see the look he threw after her as she went. "Her mother's daughter," was his muttered comment; and long past days rose before him, when there had been one at his side from whom nothing was hid. Tatting and crocheting, crocheting and tatting, Emmy gave her imagination free play. A failure in business, even bankruptcy was the solution she favoured—being still too young to face of herself the destructive thought of death. And did this happen, and Papa lose all his money, then would come *her* chance. He would learn that he had one faithful soul at his side, one shoulder to lean on. Together they would go away, he and she, right into the bush if necessary, and start life afresh. But again there were moments when she indulged an even dearer hope: at last, perhaps, Papa was beginning to see what a dreadful mistake his marriage had been.

For Emmy hated her stepmother; hated her, and sat in judgment on her, with the harshness of the young creature who has been wounded in her tenderest susceptibilities. Thus, though for the most part she rejoiced to know Lizzie among the uninitiated, she could also burn with a furious, unreasoning anger against her for living on, so blindly, so selfishly, without noticing that something was amiss. At sight of the big woman lying stretched on her *chaise longue*, idly fanning herself, book and vinaigrette at her elbow; or Papa bathing her temples for her with lavender-water, or running errands for her like a servant—at things like these Emmy clenched her fist, and averted her tell-tale eyes. She hated, too, Lizzie's vigorous, exaggerated manner of speaking; hated the full red lips that went in and out and up and down when she talked; her affected languor. . . her unwieldy figure. . . the baby that was on the way.

But with the crash came also the chance of revenge. Then it was Emmy's turn; and she could say in all good faith: "Oh, *don't* let her—don't let. . . Mamma go in to him, Aunt Mary! She worries him so." As always, there was just the suspicion of a pause—a kind of intake of the breath—before she got the "Mamma" out; a name here bestowed for the third time, and only after a severe inward struggle, because *he* had wished it.

Meanwhile John's serene and dignified existence had shattered to its foundations; carrying with it, in its fall, the peace and security of those lesser lives that depended on it. For close on six months, he had kept his own counsel. With his once full lips pinched thin in his old, greying face, he went doggedly to and from the warehouse in Flinders Lane, as he had done everyday for five-and-twenty years: driving off at nine of a morning, and returning as the clock struck six to escort Lizzie to any entertainment she still cared to patronise: and this, though his skin had gone the colour of dry clay or a dingy plaster, and he was so wasted that his clothes seemed to flap scarecrow-like on his bones. Mary's heart

HENRY HANDEL RICHARDSON

bled for him; and even Richard was moved to remark that what John must be suffering, both mentally and physically, God alone knew. But they could only pity in silence; open compassion was not to be thought of: after the one terrible night Mary had spent with John, the subject of his illness was taboo, even to her. Alone, sheathed in his impenetrable reserve, he prepared for his departure; bade farewell, behind locked doors, to a life of surpassing interest, now cut short in mid-career. In politics, his place would not be hard to fill. But of the great business he had built up he was still the mainspring; and, in a last spurt of his stiff pride, he laboured to leave all that concerned it in perfect order.— And yet, watching him with her heart in her eyes, Mary sometimes wondered. . . wondered whether the unquenchable optimism that had made him the man he was had even yet wholly deserted him. He had had so little experience of illness, and was, she knew, still running privily from doctor to specialist; giving even quacks and their remedies a trial. Did he nurse a hope that medical opinion, right in ninety-nine cases, might prove wrong in his, and he have the hundredth chance? One thing at least she knew: he intended, if humanly possible, to bear up till the child was born and Lizzie better able to withstand the blow.

But this was not to be. The morning came when, in place of rising and tapping at his wife's door, solicitously to inquire how she had passed the night, John, beaten at last, lay prostrate in his bed. . . from which he never rose again.

A scene of the utmost confusion followed. Mary, summoned just as she was sitting down to breakfast, found Lizzie in hysterics, John writhing in an agony he could no longer conceal. The scared servants scuttled aimlessly to and fro; the children, but half dressed, cried in a corner of the nursery. Emmy alone had her wits about her—though she, too, shook as with the ague.

Meeting Mary at the front door, she held out two clasped hands imploringly. "Oh. . . what is it? Aunt Mary! what is the matter with Papa?"

"Emmy. . . your poor, dear father—my darling, I look to you to be brave and help me—he will need all our help now."

Long prepared for some such emergency, Mary took control. Dispatching the groom at a gallop for the doctor, she mixed a soothing-draught for Lizzie ("See to her first," was John's whispered request) and gave John the strongest opiate she dared. The children were put in the carriage, and sent to "Ultima Thule." Then, as Richard had directed,

Mary cleared the sickroom of superfluous furniture; while Emmy bore a note to Miss Julia—Mary's sole confidante. And faithful to a promise, Miss Julia was back with Emmy inside an hour. Without her aid she at once saw to Lizzie, and brought the servants to their senses—without this sane, calm presence, Mary did not know how she would have managed, John from the start obstinately refusing to let her out of his sight. Or for that matter without Emmy either. . . Emmy was her right hand. Nimble, yet light-footed as a cat; tireless; brave; Emmy now proved her mettle. Nothing was beneath her: she performed the most menial duties of the sickroom with a kind of fiery, inner gratitude. And, these done, would sit still as a mouse, a scrap of needlework in her hand, just waiting for the chance of springing up afresh. Her young face grew thin and peaked, and the life went out of her step; but she never complained, or sought to obtrude her own feelings. Only one person knew what she was suffering. It was on Auntie Julia's neck that she had had her single breakdown, and wept out her youthful passion of love and despair.

"What shall I do! Oh, what *shall* I do?"

And Auntie Julia, knowing everything, understanding everything, wisely let her cry and cry till she could cry no more. "There, there, my little one! There, there!" But after this Emmy did not again give way. Indeed, thought Mary, there was something in her of John's own harsh self-mastery: a trait that sat oddly on her soft and lovely girlhood.

Lizzie was the sorest trial. But then, poor thing, was it to be wondered at in her condition, and after the shock John had given her? For when, that first morning he failed to present himself at her bedside, Lizzie passed in a twinkling from a mood of pettish surprise to one of extreme ungraciousness. The housemaid was peremptorily bidden to go knock at the master's door and ask the reason of his negligence. The girl's confused stammerings throwing no light on this, Emmy was loudly rung for. "Pray, my love, be so good as to find out if your Papeh, who has evidently *forgotten* to wish me a good-morning, does not intend going to town today!" And when Emmy, sick and trembling, yet with a kind of horrific satisfaction, returned bearing John's brutal reply: "No, not today, nor ever again!" Lizzie, now thoroughly roused, threw on a wrapper and swept down the passage to her husband's room.

On discovering the true state of things she dropped to the floor in a swoon. Restored to consciousness and got back to bed, she fell to screaming in hysterical abandonment—on his arrival the doctor had

HENRY HANDEL RICHARDSON

more to do for her than for John, and pulled a long face. And even when the danger of a premature confinement was over, and the worst of the hysteria got under, she would lie and sob and cry, breaking out, to whoever would listen, in wild accusations.

"Oh, Mary, love! When I think *how* I have been deceived! . . . the trick that has been played on me. . . me who ought to have known before anyone else. John and his secrecy!—he has made a fool of me, even in the eyes of the servants."

"My poor, dear Lizzie! Do believe me, he only wanted to spare you. . . as long as he could. Consider him now, and his sufferings, and don't make it harder for him than you can help. Think, too, of your baby."

But she might as well have talked to a post: Lizzie continued stormily to weep and to rail. The two older women bore patiently with her, even coming to consider it a good thing that she was thus able to vent her emotion. It remained for Emmy, Emmy with the hard and unyoung look her face assumed when she spoke of her stepmother, to make the bitter comment: "She's not really *sorry* for Papa—she's *savage*, Aunt Mary, that's what she is!"—a point of view which Mary herself was so rigidly suppressing that it received but scant quarter. "Emmy, Emmy! You must *not* say such things of your Mamma." But Richard declared the girl had hit the nail on the head. It was herself and herself alone Lizzie grieved for.

"And is it so unnatural? Has Fate not played her a shabby trick? She took John, as we all know, because he was by far the best catch that had ever come her way. Now, after a few brief years of glory, and when her main ambition was about to materialise, the Lady Turnham-to-be sees herself doomed to a widow's dreary existence: all weepers and seclusion: with, for sole diversion, the care of an unwanted infant. Not to speak of the posse of stepdaughters she has loaded herself up with."

"It *does* sound harsh. . . the way you put it," said Mary, and re-tied her bonnet-strings; she had run home one evening for a peep at her children.

However, if he and Emmy were right about Lizzie and her feelings, then what a blessing it was that John, in his illness, made no demands on her, asking neither for nor after her. With his one request on the morning of his collapse, that she should receive first attention, all thought for her seemed exhausted: just as, in the brutal answer he returned her by Emmy, had evaporated his love and care. From the sound of her pitiless crying he turned with repugnance away. Did she enter his room, with a swish of the skirts, either forgetting to lower her voice or hissing in a melodramatic whisper, he was restless till she withdrew. Except for Mary—and he fretted like a child if Mary were long absent—John asked only to be alone.

On taking to his bed he had severed, at one stroke, every link with the outside world: and soon he was to lie drug-sodden and mercifully indifferent even to the small world of his sickroom. But before this happened he expressed one wish—or rather gave a last order. The nature of his illness was not to be made known beyond the family circle.

"Trying to keep his Chinese Wall up to the end," said Mahony. "His death—like his life—is to be nobody's business but his own. Well, well. . . as a man lives so he shall die!"

But Mary was much perturbed. A dying man's whim—and as such, of course, it had to be respected. But what *could* it hurt now whether people knew what was the matter with him or not? Concealing the truth meant all sorts of awkward complications. But Emmy, overhearing this, flushed sensitively and looked distressed. "Oh, Aunt Mary, don't you *see*? Papa is. . . is *ashamed* of having a cancer."

Ashamed? . . . ashamed of an illness? . . . Mary had never heard of such a thing. But Richard, struck afresh by Emmy's acumen, declared: "That's it! The girl is right. You call it a sick man's fancy, I the exaggerated reserve of a lifetime, but Emmy knows better, sees deeper than any of us." And added a moment later: "It strikes me, my dear, that if instead of hankering after that impossible scapegrace of a son, just because he *was* a son, your brother had had a little more eye for the quick wits and understanding of his daughter, he might have been a happier man."

News of the serious illness of the Honourable John Millibank Turnham, M.L.C., brought an endless string of callers and inquirers to the door: the muffled knocker thudded unceasingly. People came in their carriages, on horseback, on foot; and included not merely John's distracted partners, and his colleagues on the Legislative Council, but many a lesser man and casual acquaintance—Mary herself marvelled to see how widely known and respected John had been. And those who could not come in person wrote letters of condolence, sent gifts of luscious fruit and choice flowers and out-of-season delicacies— anything in short of which kindly people could think, to prove their sympathy. It was one person's while to receive the visitors, answer the letters, acknowledge the gifts. Fortunately this very person was at hand

HENRY HANDEL RICHARDSON

in the shape of Zara. Zara's elegant manners and her ease in expressing herself on paper were exactly what was wanted.

She and Hempel were staying in lodgings at Fitzroy, prior to setting out on the forlorn hope of a sea voyage. For, after numerous breakdowns, poor Hempel—he looked as if the first puff of wind would blow him overboard; Richard called him: "The next candidate for the Resurrection!"—had been obliged definitely to abandon his pastorate. In the meantime he was resting in bed from the fatigues of the train journey, before undertaking the fresh fatigues to which Zara, in her wilful blindness, condemned him.

At John's, Zara received in the dining-room among horsehair and mahogany, as better befitting the occasion than the gilt and satin of the drawing-room. Lugubriously clad, she spoke with the pious and resigned air of one about to become a mourner. "My poor brother," "Our great grief," "God's will be done!" But of an evening when the rush was over, she carried to Lizzie a list of names and gifts and a sheaf of letters.

Her sibilant tones were audible through the half-closed door. "Yes, Judge O'Connor—yes, yes, my dear, himself in person! . . . with his own and his lady's compliments. . . desires to be kept informed of our dear John's progress."

And Lizzie's rich, fruity tones: "Major Grenville, did you say? . . . on behalf of his Excellency? Very gratifying. . . very gratifying indeed!"

Mary was never one to jib at trifles. But as often as Emmy heard them at it, she clenched her fist and ground her teeth. *How* she hated them! . . . hated them. To be able to care who called and who didn't call, when Papa lay dying! In her passionate young egoism she demanded that there should be no room in any mind but for this single thought.

But, as week added itself to week, and John still lay prostrate, and since, too, the most heartfelt inquiries evoked none but the stereotyped response: "No improvement," the press of sympathisers visibly declined. People ceased to call daily; came but once a week; then at still wider intervals. And at length even the hardiest dropped off, and a great stillness settled round the dying man. John was forgotten; was reckoned to the dead before he was actually of them. Only once more on earth would he, for a brief hour, play a leading part.

The flawless constitution that had been so great an asset to him in life stood him now in ill stead. His dying was arduous and protracted. Behind the red rep hangings there went on one of those bitter struggles with death that wring from even the least sensitive an amazed: "Wherefore? To what end?" Cried Mahony, watching John's fruitless efforts: "The day will come, I'm sure of it, when we shall agree to the incurable sufferer being put painlessly away. We need a lethal chamber, and not for dumb brutes alone." At which Mary looked apprehensive, and wished he wouldn't. A good job he was no longer in practice. Or what *would* his patients have thought?

"Ah, thank God, the muzzle of medical etiquette is off my jowl!"

Meanwhile, thought his wife, he was in his element, all tenderness and consideration for John—he went to endless trouble in procuring for him the newest make of water-bed—which was just what one would expect of Richard. Nor would he have him teased about religious questions or his approaching end. On the other hand, had John shown the least desire for religious consolation, Richard would have been the person to see that he got it.

But this John did not. At those rare moments when he was awake to his surroundings and tolerably free from pain, he lay exhausted and inert, his eyes closed, and with little to distinguish him from one already dead. What his innermost thoughts were, what his hopes and fears of a hereafter, remained his own secret. The single wish that crossed his lips seemed to point to his mind still occupying itself with earthly things.

Mary, sewing beside the bed, looked up one day to find his sunken eyes open and fastened on her.

She rose and leaned over him. "What is it, John? Do you want anything?"

He signified yes with his lids, sparing himself any superfluous word for fear of rousing up his enemy. Then, in a thick, raucous whisper: "I should like. . . to see. . . the boy. Yours."

Thus it came about—greatly against the wish of Mahony, who held that illness and suffering were evil sights for childish eyes—that Cuffy was one day lifted into the carriage beside Nannan, where he sat his little legs a-dangle, clad in his best velvet tunic and with his Scotch cap on his head. He looked pale and solemn. Nannan and Eliza had made such funny faces at each other, and had whispered and whispered. And while she was dressing him Nannan had talked about nothing but how good and quiet he must be, and what would happen to him if he wasn't. In consequence, directly he was set down from the carriage Cuffy started walking on the tips of his toes; and on tiptoe, holding fast to his nurse's hand, crept laboriously up the gravel path to the house.

HENRY HANDEL RICHARDSON

At the front door stood Cousin Emmy, who kissed him and led him in. Like Nannan she, too, said: "Now you must be a *very* good boy, Cuffy, and not make the least noise." Cuffy's heart began to thump with anxiety: he walked more gingerly than before. The house felt like the nursery when the Dumplings were asleep. Emmy opened a door into a room that was quite dark. It had also a very nasty smell. Someone was snoring. Cuffy tried to pull back.

"Now, be good, Cuffy!"

Then he was at his mother's knee, mechanically holding out his hands to have his little gloves peeled off. But his thoughts were with his eyes—pinned to someone lying in a bed. . . a man with a dark yellow face and a grey beard, who was asleep and snoring—like Nannan did. Cuffy did not associate this funny-looking person with his uncle; he just stood and stared stupidly. Nevertheless, something very disturbing began to go round inside him; and he swallowed hard.

Then two big black shiny eyes were awake and looking at him. They looked and looked. Cuffy stood transfixed, his lips apart, his breath coming unevenly, his own eyes round with a growing fear.

A yellow hand like a claw came over the bedclothes towards him, and someone tried to speak; and only made a funny sound—and tried again.

" . . . does you credit. But. . . at his age. . . John. . . a finer. . . child." After which the eyes shut and the snoring began anew.

Then, though he had only just come, somebody said: "Kiss your uncle goodbye, Cuffy."

This was too much. As he was lifted up Cuffy made protest, wildly working his arms and legs. "No, no!"

But his lips had brushed something cold and clammy before, his clothes all twisted round him, he was put back on the floor. And by then the face on the bed had changed: the eyes were all wrinkles now; the mouth like a big black hole. Somebody screamed. And now people were scurrying about, and there came Aunt Lizzie running in her dressing-gown, and she was naughty and cried, making the noise he had been told not to. His own tears flowed; but true to his promise he did not utter a sound.

Then someone took his hand and ran him out of the room to the dining-room, where, his eyes wiped and his nose blown, Cousin Emmy gave him a nectarine, which she peeled for him and cut up in quarters, because it was "nicer so." He was also allowed to eat it messily, and not scolded for letting the juice drip down his tunic.

But at home again, he felt the need of blowing out his shrunken self-esteem. It was a chance, too, of making himself big in the eyes of his playfellow Josey, the youngest of his three cousins, a long-legged girl of seven, who domineered over him, smacked him and used his toys without asking. There she came along the verandah, dragging his best horse and cart—with her nasty big black eyes, and the hair that stuck straight out behind her round comb.

Under seal of secrecy and with an odd sense of guilt, as if he was doing something he ought not to, Cuffy confided to her his discovery that big people could cry, too. "I seed your Mamma do it."

But in place of being impressed Josey was very angry. Grabbing the secretmonger's silky topknot, she shook him soundly. "That's a storwy, Cuffy Mahony, and you're a howwid storwy-teller! Gwownup people *never* cwy!" The fact that she spoke with a strong lisp, while a baby like Cuffy would talk plainly, always rendered Josey very emphatic. Moreover in the present case, she still burned with shame at the disgraceful knowledge that not only Mamma could cry, but Papa, too.

John died five days later at midnight.

The afternoon before, an odd thing happened. Mary and Emmy were alone with him, he lying drugged and comatose, and Mary had been fanning him, for it was very warm. Outside, beneath a copper-coloured sky, a scorching north wind blew; the windows of the room were shut against swirling clouds of dust. There was no sound but John's laboured breathing, and, exhausted, Mary thought she must have dropped into a doze. For when, warned by a kind of instinct she started up, she saw that John's eyes were open: he was gazing with a glassy stare at the foot-end of the bed. And as she watched, an extraordinary change came over the shrunken, jaundiced face. The eyes widened, the pin-hole pupils dilated; while the poor, burst lips, on which were black sores that would not heal, parted and drew back, disclosing the pallid flesh of the gums. John was trying to smile.

A second later and the whole face was transfigured—lit by an expression of rapturous joy. John even made an abortive effort to raise himself—to hold out his arms. His breath came sobbingly.

"Emma! Oh, *Emma! . . . Wife!*"

At first sound of her name, Emmy sprang from her seat behind the curtains and threw herself on her knees at the bedside, close to John's groping hand. "Papa! . . . yes, oh yes? Oh, papa. . . *darling!*"

But John did not hear her. All the life left him was centred in his eyes, which hung, dazed with wonder, on something visible to them alone. Bending over the passionately weeping girl Mary whispered: "Hush, hush, Emmy! Hush, my dear! He sees. . . he thinks he sees your mother."

Mahony knew nothing of this occurrence till long after. By the time he got there that evening, the death-agony had begun; and now the one thought of those gathered round John's bed was to ease and speed his passing. It was a murderous business. For the drug that had thus far blunted the red-hot knives that hacked at his vitals suddenly lost its power: injections now gave relief but for a few moments on end; and, hour after hour, hour after hour, his heart-breaking cry for help beat the air. "Morphia. . . morphia! For God's sake, morphia!"

But the kindly, bearded physician who sat with a finger on John's wrist remained impassive: the dose now necessary to reduce the paroxysms would be more than the weakened heart could bear. And so, livid, drenched in sweat, John fought his way to death through tortures indescribable.

At the end of the afternoon those present felt that the limits of human endurance had been reached. All eyes hung on the doctor's, with the same mute appeal. The two men, Mahony and the other, exchanged a rapid glance. Then, bending over the writhing anguished thing that had once been John Turnham, the doctor addressed it by name. "Mr. Turnham; you are in your right mind. . . and fully aware of what you are saying. Do you take the injection necessary to relieve you, of your own free will and at your own risk?"

"For the love of God!"

A moment's stir and business, and the blessed sedative was running through the quivering veins, the last excruciating pangs were throbbing with hammer-strokes to their end: upwards from the feet crept the blissful numbness. . . rising higher. . . higher. . . higher. And, as peace descended and the heavy lids fell to, Mahony stepped forward, and taking one of the dying hands in his said in a loud, clear voice: "Have no fear of death, John!"

Already floating out on the great river, John yet heard these words and was arrested by them. Slowly the lids rolled back once more, and for the fraction of a second the broken eyes met Mahony's. In this, their last, living look, not a trace was left of the man who had been. They were now those of one who was about to be—fined and refined; rich in an experience that transcended all mortal happenings; wise with an ageless wisdom. And as they closed forever to this world, there came an answer to Mahony's words in ever so faint a flattening of the lips, an almost imperceptible intake at the corners of the mouth, which, on the sleeping face, had the effect of a smile: that lurking smile, remote with peace, and yet touched with the lightest suspicion of amused wonder, that sometimes makes the faces of the dead so good to see.

John did not wake again. Towards midnight his breathing grew more stertorous, the intervals between the breaths longer. And at last the moment came when the watchers waited for the next. . . and waited. . . in vain.

All was over; the poor weeping, shattered women were led from the room. Mary, despite her grief, kept her presence of mind, and Miss Julia with her. But Lizzie was convulsed; and poor little Emmy, her long service ended, broke down utterly and had to be carried to bed, and chafed, and dosed with restoratives. Zara was bidden see to the children, John's three, who had been brought over during the afternoon in case their father should ask for them: forgotten, hungry, tired, they had cried themselves to sleep, and now lay huddled in a tear-stained group on the dining-room sofa. Mahony and the doctor busied themselves for yet a while in the death-chamber; after which, decently composed and arranged, John formed no more than a sheet-draped rising on the bed's smooth plain. Mahony locked the door behind him and took the key. The dogcart had come round, and Jerry, who was to drive back to town with the doctor, stood, his collar turned up, all of a fidget to get home to Fanny and his children. Mahony went out with them and, having watched them drive off, paused to breathe the night air, which was fresh and welcome after the fetid odours of the sickroom. And standing there under the stars he sent, like an arrow of farewell, a parting thought to the soul that might even now be winging its way to freedom, and to whom soon all mysteries would be plain. John had made a brave end. There had been no whining for pity or pardon: on his own responsibility he had lived, and he died by the same rule—the good Turnham blood had come out in him to the last. And as he re-entered the house, where, by now, the last exhausted watcher was sinking into unconsciousness, Mahony murmured half-aloud to himself: "Well done, John. . . well done!"

VI

S ome six months later the Mahonys set out on their second voyage to England. They sailed by the clipper-ship *Atrata* and travelled in style, accompanied by a maid to attend to Mary and both nurses.—And "Ultima Thule" passed into other hands.

It had proved easier to persuade Mary to the break than Mahony had dared to hope. John's illness and death paved the way. For, by the time her long vigil at his bedside was over, and Lizzie seen safely through a difficult confinement, Mary's own health was beginning to suffer. A series of obstinate coughs and colds plagued her; and a thorough change of air was advisable. A change of scene, too. Though Mary was not given to moping and, at the time, had thankfully accepted John's release, yet when it came to taking up her ordinary life again the full sense of her loss came home to her. And not to her alone but to everyone. John's had been such a vigorous personality. Its withdrawal left a gap nothing could fill.

None the less, the sacrifice she was now called on to make was a bitter one, and cost her much heartburning: when she first grasped the *kind* of change Richard was tentatively proposing, she burst into heated exclamation. What, break up their home again? . . . their lovely home? Leave all the things they had collected round them? Leave intimates and friends and their assured position? . . . to go off no one knew where. . . and where nobody knew them? Oh, he couldn't mean it!—And what about the children? . . . still mere babies—"For though you talked till you were black in the face, Richard, you would never get me to leave them behind!"—and the drawbacks of ship-life for them at their tender age? . . . the upset in their habits. . . not to speak of having to watch them grow spoilt and fractious: winding up with her dread of the sea, his antipathy to England and English life.

But Mahony, though he spoke soothingly, stuck to his guns. It was only to be a visit this time, he urged. It could hardly hurt the house to be let for a year or so. A good tenant would take good care of it; and it would be there, just as it stood, for them to come back to. Then both nurses would go with them; and as for the darlings being too young for a voyage, that was the sheerest nonsense: on the contrary, it would do them a world of good; perhaps even turn Cuffy into a sturdy boy. The same could be said for her own ailments: there was nothing like the briny for laying coughs and colds; while the best cabin in the ship would go far towards lessening the horrors of sea-sickness. As for England, they would not know it for the same country, travelling as they did today. Plenty of money, introductions to good people, going everywhere, seeing everything; and ending up, if she felt disposed, with a jaunt to the Paris Exhibition and a tour of the Continent. "It isn't every wife, my dear, has such an offer made her."

But his words fell flat: Mary only shrugged her shoulders in reply. Tours and exhibitions meant nothing to her. She hadn't the least desire to travel—or at any rate to go farther afield than Sydney or Tasmania. She had been so happy here... so perfectly happy! Why, oh why, could Richard not be content? And that he could forget so easily how he had hated England... and disliked the English... well, no, she must be fair to him. As he said, life over there would be a very different thing now they had money. (Though all the money in the world wouldn't stop it raining!) He might also be right about the voyage doing the chicks good; and it would certainly give them, tiny tots though they were, just that something which colonial-bred children lacked. But oh, her home!... her beautiful home. To have to hand it over to strangers, have strangers tramping on your best carpets, sleeping in your beds, using your egg-shell china—even the best of tenants would not care for the things as she did. She had asked nothing better than to spend the rest of her life at "Ultima Thule"; and here now came Richard, for whom even a few years of it had proved too many. Luxury and comfort, or poverty and hard work, it did not seem to matter which: the root of the evil lay in himself. On the other hand she mustn't forget how splendidly he had behaved over John's illness: never grumbling at her long absences, or at being left to the tender mercies of the servants. Many another husband might have said: let them hire someone to do their nursing, and not wear out my wife over it! But Richard wasn't like that.

And her first heat cooled, wiser counsels prevailed; the end of which was a sturdy resolve to smother her own feelings and think only of him. Two considerations finally turned the scale. One was that when, with Lizzie's convalescence, she was free to return home, she had a nasty shock at the state in which she found Richard. Without her to nag at him and rout him out, he had let himself go as never before: he had forgotten to change his under-clothing or have his hair cut; had neglected his meals, neglected the children—lost interest even in his beloved garden. And for all this they had to thank that horrid spiritualism! During the last few months it had come to be a perfect obsession with him; and from a tolerably clear-headed person he had turned into a bundle of credulous superstition. He actually sat for as long as an hour at a time, with a pencil in his hand, waiting for it to write by itself—write messages from the dead. . . and wasn't he angry when she laughed at him!

This was one thing—the chance for him of a complete break with all such nonsense. Again, coming back to him as it were with fresh eyes, she saw that he was beginning to look very elderly. He seemed to be growing downwards, losing his height, through always sitting crouched over books; and the fair silky hair at his temples was quite silvery now, did you peer closely at it. It was hard to think of Richard as old. . . and him still well under fifty. Yet the coming on of age might account for much. Elderly people did settle into ruts; and, once fixed in them, were impossible to move. Perhaps his present morbid hankering after change was a kind of warning from something inside him to shake himself up and get out of his groove before it was too late. In which case it would be folly and worse than folly, on her part, to try to prevent him.

For his sake then and for his alone. When it came to a question of Richard's welfare, all other considerations went by the board. One condition, though, she did stand out for, and that was, the house should not be let to anyone, no matter whom, for longer than a year. By then, she was positive, Richard would have had his fill of travelling, with the varied discomforts it implied, and be thankful to get back to his own dear home.

Thus it came that "Ultima Thule" was put into an agent's hands, and Mary fell to sorting and packing and making her preparations for the long sea voyage. Not the least of these was fitting the three children out anew from top to toe. Richard had forbidden them even an armband as mourning for their uncle—he was never done railing at Lizzie for having turned John's three into little walking mountains of bombazine and crepe. So Mary was free to indulge her love for dainty stuffs and pretty colours. And, thought she, if ever children paid for dressing hers did. The Dumplings were by now lovely, fair-haired, blue-eyed three-year-olds, with serious red mouths and firm chubby legs. They prattled the livelong day; loved and were loved by everyone. Cuffy, dark, slim, retiring, formed just the right contrast. People often stopped nurse to ask whose children they were. And on this, their first excursion into the big world, nobody should be able to say they were not the best-dressed, best-cared-for children on the ship!

Before, however, a suitable tenant for the house had been found—Richard turned up his nose at everyone who had so far looked over it (when it came to the point he was the fastidious one of the two)—before anything had been fixed, a note came from Tilly saying she and Purdy had travelled down from Ballarat overnight, and were putting up at "Scott's." So after breakfast Mary on with her bonnet and drove to town.

She found Tilly in a fine sitting-room on the first floor of the hotel, looking very, very prosperous. . . all silk and bugles. Purdy was out, on the business that had brought him to town: "So we two have all the morning, love, to jaw in." As she spoke, Tilly whipped off Mary's bonnet and mantle and carried them to the bedroom, supplying Mary meanwhile with one of her own caps, lest anyone should enter the room and find her with a bare pate. Then, a second chair having been drawn up for her to put her feet on, a table with cake and wine set at her elbow, they were free to fall to work. They had not met since Tilly's wedding; and Mary had now to tell the whole sad story of John's illness and death, starting from the night on which he had unexpectedly come to consult Richard, and not omitting his queer hallucination the day before he died (an incident she had so far religiously kept from Richard, as only too likely to encourage his present craze). Next they discussed Lizzie, her behaviour during John's illness, her attitude to the children and the birth of her boy—a peevish, puny infant to whom, much against her inclination, she thinking the world of her own family and little of any other, she had been induced to give John's name. And then John's will, "John's infamous will!" as Richard called it, by which Lizzie was left sole executrix, and trustee of Emmy and the little girls' money (five thousand apiece), with free use of the interest so long as she provided a home for them under her roof. "Which, as you can see, Tilly, is about as foolish a condition as the poor fellow could well have made."

Tilly nodded; but suppressed the: "Yes, but oh how like 'im!" that jumped to her lips, on the principle of not picking holes in the dead. "But what about if Madam marries again. . . eh, Mary? How then?"

Mary nodded ruefully. "Why, then it's the usual thing: she's cut off with a penny; most of her money goes to the boy; and Richard and Jerry become trustees in her stead." But, extenuating where Tilly had suppressed, Mary added: "You must remember the will was drawn up directly after marriage, when John was still very much in love."

"Lor', Mary, *what* a picnic!" said Tilly, and sagely wagged her head. "My dear, can't you see 'em? Madam, gone sour as curds, clinging like grim death to 'er posse of old maids! Poor old Jinn! Poor little kids! Caught like fishes in a net."

"Yes, well, except that. . . as Richard says. . . it's very unlikely. . ."

Their eyes met.

"Why, yes, I suppose it is," said Tilly dryly.

Thence they passed to their own affairs; and Mary told of the fresh uprootal that was in store for her—and, over the telling, let out some of the exasperation that burned in her at the prospect. Tilly was the one person who would understand what it meant; to whom she could utter a word of complaint. To the world at large Richard and she must, and would, always present a united front.

Said she: "Oh, I *did* think this time, Tilly, he would be content; when he'd got everything he could possibly wish for. It was a different matter him leaving Ballarat—and I couldn't blame him myself for not wanting to settle permanently in England. But here. . . our nice house. . . his library. . . the garden. . . And the stupid part of it is I know he'll regret it. . . tire of being on the move long before we can get back into the house. I'm making up my mind to *that*, before I start."

"Poor old girl! You do have a tough time of it."

"Besides, there are the chicks to think of now as well. Their father says the voyage will do them good, and he may be right. But the voyage isn't everything. What about the change of climate for them while they're so small?—going over into the cold as we shall do. Then, travelling isn't the thing for little children—you know what an excitable child Cuffy is.—Besides, just think what it's going to cost us, with three servants, renting a furnished house in London, making a tour of the Continent and all the rest of it. Richard has such grand notions nowadays. Economy's a word that has ceased to exist for him. The money's there and it's to be spent, and that's the end of it. But it does sometimes seem. . . I mean I can't help feeling it would be better if I had some idea what we've got and how it goes."

But having opened her heart thus, Mary came to a stop: there were things she drew the line at touching on, and though her hearer was only Tilly. You did not, even to your dearest friend, belabour the point that your husband was growing old and rusty, stiff in body and in mind. You locked the knowledge up, with a pang, inside your own heart. Again, Tilly had always made such game of spiritualism. Did she now hear that, from an interested inquirer, Richard had become an out-and-out adherent, accepting as gospel the rubbish its devotees talked, attending sittings which opened with prayers and hymns, just as if they were trying to take the place of going to church—why, at this, Tilly would certainly tap her forehead and make significant eyes, imagining goodness only knew what. So Mary kept a wifely silence.

Besides, it was Tilly's turn now to talk. Tilly had brought a rare budget of gossip with her from the old home; and no one could give this in racier, more entertaining fashion than she. Mary listened and laughed, throwing in a reproving: "Now, *really*, Tilly!" at some of the speaker's most daring shots; growing grave-eyed were the tragedies alluded to that underlay many a prosperous exterior.

Not till all the old friends had been asked after, did she press nearer home. "And now, Tilly, how about yourself, my dear? Are you. . . has it. . . come! you know what I mean!"

Tilly laughed out loud. "Indeed and it has, old girl!—and no apologies needed. Yes, love, the very best of husbands. But I was right as rain, Mary, in what I said beforehand—no spendthrift as I'm alive! Why, 'e even goes to the other extreme, love, and holds the purse-strings a bit tighter than yours truly 'as been used to. Though it's not for me to complain, my dear, considering 'ow he handles money. I'm still a bit dazed by it myself. A born knack with the shekels, and that's the truth! I declare to you, old Pa's leavings have almost *doubled* in these six months. Purd's got a sort of second-sight, which tells 'im to the minute what o'clock it is. All that was wrong with him, Mary, was never having enough of the needful to show what 'e was made of."

"Well, I *am* glad to hear that—I am indeed!"

She went home full of the news. "We were both wrong, you see."

But it would not have been Richard if he hadn't made ironical remarks. Wait till the bloom was off the grapes, said he, and then see how the land lay. For, if Purdy had started speculating already. . . "Ah, but Tilly says he has a kind of sixth sense for the ups and downs of the market."

"Many a wife thinks the same, till the crash comes. But you know *my* opinion of the national vice."

"Well, you'll be able to judge for yourself. I've asked them to dinner this evening."

"Oh, deuce take it! Have we really got to have them here?"

"Now, Richard. . . when Tilly's in town for the first time since her wedding. Certainly we have. Besides, I know you'll be interested to see what marriage has done for Purdy."

"Oh Lord, Mary! Am I not at my time of life allowed to know what interests me and what doesn't?"

"Well, I shan't see Tilly again forever so long. I do beg you to be nice to her, dear. . . to both of them," said Mary.

And when the time came he was. . . of course he was: with the near prospect of escape from people, Richard invariably found it easy to be charming to them. Another thing, she had pandered to his weak side by preparing a very choice little dinner; and she wore one of his favourite dresses—a black velvet gown, with jet trimmings, cut square at the neck.

But without a doubt, the main reason for his amiability was the immense improvement that had taken place in Purdy: it was noticeable even as the latter entered the drawing-room. In appearance he would, it was true, never be very much, what with his limp, and so on; and his lack of distinction was doubly remarkable when Richard was present, who was so slender and aristocratic-looking. But his aggressiveness had gone; he was no longer up in arms against the world. Gone, too, was the dreadful boasting that had so set Richard against him; and he had quite given over telling tiresome stories. . . thanks, thought Mary, to having married one of the most sensible of women. At the single threatened lapse into his old tone, she distinctly felt Tilly seek and find his foot beneath the table.

"Didn't I say she'd pull him into shape?" and: "Upon my word, wife, if ever there was an exploded notion, it is that the possession of this world's goods makes for evil. Why, there was actually a trace of his old self about the fellow tonight."

The ormolu clock on the drawing-room mantelpiece had just chimed eleven. Mary was giving her toes a final toast before retiring, Richard securing the hasps and bolts of shutters and French windows.

"Yes, indeed," agreed Mary; but with an absent air. She was thinking of Tilly—dear old Tilly—in whom the change had been no less marked. Looking very buxom and rather handsome in magenta velvet, Tilly had sat smiling broadly, but with less to say for herself than ever in her life before. Instead of paying attention to Richard, as she ought to have done, she had all the time been listening to Purdy, drinking in his words, and signing to Mary to listen, too, by many a private tilt of the brows. So palpably eager was she for him to shine that she had been unable to resist breaking in with a: "Oh, come now, Purd, take a *leetle* bit of the credit to yourself!—it was his doing really, Mary, and no one else's, though 'e tries now to make out it was Blake's." And at Purdy's: "Forgive my old woman's dotage, you two. . . it's still kissing-time with us, you know!"—at this Tilly had smirked and blushed like a sixteen-year-old.

Meanwhile Richard was saying from the hearthrug, where he stood nursing his coat-tails: " . . . an interesting chat after you had left the room, my dear. I was hearing all about the Mitcham case from within—the big mining suit, you know, that has created such a scandal in Ballarat. . . you must remember old Grenville of Canterbury Station, his deafness and his expletives, and those enormous black cigars—he always had one stuck in the corner of his mouth when he drove his four-in-hand to town."

"Of course I do. A very kind old gentleman I thought him."

"Yes. . . he had rather a way with the ladies.—Well, as I was saying, this fellow Blake Purdy swears by was one of the partners in the company formed after old G. had sold his mine—at a dead loss, mind you, and on the express advice of his confidential manager, who, directly after, became a promoter of the new company. When the output suddenly redoubled and the shares began to soar, old Grenville, naturally enough, thought he had been done, and sued them for fraud. The jury could not agree. Now, there's rumour of a settlement. If it takes place, it is calculated that the shares will rise in value by two to three hundred percent. Purdy stands to make his fortune—thanks to having someone at his elbow who is in the swim."

But Mary pursed her lips and looked dubious. "Well, I don't know, Richard. . . I must say it sounds to me rather shady."

"Hm. . . well, myself I prefer to keep clear of that sort of thing. All the same, Mary, I couldn't help thinking what a terrible slowcoach old Simmonds is, compared with these modern brokers one hears of. One never gets any inside information from him—for the very good reason that he doesn't know it himself."

"But so honest and trustworthy!"

"Oh, yes, there's that about it," said Richard, a trifle morosely Mary thought.

"And what do you say to the house? Wasn't it a funny thing Purdy tumbling across someone, like that?" she hastened to add, in an attempt to divert his mind from old Simmonds's shortcomings.

"A stroke of luck of the first order!"

For amongst other news Purdy had had a titbit for them. Only that very day, it seemed, in the coffee-room of the hotel, he had run up against a squatter from Darumbooli who was on the look-out for a furnished house, standing in its own grounds and not too far from the sea, where he could settle wife and daughters while the latter attended a finishing school. Purdy had at once thought of "Ultima Thule" and extolled its beauties: its lawns and shrubberies and fruit gardens, its proximity to the sea. The squatter had pricked up his ears and, if they agreed, would come out to see it early next morning.

Whereupon the last trace of Mahony's starchedness had melted, in a glow of gratitude and content.

"Upon my word, Mary, it sounds the very thing, at last!"

VII

That night he could not sleep. To begin with, he had been unused of late to an evening's talk: bits and scraps of it went on buzzing round his brain, long after he lay abed. Then, something he had eaten had disagreed with him: Cook's short-crust must have been too rich, or the pears over-ripe. He tossed and turned, to the disturbance of poor Mary; tried lying high, lying low, counting sheep and other silly tricks, all to no purpose: before an hour had passed, the black thoughts of the night—those sinister imaginings born of darkness and immobility—had him in their grip.

Their approach was stealthy. For he had gone to bed in high feather at the prospect of at last securing a tenant. Weeks had dragged by, and the house was still unlet. He fumed as often as he thought of it. To put a house like his on the market and get no offers for it! Sell? . . . yes; he could have sold three times over. But the idea of renting a place ready furnished seemed not to enter the colonial mind. Now, however, if Purdy was to be trusted. . . A rich squatter, too. . . willing no doubt to pay a good price for a good thing—though this condition was not, God be thanked, the *sine qua non* it would once have been. Still, money was money; you could not have too much of it. . . especially here. Give a man means and you gave him friends and favours, and a rank second to none. To take a petty instance: what had money not done for the very person they had had before their eyes that evening? From the seedy little down-at-heel of a year back, Purdy had been metamorphosed into. . . well, at least rendered presentable enough to bid to your table. Money had restored his shrunken self-respect. It had also brought out in him talents which not his oldest friends had guessed at. That Purdy, of all people, should prove a dabster in the share-market!—exchange to such good purpose bar-parlour for "Corner." No doubt the years he had spent hobnobbing with every variety of individual had sharpened his wits. You saw something of that in the shrewd choice he had made of a broker. For, three parts of the game, did you enter the big gamble, depended on having a wide-awake adviser at your elbow. And this man Blake, of whom they had heard so much that night, did actually seem to be one in a thousand.

One in a thousand. . . one in a thousand. . . a thousand. . . Mahony was on the point of dropping off, to the rhythm of these words, when

HENRY HANDEL RICHARDSON

a vague uneasiness began to stir in him; more exactly, when he became abruptly aware that, deep down in him, a nagging anxiety had for sometime been at work. Coming to with a jerk, he sent his thoughts back over the evening. What was it? . . . what had happened to prick him, when all had seemed to go so smoothly? He groped and groped. Then. . . ha! . . . he had it. Simmonds. The name whizzed into his mind like a dart; like a dart stuck there, and was not to be plucked out. And no sooner had he found this clue than, with a rush, a swarm of vexatious thoughts and impressions was upon him. His apparent good spirits were all humbug; at heart he had been depressed by the tale of Purdy's successes. They had made him feel a back number, an old fossil, who had to learn from someone he had always looked down on as his inferior, what was actually happening in the financial world. And for this he held Simmonds to blame. What was the use of a confidential agent who did not keep you up to the mark?—Not that he wanted to speculate; or at least not as the word was here understood. But he wished to feel that he *could* have done so, and with as much aplomb as anybody, did the fit take him. And brooding over the chances he had no doubt missed and even at this moment might be missing: at a picture of himself lying high and dry, while one and another—mere whipper-snappers like Purdy—floated easily out to fortune, an acute irritation mastered him.

He turned his pillow, and, even as he did so, told himself that the fault had been not Simmonds's, but his own. Yes, the truth was, he had had no ambition. Otherwise, why have laid his affairs in the hands of such a humdrum?—and, what was worse, have left them there. Honest?—yes: but so was many a noodle honest: and in these new countries honesty alone, unbacked by anymore worldly qualities, stood not an earthly chance. And again a vision danced before his closed lids. He saw the thousands he had failed to make—thousands that grew to hundreds of thousands as he watched—fluttering just beyond *his* grasp, though within easy reach of others. And now, to sting him, the earlier bitterness returned. . . in the form of a galling envy. To see Purdy, the foolish harum-scarum, the confessed failure, the mean little *commis voyageur*—to see such a one about to pass, surpass him, in means and influence: this was surely one of the bitterest mouthfuls he had ever had to swallow.

And here, seizing its chance, a further fear insinuated itself. What if it should not end with this? Simmonds being what he was, might he not fail in other ways as well?—let what he already held slip through his fingers, and he, Mahony, wake one morning to find himself a poor man? A shiver ran down his spine at the thought, and he made a feverish movement: he would have liked to throw off the bedclothes, and go hotfoot to call Simmonds to account. Since he was condemned to lie like a log, his imagination did the work for him, running riot in a series of pictures. . . till cold drops stood out on his forehead.

Sitting up he fumbled for a handkerchief. The change of position brought him a moment's calmness. Good Lord, what was he doing. . . working himself into such a state. It was like those bad old times when he had had to worry himself half to death about money. . . or the lack of it. He drank a glass of water, and rolled over on his other side.

Scarcely, however, had his head touched the pillow when he was off again, stabbed by yet another nightmare thought. What if it should be a case of fraud on Simmonds's part? Might not the lethargy, the stolid honesty be but a pose?—the cloak to cover a rascally activity? Like the confidential agent whose double-dealing they had heard of that night, it would be child's play for Simmonds, just because he appeared so straight and aboveboard, to fleece his clients—or at least such among them as gave him the open chances he, Mahony, had. Careless, distraught, interested in everything rather than in money, he had ambled along unthinking as a babe, leaving Simmonds to his own devices for months, nay, years, at a time. Now, he could not wait for daylight to get his affairs back into his own hands. If only he were not too late!—And thus on and on, ever deeper into the night, his suspicions growing steadily more sinister, till there was no crime of which he was not ready to suspect his man of business. A dozen times he had trapped him, unmasked him, brought him to justice, before he fell into a feverish doze, in which not Simmonds but himself was the fugitive, hunted by two monstrous shadow policemen who believed him criminal before the law. Waking with a terrific start he pulled himself together, only at once to sink back in dream. This time, he was being led by Purdy and someone strangely resembling that bottle-nosed Robinson who had played him a dirty trick over an English practice, to a cemetery, where stood a tombstone bearing Simmonds's name. Why, good Lord! the fellow's dead. . . dead? . . . and what of me? "Who's got my money? Where is it? Where am I?" cried Mahony aloud—and woke at the sound of his own voice to see pale lines of light creeping in at the sides of the windows. His pulse was bounding, Mary sleepily murmuring: "Oh dear, oh dear, what *is* the matter?"—Rising, he opened a window and stuck his hot head out in the morning air.

At breakfast-time he emerged pale and peevish, to a day that proved hardly less wearing than the night had been. One, too, that called for a clear brain and prompt decisions. For the owner of Darumbooli, Baillie by name, put in an appearance as arranged—an elderly Scot, tanned, sun-wrinkled, grey-whiskered, with a bluff yet urbane manner—a self-made man, it was plain, and wholly unlettered, but frank, generous, honourable: one of nature's gentlemen, in short, and of a type Mahony invariably found it easy to do business with. Better still, he turned out to be one of your genuine garden-lovers: as the pair of them walked the grounds of "Ultima Thule," none of the details and improvements Mahony felt proudest of but was observed and bespoken: the white-strawberry bed, the oleander grove, the fernery, the exquisitely smooth buffalo-grass lawns on which sprays were kept playing. A good garden was, it seemed, a desideratum with Baillie. And he fell in love with Mahony's at first sight.

But. . . yes, yes! now came the fly in the ointment. . . he wished not to rent but to buy: had never, he averred, had any idea of renting a house: it was entirely "that fellow Smith's mistake" ("all Purdy's muddle!"). The schooling proved another bit of fiction. His daughters were past their school years; of an age to be launched in society. Darumbooli was up for sale—Baillie had already refused a bid of ninety thousand—and planned from now on to settle in Melbourne.

Having thus cleared the air and added that, only the day before, he had seen a house at Toorak which, though not a patch on this, would serve his purpose, he offered a sum for "Ultima Thule," just as it stood, with all its contents, which sent Mahony's eyebrows half-way up his forehead.

Mary was speechless when she heard the upshot of the interview; when, too, she saw that Richard's mind—that mind which seemed unable to hold fast to any mortal thing for long together—was more than three parts made up to accept Baillie's offer. And too discomfited to meet this Irish fluidity with her usual wily caution, she no sooner found her voice than she cried: "Oh, Richard, *no!*—that we *can't* do. . . we really can't! Think of all the things we got specially out from home. . . the French tapestry. . . the carpets. . . and. . . and everything!"

Tch! now he had this to go through. . . on top of his bad night, and his own burning irresolution. His nerves felt like the frayed ends of a rope. But as usual opposition spurred him on.

"But, my dear, with such a sum at our disposal, we shall be able to furnish our *next* house ten times as well. Look here, Mary, I tell you what we'll do. We'll bring every atom of stuff out with us, from London or Paris: the very newest of everything—there won't be a house in the colony like it."

"Oh, Richard! . . . oh, I *do* think—" For an instant bitterness choked Mary. Then, she could not resist pricking him with a: "And have *you* decided to let all your books go, as well?"

"My books? Most certainly not! I made that clear on the spot.—But how absurd, Mary! What would a man whose whole life has been spent among sheep and cattle do with my volumes of physic and metaphysics?" But Mary put on her obstinate face. "Well, my things mean just as much to me as yours to you."

"Now for goodness sake, my dear, be reasonable!" cried Richard, growing excessively heated. "I suppose even a squatter can use a chair or a sofa; needs a bed and a table; but what, I ask you, would he make of Lavater? . . . or the Church Fathers?"

"It's always the same. I'm to give up everything, you nothing.—But if my wishes and feelings can be trampled on, don't you care about the children? . . . I mean about them all having been born here?"

"Indeed and I do not! I would no more have them tie their feelings to the shell of a house than I'd have mourners hang round a grave."

"Oh, there's no talking to you nowadays, your head's so full of windy stuff. But I tell you this, Richard, I refuse to have my children dragged from place to place. . . as I've been. It's not as if it's ever helped a bit either, our giving up home after home. You're always wild, at the moment, to get away, but afterwards you're no happier than you were before. And then, what makes me so angry, you let yourself be influenced by such silly, trivial things. I believe you're ready to sell this house just because you *like* the man who wants to buy it, or because he's praised up the garden. But you'll be sorry for it, I know you will, before three months are out. I haven't lived with you all these years for nothing."

"Oh well, my dear," said Mahony darkly, "I'm an old man now, and you won't be troubled with me much longer. When I'm gone you'll be able to do just as you please."

Mary's black eyes flashed, and her lips opened to a sharp retort; then she snapped them to, and said nothing. For to this there could be no real reply; and Richard knew it.

The bargain struck—for struck of course it was, as she had seen from the first it would be: thereafter it only remained for Mary to apply her age-old remedy, and make the best of a very bad job. But the present was by so much the most unreasonable thing Richard had ever done, and she herself felt so sore and exasperated over it, that not for several days was she cool enough to discuss the matter with him. Then, however, each coming half-way to meet the other, they had a long talk, in the course of which Mahony sought to make amends by letting her into some of his money secrets, and she extracted a solemn promise that, except for a mere fringe—a couple of thousand, say, for travelling and other immediate expenses—the sum he was receiving (it ran to five figures) should be kept for the purpose of setting them up anew on their return to the colony. Mahony bade her make her mind easy. They ought to be able to live as comfortably on their dividends in England, as here; and the price paid for "Ultima Thule" should be faithfully laid by for the purpose of building, when they came back, the house that would form their permanent home. "For by then my travelling days will be over. We'll plan it together, love, every inch of it; and it will be more our own than any house we've lived in."

"Yes, I dare say." But Mary's tone lacked warmth, was rich in incredulity.

VIII

And now for Simmonds.

As he made ready to go to town Mahony recalled, with a smile, his grotesque imaginings of two nights back. What a little hell the mind could create for a man's undoing! But none the less, though he now ridiculed them, his nightmares had left a kind of tingling disquietude in their train. He felt he would do well to have a straight talk with Simmonds, go carefully through his share-list, and arrange in detail for the conduct of his affairs during his absence.

He went off jauntily enough. "Don't expect me till about six."

But not a couple of hours later, as Mary was on her knees before a drawer of the great wardrobe she was beginning to dismantle, she heard his foot on the verandah, and the next moment his voice, sharp, querulent, distracted, cried: "Mary! Mary, where are you?"

"Yes, dear? I'm coming. Why, Richard, whatever is wrong now?" For with a despairing gesture Mahony had tossed his hat on the hall-table, and himself dropped heavily on a chair.

"You may well ask. Here's a pretty kettle of fish! It's all over now with our getting away."

"What do you mean? But not here. The servants. . . Come into the bedroom. Well, you do look hot and tired."

She brought him a glass of water, and while he sat and sipped this, she listened to his story; listened, and put two and two together. Arrived at his agent's office in Great Bourke Street, he had found to his surprise and annoyance that Simmonds was absent from business. Worse still, had been, for over two months. He was ill, bedridden—yes, seriously ill. "Confound the fellow! I believe he means to die, just to inconvenience me. Mary! my dream the other night. . . it flashed across me as I walked home. Depend upon it, one doesn't dream that kind of thing for nothing." Richard's tone was full of gloomiest foreboding.

"What nonsense, dear! How can you be so silly!"

In place of Simmonds he had been met by a. . . well, by a sort of clerk, who was in charge—at least he presumed so: he had never set eyes on the fellow before, and never meant to again, if he could help it! "To find a par to his behaviour, Mary, you would need to go back to the early days, when every scoundrelly Tom, Dick and Harry thought himself your equal."

"What did he say?"

Say? Well, first, it was plain to Mary, he had not known from Adam who Richard was. Without getting up from his chair, not troubling to take his head out of a newspaper, he had asked the intruder's pleasure in the free-and-easy colonial fashion which, long as he had lived there, Richard had never learned to swallow. Besides, not to be recognised in a place he honoured with his patronage was in itself a source of offence. Haughtily presenting his card (which, she could see, had lamentably failed to produce an effect), he demanded to speak to Simmonds, with whom he had important business.

"Pray, what answer do you think I got? In a voice, my dear, the twang of which you could have cut with a knife, I was informed: 'Well, in that case, doc., I guess you'll have to keep it snug—locked up in your own bosom, so to say! For the boss lies sick abed, and all the business in the world wouldn't get him up from it.' Whereupon I clapped on my hat and walked out of the place! In which, as long as Simmonds is away, I shall not set foot again. But now, as you can see, we're in a pretty fix. All our plans knocked on the head! The house sold, the agreement signed—or as good as signed. . . it's utterly impossible to draw back. Why the deuce was I in such a hurry? We shall have to go into apartments, Mary—take the children into common lodgings. Good God! Such a thing is not to be contemplated for a moment."

Mary let him talk; listened to this and much more before she threw in a mild: "We'll take a furnished house. There'd be nothing common about that.—All the same, I don't believe Simmonds, who has always been so straight, would put anyone in to look after things who wasn't honest, too—in spite of uncouth behaviour. And you can't refuse to deal with a person just because he has no manners. . . and doesn't know how to address you."

"My dear Mary, it has been a one-man show all these years; and the probability is, when the old fellow broke down he had no one to turn to. But I can assure you, if I left my investments in such hands I shouldn't know a moment's peace all the time I was away. Besides, if he does die, the whole concern will probably go smash."

Oh, the fuss and the flutter! As if it wasn't bad enough to have your house sold over your head, without this fresh commotion on top of it. There must surely be something very slipshod and muddle-headed about the way Richard managed his affairs. She didn't say so, but, had she been in his shoes, she would have known long ago of Simmonds's illness. As it was, this clerk might have been cheating the clients right and left. But anything to do with money (except, of course, the spending of it!) had of late years become anathema to Richard.

Now he went about with a hand pressed to an aching head; and after putting up with this for some days and herself feeling wholly at a loss, Mary made a private journey to town to visit Tilly. She would see what that practical, sagacious woman thought of the situation. Tilly, of course, at once laid her finger on the weak spot by asking bluntly: "But whyever doesn't the doctor take advice of some of 'is friends?—the big-bow-wow ones, I mean. They'd be able to tell 'im, right enough."

"Why, the fact is, Richard hasn't got. . . I mean his friends are not business men, anymore than he is. If only John were alive! He'd have been the one."

"Well, look here, Poll, I can ask Purd about it if you like. He may know, and if e doesn't, 'e can easily find out—I mean whether old S. is really going to hop the twig or what. Purd has strings 'e can pull."

Mary went home intending to keep silence about her intermeddling—at any rate till she saw what came of it. But Richard was regularly in the doldrums: he had to be comforted somehow. At first, as she had expected, he was furious; and abused her like a pickpocket for discussing his private affairs with an outsider. "You *know* how I hate publicity! As for telling them in that quarter. . . why, I might as well go out and shout them from the housetop."

"Richard. . . you can't afford. . . if you're really set on getting away. . . to mind now who knows and who doesn't."

But on this point, as always, they joined issue. He accused her of lacking personal dignity; she said that his ridiculous secrecy over money matters would end by leading people to believe there was something fishy about them.

"Let them! What does it matter to me what they think?"

"Why, I don't know anyone who'd resent it *more*—so proud and touchy as you are! And since home truths were the order of the day," she added: "You know, dear, its just this: you've only yourself to thank for the fix you're in. You've cut yourself off from everyone, and now, when you need help, you haven't a soul to turn to. And because I have, and make use of them, then your pride's hurt."

Which was the very truth. He had let slip friends and acquaintances who at this juncture might have been useful to him; but. . . could one nurse people, the inner impulse to friendship failing, solely from motives of opportunism? The idea revolted him. True, also, was what she said about the damage to his pride. Not, however, because they were *her* friends as she supposed, but because they were the friends they were. Again, he shrank in advance from the silly figure he was going to cut, did the story get about town how he had sold his house and packed his portmanteaux, while, all unknown to him, the chief spoke in his wheel had collapsed. What a fool he would look! Though the fact was, Simmonds had handled his affairs without supervision for so long, that he had come to look on the fellow as a kind of fixture in his life.

And, in spite of everything, his determination to get away did not weaken. In mind, he had already started—was out on the high seas. Impossible now to call his thoughts home. And the feeling that such a course might be expected of him—that Mary would expect it—only served to throw him into a frenzy of impatience; make him more blackly intolerant of each fresh obstacle that blocked his path.

Then Tilly appeared: he saw her from the window, all furbelows and flounces, and wearing an air at once important and mysterious. She and Mary retired to the drawing-room; and there he could hear them jabbering, discussing *him* and his concerns, as he sat pretending to read. This went on and on—would they never end? Even when plainer tones, and the opening and shutting of doors seemed to herald Tilly's departure, all that followed was a sheerly endless conversation on the step of the verandah. By the time Mary came in to him, he was nervily a-shake. And her news was as bad as it could be. Old Simmonds was doomed; was in the last stages of Bright's disease; his place of business would know him no more. Most of his clients had already transferred to other agents; and Purdy's advice to Richard was, to lose no time in following their example.

"Huh! All very well. . . very easily said! But to whom am I to turn, I'd like to know? . . . when there isn't one honest broker in a thousand. Swindlers—damned swindlers!—that's what they are, every man-jack of 'em. And here am I, just going out of the colony, and with all this fresh money to invest."

Said Mary: "I've been thinking" (which, of course, meant tittle-tattling with Tilly), "why not write to Mr. Henry and consult him? He's such a good business man, and knows so many people. He might be able to recommend someone to you." But with this suggestion she only added fuel to the inordinate, unreasonable grudge which Richard still bore everyone connected with the old life. "Nothing would induce me! . . . to eat humble pie before that crew!"

"Well then, *do* let us postpone our journey. . . if only for six months."

He was equally stubborn, "Sooner than that—if it comes to that!—I'll sell right out and take every penny I possess to the other side. And never set foot in the colony again."

"Now, for goodness sake, Richard! . . ." cried Mary; then bit her lip. He was quite capable of carrying out his threat, did she make the least show of opposition.

However, on this occasion his rashness took another form. After spending the whole of the next day in town, where he had gone to visit his banker, to settle with his wine merchant, arrange for the storing of his books and so on, he came home to dinner looking a different man. On her, who had gone about all day with a crease between her brows, not knowing whether to pack for a voyage or for the removal to another house, he burst in, and catching her by the waist kissed her and swung her round. "Here's your bear come home. But cheer up, Mary, cheer up, my love, and make your mind easy! All will yet be well."

"What? Do you mean to say you've actually—?"

"Yes, thank the Lord, I have!"

Over the dinner-table he gave her particulars. At the end of a bothersome, wasted morning he had dropped into "Scott's," and there, in the coffee-room, had tumbled across Purdy. ("What!—*Purdy?*" was Mary's amazed inner comment, she being as usual hard at work drawing inferences.) Purdy had met him in friendliest fashion: "I've come to the conclusion, my dear, I've sometimes been rather hard on the boy of late." They had lunched together, over a chop and a bottle of claret had got talking, and had sat for the better part of an hour. Naturally the subject of Simmonds's collapse had come up, and the fix it had put him into. Purdy—"'Pon my word, Mary, I saw today he's got his head screwed on the right way!"—had given him various useful tips how to deal with the modern broker, which an innocent old sheep like himself would never have dreamt of. And then just at the end, as they were making a move, Purdy had scratched his head and believed he knew someone who might— "*Not* Blake?"

"Blake? Absurd! Good Lord, no! . . . Blake needs watching." (Richard knew all about it tonight.) No, no: this was no flashy dare-devil, but a steady-going, cautious sort of fellow, who could be trusted to "look after your interests during your absence, and transmit *the* interest. . .

ha, ha!—Oh, and I must tell you this, Mary. When he said—Purdy, I mean—'I believe I know someone who'd suit you, Dick,' where do you suppose my thoughts flew? They went back, love, to a day more years ago than I care to count, when he used the self-same words. We were riding to Geelong together, he and I, two carefree young men—heigh-ho!—and not many hours after, I had the honour of meeting a certain young lady. . . Well, wife, if this introduction turns out but half as well as that, I shall have no cause to complain. Anyway, I took it as a good omen. We hadn't time then to go further into the matter; but I am to meet him again tomorrow and hear all details."

He rattled on in the highest spirits, seeing everything fixed and settled; and Mary had not the heart to damp him by putting inconvenient, practical questions. And having said his say and refilled her glass and his own, he sent for the children—they had been hushed back into the nursery for the past three days, while Papa had a headache. Now, setting his girlies on his knees, with Cuffy standing before him, he told the trio of the big ship that was coming to take them away, and on which they were to live—for weeks, and weeks, and weeks to come.

The Dumplings' eyes grew round. "An' s'all us 'ave bekspup on ze big s'ip?" asked Lallie, the elder of the twins.

"Bekspup on ze big s'ip?" echoed her sister.

"Breakfast *and* dinner, *and* tea, and go to sleep in little beds like boxes built on to the wall, and look out of little windows just big enough for your little heads, and see nothing, wherever you look, but the great, wide sea."

"Ooo! Bekfast, *an'* dinner, *an'* tea!"—Cuffy had to cut a few capers about the room to let off steam, before he could listen to more.

Mary took no part in the merry chatter. And when Nannan had fetched the children, she abruptly came back to the subject of her thoughts. "Of course you'll see this person Purdy speaks of, see what you think of him yourself, before actually deciding on anything?"

"Of *course*, my dear, of course!"

"It seems rather. . . I mean, it seems strange Purdy didn't. . . And as he is doing the recommending, I can't very well ask Tilly's opinion."

"And who wants you to? I'll be very much obliged if you *don't* interfere! Surely, Mary, I can be trusted to attend to some of my own business? I'm not quite on the shelf yet, I hope?"

"Oh, come, Richard. After all. . . I mean it's not so very long ago and nothing would have induced you to take Purdy's advice."

"And pray who was it brought home glowing tales of how splendidly he had got on, thanks to his acuteness and financial genius, etc., etc., etc.?"

"Yes, I know. But still. . ."

"But as soon as I come into it, or because I come into it, you lose every atom of faith. I wonder if all wives are as distrustful of their husbands' capabilities. A bad look-out for them if they are."

Mary did not deny the charge. Doubtful she was, and doubtful she remained: an attitude of mind that severely tried Mahony's temper, he having more than one private scruple of his own.

For his second meeting with Purdy, in which he had planned to be very cautious and to throw out wily feelers, was a failure. On getting to the hotel he found that Purdy could spare him but a few moments, himself having an urgent appointment to keep. They did not sit down, and their talk was scampered through at lightning speed. However, Purdy supplied him with a list of people for whom this man Wilding had acted—well-known names they were too!—and himself undertook to put in a word on Mahony's behalf. In the meantime it would be as well for him to write and summon Wilding to town.—Write? Yes; for now it turned out that Wilding's business was carried on, not in Melbourne but in Ballarat. Purdy vowed he had mentioned this fact the day before; but if so, Mahony had failed to hear him. Not that it mattered much, seeing that he himself was about to leave Melbourne. It might even, he agreed, the majority of his investments being in Ballarat mines, prove a benefit to have an agent who was on the spot.

Still, the conversation left him visibly less jubilant. While from the interview he had some days later with Wilding himself, he returned tired and headachy—always a bad sign where Richard was concerned. He met Mary with a: "Well, my dear, all our troubles are now over!"—which was true in so far as the business side of the affair had gone off smoothly. The transfer had been effected, power of attorney given, new investments arranged for, his existing share-list overhauled and revised. But. . . well, he had not been very favourably impressed by the man himself. He could find no likeness in him to the portrait drawn by Purdy—and probably amplified by his own mind, which looked for a second Simmonds—of a staid and dignified man of affairs. No, Wilding was again one of your rough diamonds: over-familiar, slangy, a back-slapper, and, like everyone else here, in a tearing hurry: he hardly bothered to listen to what you said, knew everything you were

HENRY HANDEL RICHARDSON

going to say beforehand, and better than you. His appearance, too, was against him—at least to one who set store by the fleshly screen. Wilding had a small, oblique eye; fat, pursed lips; fat, grubby fingers on which flashy rings twinkled; a diamond pin that took your breath away. Also, from an injudicious word he let drop, the idea leapt at Mahony. . . well, it might be pure fancy on his part. . . or owing to these unlovely looks. . . besides it was only a fleeting impression. . . vaguely troubling. But come! it would not do to let a personal antipathy to the man's appearance prejudice you against him. . . as Mary was never tired of preaching. What though Wilding was no beauty? Whose hands here *were* impeccably clean? Was this not just the type of your modern broker, as compared with one of the old school? The main thing, the only thing that really mattered was that he should prove alert and up-to-date. And in this respect his credentials were of the first water. What was more, it leaked out, in something he said, that Purdy had already been in correspondence with him over the affair. Might one not safely assume a hint on Purdy's part that he himself meant to keep an eye on things, during his friend's absence from the colony?

And now, at last, nothing stood in the way of their departure; and preparations were rushed forward that they might sail by the vessel of their choice. Mahony superintended the sorting and packing of his books, and saw them carted to a depository; then rearranged the furniture and bought fresh pieces to fill the bare walls where the bookcases had stood. Next he conveyed the luggage—it filled a lorry—to the wharf, saw it aboard and stowed away between hold and cabins. Of these, they had three of the largest amidships; and the best warehouse in Melbourne had carpeted, furnished, curtained them. No need, this time, for Mary to toil and slave. Like a queen she had only to step aboard and take possession.

They spent the last couple of days at an hotel. And one morning, having received word overnight that the *Atrata* was ready to sail, they packed into two landaus and were driven to William's Town. There they found a pretty crowd assembled. Everybody they knew, or had ever met, had turned out to see them off, headed by dear old Sir Jake and Lady Devine, the Bishop and Mrs. Moreton, Baron von Krause the famous botanist, old Judge Barmore and many another, not to speak of Mary's intimate personal friends, Richard's spiritualist circle, relatives and members of the family. For a full half-hour they were hard at it, shaking hands and exchanging greetings and farewells. Richard, in his new travelling rig, spruce from top to toe, was urbanity itself: as indeed how should he fail to be when, within cooee, rode the good ship that was to carry him off? There was also a generous sprinkling of children present, the colonial youngster never being denied the chance of an outing. And to Cuffy, standing stiff and important in red gloves and a tasselled sash, came Cousin Josephine to hiss in his ear: "Ooo. . . aren't I glad I'm not going? Our servant, Mawy Ann, says you'll pwobably *all* go to the bottom of the sea!" and then to laugh maliciously at Cuffy's chalk-white face.

Rowed on board, they found the cabins hardly big enough to house the masses of flowers that had been deposited in them—great stately bouquets in lace or silver holders; lavish sprays; purple and white arrangements shaped like anchors and inscribed "For remembrance." And beside the flowers were piled cases of fruit and delicacies, as well as other more endurable keepsakes: scent, and fans, and cushions, and books. Nor were the children forgotten. Over-excited, the despair of their nurses, Cuffy and his sisters rushed to and fro, their arms full of wonderful new toys.

Said Mary in tears: "I think they're the dearest, kindest people in all the world."

The last to leave the ship were Jerry, Tilly and Emmy. Emmy, looking lovely as ever in her deep, becoming mourning, broke down over the parting and cried bitterly. Mary—and Richard too—would have liked to take the girl with them; both as a companion for Mary, and in order that foreign travel might give a fitting polish to John's eldest daughter. But Lizzie vehemently opposed the plan. Nor was Emmy's own heart in it. For, since John's death, she had taken upon herself the entire charge of her little brother, heaping on his infant head all the love that had once been her father's. Hence she could not tear herself away.

Jerry, a bank manager now, the father of a family, and hailing from the township of Bummaroo, had stayed the night with them at their hotel; and, John being no more, Mary had seized this chance of unburdening herself to her staid, younger brother, of some of the doubts that haunted her with regard to Richard's present flighty management of his affairs. Bummaroo was not very far from Ballarat; and Jerry promised indirectly to find out and keep her informed of what was going on. "Don't worry, old girl. I can easily run over from time to time and see how the land lies."

Tilly sat on the edge of a bunk and was very down in the mouth. "Upon my word, Poll, I seem to feel it more this time than last—which is just what a silly old Noah's Ark like me *would* do, considering it was for always then, and here you'll be back before the kids 'ave cut their second teeth."

But the last bell went; the ship was cleared, the ladder hauled up; and all the din and bustle of weighing anchor began. The wind being favourable, the Captain undertook to reach the "Heads" before night; and he was as good as his word. They made a record voyage down the Bay; and, catching the tide before it turned, headed straight for the Bight. Mahony, in his old sea-mood of rare expansiveness, went below to announce their whereabouts. But by now, thanks to a freshening wind and the criss-cross motion of the ship, all was confusion in the cabins. The Dumplings, very sick, were being hurriedly undressed; Mary and the nurses staggered about, their hands to their dizzy heads. Cuffy alone was unconcerned: his father found him playing in the saloon, twirling to and fro on one of the revolving chairs. Here was a chip of the old block! Wrapping the child in a rug he bore him aloft, to watch the passage through the "Rip."

Perched on a capstan, Cuffy followed the proceedings with a lively interest, and to a running fire of questions. Why was the sea so white and bubbly? Where was it running away to? What were reefs? Why were light-houses? Why was a pilot? *How* did he know? Why did he have such a big boat all to himself? Why didn't he have a staircase? Did he have his own skin on under the oil? When was the sea *shut?* . . . and many another. But gradually the little voice ceased its piping and a silence fell—unnoticed by Mahony, who himself was carried away once more by a splendid inner exultation, at dancing in the open, leaving land behind. He stood lost in his own feelings, till suddenly he felt the little body his arm enclosed give a great shiver.

He looked down. "What is it, dear? Are you cold?"

But Cuffy just nestled closer into the crook of his father's arm and did not reply. He had no words at his disposal to tell what he felt at sight of nightfall on these wild, grey, desolate seas. Nor did he dare to resolve the more actual fear of Cousin Josey's implanting, and put the question that burned on his lips: "How far is it to the bottom?" . . . For perhaps Papa did not know that was where they were all sure to go.

"Come, it's long past bedtime."—And lifting the child from his perch, Mahony carried him below.

In the gloom of the cabin the hanging-lamp swayed from side to side, with a slow, rhythmical movement; timbers creaked and groaned; from the pantries came the noise of shifting, slithering china—sounds that were as music in Mahony's ears, telling as they did of a voyage begun.

Mary turned a feeble head.

"Where *have* you been? The child will be perished. Well, you'll have to see to him yourself now. We're all much too ill."

And thereafter, between convulsive fits of retching, she heard from the cabin opposite, where Mahony was undoing little buttons and untying tapes, the voices of father and son raised in unison:

> *Rocked in the cradle of the deep,*
> *I lay me down. . . in peace to sleep.*

IX

The house they took for the winter was in Kensington Gore, and the children walked everyday with their nurses in Kensington Gardens. When first they arrived, the great trees, with branches that grew almost low enough to be pulled (if you jumped), were thick with leaves, and shady like houses. Then the leaves tumbled off and lay on the ground, and, when Nannan didn't see you, you shuffled your feet through them, kicking up a dust and making a noise like crackly paper. Afterwards, men brought brooms and swept the leaves into heaps and burned them in little bonfires; and then what fun it was to run like blind men, with eyes tight shut, through the clouds of smoke. You trundled your hoop up and down these paths, but didn't go far away, because you couldn't see where they ended for mist; and Nannan said you might get lost, or fall into a round pond. And one day a strange, thick, yellow mist came down, and hid even the path you were walking on, and made your throat tickle and your eyes sting; and Nannan and Eliza, talking about pea-soup, rushed for home, feeling frightened, big as they were, and having to be helped across the road by a policeman, who made light with what Eliza said was a "bull's-eye."

After this, Cuffy got a cough and had to take tablespoonfuls of cod-liver oil, and to stay indoors while the Dumplings walked. It was dull work. The nursery was so high up that you couldn't see anybody but trees from the windows, which were barred; and you were not allowed to look out at all, if they were open. Nannan said looking over made her poor old head dizzy; and she lived in fear of seeing one of them "land on the pavement." So Cuffy hammered with his knuckles on the panes, making tunes for himself, or beat them out on his drum or xylophone, till Nannan, sewing by the fire, said her poor old head was like to split.

Cuffy gave her his gravest attention. "Are you so *very* old, Nannan?"

"Why, no, not so very," said Nannan with a queer laugh: she was buxom, and in her prime.

"How old?"

"As old as my tongue and a little older than my teeth," was the cryptic reply, which, far from ending the conversation, led on through a tangle of question and answer—why tongues grew before teeth, what made teeth, where they came from—to the eternal wonder: "Was I born, too?" and "How?"

"A caution, that child, if ever there was one!" said Nannan, in relating this "poser" and how she had queered it—"Only *naughty* little boys ask things like that, Master Cuffy!"—to Eliza and Ann over tea. This was drunk in a kind of cubby-hole off the night nursery, the three colonials having failed to fraternise with the posse of English servants who had been taken over with the house: a set of prim, starched pokers these, ran the verdict; and deceitful, too, with their "sirs" and "madams" to your face, and all the sneery backbiting that went on below-stairs.

In regard to Cuffy, however, Nannan's opinion was general: an awkward child to deal with. You never knew what fresh fad was going to get the whiphand of him. For instance his first fear, of Cousin Josey's suggesting that they would all be drowned, which had preyed on him during the voyage: this allayed, he was haunted by the dread of being lost, or at least overlooked—like a bag or an umbrella—in this great, strange, bewildering place. Even at the pantomime at Drury Lane, he suffered torments lest, when it was over, Nannan and Eliza should suddenly forget that he and the Dumplings were there and go home without them; and from the close of the first scene on, he inquired regularly every few minutes throughout the afternoon: "Is this the end?" till Nannan's patience gave way, and she roundly declared that never would she bring him to a theatre again. It was the same at Madame Tussaud's—the same, plus an antipathy that amounted to a horror of all these waxen people with their fixed, glassy eyes; and a fantastic fear that he might be mistaken for one of them and locked in among them, did he not keep perpetually on the move. His hot little hand tugged mercilessly at Eliza's baggy glove. Yes! more bother than half a dozen children put together. Just a walking bundle, said Nannan, of whims and crotchets.

Chief of these, and most tiresome of all, was the idea that he could not—or must not—sleep of a night, as long as his father and mother were out. Did they attend an evening party, he tossed restless till their return. And if in spite of himself he dozed off, it was only to start up with the cry: "Is my Papa and Mamma come home yet?" Nannan was at her wits' end what to do with him; and more than once boldly transgressed her instructions about absolute truth in the nursery. For it was not as if Master Cuffy really wanted his parents, or even wanted to see them. No sooner did he know they were back, under the same roof with him again, than he turned over and slept like a top.

The mischief was: they were out almost every night. For, in violent contrast to the hermit's life he had been leading, Mahony was now never happy unless he was on the go. An itch for distraction plagued him; books and solitude had lost their charm; and an evening spent in his own society, in this large, dark, heavily furnished house, sent his spirits down to zero. They had brought many an excellent letter of introduction with them; a carriage-and-pair stood at their disposal; and so, except for an occasional party of their own, they went out night after night, to dinners, balls and card-parties; to soirees, conversaziones and lectures; to concerts and plays. They heard Tietjens sing, and Nilsson, and Ilma di Murska; Adelina Patti with Nicolini; and a host of lesser stars. Richard said they must make the most of their time; since it was unlikely they would ever be on this side of the world again. To which, however, Mary now secretly demurred: or not till the children are grown up. For, though foreign travel meant little to her, she was already determined that her children should not miss it—it, or anything else in life that was worth having.

In the beginning, she was heartily glad of the change in Richard's habits, and followed him without a grumble wherever he wished: he wouldn't budge a step without her. But, as week after week went by, she did occasionally long for an hour to herself; to prowl round the shops; see something of the children; write her letters in peace. As things stood, it was a ceaseless rush from one entertainment to another, not to mention all the dressing and re-dressing this implied. Done, too, with Richard standing irritable and impatient in the hall, watch in hand, calling: "Now *do* come along, Mary!—can't you hear, my dear? We shall certainly be late."

She comforted herself with the thought that it was not for long: they had taken the house only for a twelvemonth; and there was talk, as soon as the weather improved, of a trip to Ireland to see Richard's sisters, and to the Midlands to visit Lisby, now Headmistress of a Young Ladies' Seminary. So, in the meantime, Mary went without her tea to sit through interminable political debates; or struggled to keep her eyes open at meetings of learned societies, where old greybeards droned on by the hour, without you being able to hear the half of what they said. "I suppose it does *somebody* some good!" thought she. Richard, for instance, who had read so many clever books and enjoyed teasing his brains. Herself, she felt a very fish out of water.

Nowhere more so than at the spiritualist seances, which, for peace' sake—and also because everybody was doing it—she now regularly attended. London was permeated with spiritualism; you hardly met a person who was not a convert to the craze. The famous medium Home had already retired, on his marriage, into private life, much to Richard's disappointment, but he had left scores of imitators behind, who were only too well versed in his tricks and stratagems. The miracles you could see performed! Through the ceiling came apports of fresh flowers with the dew on them, or roots with the soil still clinging; great dinner-tables rose from the floor; lights flitted; apparitions appeared, spoke to you, took you by the hand. But nothing that happened could shake Mary's convinced unbelief. She was of those who maintained that so-called "levitation" was achieved by standing on your toes; the "fire-test" by your having previously applied chemicals to the palm of your hand; while the spirits that walked about were just so much drapery on a broomstick. And it invariably riled her anew, to see Richard sitting solemnly accepting all this nonsense as if it heralded a new revelation. Of course, many clever men besides him were the dupes of their own imagination. Learning and common sense did not seem to go together. *She* preferred, thank you, to trust the evidence of her own eyes and ears.

However, she kept these thoughts to herself, patiently doing all that was required of her in the way of linking hands in dark rooms, hymn-singing and the rest, with only an occasional silent chuckle at the antics of the believers. But then came an evening when circumstances forced her hand. Well, yes. . . that was partly true. They were at a sitting with a medium of whom she had long had her doubts; and, on this night, the evidence for fraud seemed to her so glaring that she determined to put it to the test. For once, Richard was not beside her. Instead, on her right, she had a lady who fell into raptures at each fresh proof of the "dear spirits'" presence. Stealthily bringing her two hands together (as Tilly had long ago instructed her), Mary freed one from this person's hold; and, when "spirit-touches" were again proclaimed by her neighbour (they never visited *her!*) she made a grab, and just as she expected, found the medium easily recognisable by her bulk—crouched on her knees inside the circle, with a long feather whisk in her hand. In the dark, and in utter silence, a struggle went on between them, she holding fast, the medium wriggling this way and that, and ultimately, by lying almost flat on the floor, contriving to wrench herself free. Not a word did Mary say. But at the end, when the lights were turned up, it was announced that the "spirits" complained of an unsympathetic presence in the circle;

and after some hocus-pocus with slate-writing, etc., she, Mary, was designated and asked to withdraw.

Richard, pale and extremely haughty, made the best of the situation in face of all these strangers, none of whom but eyed Mary as if she were a moral pariah. Inwardly he was raging; and he freely vented his anger in the carriage going home.

"There you have it! Your mulish obstinacy. . . your intolerable lack of imagination. . . your narrow, preconceived notions of what can and cannot happen!" Till Mary, too, lost her temper, and blurted out the plain facts of the case. "I knew her by her figure. What's more, I distinctly felt the big wart she has on the side of her chin."

But with this, it seemed, she merely displayed her ignorance. For the spirit body, in manifestation, was but the ethereal shadow cast by the physical, and its perfect duplicate. Richard also went on to crush her with St. Paul's "terrestrial and celestial"; harangued her on the astounding knowledge of the occult possessed by the early Christians. It was no good talking. Everything she said could be turned against her.

As she brushed her hair for the night, however, she could not resist remarking, in a final tone: "Well! all I know is, if these really *are* spirits who come back, it doesn't make me think much of heaven. That the dead can still take an interest in such silly, footling things!"

"Quite so, my dear. You keep your traditional fancy picture of semi-birds and harps and crowns. It best suits a mind like yours to make its heaven as remote and unreal as possible. For the truth is, you no more believe in it than you do in the tale of Cinderella."

"*Really*, Richard! . . . what next, I wonder?—Though I must say, I don't think there's much to choose between harps and things, and playing concertinas and tilting tables. One's as stupid as the other."

"Well, how else. . . can you perhaps suggest a better way for a discarnate being to make its presence known? Every beginning is crude—and always has been. Though, for that matter, what is the Morse alphabet they use on the electric telegraph, but a series of transmitted raps?"

"Oh, I'm not clever enough to argue about these things. But I know this: if I go to heaven, I hope at least to find there'll be something something really useful—*to do*."

But when the light was out and they lay composing themselves for sleep, she heard Richard mutter to himself: "There may be. . . there probably *is*. . . fraud. And why not? . . . do not rogues ofttimes preach the gospel? But that there's truth in it—a truth greater than any yet dreamed of—on that I would stake my soul. Ours the spadework. . . God alone knows what the end will be."

The result of this affair was that Mary no longer frequented seances. On such nights Richard went out alone, and she sat comfortably by the fire, her feet on the fender, her needlework or the children at hand.

But not for long. As suddenly as Richard had thrown himself into the whirl, so suddenly he tired of it, and at the first hint of spring—it was early February; birds had begun to twitter in the parks, the spikes of the golden crocus to push up through the grass, and Richard petulantly to discard his greatcoat—on one of these palely sunny days he came home restless to the finger-tips, and before the evening ended was proposing to start, then and there, for the Continent. Why should they not shut up the house, send the children to the seaside, and jaunt off by themselves, hampered only by the lightest of luggage, and moving from place to place as their fancy led them?

Why not? There was, nowadays, no practical reason why he should scruple to satisfy any and every whim. And so his roughly sketched plan was carried out. With the sole difference that they took Cuffy with them. For, as soon as Nannan heard what was in the wind, she marched downstairs and said bluntly, she did not choose to shoulder the entire charge of Master Cuffy. The child was anyhow but poorly, what with the colds and things he had had since getting here; a walking mass of the fidgets besides; and if now his papa and mamma were going away as well, she guaranteed he'd worry himself, and everybody else, into a nervous fever. Mahony cut short the argument that followed by saying curtly: "We'll take the youngster with us," and pooh-poohed Mary's notion that travelling would be bad for the child. Much less harmful, said he, than staying behind and fretting his heart out. Besides, Ann would be there. Ann could look after him.

And so it came about that Cuffy journeyed in foreign parts, bearing with him, snail-like, all that stood to him for home.

Of these early travels, the most vivid memory he retained was, oddly enough, the trifling one of being wrapped in an opossum-rug and carried in someone's arms from a train to a ship, and back to a train. But in those buried depths of his mind to which he had normally no access, a whole galaxy of pictures lay stored; and, throughout his life, was the hidden spring that released them touched, one and another would abruptly flash into consciousness. As a small boy they put him in many

HENRY HANDEL RICHARDSON

an awkward fix; for he could never prove what he said, or even make it sound probable; and, at school, among companions whose horizon was bounded north, south, east and west by the bush, they harvested him a lively crop of ridicule and opprobrium. ("A tarnation liar. . . that young Cuffs *Mahony!*") But there *were* houses built in water—somehow he knew it—and bridges with shops on them. Boats with hoods, too, and men who stood up in them to row with a single oar. There *was* a statue so big that you could climb into its nose and sit there, and look out of its eyes: rivers, not red and muddy but apple green; a tower that leaned right over to one side; long-legged birds that built their nests on chimney-tops.—But then again, on the heel of such bold assertions, a sudden doubt would invade the speaker; a doubt whether he had not, after all, only *dreamt* these things. With no one to whom he could turn for confirmation, with every object that related to them lost or destroyed, Cuffy, throughout his later boyhood, swung like a pendulum between fact and dream, and was sadly torn in consequence.

X

Travelling from Dover to Calais and thence to Paris, the party set off on what, in thought, Mary ever after dubbed: "that mad race across Europe."

For, the Channel behind them, Richard's restlessness broke out in a new form: it seemed impossible for him to be content in any place they visited for more than a day or two on end. In vain did Mary protest: "But, Richard, we're not seeing anything!" Within a few hours of his arrival in a town, he had had enough of it, sucked it dry; and was fidgeting to be off to the next on their line of route. Nor was this itch for movement all. The strange food did not suit him: he either liked it too well and ate too heartily of it, or turned from it altogether. Then the noisiness of foreign cities—the cobbled streets, the rattling of the loosely hung vehicles, the loud foreign voices, the singing, the tambourining—got on his nerves, and, together with the unshaded windows of hotel bedrooms, kept him awake half the night: him spoilt, for how many a year, by the perfectly darkened sashes, the ordered silence of his sleeping-room at "Ultima Thule." And all the beauties in the world could not make up to Richard for lack of sleep. Or, to turn it round: rob him of his sleep, and you robbed him of all power to enjoy fine scenery or handsome monuments. And so they sometimes arrived at a place and left it again, without having really seen very much more of it than the four walls of a room.

Before they had got any distance, it became clear to Mary that Richard's travelling-days were. . . well, one could hardly say over, when they had only just begun. The truth was, they had come too late. He was no longer able to enjoy them.

It was not the physical discomforts alone that defeated him. The fancies he went in for, as soon as he set foot on foreign soil, made his life a misery to him. In Paris, for instance, he was seized by a nervous fear of the street traffic; actually felt afraid he was going to be run over. If he had to cross one of the vast squares, over which vehicles dashed from all directions, he would stand and hesitate on the kerb, looking from side to side, unable to resolve to take the plunge; and wasn't he angry with her, if she tried to make a dash for it! His own fears rendered him fussy about Cuffy and the maid's safety, too. He wouldn't hear of them going out alone; and insisted every morning on shepherding them to their walk in the Public Gardens. If he was prevented, they must drive there in a *fiacre*. Which all helped to make the stay in Paris both troublesome and costly. Then there was that time in Strasbourg, when they set out to climb the tower of the cathedral. It was certainly a bad day to choose, for it had rained in the night and afterwards frozen over, and even the streets were slippery. But Richard was bent on seeing the Rhine, and the Vosges, and the Black Forest from the top of the steeple; so up they went. As far as the platform, it was plain sailing. But on the tower proper, when they were mounting the innumerable stone steps—all glassy with ice, and very tricky to keep a footing on—which led to the spire, he turned pale, and confessed to giddiness. . . it was true you looked through the wide-open stonework right down to the street below, where people crawled like ants. And after another bend in the stair, he clinging fast to the iron hand-rail, he had ignominiously to give in and descend again: backwards, too! "I felt I should either fall through one of the openings or throw myself out. Great heights are evidently not for me."

And this was not wholly due to imagination. For, after going up the Leaning Tower of Pisa and taking a peep over the side, he felt so sick on reaching the ground that he had to go back to the hotel and lie down.

Again a beautiful city like Munich was ruined for him, by the all-pervading smell of malt from its many breweries. The whole time they were there he went about with his nose in the air, sniffing; and he never ceased to grumble. Next, as the Tyrolese mountains were so close, they took train and went in among them; but this didn't suit him either. The nearness of these drear, dark masses wakened in him, he said, an overpowering sense of oppression; made him feel as if he *must* climb them; get to their summits in order to be able to breathe. One moment abjuring heights, another hankering after them! . . . who could keep pace with such inconsistencies?

Of course there were times when he smiled at himself; saw the humour of the situation; especially when he had just escaped from one of his bugbears. But then came the next (he was never prepared for them) and hit him equally hard. The thing he *couldn't* laugh at was his—their—"infernal ignorance of foreign lingos." Not to be able to express himself properly, make himself fully understood, riled and fretted him; though less, perhaps, than did her loud and unabashed efforts to say what she wanted. And because he couldn't argue, or expostulate, with porters, waiters, cabbies and the like, he constantly suspected these people of trying to do him. The queer thing was, he preferred being diddled, putting up with it in gloomy silence, to trying, in broken French, German or Italian, to call the cheats to account. Many an extra franc and taler and lira did this hypersensitiveness cost him. But his dread of being laughed at was stronger than himself.

Yes! there was always something. He never let himself have any real peace or enjoyment. Or so thought Mary at the time. It was not till afterwards, when he fell to re-living his travels in memory, that she learned how great was the pleasure he had got out of them. Inconveniences and annoyances were by then sunk below the horizon. Above, remained visions of white cities, and slender towers, and vine-clad hills; of olive groves bedded in violets; fine music heard in opera and oratorio; coffee-drinking in shady gardens on the banks of a lake; orchards of pink almond-blossom massed against the misty blue of far mountain valley.

Of all the towns they touched, even including Naples and Rome, Venice suited him best; and this, she firmly believed, because he went there with the idea that, having neither streets nor wheeled traffic, it must of necessity be a quiet and restful place. Herself she noticed nothing of this. Dozens of people walked the narrow alleys—you could really go everywhere on foot—and the cries of the gondoliers, the singing and mandoline-playing lasted far into the night. But Richard throve on it; though it was June now, and very hot, and alive with mosquitoes. He bathed daily on the Lido, and for the rest of the day kept cool in picture-galleries and churches, of which he never seemed to tire. Whereas she, after half an hour of screwing up her eyes and craning her neck at ceilings, had had more than enough.

They had been there for a whole fortnight, and there was still no talk of their moving on, when something happened which cut their stay through as with a knife. The smallest details of that July afternoon—it started with one of Cuffy's outbreaks—were burnt into Mary's brain.

Richard had gone after lunch to the British Consul's, to fetch their Australian mail: Mary was anxiously waiting for news of the birth of Tilly's child. She wrote at her own home budget while expecting his return, sitting in the cool hotel bedroom with Cuffy playing on the floor beside her. Deep in her letter, she did not notice that the child had strayed to the balcony. How long he had been there, still as a mouse, she did not know; but she was suddenly startled by hearing him give a shrill cry.

"Oh, no. . . *no!*"

HENRY HANDEL RICHARDSON

Laying down her pen, she stepped through the window. "What's the matter with *you?*"

On the opposite side of the canal some men were engaged in drowning a puppy. They had tied a weight to the little animal's neck before throwing it into the water, but this was not heavy enough to keep it down; and again and again, in a desperate struggle for breath, it fought its way to the surface, only to be hit at with sticks did it come within arm's reach. Finally, amid the laughter of the crowd, the flat side of an oar caught it full on its little panting snout and terrified eyes. With a shriek that was almost human, it sank, not to rise again.

"Run inside, Cuffy. Don't stay here watching those nasty cruel men," said Mary, and took him by the arm. But Cuffy tore it away and remained standing with dilated eyes and open lips, breathing rapidly. The last blow struck, he burst into a passion of tears and, running to a corner of the room, threw himself face downwards on the floor.

There followed one of those dreadful exhibitions of rage or temper which Mary found it so hard to reconcile with her little son's usual docility. Cuffy kicked and screamed and wouldn't be touched, like the naughtiest of children; and at the same time was shaken from head to foot by sobs about which there was nothing childish.

She was still bending over him, still remonstrating, when the door opened and Richard came in. One glance at his face was enough to make her forget Cuffy and spring to her feet.

"Richard! Why, my dear. . . why, *whatever* is the matter?" For he had gone out, not an hour earlier, in the best of spirits; and here he came back white as a ghost, with dazed-looking eyes and shuffling feet. "Are you ill? Has the sun. . . ?"

Midway in a sob Cuffy stopped to listen. . . held his breath.

Pouring himself out a glass of water and spilling it as he poured, Richard drank, in a series of gulps. Then, from a bundle of newspapers and letters he was carrying, he drew forth a folded sheet and handed it to Mary.

"Read this."

In deep apprehension she took the paper. As she read she, too, went pale. It was a telegram from Jerry, forwarded by their London banker, and ran: RETURN IMMEDIATELY. MOST URGENT. WILDING ABSCONDED AMERICA.

Mary could not all at once take in the full sense of the words.

"But how. . . what does it mean, Richard? I don't understand."

"Mean? Ruin, I suppose. In all probability I am a ruined man." And dropping heavily on a chair, Mahony buried his face in his hands.

Cuffy sat up, and peeped furtively at his father and mother, with round eyes.

"Ruin? But how? . . . why? Oh dear, *can't* you speak? No, no, Richard! What are you thinking of? Remember the child." From under his hands tears were dripping on the table.—"Go to Ann, Cuffy. She shall take you out or give you your tea. Run away, dear. . . quickly!—Now, Richard, pull yourself together. It's no good breaking down. *What* has happened? What do you intend to do?"

"Yes, what am I to do? Oh, help me, help me, Mary!"

"Of course, dear, of course I will."

Stifling her own alarm, Mary sat down at his side and took his hand in hers. It was plain he had had a severe shock. He admitted as much himself: the thing had come so suddenly. He told how, out of the dazzling sunshine he had stepped into the cool office at the consulate, had passed the time of day with a clerk, had been chatting with the fellow when the telegram was handed him.

"This has just come for you, sir. I was about to send it on to your hotel."

Yes, he had not even stopped talking as he tore it open. The next moment the room had started to swing round him; he had been obliged to take a seat, everyone staring at him, eyeing him askance. How he managed to get out of the place and home, he didn't know. His mind seemed to have escaped control: felt like a child's puzzle that had been rudely jolted into hundreds of pieces, and had now all to be re-set. "Which I don't feel equal to, Mary—and that's the truth. Something seems to have broken inside me."

Oh, how like a bad dream, the remainder of that day! For the practical side of the matter could not wait—not for a single hour. Richard half-way restored to composure, they had to set to work in cold blood to discuss the situation. It was clear to both that he must return to Melbourne with the least possible delay. Till then, he would not know how he stood. Things might not, urged Mary, be quite so black as they looked at first glance, Wilding's absence yet prove capable of a rational explanation. But Richard, she could see, feared the worst. . . had no real hope of this. (And in her heart even she thought the tone of Jerry's message belied it. Oh, where would they have been, had she not had that private confab with Jerry the night before sailing!) No, the conclusion Richard had jumped to at first reading, he still maintained: after the fashion of many a dishonest broker, Wilding had sold the scrip he held from his clients and bolted with the proceeds. Now, the only question was: what was left; what could be saved from the wreck.—A mail steamer was due to leave Venice sometime during the week; and on this Richard must, if humanly possible, secure a berth. And the rest of the day passed in running from wharf to agent, from consul to banker. The money question had also to be gone into: what he still had in hand; how much remained on his letters of credit; what balance lay in the London bank. Then they had to think of the furniture, the curios and pictures they had bought on their travels, and sent back to England. The London house would have to be got rid of; the servants paid off, and so on. Before evening Mary's brain was reeling with all the details it was necessary for her to take in. But this rush and flurry was exactly what Richard needed. And she kept him at it, kept him on the go till late at night, with the result that he went to bed dog-tired—too worn out to think.

But he had hardly dozed off, when they were roused by Cuffy starting up in his sleep, screaming: "No, no! . . . don't hit him. . . oh, *Doggy!*"

Hastily informed what had happened, Mahony struck a light and rose; and forgetting himself over a trouble even more pressing than his own, he lifted Cuffy out of bed and set him on his knee There he talked to him as, thought Mary, only Richard could talk. He went through the scene of the afternoon, made the child, amid tears and frantic sobs, live through it afresh; then fell to work to dispel the brooding horror that lay over it. Such things as this were often to be met with in life; Cuffy must be a brave little man and face them squarely. Somehow, they all fitted into a great scheme on God's part, which our poor brains were too puny to understand. To be pitied was not only poor doggy, whose struggles had soon ceased, but also the men who could act so cruelly towards their little brother—no less a brother because he had not the gift of speech. Cuffy must try to feel sorry for them, too; they had probably never had anyone to teach them the difference between right and wrong. And he must make up for their want of love, by being doubly kind himself to all dumb creatures.—And so on and on, in a quiet, soothing voice, till the child's terror was allayed and he slept, his arms clasped like a vice round his father's neck.

Forty-eight hours later Richard, with for luggage a single portmanteau, boarded the Overland Mail for Egypt—and thus ended a two days' nightmare in which he had never ceased to torture himself with the bitterest reproaches. "It is all my fault. . . my own fault. . . I alone am to blame. If *only* I had not been so headstrong. . . had listened to you!" The last glimpse Mary had of him showed him standing at the taffrail of the tender that carried passengers to the steamer; standing very erect, and even making a brave attempt to smile, as he waved his hat in farewell; for, when the time came, his chief thought was of her, and how he could ease the parting.

Till now Mary had kept up; had had, indeed, not a moment to think of herself, so busy had she been consoling, supporting, encouraging. But now that everything was over and she sat alone in the hotel bedroom, all she had gone through, all the conflicting emotions of these two past days—not the least of which were self-reproaches every whit as bitter as Richard's own—took toll of her. Behind locked doors she broke down and wept bitterly.

The thought of her coming loneliness appalled her. For over twenty years she had never been absent from Richard for more than a few weeks at a time. . . had never been parted from him by more than a couple of hundred miles. Now, this violent abrupt separation, with all the seas between, made her feel as if she had been roughly torn in two. For months and months to come she would have no one to lean on, no one to consult—oh, *What* if one of the children should fall ill and Richard not be there? She also shrank, with the timidity of unuse, from the prospect of having to emerge from her womanly seclusion and rub shoulders with the world. Her work had invariably been carried on in the background. When it came to a personal contact with business and business people, Richard had always been there, to step forward and bear the brunt. Now she, who had travelled but the briefest of distances unescorted, was called on to undertake by herself, not only the far journey across the Continent, but the infinitely more trying one of a two to three months' sea-voyage round the Cape. And until she got on board! To be faced, before that, were railway officials, porters, house-agents, shipping companies, bankers; the drawing of cheques and the paying of bills; the dismissing of servants; the packing and transport of baggage and furniture, the embarking, the long, long voyage with but one nurse for the children, and nobody at all to look after her. But hardest of anything was the knowledge that she would have to remain in her present state of ignorance and uncertainty, knowing nothing of what had actually happened, or of how Richard was bearing up, and whether he was well or ill, until she herself landed in Melbourne more than six months hence.

But the barest hint of illness in connection with Richard was enough to make her mind swerve, with a sudden jerk, from herself and her own troubles, to him. Desperately as she would miss him, and need him, yet she had small doubt—something within told her so—that, when she stood face to face with things, she would contrive to get on somehow. But he!—how would he ever manage without her? . . . to nerve him and to soothe him, and to listen to his outpourings—away from her, he quite literally would not have a soul to speak to. She saw him on the outward voyage, eternally pacing the deck, a prey to blackest anxiety—and the last thought of self went under, in a fierce uprush of pity for him, so solitary, so self—centred, so self-tormented. Oh, that he might be spared the worst! He was old for his age; much too old to have to begin life afresh—life which, with every caprice satisfied, had yet become so hard for him: an hourly tussle with flimsy, immaterial phantoms, whose existence other people never so much as dreamed of. And to know him pinched for money again, going short, denying himself, fretting over the straits to which he had brought her and the children. . . no! Mary felt there was nothing, absolutely nothing she would not do, to help him, to spare him.

Well! . . . sitting crying wasn't the way to begin. That was a fool's job. She must just set her teeth and make the best of things—separation, uncertainty, responsibility—endeavouring, when it came to business, to stand her ground, even though she was but an inexperienced woman. And as a first step she got up, dried her eyes, and bathed her face. After which she had trunks and saratogas brought out, and fell to packing.

But more and more, as the day wore on, did a single thought take possession of her—and, in this thought, Mary came as near as she ever would, to a conscious reflection on the aim and end of existence. It began with her suddenly becoming aware how she longed to hug her babies to her again, and how much she had missed them; a feeling until now resolutely repressed. . . for Richard's sake. Now, as, in imagination, she gathered her little ones to her heart—and gathered Richard with them, he, too, just an adored and absent child—it came over her like a flash that, amid life's ups and downs, to be able to keep one's little flock about one, to know one's dearest human relationships safe and unharmed, was, in good truth, all that signified. Compared with this, hardships and misfortune weighed no more than feathers in the balance.

"As long as we can be together... as long as I have him and my children... nothing really matters. I can bear anything... put up with anything... if only they are spared me!"

THE END

A Note About the Author

Henry Handel Richardson (1870–1946) was the pen name of Australian novelist Ethel Florence Lindesay Richardson. Born in East Melbourne, she was raised in a series of towns across Victoria with her mother and siblings following her father's death. At thirteen, she left Maldon—where her mother worked as the local postmistress—to attend Presbyterian Ladies' College in Melbourne. Her time there would inspire her bestselling coming-of-age novel *The Getting of Wisdom* (1910). Upon graduating in 1888, Richardson moved with her family to Germany to study music at the Leipzig Conservatorium. In 1894, she married John George Robertson, whom she met in Leipzig while he was studying German literature. They moved to London in 1903, where Richardson would publish *Maurice Guest* (1908), her debut novel. In 1912, Richardson returned to Australia to begin researching for her critically acclaimed trilogy *The Fortunes of Richard Mahony*, which consists of the novels *Australia Felix* (1917), *The Way Home* (1925), and *Ultima Thule* (1929). Partly based on her own family's history, the trilogy earned praise from such figures as Sinclair Lewis for its startling depictions of a man's decline due to mental illness and the lengths to which his wife must go to care for their young family.

A Note from the Publisher

Spanning many genres, from non-fiction essays to literature classics to children's books and lyric poetry, Mint Edition books showcase the master works of our time in a modern new package. The text is freshly typeset, is clean and easy to read, and features a new note about the author in each volume. Many books also include exclusive new introductory material. Every book boasts a striking new cover, which makes it as appropriate for collecting as it is for gift giving. Mint Edition books are only printed when a reader orders them, so natural resources are not wasted. We're proud that our books are never manufactured in excess and exist only in the exact quantity they need to be read and enjoyed.

Discover more of your favorite classics with Bookfinity™.

- Track your reading with custom book lists.
- Get great book recommendations for your personalized Reader Type.
- Add reviews for your favorite books.
- AND MUCH MORE!

Visit **bookfinity.com** and take the fun Reader Type quiz to get started.

Enjoy our classic and modern companion pairings!